"This is foolish, my lord. We should not be here together like this."

"No. We should not." His finger left her lip and trailed over the smooth curve of her chin. It sailed light as a feather down the slim column of her throat and paused at the indentation at its base. "But we were not speaking of shoulds and propriety. There is only you and I. And no one to deny us."

"The world . . ."

His finger rose to her lips to stop her speech. When she glanced up in affront, he smiled. "The world is not with us. There is only you." He lifted his finger from her mouth. "And I. For you I will be any and all you ask of me."

She should send him away, order him out of her room and her life. Instead, she held tighter to him and hoped he would not leave. Madness, surely. Somehow she must find a way to hold something of herself back or she would be lost.

BOOK YOUR PLACE ON OUR WEBSITE AND MAKE THE READING CONNECTION!

We've created a customized website just for our very special readers, where you can get the inside scoop on everything that's going on with Zebra, Pinnacle and Kensington books.

When you come online, you'll have the exciting opportunity to:

- View covers of upcoming books
- Read sample chapters
- Learn about our future publishing schedule (listed by publication month *and author*)
- Find out when your favorite authors will be visiting a city near you
- Search for and order backlist books from our online catalog
- Check out author bios and background information
- Send e-mail to your favorite authors
- Meet the Kensington staff online
- Join us in weekly chats with authors, readers and other guests
- Get writing guidelines
- AND MUCH MORE!

Visit our website at
http://www.kensingtonbooks.com

MISCHIEF

Laura Parker

ZEBRA BOOKS
KENSINGTON PUBLISHING CORP.
http://www.kensingtonbooks.com

PART ONE

Say what you will, 'tis better to be left than never to have been loved.

—William Congreve

Chapter One

Persia, 1808

"Alhamdolillah! Let me have one great adventure before I die!"

Japonica Fortnom peeked through the window's *mashrabiyah,* a closely woven screen of carved wood that allowed viewing out of a room but not into it. The oriel window looked out on the Bab al-Shaykh, an ancient quarter of old Baghdad where the turquoise-tiled domes and spindly minarets of mosques glittered in the morning sun. Once the home of Caliphs and the legendary Ali Baba's forty thieves, this was a city where intrigue and betrayal still rivaled mercantile concerns as the chief enterprise. It seemed a place where her prayer might be answered. After all, adventure was in her blood.

She was a third generation Fortnom, a branch of the famous London Fortnums who helped established Fortnum and Mason grocers. Many years before, her grandfather had come with The East India Company to Bushire, a port city along the ancient trade routes of Persia. Settling in permanently, he married and began a family who, for reasons never given, changed the spelling of their name to Fortnom. While the head of the English branch continued his climb in service to Queen Charlotte from royal footman to Page of the Presence, Fortnoms became adventurers. As part of The Company, father and then son roamed the subcontinent seeking teas, spices, and condiments with which to supply their London cousins. The Fortnom preference for exotic lands quickly earned them the nickname "the Indians" among their English cousins. A title not altogether complimentary, her mother once admitted. But life was never dull.

Japonica sighed. That was not quite true. Life had been very sad, dull stuff since her father's ship sank in a monsoon off Calcutta two years before. With nothing left of her old life or her long-held dreams of adventure, she had continued as a Company employee specializing in herbs. At times she felt as if the world could swallow her whole and no one would ever notice.

Then, miracle of miracles, The Company requested that she to go to Baghdad. Known for her skills as an herbalist, she had been sent here to nurse Lord Abbott, viscount Shrewsbury, who was stricken with a fever no physician could cure.

Perhaps she was tempting fate this day by whispering her prayer but she could not hold it back.

"*Alhamdolillah!* Let me have one great adventure before I die!"

She had first composed the prayer the summer she turned ten. That was the first time her parents sailed away on their yearly expedition and left her behind.

They proclaimed that it was time their only child began lessons in literature, elocution, deportment, dancing, and drawing. In other words, it was time she became cultured.

"One day you will be more than a shopkeeper's daughter. You will be a wealthy lady," her mother would say. "Beautiful ladies have all sorts of lovely adventures."

Japonica sighed again and turned away from the window. "Oh, Mama, what a disappointment I must have been."

She'd inherited her father's quick mind and tenacity, a by-product he claimed of their heads of red hair. Alas, she did not inherit his fabled charm or a single feature of her mother's remarkable beauty.

She rose from her cot and went to pour water into a basin to wash her face. Unlike her mother, she seldom looked in a mirror. She knew her appearance only too well. Carrot curls framed apple cheeks, an indifferent nose, and a mouth other women often remarked upon as "a little too generous" and certainly too pink for the shade of her hair. It was not a face to lure gentlemen from their self-possession or their consequence. It certainly was not a face to launch a thousand ships or topple a crown. No, it was a face to make a young woman compose prayers for deliverance from dullness.

Japonica dried her face, then reached for her India muslin gown. At twenty years of age she had learned that adventures were not for shy, funny-faced girls with pale red hair. Nor was romance.

Even so, if her mother had not succumbed to a fever before her daughter reached the presentable age of sixteen, she might have steered her successfully through the marriage market of Bushire. English-women were rare in this part of the world. By age sixteen even she, an ugly duckling, was being courted by a constant succession of English military officers. That brief joy collapsed when her ever-pragmatic father refused the suit of a young lieutenant in the Life Guards, threatening to disown her.

"Aristocrat, my arse! You can do better! Poor as church mice, these younger sons. Parents bought them colors that they might not starve. I could buy and sell any baker's dozen of them, and they know it. 'Tis the gleam of my gold in his eye when the lieutenant bends a tender gaze on you, daughter."

She winced at the remembered pain of realizing that her father's harsh words were no more than truth. The lieutenant never found reason to call again. When word spread that no mere soldier would ever be good enough for the rich merchant's daughter, she found herself a wallflower even at affairs with sparse female attendance.

"*Sobhanallah!* I shall die an untried old maid!"

The Persian curse, something her mother would have abhorred, came naturally to the lips of a young woman reared in the realm of Shahs and scented gardens and hagglers' bazaars. While she was no longer allowed to travel after age ten, her father still took her, dressed as a servant, with him when he did business in the local marketplaces. At his urging, she learned to buy and use herbs, to judge the quality of incense, pearls, silks, and furs. And, when there was a much-needed bargain to be made, never to take no for an answer.

"Independent! That's my girl!" her father would say proudly. "When you're a lady of considerable fortune, it ain't necessary that you be wed to be respectable."

A shadow of emotion crossed Japonica's face. As an heiress, she was respected but it might have been nice to be loved. Unfair! Unfair! The warm hard-beating heart inside her yearned for bright, wild adventure. Yet hers was a silent rebellion of the soul that went on behind lowered lids and closed lips.

"So ye're awake!" said a dour voice. "I thought ye'd lie abed all mornin'."

Japonica turned with a smile for her former nanny who was now a trusted friend. "Good morning, Aggie." When she noticed the older woman's somber expression her own brow wrinkled. "Did the viscount have a difficult night?"

Aggie harrumphed. "He sleeps the restless sleep of the wicked! Such tossin' an' turnin'! I'd ken he saw all the evils of hell awaitin' him."

Aggie clucked her tongue as she set a tray of tea and biscuits before Japonica. Predicting calamity was her favorite pastime and the last days had given her much fodder for her dire predictions. "The Resident will have to answer for it should ye perish alongside his lordship. Bringing ye under a roof with a festering fever in a town plagued by the French! Either of which may kill us at any moment!"

Japonica winced at the reminder that despite her meticulous care, the viscount's health was failing. She and Aggie had arrived in Baghdad two weeks ago, and she soon realized there was very little she could do for the viscount other than make his last days comfortable. The French were another matter.

Like the rest of the population she'd learned of the Shah's secret treaty with Napoleon when French Hussars began arriving in the city a few days ago. The French were already at war with the English in Spain, Portugal, and Egypt. The new treaty made Persia officially at war with Britain.

"You better go in to him," Aggie said when Japonica had finished her tea. "His lordship's agitated over the contents of a letter what come last night."

"Last night?" Japonica sprung up. "Why didn't you say so before?"

"And ruin yer breakfast? For all he says, he'll keep well enough."

Japonica hurried toward the viscount's chamber but paused to knock before entering. His voice was so weak she barely heard his reply.

Despite the brilliant day, his room was shuttered into semidarkness. Lying beneath a thin muslin sheet, he appeared no more than a series of long thin bones. His wispy hair was the color of the pewter goblet on the table beside his bed. His complexion had the unhealthy pink of a consuming fever.

"Good morning, my lord."

He opened his eyes, sunken and rimmed in red. "My sweet Japonica. We have news." He fumbled with the missive under his fingertips on the bed. "A messenger delivered it during the night. Will you read it, child?"

"Certainly." Japonica took it, noticing that his fingers were icy while the rest of him seemed afire. Not much time left.

She moved to a window and held the message up to rays of the sun filtering through the wooden slats. The contents lifted the soft hairs on her forearms. It was from the East India Company. Brigadier-General John Malcolm's mission to the court of Fath Ali Shah had collapsed before reaching Teheran. Napoleon's treaty stood. No Englishman's, or woman's, life was safe in the country's interior. The viscount and all in his party were directed to return to Bushire at once.

"At once," Japonica murmured. *"Bismallah!"*

"What do you say?"

"Nothing, my lord." She bit her lip. How by Mercy's Grace was she to see so gravely ill a man safely out of a city swarming with French soldiers?

According to her father there were always tribal men in the hills whose loyalty was not so fixed upon the Shah that it could not be bought by the color of gold. A few of them might be persuaded to smuggle the viscount's party south. But her patient was too ill to hazard a run from the city into the hills. She would need assistance just to reach them.

"You will need help, of course," Lord Abbott said after a moment, as if reading her mind. Japonica saw a thin smile on his fever-ravaged face. "We need the services of a very particular man. The only man in all of Baghdad who holds himself above the influence of the Persian Shah, the English, and the French."

"The *Hind Div?*" Japonica suggested in amusement.

"The very same." He nodded weakly. "The *Hind Div.*"

"I was not serious." Her abashed smile deepened. Indian Devil, indeed! Lord Abbott's fever must have caused his mind to wander into fancy. "No doubt he is a resourceful fellow but I don't think he is to be trusted."

"What have you heard?" The viscount tried to sit up and, failing that, rolled to push himself up painfully on one elbow.

Japonica rushed over to help him. As she rearranged his pillows to ease his posture she said, "He is said to be a spy, thief, assassin, and worse."

Lord Abbott nodded weakly. "Indeed, he may be. Some claim he is in the service of Zaman, Shah of Afghanistan, who raids both Persian and Indian territories. Still others believe that he is the specter of a murdered Sultan returned to life by Mohammed to scourge all *Farang.*"

"Scourge all Europeans!" Japonica felt a fresh thrill rush up her spine but she was not about to quail before mere rumor. "A boastful reputation has its uses, I suppose. It makes him known and feared by all."

"Exactly!" The viscount gave her a measuring

glance. "He is a reputed magician, as well. 'Tis said that for the right fee he can make people disappear or appear at will."

"Would that were true," Japonica murmured to herself. Their little party needed very badly to disappear from Baghdad and reappear safely in Bushire. "In any case I would not even know where to find such a person."

"I have written you an introduction." He smiled and pointed weakly to a sealed missive lying on the desk across the room.

"You know him?"

His smile widened as he saw her amazed expression. "I've been in the Orient too long not to be prepared for abrupt changes of fortune. I've written down such directions as I could glean from the servants on how to find him." His fever-ravaged eyes scanned hers. "The only question is, do you have the courage to seek him out?"

A shiver of anticipation slipped through Japonica unlike any she had ever before felt. To visit the *Hind Div* would be adventure, indeed! Did she have the courage?

Nodding solemnly, the daughter reared in the shade of flamboyant parents made the first independent decision of her life. "I do."

"I dunnae like it." Aggie hitched up her right shoulder, thin lips disappearing into the pitch of her displeasure. "Look at ye, brown as a wren and eyes to make a *houri* blush! Yer own father would nae know ye."

"Let us hope my disguise will fool all eyes," Japonica replied. She glanced down at her dark hands and smiled. She had stained them, as well as her face, with ground walnuts. Kohl made her eyes water but lent an exotic touch to their color. Her hair was another matter. A heavy black veil was required to conceal its red luster. The disguise was a trick her father had taught her in order that she might get better prices in the bazaar. Her Persian, at least, was so fluent that no one would suspect she was English. Yet there had never before been lives at stake if she were discovered. Her skills with medicinal herbs had brought her to this city. Now it was her wits she must use most cleverly or she could well lose her freedom and that of those counting on her.

To still the qualms of second thoughts, she snatched up a heavy black cloak to cover her elaborately embroidered silk gown. "I must leave."

"You should be taking me with you. You should nae be wander—"

A gruff male shout from the street below snared their attention. Aggie turned and looked out the latticed window. "Aw Gawd! 'Tis the frogs!"

Japonica hurried over, pressing in against the older woman for a better view. A small cadre of French Hussars on horseback had entered the alley. The two women held their breaths as the sounds of horses' hooves slowed before their door and one of the men dismounted.

"I'd like to see them try and arrest us!" Aggie huffed, pulling back her sleeves in anticipation of a brawl. "Me and me rollin' pin's bested better!"

"Softly, Aggie!" Japonica cautioned and tugged the older woman's arm to pull her back so that they would not cast shadows on the window.

But they heard no knock. Instead they listened to the sounds of men drinking from the public fountain. After a short pause, they heard sounds of the soldiers riding on.

"Thank heavens!" Japonica murmured in relief. "But it can't be long before we are discovered."

Aggie gave her a severe look but it softened almost instantly into a smile. "Then ye'd best be on your way."

Moments later, with a hand clutched tightly over a heavy purse she had tied beneath her gown, Japonica slipped from a side door and into streets deeply shadowed by the late-afternoon sun.

The city's original two thousand-year-old lanes had been built wide enough for use by camels and horses. Yet successive building projects through the centuries had turned poorer sections into a nearly impenetrable maze of alleyways. She picked her way slowly through dusty streets full of people baked in their own sweat, and refuse and other evil smells best left unguessed at. Several times she had to stop and backtrack as she attempted to follow the meager instructions. Every delay cost her precious time. All the while the sun lowered relentlessly, turning the stifling alleys to umber-shaded canyons under a deepening azure sky.

Finally she had to pause to turn her face to a stone wall in a public courtyard as a delegation of men in richly embroidered robes, preceded by an incense bearer, made their way through the crowd. The deference due nobles was formidable and defiance brought swift retribution.

When they had passed she looked right and left, confused once more, for the streets leading away from the plaza looked like so many spokes of a wheel. Giving herself up to intuition and fate, she moved purposefully toward the lane the nobles had taken. Miraculously, when she reached the end of it she found herself in the heart of the *suq*.

A great din arose from the bazaar around the great Mosque al-Kazimayn where the voices of hagglers joined the clank of coppersmiths' hammers and the braying of impatient camels. This was the place marked on her map!

She quickly passed stalls offering carpets, prayer beads, and finely printed copies of the Koran bound in leather and stamped in gold. Other vendors dispensed holy water from pottery. Still others offered more corporeal delights such as dates and almonds and kat, a plant whose mild stimulant effect could be best appreciated by chewing it. Ordinarily she would have stopped to sample the bins of spices and herbs filling the air with a pungent if bewildering blend of aromas. Nothing delighted her more than a bargain. She was curious to test the reliability of the prayer compass said to orient itself toward Mecca from any spot on Earth, yet she waved aside the eager merchant who thrust it toward her with a hopeful smile. Time was slipping away from her.

Then she passed through the white plume of sweet piney balsam scent arising from the incense burner. Her footsteps faltered. This was no ordinary incense. Unless her nose deceived her—an unlikely event, for her sense of smell was highly trained—she had happened upon a rare prize.

She turned quickly to the merchant but kept her gaze lowered as she pointed to a bowl of small amber beads. "How much?" she asked in Persian.

"Four hundred tomans, gentle lady." The exorbitant amount, nearly eighty English pounds, made her gasp and quickly turn away with a shake of her head.

As expected he hurried after her crying, "What would the *memsahib* offer me?"

She turned slowly to him, as if reluctant. "From where does your frankincense come?"

"Dhofar," he answered promptly.

Japonica smiled behind her veil. The best frankincense in the world came from Dhofar. Therefore, every seller made such claims of his wares. Only an experienced buyer could recognize its distinctive aroma. Without a word she pulled several coins from her pocket.

Seeing the gleam of gold, the old man took it and then poured a handful of small translucent gold beads into her palm.

She pocketed the precious incense as the keening sounds of the call to the faithful arose from the nearby minaret. According to custom, all women must leave the streets at the Moslem call-to-prayer.

In a low husky tone she hoped would not travel beyond the stall she asked, "Where may I find the home of the *Hind Div?*"

The merchant's eyes grew so round she thought he would faint. "No, no, dear lady! You cannot mean to go there. That is where the devil resides!"

She did not miss the implication that he knew that there was a "there" to go to. Since he had already seen the gleam of her gold, she dug into her pocket and produced an amount similar to that which purchased the frankincense.

His ogle of horror turned quickly into a squint of calculation. "You wait," he said, then turned and ran to the nearby stall to confer with two of his neighbors. They eyed her suspiciously as they spoke, using a mountain dialect of lisps and nasals sounds with which she was unfamiliar. The animated conversation drew the curiosity of other merchants until the group of three swelled to well over a dozen.

As the seconds ticked past she wondered if she had made a mistake in revealing her destination. But finally the merchant hurried back to her.

He motioned for her money and when she handed it over he said quickly, *"Ala alshemal.* Keep left. Forty paces!"

"How far is that?" But he had turned away and

she knew she had been told all she would hear from him.

"Forty paces," she murmured to herself. The number was of little use in a country where "forty" was used to express any large sum. Forty paces might mean forty or four hundred.

She did not bother to count her footsteps but she realized as soon as she entered the narrow lane he had pointed out that she was suddenly out of earshot of the marketplace. What's more, there was music in the air. Someone was playing a hornpipe, an English sailor's instrument, and the tune was none other than the Scottish air, "The Bob-tailed Lass." What brazenness for the player to identify himself as an enemy of the French!

Yet that waggish insult might also be her luck. Surely this was an omen that she had found the lodgings of the *Hind Div*. He would fear nothing.

She hurried to the single narrow door in the high wall of the house and pulled the woven bell rope hanging beside it. She did not hear the bell sound but the music ceased and after a moment she heard a shout from above.

"You there! Go away!" a man dressed as a servant yelled out in very poor Persian. "We accept no visitors and want no peddlers!"

"I'm not a peddler!" she cried out in her own language and then immediately wondered if that had been a wise thing to do.

"English?" The man's own voice was unmistakably accented in soft Scottish burr. "Do nae bestir yourself, lass, 'til I come down!"

In less than a minute a narrow panel opened in the door shadowed by latticework so that she could not see the face behind it. She moved in close to whisper, "I am looking for the man they call the *Hind Div*. Are you he?"

"Won't say I am and don't say I'm not. Only ye best come back tomorrow. 'Tis no night to brave the *Div*." He snapped the little window shut.

She rapped on the door impatiently. "I have money."

The panel swung open again. "How much?"

"Let me in and you may see for yourself," she answered, sounding much braver than she felt.

To her amazement the door opened. After a quick look left and right down the strangely empty alley, she stepped inside.

The moment she crossed the threshold a cool sweet breeze enveloped her with the scent of jasmine and orange blossom. The heat and dust and altogether unpleasant odors of the street were absent. She took several steps away from the entrance before the impression of otherworldly beauty brought her to a halt. This was the home of a very rich man.

She had been told that the most seductive quality of a Persian house was that it looked inward on a scented realm shaded and cooled and sealed off from the world. Now she understood. Pure white columns and archways gleamed dully in the indigo shadows surrounding a large courtyard. Gold-fringed pomegranate silk curtains fluttered on a breeze seemingly of its own invention, for the street had been stifling still. Flanked by the lush green of orange and lemon trees and lit from a mysterious source, a fountain stood in the courtyard's center, shimmering with crimson and azure and gold mosaic tiles set in floral designs. This was the source of the single sound in the air, a charming burbling.

The sound of the door slamming shut behind her startled Japonica from her thoughts and she swung around saying, "I have come . . ."

She spoke to emptiness.

No one stood near the door. Nor, as her eyes

became accustomed to the gloom, did she see anyone in any part of the courtyard. Sensing that she had made a mistake by entering a stranger's home so precipitously, she rushed back to the door and pulled repeatedly at the latch but it did not budge.

"Bismallah! What trick is this?'' she asked in Persian. No answer came back save for the distant echo of her own voice.

"Very well." She straightened and turned back to the courtyard. Though her heart beat a tattoo worthy of a dervish dance, she would not show her fright. She lifted her voice and said coolly, "Tell the *Hind Div* I will wait for him by the fountain."

She waited several long minutes in the silence. More than once the prickly sensation of being watched made her suddenly glance back over her shoulder. There was never anyone there.

She suspected the *Hind Div* was deliberately testing her resolve. Such a man would only respect a show of courage. To dispel her nervousness, she reached out to splash a little in the water of the fountain. At the bottom of the crystal depths she saw a flash of a silver-white fin and then a red-gold tail as exotic fish swam in lazy circles among the lily pads and lotus flowers.

Moments later the tinkling of an unseen bell drew her to a nearby alcove. Unnoticed before, a large copper dish rested on a ledge, filled with skewers of lamb, fragrant rice, eggplant, tomatoes, hummus, baba ghanouj, several kinds of olives, and a large disk of bread. Beside it stood a cup of tea. Parched from her journey, she reached for it. Her host might be illusive but his hospitality lacked for nothing.

Only as the sweet brew touched her tongue did it occur to her that the sumptuous feast might be a trick to drug the unthinking. Quickly, she spit the tea back into the cup and put it down.

"Are you always so wary of your host's offering, *memsahib?*"

That deep and mellifluously masculine voice, she knew at once, must be that of the *Hind Div.*

She turned slowly to look at him and nothing after that seemed quite real.

Chapter Two

He stood on the opposite side of the courtyard dressed from head to toe in black, his features hidden behind a tuck of cloth from his turban. Only his eyes were visible and even from a distance they seemed to glow like a cat's in the dark.

Behind her own veil, Japonica gaped in amazement. Her father had once kept a Caspian tiger in a bamboo cage until he could ship it to a menagerie in London. With a singular frightened fascination she watched that tiger slowly pace day after day, wanting to tease from its watchful gaze the thoughts of such a magnificent creature. The *Hind Div* possessed that same feline grace as he approached on silent feet.

He paused in half shadow two-arms' lengths away, then he reached up and stripped away his mask. Japonica shrank back with a quick breath of alarm. The visage he revealed was striking! And terrifying!

He bore on his face the markings of the Arabian cheetah!

Bold black lines slanted outward from his kohl-rimmed eyes toward his temples. Others scored his bronze skin from the inner corner of each golden eye toward the corners of his upper lip where thin stripes of black beard outlined his mouth then came together in a silky black twist of a tassel at the end of his chin. She had been wrong to scoff at his name. The being before her seemed the embodiment of an Oriental demon.

Lines from a fairy tale about an Arabian sorcerer flittered through her amazed mind. "A charismatic man with piercing eyes and seductive airs/When he came into the room the mice jumped on chairs." As she gazed into his golden eyes, as rich in color as the frankincense beads in her pocket, she believed this man capable of magic, and more.

"My servant claims you would break down my door." He threw back his cloak and rested his left hand on the jeweled hilt of a wickedly curving scimitar tucked into the wide sash about his waist. As his golden gaze moved deliberately over her she felt a chill that had nothing to do with the mysterious breeze. "You are either very brave . . . or very foolish."

Foolish! her dazed senses whispered. Just by staring at him she violated a rule of etiquette for any Persian woman. Yet who could look away from this glorious, frightening being who seemed not quite real?

Heart pounding as though it would break free of her ribs, she bowed her head and answered in her most formal Persian, "I beg your indulgence, *burra sahib.* I am abashed with awe to be in the magnificent presence of the *Hind Div.*"

He was silent so long she cast a dubious gaze upwards. Nothing in the dark shadows cast upon his face offered her reassurance. "For this pitiable utterance I am roused from my slumber? *Sobhanallah!*" he pronounced in disgust, then turned and strode away.

"Wait! Oh no, wait!"

She started after him but his footsteps quickly outpaced her. When he disappeared behind a curtain she paused. Was he truly insulted by her greeting? Or was he incensed by her refusal of the hospitality of his house? There were few greater insults in this part of the world.

From out of nowhere a hand grasped her upper arm from behind. With a cry she swung round and up into the arresting face of the *Hind Div.*

"*Bismallah!*" she whispered in true fright, for it seemed impossible he could have doubled back so quickly.

He smiled but it did not touch his penetrating gaze. "You are impetuous, are you not?"

"You speak English!" To be perfectly accurate, he spoke with the cultured tones of a London aristocrat.

"You begin to bore me, *ayah,*" he replied, slipping back into Persian. His hand dropped away from her arm. This time he did not simply disappear but crossed the courtyard at a leisurely stride.

Her first impulse was to flee while his back was turned. She began to tremble. His cheetah gaze and stealth terrified her. Yet, if she fled how would the viscount escape Baghdad? No, she must not fail. But how could she match the audacity of a being who did not seem quite mortal? She had no skill in sorcery and beguilement. She had only the desperation of fear.

She took a few steps after him and called out, "Impatience seldom yields a handsome reward, *burra sahib.*"

He continued on as if he had not heard her. Yet, before he entered the tented pavilion at the far end of the terrace he glanced back. "Are you worth my patience, *ayah*?"

She drew in a long breath scented by the first waft of night-blooming jasmine. He addressed her with a term for a lowly servant. Her fear vanished before a rare spurt of Fortnom temper. When he disappeared into the pavilion she hurried after him. Man or magician, he would not so easily dismiss her!

Unseen hands parted the curtains when she reached the entrance. This time she betrayed no surprise. Her guard was set against his charlatan tricks. He would not amuse himself at her expense a second time. Yet the man who stood in the center of the room lit by torches mounted at each of its corners could not be ignored. Repulsed yet attracted by his exotic countenance, she had to admit his fascination and his capacity to surprise.

In the miraculous space of seconds he had replaced black garments for an *abe* of richly embroidered gold silk over loose-legged trousers. His turban was gone. Long silky black hair flowed onto his shoulders yet there was nothing in the least feminine in the display. As he turned toward her she saw the seductive line of his mouth curve upward and knew she was about to be tested once again.

As he approached she felt no inkling of danger, only the presence of a power so strong it withered the urge to resist it. The feline markings made it impossible to determine the true features of the man beneath. That very ambiguity made him at once the most hideous yet masculine man she had ever encountered . . . if he were a man.

When he was closer to her than was proper he bent to whisper in a breath scented by cloves, "When, I wonder, will you astonish me, *bahia*?"

For one amazed moment she felt the tantalizing heat of his skin against hers through her veil as he rubbed his cheek catlike along hers. Through the thin silk the rougher texture of his beard grazed the summit of her nose. Then he drew back. He was smiling but it did not put her at ease. "You smell delicious, *bahia.*"

"It is a perfume of my own design," she answered, then wished she had not.

"Ah, so that is the source of your magic." He reached out to touch her, the merest contact of a single finger stroking the upper edge of her veil, and it sent a ripple of pleasure along her cheek.

She jerked away, hoping he had not seen her response. She should resist the lure of his gaze. That was where his potency lay, in the thrall of those golden eyes.

"What other skills do you possess, *bahia?*"

She glanced up again and met the frightening strength of will behind those topaz eyes. "I have come on a most urgent matter, *burra sahib.*" She reached into her sleeve and produced the letter Lord Abbott had given her.

He took the missive and without even a glance tossed it onto a nearby table inlaid with rare woods and mother of pearl. "Have you so little courage you cannot speak for yourself? Come. I show myself to you." He reached out toward her again. "Will you not unveil for me?"

"No!" She backed away and received the derision of his rich laughter.

"So then, you have a little courage. Beautiful women usually do."

There was no answer she could think to make to his compliment. How disappointed he would be if he knew only a drab wren stood behind her *abeyya* and veil. So rich and powerful a man must have a harem, each concubine more lovely than the next, the least of them a dozen times more beautiful than she.

He moved toward the center of the room and a low wide divan covered in silk and furs. Climbing nimbly upon it, he then reclined in a supine position upon the pillows and shut his eyes. After a few moments she heard the soft sounds of sleep coming from the bed's occupant.

She approached the bed warily, her gaze darting into distant corners shaped by draperies undulating on the breeze. Surely he did not mean to keep her waiting while he dozed? If this were another prank she would be ready.

Yet the strangely painted face she looked down upon bore the unguarded expression of a man in repose. What insolence! She had to resist the urge to prod him with the toe of her slipper. Instead she folded her arms under her bosom and said in her most disparaging tone, "It is said the *Hind Div* is a being of infinite resourcefulness. Alas, I have witnessed only the shabby tricks of an commonplace conjurer who soon wearies of his own sad antics."

Though his eyes remained closed she saw a smile of bright ambiguity blossom on his mouth. Was it amusement or derision? Without the witness of his eyes she could not guess. "Ask your favor, *ayah.*"

This time she did not hesitate. Unlike the convoluted formality of the Persian language, the directness of English best served her purpose. "I seek your services to carry three people from Baghdad to Bushire."

"Any camel can discharge that errand," he answered in an obscure dialect of the northern provinces. Did he think by doing so he would confound her?

"Not *any* camel," she answered in kind, for she had become familiar with many of the tongues in which the spice business was transacted. "The one I seek must be able to conceal its passengers inside its hump."

He sighed deeply, eyes still closed. "I know of no such beast."

"Surely the *Hind Div* could conjure one."

She expected a greater reaction to her taunting but he merely shook his head against the shimmering surface of the pillows. "The fate of three *Farang* is of no great moment in Persian affairs. The *Hind Div* denies you."

She bit back the retort that came to her lips. So he had guessed she was *Farangi*, English. Yet who was he to reject her plea? He was not a Caliph to wield despotic authority over defenseless subjects. He had not even heard out her offer.

"A wise man never hears the 'no' in a refusal, only an invitation to continue until a bargain has been struck." Her father's advice came back to her now. The *Hind Div* must have a price.

She said softly, "Do you not find it strange that despite his treaty with the French, the Shah has not ordered the English from his land?" She glanced at him dozing like a cat. "Perhaps it is so that he may frustrate the cause of the one with the other. It is a prudent man who keeps his enemies and his friends equally close."

The *Hind Div* turned his head sharply toward her and opened his eyes. "You are wiser than is to be expected in a female. But why should you wish to impress me with your meager knowledge of state affairs?"

The words were not spoken harshly yet his judgment of her inferiority shamed her. She looked away, afraid that he would see that vulnerability in her gaze. "In a country where loyalties are as fluid as lamp oil the weak constantly shift allegiance with the changing fortunes of the strong."

"My loyalties are to myself alone, *ayah.*"

A second refusal. "And yet it is known that the *Hind Div* may be persuaded to lend his talents to a cause by a shower of rupees."

"I would prefer a deluge of lakh." His expression was skeptical. "Have you the capacity to produce such a downpour?"

"I have but a minor skill," she said carefully. She certainly did not have the capacity to produce the sultan's ransom he suggested. One lakh was worth one hundred thousand rupees! If only she had not bought frankincense in the market she might make a better showing. Yet, he seemed to value cleverness.

She pulled out the last of her coins and tossed them in the air saying, "Does not a sprinkling of dew refresh the garden better than the flood of a monsoon?"

The meager shower of gold that fell upon him provoked a single harsh bark of laughter. *"Bahia,* you sadly underestimate my indifference to your situation. Be gone. I am weary of the game."

Leaning back, he braced the arch of his left thumb and forefinger across his brow and rubbed hard at his temple, betraying a trace of weariness. It was the first unguarded gesture he had made, she realized. Perhaps he had not been feigning sleep. This sense of his mood surprised her. Yet she knew without a doubt that something weighed greatly upon his mind. Perhaps in that vulnerability lay a way to gain his help.

She moved quickly to the brazier near the foot of the bed. Using the tongs left there for that purpose, she picked out three glowing coals and transferred them onto a copper dish nearby. Taking two frankincense beads from her pocket she dropped them onto the coals. Almost at once a heady woodsy aroma arose in a thin plume of smoke. Fanning it with a palm frond, she carried the dish to the head of the bed and placed it on the floor near him. "I offer for your pleasure a gift of the finest incense to be had at any price. Breathe deeply, *burra sahib.*"

He did not move or speak.

Undeterred, she spied on a low table a long-necked wine pitcher inlaid with semi-precious stones. Beside it stood two matching goblets. She had refused his hospitality but that did not mean she could not offer it back to him. She poured a generous portion of wine and brought it to his bedside.

"Will you not at least accept this small offering as a token of good faith?"

"Good faith too often turns bad." He sat up with a swiftness that was startling and grabbed the wrist of the hand holding the goblet. "Are you the assassin sent to poison me?"

"I am no assassin!" She winced as his fingers bit into her wrist. "You are hurting me."

"I shall do more than that if you lie." The markings on his face seemed to alter with his anger, changing him into a preternatural predator.

"I do not lie."

"Then drink from the cup." Releasing her, he reached up and snatched away her veil.

Japonica looked down, not wanting to see the disappointment she knew would come into his eyes when he realized how plain she was.

He did not seem to notice. "Drink, *bahia,* or you will not like what happens next."

She steadied the goblet in her shaking hands and took a great gulp of the wine. She did not expect it would be so highly spiced, and choked. Sputtering and gasping, she tried to catch her breath as she passed it to him.

But he did not take it. He lifted the goblet by its base and pushed it toward her mouth. "Again," he ordered.

Though her throat and eyes burned she took another small sip.

When she would again have lowered the cup he took it from her and grasped her by the back of the neck. "Drink!" he commanded and held it to her lips.

When she tried to sip slowly, he forced her head back and poured it into her until she had swallowed most of its contents. Only when she was gasping for breath with tears streaming down her face did he relent.

"Now then, I will drink." Smiling, he took the cup and turned it up, draining it completely before tossing it away.

The inordinate sound it made as it bounced on the marble floor reminded Japonica with renewed trepidation of just how isolated they were.

He seemed to read her thoughts because he was smiling again. That wicked smile cut into the last of her courage like the sharp edge of a scimitar. "Now then, *bahia*, what did you truly come here for?" She held her breath as he reached up to touch her face, skimming a finger lightly over her lips. "Or shall I tell you?"

She could not look away from his golden gaze, brilliant with an emotion as old as sin. Yet she did not believe she provoked his lust. Now that her veil was gone he knew she was no beauty.

Something altered in his expression. He watched her with the same intensity yet in it was now a hint of detachment. All at once she understood. His interest lay in gauging the affect he was having on her.

A flush of anger made her tremble. He was mocking her, toying with her again. And this time he had chosen her most vulnerable spot, her confidence as a woman. Did he think her vain as well as foolish? She knew what men saw when they looked at her. But oh, for an instant, she wished she were a match for the lie in his eyes!

She pushed away the hand he rested on her cheek. "You do not frighten me," she said in a voice thickened by wine and resentment.

He took her by the shoulders and drew her in slowly until his face was only an inch from hers. "Say . . . not . . . yet."

Sensation quaked along every one of her nerve ending as his lips parted over hers, offering her first the heat of his breath and then the shocking length of his tongue. She gasped and tried to pull away but his arms were suddenly around her, holding her fast. She went still. Perhaps he wanted her to struggle, to plead with him, to beg for her life. If that were his intention, he would be disappointed.

The torment of his kiss lasted only a few seconds more before he lifted his head. "Do I frighten you yet, *bahia?*"

She merely glared at him unwilling to admit the "yes" that her heart proclaimed in its rapid pounding. Cast away her courage because of a kiss? Never!

Something new entered his gaze, a calculating intelligence that ruled even the wild look in his eyes. "Pass the night with me. Relieve me of the torment that plagues me and perhaps I will aid you."

A surge of heat from within stung her cheeks and put a quiver in her voice. "A man of genuine persuasion would not need to bargain for an unwilling lady's favors."

His smile was a tricky thing. "How little you know of men."

His hands found and cupped her face and then he sank his teeth into her lower lip, startling another gasp out of her. Given entrance, his tongue slipped between her lips and plied her mouth with a gentle in and out motion. This time she tasted in his kiss the spice of cloves, tang of wine, and it seemed something of the mysterious essence of the man himself.

Let him have his way! a heretofore unacknowledged part of her whispered. *Learn what it means to be desired!*

Wherever had that thought come from? She possessed twenty years of modest living to go against the strange sensations uncurling inside her.

He is a seducer! The conventional part of her warned. *You will live to regret it!*

In answer to her struggling thoughts a dizzying spiral of longing thrust up suddenly from the depths of her being. She felt a tear splash her cheek and was astonished. What was this unbearably, frighteningly sweet sensation provoked by his kiss? More of the *Hind Div's* magic?

"Do you like it, *bahia?*" The amusement in his voice came to her from afar. She was not a woman to set a man aflame. Yet this man had done so to her with only his lips. If he mocked her, she no longer cared. "Yes!"

He lay back and drew her onto the bed beside him. She did not think of resistance. Instead, she reached up and touched his cheek, feeling the hard ridge of his jaw beneath the bristle of shaven beard. He was no metaphysical being but wholly man. And that was more than enough. She slid her other hand up behind his neck to bring him closer. She needed him to be closer—much closer!

He followed her invitation, adding and elaborating on the kisses that had come before. And with each heartbeat her sense of touch became more achingly acute. She found the subtle variations of pressure and tastes of his lips enthralling. The fine weave of his silk *abe* became thick as burlap beneath her fingertips.

From its folds rose the heady perfume of a Persian garden: orange blossom, jasmine, and carnation as well as the bolder essences of amber and musk. The fragrances seemed to take on colors that spiraled in and about them like an aurora. Through the thick delicious tension rising in her, she realized too late that his hands were removing the veil from her hair.

"Red hair!" she heard him say in astonishment. His fingers plowed through her curls, lifting and spreading them on the pillow beneath her head. An exultant chuckle rumbled from his chest onto hers as he rose up over her to whisper, "You are the rarest of harem beauties, *bahia.*"

He could not be talking to her. She, a beauty? She tried to meet and hold his stare but her eyes would not focus. "I—I feel . . ."

Even as his features blurred she saw his smile change. "You were wiser when you were suspicious, sweet one. It is only the effects of the potion in the wine."

She saw his lips moving but his words no longer made sense. Caught up in the wonder of the feelings coursing through her she could only gaze in awe at the creature poised above her. So many questions half-formed in her mind only to slip away. . . .

She had never embraced a man before, never felt the heat of a man's body against her skin. That heat warmed her and soothed her yet made her restless for things she had no words or experience to give a name. It was all too bright, too feverish, too much!

"Oh please, help me!" she cried out and again reached for him.

"Yes. I will help you, *bahia.*" He sounded so certain of what she needed and so pleased that she had asked it of him.

He rolled her over on her back and slid the weight of his body over hers. His powerful hands glided down then up over her, lifting her robes. "Oh yes, I will help you and me to happiness."

She was drifting on a melody. The music, a forlorn tune played on a flute and accompanied by the complex tempo of a drum enfolded her, moved inside her, then carried her along in a rhythm all its own. The beat changed, the drumming faster and stronger as if she were being chased by it.

Dizzy, impatient, curious and frantic, she tried to keep the pace, matching the undulations of her body to the insistent urge of the rhythm . . . until she was spinning like a dervish out of control, complete in the madness of the moment.

The Milky Way traced a pale smudge through the midnight sky. From a distance the sound of singing carried on the breeze with a melancholy sweetness as exotic as it was plaintive. Desert blooms laced the air with heady perfume. But the beauty of the night was lost on the *Hind Div*. His mind was afire with thoughts untouched by his half-drugged state.

A virgin!

He had not expected that.

He had been awaiting an assassin.

For weeks carrion birds had been circling, banded together in their fear that he knew too much and might be captured by the English, the French or the Afghans and tortured to tell all that he knew. There was nowhere to turn. No ally to trust. Several attempts were made on his life before he shut himself up in his house three days earlier. Yet there were worse ways to die. Better, for instance, to die quickly at the hands of an assassin than ignobly on the rack or in boiling oil.

Fitting, too, that he should then choose the moment to allow the assassin in. He had issued an invitation the day before. Tonight he would be at home to all visitors.

It was to be the last night of his life. He had prepared for it carefully, bathed and dressed, and painted his face for the occasion. A few puffs of opium-laced tobacco in his *huqqah* had taken the edge off his eagerness for the matter to be over. When a stranger finally appeared at his door he was almost relieved. It seemed fitting his life would be given up at the hands of a woman.

So young, so innocent seeming, he had thought when she first spoke to him. How deadly she would prove to a man who had any ounce of goodness in him. But he was not a good man and so had prepared a surprise of his own for his guest. For he had discovered that life, even when freely offered up, is hard to give away. He would die, but not before he had taken his last pleasure with her.

Many who sought his favor sent their mistresses or harem slaves to the *Hind Div,* believing that a feminine plea would more easily gain his sympathy. He learned after taking a knife in the shoulder from a *houri* who came to do her master's bidding that women could be as treacherous as their brethren. Oh, he continued to bed those who offered themselves, but only after he had defanged them with drugged wine. Some were quite skilled. Others played reluctant. Afterwards, there was always a smile of triumph. Even if they went away with other hopes unmet they could boast that they had lain with the legend known as the *Hind Div*.

Except this one. She had stared up at him afterwards with the teary confusion of one who did not understand what had occurred.

A virgin!

If only she had not reached for him a second time, begging him to ease the passions he aroused in her, he might have been more wary. But he had been heedless of doubt as she so recklessly embraced him, so certain that she was as practiced as he in the erotic arts. The barrier was broken before he understood its significance. She had not presented herself as a seductress. Now he knew why.

"*Sobhanallah!*" Who would send a true innocent into the lair of the *Hind Div*?

That maddening thought had sent him roaring out of his bed as soon as the deed was done to find the note she had tried to give him earlier. Instead of the triumphant taunt he'd expected from an enemy, it was addressed to the man he had once been. He had to read it twice before the full import made itself clear to his drugged senses.

Dear Boy,

I have found for you a bride! Wondrous creature! She is that rarest of women: resourceful, levelheaded, and with a true loving heart. I send her to you for your approval. And then I shall borrow her back for a time. No doubt you've made an impression upon her to last a lifetime.

Until you are ready, she will be in my care.

But don't make her wait too long, my proud young cock. I would not like to think of her shackled to a less deserving man.

George Abbott

A bride!

He cursed again in astonishment! For such innocence there was no less-deserving man than he.

He had rushed back to the bed to ply her with questions. Though she appeared to be sleeping she answered readily enough. In fact, she had reached for him again, tried to kiss him. No surprise, in that the potion in the wine was an aphrodisiac, which was why he had willingly drunk a portion. The answers he received to his questions dampened what was left of his lust and deepened his self-disgust.

Miss Japonica Fortnom! An English merchant's daughter.

He knew the name. Had known her father, slightly, through his dealings with The East India Company.

So then, it was true. She was no assassin. He had seduced a complete innocent!

Below him a quarrel began, male voices raised in belligerence. The sounds grew louder as they spilled into the street below. Sounds of a scuffle followed, then a cry of triumph and laughter. After a minute, the men moved on and silence again fell upon the night.

An emotion he did not at first recognize stabbed him. Regret. It was an emotion he could ill afford. Not after the life he had led. Recanting one's sins at the hour of one's death seemed a cowardly act. He realized that he was no longer a gentleman or even, he sometimes suspected, wholly human. He felt a thousand years older than that idealistic young lieutenant who had come to Persia ten years earlier to seek his fortune. No, he could not do the honorable thing.

Men such as I, who see how the grains in their hourglass dwindle, will always seize the moment. To my everlasting glory or shame, I am such a man. He had written those words as part of his last will and testament before he left his post in Calcutta.

So then he would remain true to his nature . . . until the assassin found him. He had not forgotten that, if she were not the one, another awaited for him this night. The last grains in his hourglass dwindled, indeed.

He did not consider the feelings of the young woman in his bed as he turned back to the room and allowed himself no thoughts at all as he moved toward her on a silent tread, wanting only to savor the moments strung between his first despicable act and the next.

She lay as he left her on her back. Her face held the blurred softness of one in the embrace of sweet dreams. She was no beauty but there was charm in her snub nose and enough sweetness in her generous mouth to shame the stingy kisses of many greater beauties.

Such sweetness! He ached with the need to love her again.

He bent and kissed her. Her lips softened under his but as he brushed a caress over one breast she suddenly shied away. Even in sleep, it was her nature to resist what she would certainly have refused had she had her full senses. A better man would have relented.

He was not a good man! He was the *Hind Div*. He showed no mercy. Took what he wanted. Helped no one but himself. And so then he would help himself to what he had never before had and would never have again.

He made love to her slowly and completely. The fierce need gripped him to stretch out each moment to its fullest, to hold her and pleasure her, even though the look in her dazed eyes was more wonder than recognition. But she did respond. He found the wanton beneath the innocence, turned her sobs to cries of pleasure, until together they tasted paradise.

And when he was spent, he pulled her so tightly to him that she unconsciously struggled to ease his embrace. But he did not yield. The *Hind Div* never yielded to a weaker nature. Never!

He had only this night to lie in the embrace of
Japonica Fortnom, his never-to-be bride.

Japonica jerked awake, as panicked by the darkness
as if she were suffocating. Yet she drew breath easily
and all she had to do was open her heavy-lidded eyes
to chase away the deep gloom. They fell shut again
almost immediately. Behind her lids, the world was
a whirling dervish, yet sensations penetrated the turmoil. Beneath her hands were the textures of silk
and velvet. And surely a down pillow cushioned her
head. Then she reached out and met the solid wall
of a bare chest.

"Ah, you awaken."

Confused and incredulous she looked up into the
painted face of the *Hind Div*.

He leaned on an elbow as he lay beside her, an
expression of amused tenderness on his face. "So
now you've learned something of the nature of men."
He placed a hand on her stomach and she felt with
a distinct shock the heat of his palm on her bare
skin. He kissed her before she could move away, a soft
quick kiss, then he reached out and lay his forefinger
against her right cheek. "I am honored by your gift,
bahia."

Panicked by his words, she brought her arms up
to push him away but they were curiously weak and
folded at the elbows instead of providing resistance.
He gathered her close, rolling with her until she was
above him. And then he shoved her roughly from
the bed so that she fell on her knees on the rug. "Go
home, Miss Fortnom."

Japonica stared up at him from the floor in stark
horror. She had been lying in bed with a naked man.
And worse, he knew who she was!

He reached across the bed and picked up her

things. "You will want these." He tossed the items to her and they scattered about her.

Tears of humiliation welled up in her eyes as she scrambled about in her nakedness trying to gather her clothes. Her thoughts swirled and twisted with angry vigor as she slipped her *abeyya* over her head with shaking hands. Why could she not remember exactly what had occurred between them?

She put a hand to her brow. Her thoughts would not come together. She felt as if she had been ill with a fever. So many questions needed answers but she could not even speak to the naked man sprawled out so shamelessly before her.

As she slipped on her shoes she looked nervously about. How long had she been here? The shrouded room gave no hint of the hour. The only clues to the last minutes—hours?—were in the swollen feel of her lips and a strange aching low down. Then she remembered. He said he had drugged her!

She kept her gaze deliberately away from the *Hind Div* as she rose to her feet. Thankfully, he did not move or speak. But the unspoken question danced a frenzy inside her. What else had he done to her? Had he violated her? Surely not—! This was just another of his tricks. He liked to torment and tease. Perhaps he had undressed her, taking delight in her helplessness, as she lay naked before him. But surely he had not—!

She cast an angry glance to where he now sat absolutely expressionless on the side of the bed, dressed in his *abe*. No doubt he was waiting for her to rail at him for drugging her. The honeyed taste of spiced wine still hung in back of her throat and threatened to gag her.

She drew in a shuddery breath. Very well. He had amused himself at her expense. Yet, he knew who she was. Most likely he had read Lord Abbott's letter while she dozed. If he had violated her, he would not have just ordered her to leave when he knew she would be returning to the viscount, who could have him arrested. Surely it was only embarrassment that made her dance on a knifepoint of doubt.

She covered her head with her shawl, her mind racing. Every instinct told her to flee. Yet how could she explain to Lord Abbott that she had been unsuccessful?

Shame was not a thing she could use to advantage with the *Hind Div.* There was only audacity. "Astonish me!" he had challenged.

As she turned to look fully into his eyes, an idea sprung to life. "By your words just now you admit that you are in my debt."

She saw his gaze flicker. Nodding once, he rose from the bed. "Name your price. Afghan rubies? Burmese sapphires? This, perhaps?"

With a flick of his wrist he produced into his palm a turquoise ring worthy of a Sultan and held it out to her. "It is yours."

She shook her head. No jewel in the world would ever assuage her anger for his treatment this night. But there was something. "You said that *I* may name my price. I want passage for three—immediately— out of Baghdad in safety to Bushire."

For an instant she saw surprise in his golden gaze. At last she had astonished him! Then it was eclipsed by a smile that reached all the way up and out through his eyes. "I have misjudged you. I am glad."

"Does that mean you agree?"

He did not answer but took her by the arm and pushed her to the pavilion's edge and lifted a curtain. "Go home, *Uzza.* My servant will see you to safety. But sleep lightly."

Japonica stared at him, unable to determine from either his words or his expression if a bargain had been struck. Then her gaze settled on the wicked curve of his mouth. It had!

Without thinking an instant beyond the impulse, she leaned toward him on tiptoe. "Thank you, *burra sahib.*" Then she astonished herself by kissing him full on the lips.

When she was gone he smiled to himself. She was made of sturdier stuff than he had supposed. These last minutes must have been as difficult for her as anything she would ever experience. By braving it out she had won from him something rare; his respect. So, then, the night had not destroyed her spirit or her honor. There would be no consequences beyond the memory of his never-to-be bride and himself.

Just to be certain his mind had not played a trick on him, he reread the letter. Then he went to his writing table and composed a note. When he was done, the laughter which burst from him could be heard beyond the high stone walls of his house.

Chapter Three

Japonica's slippers made soft, swishing sounds on the marble floor as she paced outside the office of the Resident of the East India Company in Bushire. Lord Shrewsbury was now a guest in the Resident's home and she had been summoned for a briefing on his condition. All agreed it was a miracle that he survived the trip from Baghdad by a whole week.

She had not seen the *Hind Div* again, yet he had kept his part of their bargain. Before daylight of the day following their meeting a *takhi-I-ravan*, a Persian coach comprised of a covered litter carried by horses harnessed before and after, had arrived at the viscount's door. Accompanied by uniformed guards she, Aggie, and Lord Shrewsbury had been whisked out of Baghdad.

She should be relieved and ready to put the entire experience out of her mind. Yet nothing soothed or satisfied her. Not the return to the comfort of her home or the pleasure of her herb garden, or even the company of her friends. Nothing she did could long keep her thoughts from the memory of her encounter with the *Hind Div*.

He *had* ravished her!

Japonica gripped her Paisley shawl more closely about her shoulders, her step quickening as if she could outpace her thoughts.

Once the drug wore off, bits and pieces of that night came back to her along with the realization of what he had done, what *she* had done.

The truth should have shocked her. Remarkably, it had not. The memories did not seem quite real. Yet she did not doubt a single fleeting shadow of that night. She had wanted adventure. She had very nearly met with disaster.

Japonica looked up at the cry of a peacock in the courtyard. He was strutting toward a drab peahen, his tail feathers spread in vivid array. Yet the *Hind Div* could give the fowl lessons in dazzlement. Even now all she had to do was close her eyes to see his fantastic countenance, the enticement in those golden eyes. Like the peahen watching in rapt fascination she too, in an unguarded moment of awe, forgot to beware of his sorcerer's skill.

She turned sharply away from the mating dance. His treatment of her was what she could have expected from a brigand and spy. Moreover, it galled her to admit that she was to blame for the success of his vile plan. She had poured for him the wine that was her downfall! Most damning of all to her character was the fact that she had been so unaware of her true circumstance that she had voluntarily kissed the rogue!

"Wanton!" Japonica murmured the word of forbidden longing under her breath. It was the drug that had overrun her sense of decency, she told herself each time memory assailed her. But she did not quite believe it. She once feared she would die an old maid. Desire. Now she knew it, to her regret.

"Fool!"

"What did you say?"

Japonica turned quickly to the speaker. The Resident had opened his door and stood gazing inquiringly at her. "I beg pardon, sir." She curtsied to cover her embarrassment. "I did not realize I was no longer alone."

He cocked his head to look down the length of the veranda before he said, "Come in, Miss Fortnom."

The preliminaries of good manners took up the next several minutes as he offered her jasmine tea and ginger biscuits. Finally, when the servant who served them withdrew, the Resident set his teacup aside and leaned back in his chair with a broad smile. "So then, you have done well for us, Miss Fortnom. Well, indeed."

"I would feel better if Lord Shrewsbury's recovery were assured."

The Resident shook his head slowly. "You cannot fail to be aware, as he is, that he is dying."

"It is my greatest regret."

"But not your fault. Lord Abbott speaks daily of your excellent care. Says you alone are responsible for what little ease he has had these last weeks." He reached into the pocket of his coat and took out a sealed document. "In fact, he has put me to the task of laying before you yet another matter. It is most unorthodox and I cannot in good conscience request it of you. But . . ."

She took the document and read the first lines of several thick pages of foolscap. "Lord Abbott proposes to make me viscountess and guardian to his . . ." She looked up in astonishment. "His five daughters!"

The Resident nodded with a smile. "It is an offer of marriage."

Distinct shock ran through Japonica. "To me? Why?"

The Resident cleared his throat. "It is all written there. I think you will find the details of such an alliance decidedly to your advantage." He smiled warmly. "And I believe your father, knowing him as I did, would approve."

Japonica shook her head. "But marriage to a dying man? It is . . . unseemly."

He nodded solemnly. "It would seem irregular at first glance. Yet do not think badly of him, Miss Fortnom. He is but thinking of his daughters who would otherwise become destitute at his death. There is the usual entailment upon the Shrewsbury title. All properties and income derived become the sole property of the new viscount. Had Lord Abbott produced a son, this would not be a problem. It is not incumbent upon the new heir to care for Lord Abbott's offspring. Still, the dowager's portion would allow his widow to live in any of the Shrewsbury residences with a stipend generous enough to care for the children."

Japonica nodded but she did not, in all honesty, understand the peculiar ways of nobility that sacrificed the security of many for the continued prosperity of the few. "Perhaps there is someone else more suitable in Bushire. A widow?"

"It's been considered. There is no one else . . . ." He let the thought trail away, as it began to sound as if she were the viscount's last choice. "But think, my dear Miss Fortnom. Such a marriage would elevate you to a level of society to which you might never have aspired."

"I do not hope to rise above my situation," she murmured.

"It is to your credit that you demure. Of course, your father left you a sizable inheritance . . . ."

"Which marriage would give control of to my spouse," she added.

The Resident had the grace to look abashed but continued with the assurance of one who has already composed his argument against all debate. "Lord Abbott disavows all claim to your inheritance." He pointed to the document she held. "Read it all for yourself. But before you do, allow me to show you something else."

He walked over to his desk and picked up a velvet pouch. After loosening the drawstring he withdrew five oval frames and arranged them on the desk. "Come, look you here."

She approached and saw five miniature portraits lying on the desktop.

"Their names are Hyacinthe, Alyssum, Peony, Cynara, and Laurel." The Resident smiled. "Fanciful, perhaps, but being an avid horticulturist, Lord Abbott chose names from his gardens. 'The Shrewsbury Posy' he calls them."

Japonica touched each portrait with a fingertip as she repeated the names aloud. The eldest was perhaps ten, the youngest an apple-cheek cherub in swaddling. Spread between them were the likeness of girls four, six, and eight. Her bosom swelled with the compassion she would have felt for any about-to-be-orphaned child. Five children! It was an enormous charge.

She looked up at her host. "Will Lord Shrewsbury's family approve of his children being given into the care of a commoner?"

The Resident pulled at his lower lip before answering. "I won't quibble. There will be the usual obstacles in a marriage many will consider a misalliance. Yet I cannot think of a readier spirit for the project than yours, Japonica. If I may be so bold to call you Japonica." He reached out and took her hand. "Your father was a particular friend of mine and I would see to it that his daughter is placed safely out of danger."

She looked up from her perusal of the portraits. "What sort of danger?"

His expression grew serious as if he debated his next words. "You have made yourself known to those best left in ignorance of your existence."

"You mean the *Hind Div?*" Her eyes widened as the Resident looked away, clearly discomforted by her question. Mercy! What had he heard? "You fear he means me some mischief?"

"No, not he." He squeezed her hand before releasing it. "The viscount fears that in urging you to seek out the *Hind Div* he put your life in jeopardy. This is a country in which revenge is often exacted upon the friends as well as the households of one's enemies. The *Hind Div* was a man with many enemies."

"You say *was?*"

He looked at her, his eyes full of concern. "The *Hind Div* is dead, my dear."

Japonica turned sharply away. Despite her anger and hurt at her humiliation at his hands, she had never once wished the *Hind Div* harm. A dozen things ran through her mind, questions to which there would now never be answers. At the end of that brief torment all she could think to ask was, "When?"

"Shortly after you left Baghdad. It is said an assassin murdered him after Afghan rebels put a price on his head."

"Are you certain?" Doubt bolstered her disbelief. "The *Hind Div* is known for his trickery and magic. Perhaps this is just another of his deceptions."

He smiled a little sadly. "We have our ways of knowing. I should not have brought it up. The matter may rest with his death."

"I see." The *Hind Div* was a violent man who lived a violent life. What other end could she expect for him? She should not be so shocked. She should not feel as if a bit of her own life were draining out of her. "You will forgive me if I resume my seat," she said in a wooden tone, crossing on unsteady legs to her chair.

"Dear child, I have distressed you." The Resident poured her a cup of tea. "I assure you, as long as you are in Bushire, you are safe. However, if you agree to marry the viscount, you will be sent to England." He indicated the document she still held. "Read it very carefully before you decide. If you so choose, you can leave for England almost immediately."

"I've never been to England," she said absently. *Dead!* So vital a being gone from this earth? It did not seem possible.

"Then you shall find the experience most interesting, I expect."

"Perhaps." She forced her thoughts away from the pavilion room of a house in the old *suq* of Baghdad. "What do you suppose Lord Shrewsbury's heir will have to say in the matter?"

The Resident smiled. "I believe that he is unaware of the future pressing in upon him. He's in the army, in India."

"I see." So even his future was uncertain. He might well die before the coronet ever rested officially upon his brow. *Dead!* Was it possible that those golden eyes no longer looked so boldly upon the world?

". . . act of mercy, Japonica Fortnom." He squeezed her shoulder. "Give it due consideration."

She regarded him with frank doubt as a new thought occurred to her. She was damaged goods, as Aggie would say. Would the viscount still wish to marry her if he knew? To keep him in ignorance of the fact would be to cheat a generous man, even if he were dying. If she were to agree to wed him, she would first tell him about her visit to the *Hind Div.* No, she should say nothing, do nothing. No good would be done in telling that truth.

The room seemed all at once much too warm. The urge to burst into tears pressed upon her so hard she abruptly stood up. "I think I must decline. I believe . . ."

Her gaze wandered to the dear little faces on the desk. How unfairly life dealt with females, even those born in its loftiest realms. Their father's hasty marriage was all that stood between them and poverty. How could she abandon helpless infants? She could not.

She turned to the man who had been her father's friend and now saw himself providing best counsel for her. "Very well. You may tell the viscount I accept his—his offer." Had any wedding ever been so coolly arranged?

"You have yet to read the details," the Resident reminded her.

She shook her head. " I cannot see that they matter against the happiness of five helpless orphans."

The man positively beamed. "Well said, Miss Fortnom. Well done!"

Japonica walked the windy deck of *The Griffin* on unsteady legs. Three weeks out of the port of Bushire, the ship was beating up the coast of South Africa. She had learned many things in recent days. Foremost, she was not a sailor. Rounding the Cape of Good Hope a few days before, in what the captain called a "right nice blow," sent her to her bunk with a green face and a bilious stomach. To her chagrin, she had tossed up a meal a day ever since. That was enough to convince her she would never see Bushire again if it meant an ocean voyage.

Aggie had said it was just nerves and would pass once she got her sea legs.

"Morning, your ladyship."

She glanced up with a start. As the first mate tipped his hat to her, she nodded and hurried past him. She was not yet accustomed to being addressed as a ladyship, let alone Lady Abbott or the more formal Viscountess of Shrewsbury. Perhaps she never would be. Not even with her husband's coffin resting in the hold of the ship carrying them toward his homeland.

Though two months old, their marriage was still the talk of Bushire when she set sail. Lord Abbott had been adamant that the ceremony be public so that he could in his words "give proper due" to his new wife. Japonica suspected that he hoped to save her the embarrassment and inevitable gossip of a hushed and hurried affair. Hurried it was. Hosted by the Resident and his reluctant wife, they married in The Company chapel with a vicar presiding and a small contingent of the "right" people invited. Despite Lord Abbott's grave condition, the ceremony was held with all the pomp possible for a man who could not rise from his chair to make his pledge to his new bride. Afterwards, he retreated again to his sickroom while she was left to accept the best wishes of the guests at the wedding breakfast.

Within the week she was in widow's weeds, a show of mourning that she took very seriously. One week a bride, two months a widow. Was it odd that she genuinely grieved for a man she scarcely knew?

The second thing she had learned about herself on this voyage was that she could no longer predict what her reactions would be to events even stranger than her sudden widowhood. That had been confirmed only this morning when Aggie insisted on examining her after noticing that Japonica's stomach seemed distended. Expecting to find signs of a septic bowel she had instead made a very different sort of discovery.

"Glory be! Can it be? Ye're with child!"

For a moment they had shared in equal parts the shock.

Japonica reached for the older woman's hand. "Oh, Aggie, what shall I do?"

"You've done enough, I'd say." A hard look came into Aggie's face. "So who was the rogue?"

Japonica had held on to her secret for nearly two months but the shock of the unexpected demanded it be spoken at last. "It was the *Hind Div.*"

Aggie's expression soured briefly. "Ah well, that I'd nae have suspected." The older woman sat down heavily and raised the edge of her apron to wipe her face before she said, "You'd better begin at the beginning, lass, if I'm to know what to advise."

Japonica told her all that had occurred that night and heard for the first time in her life Aggie utter a profanity.

"Drugged ye, the very devil he is!" she finished. "*Och* well, the law will know how to deal with his sort."

"There's no need." Japonica looked away. "The *Hind Div* is dead. I'm told he was murdered the day we left Baghdad."

"Not soon enough," Aggie said grimly.

"He—he didn't hurt me." When Aggie's gaze met hers she blushed, not knowing why she chose to defend a man whose actions were indefensible. "I just meant, he was not callous."

"The practiced sort often aren't." Aggie shook her head and sighed. "Wed, widowed, and with child all in the space of a fortnight. 'Tis no fit way to begin married life, I'm thinking."

"Aggie, I'm so ashamed! What will people think?"

There was not a sentimental bone in her body but Aggie's protective spirit was an awesome force. "Not a thing, to my way of thinking. 'Tis only to be expected that a healthy bride should soon be breeding."

"But, Aggie . . . ." She blushed furiously. "The viscount was too ill to—to consummate the marriage."

Aggie bent a hard gaze on her. "You know naught of men if you think a wee thing like the shadow of death would keep all of them from a young bride's bed." She folded her arms across her chest, her expression implacable. "You're a married lady. What other explanation is there?" Something in her tone made it plain she did not expect an answer.

"People will talk," Japonica said.

"Aye. But they cannae prove a thing." She frowned as she gave hard thought on the matter. " 'Twas only two weeks between the deed and marriage, so the babe's birth date will no' catch you out."

"But what of the child?"

Aggie met her gaze with a pale blue stare. "Do you want it?"

"I—yes." As much as the answer surprised her, it was a completely honest one. "I never thought to marry so I never thought to be a mother. Now I am one and soon to be the other. It's a miracle, in a way."

"There's ways and there's ways," Aggie answered noncommittally.

Japonica flung her arms about the older woman's neck and pressed her cheek to her bosom as she had often done as a child. "Aggie, am I so very bad a woman?"

"Nae, lass." Aggie patted then stroked her hair.

"You're nae the first and nae the last to be tricked out of yer virtue by a devil of a man."

"But what then shall I do? I can't have the child in England."

"And why not, I'd like to know?" Her expression became shrewd. " 'Tis only right that Viscountess Shrewsbury's child be born in the ancestral home. Rumor will quiet soon enough with the viscount's other children there as witness."

"But it's not the viscount's child!" Japonica protested.

"The world will care naught for the truth but to use it agin you." She took Japonica's face between her rough hands. "You're a lady now. Whatever they may think, none will dare declare that this is not the viscount's child."

Japonica smiled weakly. "What if the babe is foreign-looking like the *Hind Div!*"

"Ah well then, you can toss the little devil in the sea."

"I would never!"

Aggie smiled, a thing so rare it transformed her face. "Then we will think of something else, won't we?"

For the first time in days Japonica smiled. "You seem to think we shall come through this with ease."

Aggie's naturally sour expression came back. "A body does what a body must. Sometimes the hardest things are the things that must be."

But it would not be easy.

Japonica turned to the railing and looked out at the vast expanse of ocean rolling away from the ship and felt as bereft as if stranded on the dunes of a desert. She was a month away from England. She was far from home. She could not go back and she did not want to go forward. What, then, was she to do?

"Astonish me." The *Hind Div*'s voice seemed to come to her on the wind of the sea.

Beneath her cloak she touched her slightly swollen belly. She had thought him dead and gone. Now she knew a part of him had taken root inside her. This then was the *Hind Div's* final death-defying act of beguilement.

A new adventure awaited her after all.

PART TWO

*To mourn a mischief that is past and gone
Is the next way to draw new mischief on.*
                              —William Shakespeare

PART TWO

Chapter Four

England, November 1809

A roaring fire chased the chill of an early and rare snowfall into the farthest corners of the breakfast room at Croesus Hall. The fancifully named domicile was the family seat of Viscount Shrewsbury. Situated some twenty-three miles from London, Croesus Hall was an easy distance from fashionable society. But for all the good it did the Abbott sisters, it might as well have been three hundred and twenty. Bored to bits by gentle hillocks, seasonally verdant fields, and the bucolic cares of village life, they dreamed and schemed of the day they would be presented in town. Such a thing was impossible, for they had no female sponsor to launch them on the often-perilous sea called the London Season. Nor were they likely to find such a person. Through a false sense of their own consequence and a lack of discipline that had allowed their high spirits to run wild these many years, they had managed to alienate the affections of every female relative of their acquaintance.

Lady Wellsey, a distant relative, who had recently made the mistake of inviting them to tea, put it precisely. "The Shrewsbury Posy? Rather call them The Shrewsbury Poison!"

The staff, run with precision by Bersham the family retainer, routinely avoided their mistresses' attention. On this morning, however, every ear in the household was cocked toward the young ladies' chatter. Even the Shrewsbury governess Miss Willow, who sat next to a sideboard that groaned under an enormous breakfast of which she had not been invited to partake, listened with ears pricked. For this morning, the sisters discussed the imminent arrival of their new step-mama!

Miss Hyacinthe Abbott led the discussion. Long of limb and with a coltish awkwardness, she had a narrow, horsy face emphasized by a center part in her heavy dark hair. "I shan't speak to her. Not a word! Why give her the consequence? I can't think why Papa would marry his nurse."

"What kind of nurse was she? Papa is dead. I believe she poisoned him and I shall say so to her face," declared Miss Laurel Abbott between generous bites of broiled kidney. An unregulated fondness for partridge, scones, and pudding had puffed her flawless complexion into full-moon roundness and her body into curves that threatened to snap her stays.

"I cannot believe so vile a thing. Papa would never consort with a woman capable of—of ..." Words failed Miss Alyssum Abbott, the middle sister and the only one possessed of true beauty.

"What but evil influence could induce Papa to align himself in marriage to a woman so obviously beneath him in rank and breeding and ... ?" Fourteen-year-old Miss Cynara, prickly at the best of times, paused to spear the plumpest kidney viciously with her fork and lift it onto her plate. ". . . In every way."

"P-p-perhaps she is better than we dare hope." Miss Peony, the youngest at the tender age of twelve, glanced around with the hope of finding an ally among her older siblings.

"Oh, you would think kindly of the snake who bit Cleopatra!" Cynara pushed away her plate in disgust, the coveted kidney untouched.

"Who is Cleop-p-patra?" Peony questioned.

"Never mind, dear." Laurel took a piece of toast and inspected it for weevils, which she believed the cook deliberately introduced into their wheat out of spite. Perhaps she had been a bit rash, accusing the cook of stealing, but then the bills certainly seemed to mount up to more than five young women could consume.

" 'Tis all very odd," Alyssum said quietly. "Why has she waited a full year before coming to England?"

"Perhaps she was too sad to make the journey," Peony suggested, for only she among her sisters still mourned a father they scarcely knew.

"It did not prevent her from promptly shipping poor Papa home like so much cured beef," Cynara pronounced.

"More likely she ran through whatever sum Papa gave her and hopes that by coming here she may extract more from us." Laurel boldly voiced the concern uppermost in the four sisters' minds. "It must be that she is after the Shrewsbury fortune!"

"Which makes her no better than she should be." The tip of Hyacinthe's nose twitched. "One could expect little else from an Indian."

"She ain't Indian." Laurel looked quite smug. It was due to the woman's letters to the family solicitor that they knew something about their new step-mama. "Her parentage is English."

"Yes, but who were they?" Hyacinthe, too, had read the solicitor's replies. "Cousins of a London grocer!" She shuddered. "Mark my words. She will stink of the shop."

"But may, no doubt, expect that this marriage has raised her above her lowly birth," Laurel added.

"She may believe it raises her above us," Alyssum exclaimed.

"Precisely!" Laurel declared. "If we do not strike first, we shall soon find ourselves at her beck and call. That we must prevent."

"How can we?" Peony scratched her head vigorously, an action that caused her sisters to shy away.

"Are you lousy again?" Alyssum asked in concern.

"No," Peony answered quickly though she could not honestly swear to it. Her fondness for the woods and stables made it a chronic condition with her.

"You should not even be here," Cynara scoffed. "Lenora Parkinson says her little sister is kept in the nursery and allowed below stairs only when expressly sent for. Go up to your room at once!"

"I won't and you can't make me!" Peony shouted. Cynara balled up her fist and shook it. "Can't I just!"

"Sisters, please!" Hyacinthe rapped her fork on her plate. "Is it not enough that we must deal with this—person?"

"I believe I have found the antidote to our new step-mama." Laurel glanced around the table, her expression brimming with mischief as she met the looks of expectation on her sisters' faces. "We shall appeal to the new viscount for protection."

"We do not know him," Alyssum said.

"A mere formality. He is a distant relation, after all. And unmarried!" Laurel leaned forward against the table in the way that brought prominent attention to the abundance of womanly charms exposed by her too-low-cut bodice. "And therefore open to feminine persuasion!"

"A single gentleman possessed of title *and* fortune should not escape obligation to his female relations," Hyacinthe agreed.

"Some consideration must be made of the possibility," Alyssum said, although, as third in line of her marriageable sisters, she would have no chance to set her cap for the new viscount. Not that she cared much. The new rector at Ufton Nervet, a Mister Charles Repington, had made an impression she could not quite forget. Unless she was mistaken, the serious-minded and quite handsome youngest son of a baronet had held her gaze a fraction longer than necessary as they were introduced after services a week ago. His "living" was said to be worth nearly one thousand a year! She hugged that tiny secret to her heart in consolation for the lost viscount.

"For all we know the new viscount is doddering and poxed," Cynara declared, always eager to cry "fly in the pudding."

Laurel's smile remained smug. "He is not above thirty years old and a decorated officer recently discharged from the army at Calcutta!"

"A s-s-s-soldier?" Peony breathed with shining eyes. "I am partial to a gentleman in a red coat!"

"He is expected to arrive in London no later than the end of the month," Laurel finished triumphantly.

"How do you know so much?" Cynara asked suspiciously.

"I read the gazettes," Laurel answered. But in point of fact, she had not handed over every letter she received from the solicitor. Self-promotion in a household of women, she decided early on in her young life, required a bit of subterfuge.

"Such a gentleman," Laurel continued, "so long away from good society, will be in need of a stylish wife who can preside over his home in a manner equal to his new consequence."

"What home?" Peony questioned.

"Why, this house and all the Shrewsbury possessions." Laurel waved her fingers about. "There is even a house in London which, I should think, he would prefer to the country. So this is what I propose: we go to London immediately so that we may be there to greet him upon his return."

"Yes, yes!" was the rare unanimous agreement.

"We can all buy new bonnets!"

"And shoes!"

"And gowns!"

"And inquire about our yearly allowance," Laurel said, hoping to bring renewed sense to their purpose.

Though Hyacinthe was nominally head of the household, she spent her time looking after their father's extensive gardens, which he had entrusted her to oversee in his absence. Laurel kept the books. There had been no direct answer from their solicitor to her request for their annual allowance, usually issued right after the fall harvest. Instead, Mr. Simmons had informed them of the dowager viscountess's imminent arrival in England, which would, "settle all matters material to the question." That, thought Laurel darkly, meant they were to lose control of what little they had.

"So then, it is agreed." Hyacinthe nodded with a rare look of satisfaction upon her face. "We shall pay a visit to London to meet the new viscount."

Laurel glanced suspiciously at Alyssum, thinking that she must encourage her sister's tendency to dress in insipid colors in the hope it would obscure her natural beauty. "With very little effort I believe I shall soon convince our newly titled relation that marriage to one of his orphaned relatives is the right thing—nay, the only honorable avenue open to him."

"You mean to marriage to *you*," Cynara taunted. "It should be Hyacinthe, the eldest, who instructs him in his duty to us."

"Not I." Hyacinthe drew herself up. "I will not parade before any gentleman like a cow at market. If he has not the good sense to recognize the advantages of the alliance, I shall forbear to apprise him of it."

"I, on the other hand, have no such scruples." Laurel smiled. "I shall cast my lures before the viscount, depend upon it!"

Peony clapped her hands. "If Laurel marries the new viscount, th-th-then we need never leave Croesus Hall!"

"As to that, I shouldn't wish to have four sisters underfoot while I establish myself as Croesus Hall's new mistress." Laurel dimpled with as much pleasure as if the match were already writ in the parish book. "I would see you comfortably placed once I'm wed. Perhaps Papa's hunting lodge in Edinburgh."

"You wouldn't dare!" four voices chorused together.

" 'Tis a great drafty place . . ."

"Without a single comfortable bed . . ."

". . . Or proper servants!"

". . . Or heat!"

By the time the butler stepped inside the door, the chorus of invective had degenerated into an all too usual public school-style brawl complete with volleys of food and tableware.

Hyacinthe spied him first and clanged her fork against her teacup for silence. "Yes, Bersham?"

The long-suffering family retainer did not blink an eye as a late-launched biscuit skimmed past his shoulder. "Misses Abbott, the mail coach has been spotted coming up the drive."

Laurel lowered the spoon she was about the send hurtling toward Cynara. " Did you say *mail* coach?"

"Yes, miss." He glanced quickly at the wallpaper to see what would be required to remove the jam that had been flung at it.

"We'll just see about that." Hyacinthe rose, her features set in consternation, and headed for the exit.

The remaining girls overset chairs in their haste to beat one another to the dining-room door where they pushed and shoved and even tore the sash of one gown and stepped on the hem of another before they had successfully passed through.

They all reached the windows of the front hall in time to see a great black coach rock to a halt on the drive. Its team of heavy horses pulled up short under the driver's virulent cursing and sawing on the reins, spewing gravel beneath heavy iron-shod hooves while shivering and snorting great clouds of breath into the chilly air. It was a singular sight for the sisters who had never had need to even consider a public equipage.

"Remarkable display," Hyacinthe murmured under her breath and withdrew a little lest the passengers notice her at the window. "Bersham. Ask that fellow what he means by plowing up our drive with his great beasts."

As the butler hurried to the front door the postillion leapt down from his perch.

"Croesus Hall!" the driver bellowed in a voice better suited for the coach yard of a travel inn. "One-minute stop to unload a passenger!" he added as the postillion opened the coach door and lowered the steps.

"Oh, Lord!" Cynara jumped up and down. "I'll bet it's *her!*"

Laurel, stung with excitement at the possibility gushed, "This is too delish! Our new step-mama come to Croesus Hall in a common conveyance!"

As passengers began piling out into the chill morning air, the five sisters pressed to the windows for a better view.

"Is that her?" Cynara questioned impatiently when she spied through the lace curtains a woman of middle years.

"I have no way of knowing until she presents herself," Hyacinthe answered. Yet, she, too, had picked out for her particular inspection the woman in brown serge whose face, beneath her bonnet, was broad and plain-featured.

"She ain't brown like an Indian," Cynara observed.

"She scarce seems a lady," Alyssum mused aloud.

"One supposes the Indies do not provide much opportunity for brilliance in womanhood," Laurel murmured in satisfaction. "We must expect oddity."

None of the other passengers appeared, in the least, a more likely candidate. Two of them were male, a farmer and a military officer. The fourth and final passenger was a young female who scarcely reached the shoulder of the officer who offered his hand to help her down. She wore a deep black bonnet and a wholly unfashionable sheepskin garment that looked like something a shepherd had stitched together for warmth on a winter heath.

In short order, three small valises and one very large trunk were unlashed from the back and placed on the drive. Then as briskly as before, the postillion ordered the passengers to climb back onboard. Every one of them did so but the young woman in the fleece-lined cloak.

"Is that h-h-her?" asked Peony as she danced on tiptoe behind her taller sisters.

"Surely not!" murmured Alyssum in doubt.

"But she's young!" Laurel exclaimed in vexation. "Remarkably young!"

"Younger even than . . ." Cynara began.

Hyacinthe held her silence but her opinion was writ large on her face. Her eyes, rounded with amazement, were fully trained upon the frightful creature moving toward Bersham with a bright smile. In her hand was a valise bearing the Shrewsbury crest!

"That'll be Ufton Nervet, ma'am." The speaker, a young military officer, tilted his head toward the window of the mail coach. "Croesus Hall lies not far on the other side." When Japonica looked up, he winked at her. "You are coming into service there? As governess, perhaps?"

Japonica turned her head, ignoring his too-friendly manner as she had all his other attempts to draw her into conversation since the day's journey began. She supposed he had bribed the driver in order to learn her destination. He could not learn the reason behind it for she had told no one. The squire and his wife who formed the third and fourth of their group had not spoken a word to her, which was just as well. She found very little reason to represent herself to the world as a viscountess when she meant to renounce the title.

Pushing aside the coach's leather window shade, she glimpsed townspeople so layered in wraps they appeared like so many bales of cotton. Many of them paused to watch the passing coach. In turn she watched them until her breath turned to frost before her nose, obscuring her view. The most amazing discovery of her journey so far was the climate.

Two evenings ago when the coach halted at a posting inn for the night, she had stepped out into a silvery fall of tiny white points of light from the night

sky! She had heard of it but never before seen snow.
Delighted, she had danced about trying to catch a
few flakes in her palm. But the cold had soon lost
all fascination for her.

Born and bred in a climate where flowers bloomed
year round and the only seasons were dry and monsoon, she soon found the cold a torture. Today her
hands and feet ached from the chill as bursts of wind-
borne rain and snow continuously found every crack
and cranny in the coach. Her travel clothes were near
ruined, as were her spirits. She would not be here
now but for the promise she had made to Lord
Abbott, one she had thought many times in the past
year that she would not keep.

Would she have been brazen enough to carry out
the deception of giving birth to her child beneath
Lord Abbott's ancestral roof? She would never know,
as chance once more took charge of her life and
changed its course utterly.

Their ship had sailed into port at Lisbon last spring
only days before Napoleon's forces seized the port
city. For the next few months they were stranded as
unwilling guests of the French, until Lord Wellington's troops arrived in summer to liberate them. By
then, she was too close to her confinement to risk
another long sea voyage. Meanwhile, Wellington himself saw to it that Lord Abbott's body was shipped to
England.

On August 1, under the Sign of The Lion, she
gave birth to a child with black hair and eyes with a
strangely golden tint behind the natal blue haze. She
should have suspected that the *Hind Div* had yet to
cast his final spell upon her life. She had a son!

So much for Aggie's perfect apple of advice! At its
center now lay a worm of complication: her impossi-
bly sweet son. If he had been born in England and
accepted as Lord Abbott's child, that would also have

made him heir to the Shrewsbury inheritance! That
was a lie she could not perpetuate. That meant no
one in England must know about Jamie, named after
her father.

Japonica bit her lip to still its tremor. She could
still scarcely believe that she had had the strength to
leave Jamie behind with Aggie in Lisbon. Yet there
was very little choice. She could not risk his health
or the questions his appearance would give rise to.
The world would call her son bastard and the truth
would do nothing to ease the shame. Her son would
not have the legal protection of a father's name.
Would she one day find the words to tell him the
truth? How to explain to a child the duplicitous
nature of a father the world knew as the *Hind Div*?
No, better he not know.

Love born of deception was still love. The fierce
protectiveness which rose up within her when she first
gazed upon her swaddled son remained unalterably
powerful. Nothing and no one would harm him as
long as she lived.

But first she had a promise to keep.

A scandalous and wicked woman she might be, but
she was also an honest and trustworthy person. She
had given her pledge to Lord Abbott to look after
his little girls. She would not be free to live her own
life until she had found a way to fulfill that pledge.
And that required this journey to England.

Japonica suppressed a sigh of misery. It was the
right thing, was it not? No, she must not think about
it all again, not any of it, not when she was about to
meet her new family.

The mail coach suddenly swung off the main road
and the driver yelled out, "Next stop, Croesus Hall!"

Leaning forward, she twitched open the leather

curtain. She had been expecting a fine house. The imposing breadth of the large, handsome stone mansion she glimpsed through a copse of leafless trees quite took her breath away. Three stories in height, with smoke rising from several chimneys along the roofline trimmed in snow, Croesus Hall was a study of stately order surrounded by rambling woods. Through the countryside snaked a silver-backed river culminating in a lake before the palatial home. Had the viscount lived, this would have been her home.

That thought surprised her anew as the mail coach rounded a curve, carrying her at breakneck speed toward the edifice. She was accustomed to managing her father's household of five servants. A place of this size must command the attention of dozens of servants! It was just as well that the burden would not be hers.

When the driver had brought the great black coach rocking to a halt, the other passengers rushed to step down, using the stop as an excuse to stretch their legs. Japonica deliberately waited to be last, attempting to dust off a little of her travel dirt. She had hoped to make a better first impression. In correspondence with the Shrewsbury solicitor in London, he had promised her that the Shrewsbury post chaise would meet her upon arrival at the dock in Portsmouth. But an autumn squall off the French coast had forced her ship to make port instead in Falmouth in far west Cornwall. To her dismay, there was not a private chaise to be had at any price in that town.

"Hired away by officers of the fleet, what with the weather forcing so many ashore," the coaching clerk had explained. "There's only the Mail coach going out today, miss. If ye idle by a few days, 'twill come a coach for hire."

She did not want to add even a day to her time

away from her son, so she had made the two-hundred-mile journey by public coach.

She stepped down with the help of the young officer's proffered hand, forcing an expression of cheerfulness she did not feel.

"Good luck to you then, miss." The officer pinched her elbow familiarly before he climbed into the coach.

Ignoring the insult, she picked up her valise and approached the elderly man dressed as a servant who stood staring at her with a frown on his long face. She smiled at him. "Good day. I am Japonica For . . . ."

"Who is she, Bersham?"

Startled, Japonica looked up toward the owner of that commanding voice. At the top of the steps stood a tall young woman in the most unforgiving shade of lavender.

"Good morning," Japonica called out, and made her way toward them.

By the time she reached the first step, four other young women had joined the first. They were too elaborately dressed to be servants, yet poorly groomed. If she did not know better she would think that they had just been in a fight, for there was not a neat head of hair between them and their gowns were soiled and wrinkled. Perhaps they had donned the castoffs of their betters in hopes of making a good impression on their new mistress. But how had they known when she would arrive?

Uncertain how to present herself, she chose the most direct method. "I am Japonica Abbott, wife of the late Lord Abbott."

"Oh Lord!" cried the pudgy one. "It's her!"

"Our new step-mama?" said the youngest.

Without a word to her, the tall woman lifted her gaze past Japonica. "You there, fellow, drive on!" she ordered in her deep contralto. The coach horses apparently understood that the order concerned them for they stepped immediately into stride.

She waited until the rattling noise of the coach had subsided before bringing her gaze back to Japonica. "I am Hyacinthe Abbott, Lord Abbott's eldest child. I suppose you must come in. For now."

Chapter Five

"There must be some mistake." Japonica stared uncomprehendingly at the five hostile gazes glaring at her across the morning room. In the bag at her feet were ribbons and sweetmeats for the children she thought she would be greeting. "I was told Lord Abbott's daughters were still in the nursery."

"And we were told to expect a lady." Hyacinthe looked over the younger woman's road-worn appearance. " 'Twould seem we were all misinformed."

Japonica tried to adjust her thoughts to this new circumstance. The Shrewsbury Posy was not comprised of cherubs. They were young women, and not all so young, to judge by the eldest. In her frosty severity she seemed a dozen years Japonica's senior! Still, there was nothing for it but to begin again.

She smiled as brightly as her fatigue would allow. "Surprise need not be unpleasant. I am certain we shall get on beautifully once we come to know one another.''

"I very much doubt that," Hyacinthe answered. "You are as we surmised, as far beneath us as we are above you." She drew herself up to her full height, five inches above the intruder. "Your decided lack of propriety in arriving by public coach is nothing short of shocking! I presume your maid follows by pony cart."

"I have no maid," Japonica answered forthrightly.

"No maid?" Laurel repeated in a tone that made Japonica flush.

"Every lady has a maid," Alyssum said, as if she could save the moment.

"Every *lady,*" Laurel responded with emphasis on the last word.

A dull throbbing began at Japonica's brow. "It has been a very difficult journey. I made it only that I might make the acquaintance . . ."

Hyacinthe cut her off with an abrupt gesture, hugely enjoying her position of power. "The reason for your presence isn't in the least of interest to us. If you had any finer feelings you would have come directly to England upon father's death."

In satisfaction, she saw the younger woman pale. "I wrote to explain that I was unavoidably detained."

"So you say." Hyacinthe sniffed. "You may as well understand that there is no place for you here. No one in this house will ever think of you as any sort of relation."

"Certainly not a step-mama!" added Laurel.

"Never!" chorused the remaining three.

Japonica lowered her gaze, caught between anger and embarrassment. She had not expected to be welcomed with open arms, but the depth of the hostility of these five young women made her feel a little sick, which brought to mind the smells of broiled meat and warm bread emanating from deep in the house. She had not eaten properly in days, but she brushed the thought aside. What she needed most at this moment was a chance to collect her thoughts.

She glanced about for a distraction and noticed a fire blazing beyond the room in which they all stood. "Oh, lovely. A fire!" She moved deliberately toward it as if she had been invited. She did not care if they followed, so long as she could for a moment remove herself from their collective censure.

She pulled free the ribbons of her bonnet as she passed from one room into the next and lifted it from her head.

"Red hair!"

"Do Indians have red hair?"

"Mongrels do!"

The words were whispered behind her but loud enough for her to overhear. Japonica did not glance back. She paused to lay her bonnet on a side table then swung her heavy Afghan sheepskin cloak from her shoulders and draped it over the back of a settee before continuing toward the hearth. When she thrust her hands toward the fire, the stinging warmth greeted her like an old friend. Ah, but this was exactly what she needed!

After a moment she turned with a smile to see the Abbott girls had joined her, at a distance. "We should become acquainted. Won't you tell me a little about yourselves?"

"I see no reason to do that," Hyacinthe answered.

"Then I will give you one." Japonica rubbed her hands together. Chapped raw by the cold, they stung and turned an angry red. She had not meant to begin with the terms of her bond to them but it was as well that they understood it from the beginning. "I made your father a solemn promise that I would act as your guardian until each of you are wed." She glanced doubtfully at Hyacinthe. "Or other suitable arrangements can be made."

"You expect us to believe Father would willingly have made you his viscountess?" Hyacinthe eyed the stranger as if she were a sickly sow. "You have no style, no polish. Your features, like your accent, betray your common roots. Impossible!"

As if cued to do so, Laurel pressed a hand to her ample bosom and cried rather too theatrically, "Poor father! Old and ailing, alone in a strange land."

Cynara took a step toward Japonica. "Admit it. You forced this marriage upon Papa!"

"If, indeed, it ever took place." Hyacinthe spoke this last with a self-satisfied smacking sound.

Japonica noticed the remaining two girls watched this confrontation with avid interest yet they made no effort to take part in the attack. Perhaps they were more willing to hear her out. "As a matter of fact, your father's proposal of marriage came as a complete surprise. My first inclination was to refuse it."

"I don't believe you. You are a liar!" Cynara's face flamed with indignation, which only brought to prominence the angry color of her pimpled skin. "Why would Papa propose to you?"

"I believe you poisoned Papa!" Eyes blazing and bosom still heaving, Laurel took a step toward Japonica, drama as innate a part of her as breathing. She trod on her torn sash and might have tripped had fury not carried her forward. "When he was too weak to protest, you forced your vile plan of marriage upon him!"

"Slut!" Cynara whispered.

Japonica saw Hyacinthe smile at last. But it possessed a mean thinness. "If you have the least feeling for our father's memory you will leave at once!" She looked left and right and gave a nod to her younger siblings who quickly followed her as she stalked away.

"I certainly carried that off well," Japonica declared under her breath, but her hands were locked so tightly together before her that the skin had cracked and begun to bleed. Ignoring the pain, she moved to a nearby wing chair and collapsed gratefully into its concealing depths.

Lord Abbott, it seemed, had played a nasty trick on all of them!

"Why would he do such a thing?" she murmured. Did he think her more likely to accept the role of mother to infants than young ladies? Not only were they far older than she had been led to believe, but also considerably less well bred!

She had supposed that aristocratic children would be beautifully groomed, with the serene nature of swans. Instead they looked and behaved like wealthy fishmongers' children. Only the eldest appeared to have washed before dressing. And their hair, well that did not bear thinking about just yet. The instant impressions she had formed of them did not bode well for the person who would assume the responsibility to marry them off.

"*Bismallah!*" Japonica muttered. Three grown stepdaughters and two nearly so. What was she to do with them? She had thought—oh, but what she thought did not matter. Toddlers or debutantes, they would not long be her concern.

"Miss—My lady?"

Japonica leaned forward until her vision cleared the wing of her chair. A thin middle-aged woman in dustbin brown stood a little distance away wringing her hands.

"I don't mean to disturb you, my lady." She dipped into a curtsey. "I'm Miss Dorothea Willow, the Abbott governess."

"Hello, Miss Willow." Poor dear, she thought. The reed-thin woman seemed intimidated by her own shadow. The Abbott girls must bend this "willow" to their whim at every moment of the day. "What may I do for you?"

The governess's gaze faltered before her new mistress's. "With your permission, my lady, I should like to tender my resignation."

"Resign? But you mustn't. I shall need every sort of ally I can muster in this household. Say that you will stay."

The sudden droop in the governess's posture answered before she did. "With your indulgence, I must insist, my lady. The young ladies are of an age . . . ."

The door opened behind the governess and the butler strode in. "You'll be wanting the Shrewsbury carriage then, madam?"

Japonica cocked a brow in surprise. "To what purpose?"

"I was told . . . ." The elderly man exchanged glances with the governess. ". . . that madam would be retiring to the coaching inn at Ufton Nervet."

The Abbott girls' second volley had been fired. Japonica sat forward. "Quite the contrary. Please see that my things are taken upstairs. I do not care which room I am given. I wish to rid myself of travel dust before tea."

She saw him glance back over his shoulder to the open doorway where two footmen stood in the hall with her things in hand. So then, her position within the household was in doubt. The last ember of her strength flared to life as anger. She might have been too startled to adequately defend herself with the Shrewsbury Posy, but she had had a moment to regroup.

She stood up, seeking to reach every quarter inch of her five feet and two inches. "Are you new to service?"

The butler's head snapped back toward her with a startled expression. "No, madam."

"Then we will not stand on formality this day as it is my homecoming. But do not mistake my informality for lack of understanding of how things work. I am the viscountess and you are the butler."

The flick of anger in her voice made the older man stiffen. "Yes, my lady."

"You have your instructions. That will be all for now."

She picked up a handful of her damp India muslin gown and moved toward the exit. She did not allow her eyes to focus on any one of the male servants in the hallway as she headed for the main staircase. She was too angry to risk a confrontation should anyone take the opportunity to test her authority. All she had in her favor was rectitude and that, she knew from experience, would carry her only so far.

When she had climbed half the way to the second floor she turned back to the people below. "Oh yes, Miss Willow, you will join me for tea. Until I have time to think over the matter, no one is sacked or may resign. Please inform my stepdaughters that they are also invited to join us."

Miss Willow pinkened like a berry. "I meant no insult, my lady, but . . . ."

All cast startled gazes upwards as a crash sounded above their heads, followed by screams of rage.

"Mercy!" Japonica cried. "What was that?"

"The mistresses possess high spirits, my lady," the butler answered with a sigh of long-suffering.

"Do they indeed?" Japonica firmed her mouth. "They stand in need of someone to curb them."

"Indeed, my lady." The old retainer gave her a significant look from beneath his bushy brows.

It shan't be I, she added in afterthought as she continued her climb. She had detested every second of her time in England so far. Nor did she intend to spend a minute longer than necessary beneath this roof. It was clear what had to be done. She must go to London at once to see the Shrewsbury solicitor and learn how she might rid herself of the duty of caring for Lord Abbott's daughters.

Sweet resinous essence of frankincense and the pungency of orange saffron perfumed the air. Overhead, the clear deep blue of a turquoise sky mocked the presumed perfection of a Pasha's ring. Ancient hills buckled by time and sculpted by timeless winds lay beneath the ageless sun. Gray snags of *nabug* trees rooted in the outcroppings, their branches swelling with plumlike fruit. Far below spread orchards of date trees, green limbs fed by the curving path of a silver river. Farther on, orange groves, then acres of pomegranates grew along the banks of this blessing in the desert.

The day abruptly dwindled into evening, twilight resting like a glowing azure jewel on a horizon banked by a lapis heaven. Cool and sweet, the night air issued an invitation to slumber . . . .

Something stirred in the shadows, golden feline eyes gleaming in the dark. Movement of sleek musculature rolled beneath the rich striped pelt of an Arabian cheetah with a mortal face. Not animal, yet not quite a man. A face to fascinate and frighten and beguile, an exotic visage with a penetrating gaze that held a promise of adventures unknown—a chimera made real.

His kiss! Such pleasure! Yes, yes, here in his embrace is pleasure. But the cost! There is a cost.

Blood on the sheets. Flowing crimson bright, like an overturned jug of wine. It flows from the wounds of the creature stretched over her.

Japonica sat up in bed gasping for breath as tears streamed down her cheeks. Her eyes and cheeks burned but the rest of her was icy-cold. The fire had gone out, leaving her in utter darkness. For a moment she did not know where she was. The room no longer smelled of incense and spice. Then she remembered. Far from Persia, she lay in a bed that smelled of mold and damp wool in a room smelling faintly of smoke and dust. She was in England. So then it was only a dream.

The *Hind Div* is dead.

She collapsed back against the bedding and squeezed her eyes tightly shut. After all this time she should be free of his memory. To mourn for a man she despised made no sense. The tears on her cheeks must be from fatigue and worry.

She sighed, pressing a hand deep into her middle where until four months before life lay . . . .

"Oh, Jamie, my love."

With each passing hour she felt less certain that she had chosen right in coming here. After the unpleasant shock of the morning's events, she wanted nothing to do with the Shrewsburys!

A feeling of tightness in her chest came whenever she tried to reason her way through the complications of the day. On this night it had so tight a grip, she could scarcely breathe. She tried to sit forward again to ease the struggle of her breaths but she felt so weak.

The first spate of coughing caught her halfway through an indrawn breath. The hacking seared her throat and brought tears to her eyes. She fumbled around in the dark for the tumbler of water she had placed by the bedside but sips of it did not help for long. Dizzy and weak, she fell back among the pillows, wheezing for breath, her face covered by sweat but her limbs beginning to shiver. She could not be sickening, must not. There was no time to lose. She needed to get away, go back to Lisbon and then . . .

The coughing began again. The second round seemed about to bring up the lining of her lungs.

When she could finally draw a steady breath, she found the tinderbox and lit a candle. She had brought with her a variety of herbs and elixirs for just such an emergency. Chamomile was good for the throat, as was anise and an infusion of marjoram. But when her feet touched the floor she found she had to grab onto the bedpost to keep from falling.

"I am sick," she whispered because she could not be louder. No, no, she mustn't be ill. No time for it. She was simply tired, oh so very tired. She would just go back to bed and sleep. In a week or two, when things were nicely settled, she would return to the two people who she loved most in the world and forget she ever was the dowager countess or even married.

She took a step toward the bed and instead stepped off into darkness.

"Should we send for a doctor?"

"Certainly not. You heard her yourself. She wishes only to be left alone."

Japonica opened her eyes a slit to find two women holding handkerchiefs to their faces as they stood over her. Had they been there long? She could not remember. Only that there were occasionally voices about her bed and some kind soul spooned broth into her at regular intervals.

"She's been down with the fever for three days. What if she should die?"

"She would not be that obliging."

"Laurel!"

"You know what I mean. Besides, there's Miss Willow to care for her. Come away before one of us sickens. It would be like her to bring an Infidel fever with her. Mercy! We might all perish!"

"Quinsy," Japonica murmured through a throat so swollen she could barely breathe.

"Did she say something? What did she say?"

Hyacinthe bent down low over Japonica. "We cannot hear you."

"Quinsy," Japonica whispered a second time.

"Ah." Hyacinthe stood up. "She says 'tis a vile infection of the tonsils. Not usually deadly."

"Her illness buys us a bit of time. I've been through her things but I—*Ouch!* Why did you pinch me?" Laurel asked crossly.

"Do shut up and come away!" Hyacinthe ordered. "She may hear you."

"She will not remember what we say. Her fever's too high," Laurel assured her elder sister. "If she has squandered the fortune Father left her, she did not bring the results with her. I could not find one piece of good jewelry or a single lovely gown! Yet I did find something of consolation for all my efforts. Five tins of Turkish Delight from Fortnum and Mason! My favorite! She will not miss one, I'm sure."

The voices drifted away and the light with them. Japonica could only be grateful. No, she was not going to die. Nor was she alarmed by the news that her belongings had been searched. One thing did bring a smile to her fever-chapped lips. She now knew her stepdaughters were not above spying. She had been right to tuck her half-finished letter to Aggie beneath her mattress.

Chapter Six

December, 1809

In a private room in the inn at Hartford Bridge, some thirty-five miles out of London, a retinue of five British officers shared a late supper. Augmenting the inn's own fare of chops and oysters were boned pheasants in aspic decorated with lobsters and prawns, potted meats with savory jellies, slices of fresh ham, and iced cakes soaked in brandy, all shipped by their request from London's renowned grocer, Fortnum and Mason. No John Company of officers with any pretense to fashion would have done without such delicacies. Fortified by tobacco and claret, successfully smuggled into the country beneath the watchful eyes of customs men, they played cards for high stakes.

"Gad! I had forgotten how dismal England is in winter!" declared Mr. Hemphill, a lieutenant in His

Majesty's Indian Army in Calcutta. He had played his hand badly and needed something to blame for his present ill temper. "There's only six hours of daylight on the best day. Damnable rain and snow turns even that to twilight!"

"Foreign Service has made you soft." Mr. Howe rested a foot shod in gold-tasseled Hessian on the ornate brass fire screen.

"And lazy." Mr. Frampton broke the seal on a fresh deck of cards with his thumbnail.

" 'Tis the country that's grown soft and lazy," Hemphill rejoined, picking up the newspaper he had been perusing earlier. "It says right here the war with France goes badly. Seems to be little hope of it going otherwise."

"The fault of command." Mr. Winslow smoothed the spot on his upper lip where a mustache grew until a week ago. "Since the Duke of York was forced to resign, the army's been without a Commander-in-Chief. Over a petticoat scandal! The worst sort of folly!"

"Bloody right!" Hemphill echoed. "Better to die in battle than sicken like those poor bastards idling off Antwerp last spring."

His compatriots nodded in agreement. While stranded on the isle of Walcheren after an aborted attempt to rout Napoleon's forces at Antwerp, illness swept through the English troops. Nicknamed the "Walcheren Fever" it killed four thousand and disabled eleven thousand more.

"Blame not the army but Parliament!" Howe muttered. "It has damned little to show for itself beyond a dreadful inertia."

"Worse yet, the Americans dare aid the French by carrying on continental trade! Mark my words, we are not done there," Frampton added. "It will come to war again with the colonies."

"I shouldn't think you'd care to be part of it." Winslow smirked. "How will you keep all that lace and those medals clean in the wilderness?"

"We'll not be gone long enough to stink." Frampton winked at Howe. "Shouldn't take a crack brigade long to sort them out."

Howe and Frampton were boastfully aware that their positions as captains in the Royal Household Cavalry gave them social superiority over their fellow officers who, though of higher rank, served in the Indian Army. Those officers were serviceably dressed in simple jackets and overalls. The Cavalry officers wore expensive red jackets with gold buttons replacing the regulation brass, gold lace cuffs, and spotless white breeches tucked into mirror-bright boots. Even at play they kept strapped to their waists the sword of their rank with its unique gilt half-basket hilt.

"Disgraceful, the loss of the American colonies," Mr. Howe continued. "That blunder I place on the shoulders of the monarchy." He leaned in with lowered voice to mutter, "A mad old King teeters on the throne!"

The Indian officers glanced at one another. Few Englishmen dared speak of the King's ill health. Considering their present mission, it was a taboo subject. They were an English honor guard of the Persian envoy, Mirza Abul Hassan Shirazi, who had arrived in England aboard the *Formidable* exactly one week earlier.

As the next hand was dealt, Howe glanced at their fifth and so far silent companion. "Have you nothing to say on the matter, Sinclair?"

The only man in civilian dress among them, Sinclair sat a little apart. The depression of two vertical lines drew together black brows over his tawny-eyed scowl. Candlelight played along the severe planes of his face, etching the deep scar on his forehead that hinted at a calamitous experience he never spoke of. Now his disturbing gaze singled out Howe. He did not, however, speak.

"Have you nothing to say, sir?" Howe repeated in challenge, for he did not like to be afraid and Sinclair's gaze discomforted him more than he cared to admit. "Or do you admit to ignorance on the subject?"

Sinclair reached with his left hand for the cards Winslow had dealt him. "Had I the ear of the Duke of York or the Duke of Portland or even the monarch himself I'd have advised them to better effect."

"I'm sure you would," Frampton drawled good-naturedly. "That is why we must needs travel cross-country in a blizzard to help you three play handmaidens to a gibbering Infidel who fancies himself an ambassador."

"One who dresses in women's silks!" Howe added. "Only Sinclair seems to understand him, even when he's attempting English. But I suppose that is to be expected," he rolled his eyes in Sinclair's direction, "for one who went native."

Unease passed like a ripple through the room. All gazes swerved toward Sinclair but he gave no sign he'd heard a slur in the phrase.

Until six months ago his fellow officers had thought Devlyn Sinclair dead, lost in a mountain skirmish with the Afghans in 1807. Then this past July he had miraculously appeared at the home of the Governor General of Calcutta. Alive, but just barely. It was obvious he had been tortured.

Dressed in rags and suffering sepsis in several severe wounds, he lingered near death for a month before recovery seemed certain. When he became rational he could not—or would not—explain the last two years of his life.

Rumor bloomed in the wake of conjecture. Some

said he had been a prisoner of the Hindi. Others had it that he, having escaped the Afghans, had been in hiding with the tribes that lived in the mountains along the Afghan-Persian border. Detractors whispered the suggestion that he had been consorting with the Russians. The governor, ever a practical man, chose not to put Sinclair to an official inquiry. Declaring Sinclair a captive of English enemies, the governor nonetheless took the first opportunity to send him back to England and out of the way of lingering disconcerting questions.

Friends rallied round but admitted among themselves that Sinclair was no longer the man he had been. During the voyage to England he sometimes cried out in his sleep in languages none of his fellow officers recognized. None had the heart or the nerve to mention it. His temper, always formidable, had become unpredictable.

Howe leaned back and rested a second booted foot on the brass screen by his chair. In the week since he had joined up with the Mirza's party in Portsmouth, he had grown jealous of the way Hemphill and Winslow deferred to a man he considered half-mad. Most often he avoided Sinclair, but tonight he decided that he would no longer suffer being ignored by him.

"Diplomacy is dull stuff! No job for a real soldier." He glanced sideways at Sinclair as he played a card. "Leave it to the aged and the unlucky bastards who can no longer pass muster."

"I'd sell me commission in a whisker were I, like Sinclair, to inherit a viscount's coronet," Winslow said with a forced cheerfulness.

"I'll not sell my commission before my dotage," Frampton said as he played from his hand. "Better off dead than old or maimed."

Sinclair did not give either man the satisfaction of

a stare. But after a few moments he lifted his right arm and laid on the table not a hand, but a curved length of metal in the shape of a hook, which glinted in the candles' flame.

Howe looked away with a visible shiver, muttering something profane under his breath.

"They say this Mirza keeps a harem of little boys in Teheran," Frampton offered into the stalled conversation.

"That would explain why Sir Hartford sent for Hemphill," Howe rallied.

Hemphill's fair skin mottled with embarrassment and he played a card. "No reason to impugn a man's reputation with that kind of talk, sir."

"Ho! The lad's offended," Howe crowed, pleased to have struck a spark off one of the gathering. "The Persian travels solely in the company of men. If he is the delight of women that he claims, where is his harem?"

"I have read of the practices of the Mohammedans." Frampton offered the others a smug glance. "I dare swear the eight male servants who hover about him are not there for protection only."

Sinclair's gaze moved with deliberation from his cards to Frampton. "The Mirza has been known to entertain half a dozen women per night."

"Half a dozen. By Jove!" murmured Hemphill in admiration.

"How would you know such a thing?" Howe demanded.

"I was present on one such occasion."

"I thought you had lost your memory," Howe pressed.

Sinclair's expression altered, as if he were momentarily as surprised by the revelation as any of them. "It is—unreliable."

"Much, we're told, like your past." Having found

a weakness, Howe could not resist pursuing it. "Some say you are a hero. Other rumors would have it you're a coward and a traitor."

"Rumor is the meat of fools."

Howe swelled with indignation as the others chuckled. "Would you care to make yourself perfectly clear, sir?"

Sinclair did not look up from his contemplation of his cards but a muscle ticked in his jaw. "I dare say you'd not like me to do so." He launched a card from his left hand with the flick of his thumb then moved it to the center of the table with his hook.

Winslow whistled when he saw the card. "Satan take your luck, Sinclair. You haven't lost a hand!" The second the words were out, Winslow went scarlet. "Sorry, didn't mean . . ."

Sinclair caught his wineglass in the curve of his hook and brought it to his lips. The glass shifted precariously in its steel cradle as it met his lips, yet he tipped it up and drank it dry. When he set the glass on the table again a single drop of blood-red claret hung from the wicked tip of his hook. It drew all eyes, an impressive reminder of the deadly enemy its wielder had once been.

Annoyed by the fascination with which the other men watched his adversary's every move, Howe could not still his contempt. "I can but admire a man of parts. Even if they are not all his own."

Sinclair stood up suddenly. *"Bismallah!* This is a waste of an evening!"

Seeing this as a retreat, Howe could not resist a final jibe. "But you're not done entertaining us? Come, don't be shy. What other parlor tricks do you have up your sleeve?"

Sinclair swung about and caught Howe's jacket front on the prong of his hook and dragged him in close. "What do you think of this one?"

"Release me at once!" Howe ground out between his teeth though he did not try to tear away. His assailant's cold-eyed gaze was that of a man who would act without mercy or conscience.

The other men stood up together. Winslow was the first to speak. "He ain't worth it, Devlyn."

Hemphill laid a restraining hand on Howe's shoulder. "Nothing but boredom and the weather to hold accountable for the night's incivilities."

"Give over, Sinclair," Frampton said in a bored voice. "Have another glass of claret."

With his left hand Sinclair grabbed a full glass of claret off the table and flung it in Frampton's face. "You drink it!" He turned and focussed once more on the man tethered by his hook. "Do you really wish to challenge me?"

Howe snorted, his spirit rallying as he perceived the men watching them were now on his side. "I'll not touch a cripple!"

Emotion spasmed in Sinclair's expression. "Until you have lived as I've lived you will never know what I know!" He released Howe with a shove.

Howe jerked away, betraying to them both his incomplete mastery of his anxiety. To cover his blunder he said, "We've all heard tales of your unstable temperament." Howe pulled his dolman straight. "But occasionally even a *sepoy* officer must answer for his outrages."

"See here, sir!" Hemphill protested, for the term for a native soldier was a slur to an English officer. "You insult more than one present."

"Allow me to show you how well a *sepoy* can defend himself." Sinclair reached for the carving knife lying in a plate of bloody beef juices on the sideboard.

Alarmed, Winslow leaned in close to whisper, "Not like this, Devlyn. You disgrace yourself."

"Stay back!" Sinclair swung out an arm. It caught

Winslow full in the face and sent him flying backwards to crash into the card table, spilling wine and sending cards to scatter on the floor.

Just as suddenly, he tossed the knife away and raised both arms to his head. "Good God!"

"What is it?" Frampton asked, but Sinclair turned and stumbled out of the doorway like a man being pursued by his own special demons.

"Foxed!" Howe declared in contempt. "I do believe Sinclair's quite drunk!"

"It's his damnable temper," Frampton answered. "It will one day land him in Bedlam."

Hemphill approached Winslow as he righted himself. "What the devil was Devlyn on about?"

"Damned if I know." Winslow's face reflected his sense of outrage. "Though we are friends, sometimes even Devlyn goes too far."

"Damnable head!" Devlyn Sinclair muttered as he lurched across the open road opposite the inn, pressing his forehead with the heel of his left palm. His head seemed about to burst like an over-ripe melon. The pain always came when he tried to remember some shred of his forgotten past.

Sometimes the pain built gradually until a blood-red veil rose before his eyes. At those times he voluntarily withdrew from all human company. Other times, like tonight, it exploded in anger equal to a cannon put to short fuse. The indignity of losing control of himself humbled him as nothing ever had.

When he reached the railing of Hartford Bridge on the far side of the road, he began tearing at his coat with hand and hook. The heavy woolen jacket seemed to bind his chest. Finally he managed to struggle out of it, though breaking a button off; he heard it skip away in the darkness. Breathing hard, he lifted his arms and face to the frigid night. The cold helped. It numbed his senses.

He inhaled sharply and willed away the memory of the expressions of shock and mistrust on the faces of the men that he had just left. What must be clear to all after tonight was that he was not fit for the post to which he had been assigned.

The black rages, as he called the sudden fits, were often followed by headaches so horrible he wanted to beat his head against stone until it burst. Other times, phantom pains from the missing hand plagued him, awful poker-hot pains that shot up his arm until he would have gladly chopped the hand off again to be rid of the torture.

Physicians from Calcutta to Teheran had probed and clucked like nervous hens over his affliction but none could cure him. If only he could remember the past two years, they counseled him, he might be cured. To that end they offered opium and prayers. He did not trust the one and did not believe in the other.

The Governor of Calcutta believed that returning to England would give him some peace. But by agreeing to be part of the diplomatic retinue accompanying the Mirza to London, he had put himself in an untenable position. The enforced camaraderie aboard ship with men who knew him well but to whom he no longer felt any connection had driven him to the edge of his powers of control. Now, traveling to London by coach, he knew himself to be very close to the edge of an abyss.

Self-loathing roiled in his middle like pythons. What good was a man who could not hold his horse's reins? One who could not even cut his meat or easily fasten his breeches? Once, he had been thought a bruising rider and accomplished swordsman. Today any child of five could best him in the simplest tasks.

Yet to be baited with questions he could not answer was worst of all.

"Better off dead!" he repeated through clenched teeth.

The pain seared like a white-hot blade at a point beneath the scar which ran diagonally from his right temple to bisect his right eyebrow. Groaning, Devlyn thumped his forehead repeatedly with his left palm, striking almost hard enough to leave a bruise. He had made a mistake in accepting a new post. He was no longer what he had been. What he had become he could not abide.

He was not afraid of death. Death was a soldier's constant if capricious companion, capering through the lives of friend and foe alike. No, he was not afraid of death. He feared only the unseemliness of disgrace.

Gradually he became aware of the gentle slap of waves in the darkness below him, of dampness on his lips that was not a tear. He lifted his head and reached for support to hoist himself onto the bridge railing, contemplating an action he could not quite bring himself to name.

Dark cold water. Easy enough to slip quietly down into it. Simple enough to drift away. Silent. Unseen.

An accident. It would seem so. Not unheard of. The cloak of night. An icy bridge on a night laced with snow. A misstep.

How easy to tumble headfirst into oblivion. How much better for all.

"For me . . ."

He squeezed his eyes shut, tears streaming unchecked down his face. He was not a coward. He was not sure why he clung so tenaciously to that thought. It was the one thought that stayed in his mind long after the pain had blinded and deafened him to all his surroundings. If only he were a coward he might have ended the torment. This pain that . . . blotted . . . out . . . everything!

He did not know how long he stayed on the bridge. When he came to himself again his shoulders were covered in a light mantle of snow and his face felt stiff from tears long since frozen by the night. He was kneeling on the road. When he rose, his breeches were stiff with frozen damp. He felt sick to his stomach, but the rage and the pain had passed.

He turned and staggered like a drunkard toward the inn, wondering if Winslow would allow him to share his bed this night. Traveling companions, even officers, often slept two to a bed. He had deeply insulted Winslow. Every man had his pride. If the quarrel was serious enough, even friends might find themselves at the business end of rapiers at dawn. So then, perhaps he would not risk another confrontation with Winslow, as he did not trust himself to keep his shaky grip on his temper.

He was in the stables before he thought better of what he was doing. Some would say he was deserting his post. Yet he had, just the morning before, asked permission to take leave of the Mirza's party for a few days once they reached London. Personal business in London required his attention. He had decided that once his business was done, he would leave England, and the army, for good.

He ordered a horse and left directions for his belongings to be sent along with the rest of the party.

As he awkwardly climbed into the saddle his mount shied, unaccustomed to the reins being directed by a left hand. Murmuring a curse, he fought to bring the horse under control. If he were thrown and killed here and now, he would be spared the ordeal ahead but not the ignominy of knowing that his last act was one to shame any former Hussar. After a moment, he dismounted and ordered a carriage readied.

While he waited, he fretted like a schoolboy about to face the headmaster. He did not want to be a viscount. What he wanted he could no longer have, the life of a soldier, a hero. He could not imagine that anything else in life would ever again engage his passion or intellect. Better he should disappear into the desert than become a mad recluse in London.

When they were ready the coachman pulled up before him and cried down, "Where to, sir?"

Devlyn climbed in saying, "The Shrewsbury residence in Mayfair!"

Chapter Seven

The sound of crystal breaking caused barely a ripple in Japonica's expression as she continued to ladle soup into her bowl. It was the third such crash that morning. It was quite clear to her now. She had landed in an asylum. Her stepdaughters shouted and cried and fought like lunatics at every hour of every day.

Despite her best efforts and the offer of a generous raise, Miss Willow had departed with an alacrity that spoke her feelings towards the girls.

"I shan't be far behind her," Japonica said to the empty dining room. The only way to achieve peace at breakfast was to refrain from coming in until they had abandoned the table.

A fortnight beneath the roof of Croesus Hall was more than enough time to convince her that she could be of no use to girls who had no wish to be other than they were. The older two belittled, ridiculed or ignored her every attempt to be friendly. Caught between their siblings' hostility and a stranger, the younger three most often remained silent in her presence.

She had written to the Shrewsbury solicitor in London to alert him of her intention to visit his chambers, along with the Misses Abbott, this very day. If not for the illness that had kept her in bed for nearly two weeks and still sapped her strength, she would have settled the matter before this.

She resisted gazing into a mirror until she prepared herself for the day's journey. When she did, the reflection was what she feared. The fever had left her with a sallow complexion, sunken cheeks, and eyes that seemed too big for her face. Even her hair had lost its shine, looking so dull and woolly she had chosen her deepest bonnet to conceal it.

" 'Tis not a social event," she reminded herself. Which was just as well. The only gown she possessed that had not been altered to accommodate her pregnancy was a black mourning frock of corded muslin with a high collar.

"The carriage is brought round, my lady." Bersham stood in the doorway of the dining room. "And your belongings have been loaded."

"Thank you." She had yet to tell the girls she would not be returning to Croesus Hall. After settling affairs with the solicitor she meant to stay in London and book passage on the first ship leaving for Portugal.

She glanced up wearily as the sound of a door being slammed echoed in the house. "You may inform the Misses Abbott that the carriage leaves in a quarter of an hour. If they are late I shall go to London without them."

Half an hour later, six ladies sat in the Shrewsbury chaise, traveling at the spanking speed of fifteen miles an hour toward London.

Behind the veil of her lowered lashes, Japonica surveyed her charges. She had dressed for the cold weather journey with sturdy boots and her Afghan cloak. The sisters wore what seemed to her outrageous traveling gear. Over sheer gowns of white muslin they sported feather boas and silk pelisses with pointed tails dripping tassels. Their white chip bonnets trimmed with an assortment of pastel ribbons and spring flowers were at odds with the wintry season. The effect of their finery was much like girls playing dress-up from their mother's armoire.

Unfortunately, they had not taken such pains with their toilette. Laurel's perfume overpowered the small confines of the carriage while, Cynara, who sat next to her, had a distinctly unpleasant smell. If the day were warm, Japonica suspected she would gag from the child's rankness, a peculiar odor combining boiled cabbage and old cheese. She tucked her chin into her cloak and tried to concentrate on the book of poems she had plucked from the library.

Thankfully the girls too brought things along with which to amuse themselves. Hyacinthe worked a piece of embroidery, while Laurel contented herself with studying the fashion plates in a copy of *Lady's Magazine.* Cynara and Alyssum played Beggar My Neighbor. Only Peony slouched in her seat, clutching a dilapidated French doll with a sagging pompadour wig and one glass eye missing.

After a while, a subtle wiggling and whispering began between Peony and Cynara, who shared Japonica's seat. She ignored their gazes and whispers until Peony burst out with, "Are there really t-t-tigers that drink t-t-tea from cups?"

Japonica smiled slightly. When she had attempted the day before to draw out the child by entertaining her with a story about Persia, Hyacinthe and Laurel had quickly stifled their youngest sister's curiosity. "I should be happy to tell you the story but your sisters believe I fill your head with drivel."

"It is drivel," Hyacinthe murmured.

"I don't care. I *want* to know about the t-t-tigers," Peony exclaimed as she addressed a scalp itch. "Tell me, oh please, do."

Japonica met Hyacinthe's sour-milk expression. "As my tale is of little interest to you, you are free to concentrate on your needlepoint."

Thus dismissed, Hyacinthe had no choice. "Drivel!" she declared again under her breath as she reapplied her needle to her linen square.

"So then, where were we?"

Peony leaned forward in anticipation. "The part where the tiger drank up all the tea!"

"Ah yes. It is a story my mother told me when I was half your age. Whenever the weather permitted, our neighbor always had her tea in her garden. But one afternoon she was interrupted by a great fracas. A servant came running to tell her that her pet mongoose, brought with her from India, had cornered a rat in the pantry."

"What's a moon goose?"

"Mongoose. I'm told it's like the English ferret."

"Vermin," Cynara pronounced in a worldly tone.

"Really? In India the mongoose is often kept as a house pet, much like a cat. But they are fiercer. They can even kill poisonous snakes."

"Snakes?" Laurel cried. "What a very horrid conversation you are having!"

"W-w-what about the tiger?" Peony insisted.

"Ah yes, the uninvited guest." Japonica tapped the end of Peony's nose with her fingertip. "When the lady of the house had seen to the disposal of the rat and returned to the garden, she found her cakes eaten and her teacup empty. As she bent to pick up the teapot, she noticed a trail of crumbs leading from the table into the nearby foliage." Japonica pretended to sprinkle crumbs with her fingers, aware that she had an audience of five, although three would not admit to it. "Curious, she followed that crumb trail to the edge of yard where she stared into the jungle leaf. And what do you know? A pair of golden eyes peered right back at her!"

"Oh my!" Peony gasped. "What then?"

"Why, before the lady could move a muscle or even cry out in alarm the eyes disappeared."

"Disappeared?" Peony echoed in disappointment.

"Only the eyes," Japonica assured her. "For just then the lady saw the telltale black stripes on the golden coat of a tiger gliding among the tall reeds near her pond. When he reached the clearing, she noticed one of her best linen napkins tucked about his neck. Upon it was a jam smear from her very own jam pot. She could come to only one conclusion, the tiger had come into her garden and helped himself to tea!"

"I don't believe it." Cynara sat back and crossed her arms.

"I do not blame you." Japonica nodded. "As no one had ever seen a tiger so far south, her friends did not at first believe the lady either. Yet as the days went by, several other neighbors reported seeing the tiger at teatime near their own homes. Not long after, the news reached Bushire that a local tea merchant, lost in the wild of India some weeks before, had been eaten by a tiger. Rumor soon began that the unfortunate man's spirit, now residing in the tiger, had journeyed all the way from the India so that he might still take tea with his friends. After that, every afternoon his friends set out a cup and a biscuit with jam in hopes that he would feel welcome.''

"I think that is a lovely tale," Alyssum said with a shy smile.

"I think it is very silly," scoffed Laurel.

Peony leaned in close with an upturned face. "Are there many such m-m-monsters lurking about in P-P-Persian gardens?"

"Tigers aren't monsters. They are magnificent wild creatures."

"Magnificent wild creatures who eat people!" Laurel rejoined.

"And people eat creatures in return."

"I'd never eat a creature!" Peony declared.

Japonica gave her a gentle smile. "Oh but you do, dear. Where do you suppose the kidneys and ham and sausage you ate for breakfast come from?"

Hyacinthe sniffed and looked away.

"There are many animals in Persia that are quite wonderful and not dangerous at all," Japonica continued. "There are antelope. And camels, which are not dangerous but very rude." She could not keep from glancing at Hyacinthe. "Near the rivers you will find egrets with fine white plumes which English ladies buy to wear at Court. Also peacocks, with such wonderful feathers you cannot count all the colors contained in them."

"Laurel has a fan of peacock f-f-feathers," Peony said. "She won't allow us to touch it."

"Father sent it to her," Alyssum offered by way of explanation. "He always sent each of us such nice gifts."

"He was the best most wonderful father in all of England," Hyacinthe added, then looked quickly away for she was not supposed to be listening.

Japonica fell into thoughtful silence. Wonderful father? Lord Abbott had neglected to give her the proper ages of his children. Or, perhaps, he still thought of them as little girls. "When was the last time you saw your father, Peony?"

"Five years ago."

"So long?"

"Little nodcock!" Cynara admonished. "Papa was home two years ago."

Peony's expression drooped. "But I had the measles and Papa did not wish to be exposed to it."

"He refused to see you?" Japonica could not contain her astonishment.

"He was never long at home but we were never far from his thoughts." Hyacinthe answered this time. "We received packages monthly."

"You mean the gardener received packages," Cynara said sourly.

"Father's gardens were his prized possession," Hyacinthe said in defense. "They are the result of his life's work." She glanced disdainfully at Japonica. "I doubt you are aware of his renown as a horticulturist. I am familiar with his entire collection. Every plant!"

"I am a little familiar with plants myself and should be interested in a tour of Lord Abbott's garden ... at some point." Yet, if the reason for her trip to London were successful, she would have no opportunity to take such a tour.

"Papa loved all of us equally," Laurel said, for she did not like to be long out of the conversation. "He named us after his flowers."

"Only sometimes he forgot our b-b-birthdays." The youngest member of their party could not have looked more dejected. "I wish Papa had stayed home with us."

Japonica reached out and patted the twelve-year-old's shoulder. "You are fortunate to have so many sisters."

Hyacinthe must have read pity in her expression for she lifted her chin in challenge. "Aristocratic households do not coddle children. We are bred to different standards. Maudlin expressions of affection produce weak minds."

"It seems a lonely standard for a child," Japonica replied mildly. "I have lived quite differently in every way from you."

"Where did you live?" Cynara asked in frank curiosity.

"In a hut of s-s-straw and m-m-mud?" Peony suggested. "Hyacinthe says that's the only kind of shelter foreigners can afford. Or they s-s-sleep on the ground," she finished with a faltering conviction that matched her stutter.

Hyacinthe did not meet Japonica's eye. Smiling to herself she said, "Hyacinthe is right about one thing. Some of the richest people in Persia have houses without doors and they do sleep on pallets on the floor."

"And do the wild animals roam about drinking the owner's tea?"

"Oh no. Only the most civilized people live there." Yet even as she spoke, the painted visage of the *Hind Div* came to mind. She felt her cheeks suffuse with anger and another emotion less easily named.

"What's wrong? You look odd," Peony said with childish candor.

Belatedly Japonica realized five pairs of eyes watched her intently. "I was just reminded of one owner of a house in Baghdad who was a cheetah."

"You will insist upon nonsense," Laurel said disparagingly.

"Ah, but I met the owner myself. His name was the *Hind Div*. His house was very beautiful and very grand, with marble floors and many fountains. Instead of doors the rooms were hung with the most beautiful curtains. Some were made of glass beads, others of silk, the colors of the sunset. No matter how hot the day, the air beneath his roof was cool and fragrant. Most amazing of all, a guest had only think of a desire, like a wish for a cool drink, and it would appear without so much as the whisper of a servant's slippers.''

"Where did the cheetah sleep?" Peony asked, fully caught up in the tale.

"His bed was a low wooden platform upon which dozens of scarlet and sapphire and gold pillows were piled.''

"It sounds like a fairy castle!" breathed Alyssum. "Except for the cheetah."

"What fairy tale doesn't have its troll or ogre or serpent lurking?" Japonica answered thoughtfully, for she knew only too well the price of enchantment.

"Tell us more about Persia," Peony coaxed.

Feeling that she had at last made progress with at least one of the Shrewsbury Posy, Japonica resisted the urge to press the point. Instead, she reached into the portmanteau at her feet and retrieved four hand-painted tins. "Who would like some Turkish Delight? I was certain I had five tins but one seems to have disappeared." From the corner of her eye she saw Laurel's mouth become prim.

As he summarized the document before him, Mr. Simmons, the Shrewsbury solicitor, took pains to frequently glance over his pince-nez to offer his little audience brief reassuring smiles. At the behest of his wife, he took particular notice of the new viscountess each time he did so. Nothing less than a full accounting of the day's events would satisfy Mrs. Simmons, who prided herself on being an encyclopedia of information on the *ton* for her friends. But he did not need her directive on this particular occasion.

Though an unexpected and unpleasant previous visitor had left him flustered and distracted, his attention was riveted from the moment the dowager viscountess entered his offices.

The late Lord Shrewsbury had married a girl younger than his eldest child!

Then there was her peculiar accent that, although cultivated, spoke distinctly of the colonial class. Sallow of complexion and on the slight side, he was satisfied at once of his own error in speculating that the new viscountess's pulchritude had played a greater role in the viscount's decision to wed her than the considerations the peer had set forth in his last letter to him. To be sure, reddish lashes and brows were a mere hint of the red tresses that lay beneath her weathered bonnet. Still and all, "ordinary" was the only word that fit her.

He would also report to his wife that, as usual, the Shrewsbury Posy were overdressed, overscented, and underimpressed by the niceties of the fashionably new toilette that demonstrated the virtues of soap and water. A disciple of Beau Brummell, he periodically lifted a vetiver-scented handkerchief to his nose to disperse the odors in the overheated room. "There you have it, my ladies, the short and simple truth."

"I cannot believe it!" For once, Hyacinthe's face had lost its hauteur. In its place was alarm. "There is no mention of our settlement."

" 'Tis an easy matter to explain." Mr. Simmons's hearty chuckle failed to infect his clients. Truth to be told, he had begun to sweat under his neck cloth as he met the eldest daughter's Medusa-like stare. Miss Hyacinthe would unnerve a bulldog. "You are provided for through the dowager's portion."

"Dowager's portion?" Hyacinthe's gaze swiveled sharply toward her stepmother and Mr. Simmons could only admire the aplomb of the receiver of that withering stare. "Is there to be no continuance of our allowance? No separate settlement? We are disinherited, Mr. Simmons?"

Feeling the sting of her stare once more, he hurried into speech buttered by a groveling tone. "Never so harsh an expedience, my lady. There was nothing for you to inherit."

"What of Father's personal funds?"

"*Ahem.*" Mr. Simmons adjusted his lens. "I'm afraid there is nothing left. His lordship's personal finances went to fund his horticultural pursuits. Still, there's no cause for alarm. Lady Abbott is now your legal guardian."

"But that is what we've come to prevent." Laurel rose from her chair and flung one end of her long boa over her shoulder. "We wish to appeal to the new Viscount Shrewsbury to be our benefactor."

"I, too, believe it is the best solution," Japonica put in, much to the astonishment of the five girls surrounding her.

"Now, now! Let us not be hasty, my ladies." Mr. Simmons applied his scented handkerchief this time to mopping his brow. He was most definitely sweating! He well knew that the very last person any of them was likely to receive relief from was the new viscount.

Full of threats and bluster, an earlier visitor had been none other than the new viscount himself. The nobleman had said first he did not want the title. Moments later he owned that if he did accept, he would refuse all the usual encumbrances of inheritance.

Mr. Simmons muttered to himself. He would never

forget his chill at the sight of Lord Sinclair's wicked hook! Lord! If the Abbott sisters poked that rabid dog, they would no doubt all be devoured in retaliation.

Out of habit, he reached for the decanter on his desk, only to pause in mid-action as he spied Hyacinthe's sharply arched brow of disapproval. Bitterly regretting the lack of fortification, he cleared his throat while searching for the words to skirt disaster.

"The entailment is quite clear." He cast a nervous glance at Hyacinthe. "The viscount is under no legal obligation to his female relations."

"But that's unfeeling!" said Hyacinthe.

"Now, now," he continued in his most calming voice. "That is why the provision was made for a dowager. With Lady Abbott in residence you may continue at Croesus Hall in a quite comfortable situation."

Japonica felt the hair lift on her arms as five pairs of eyes shot daggers at her.

"How could such a horrid document be allowed to stand?"

That teary voice, coming as it did from Alyssum, the loveliest of countenances, deeply moved Mr. Simmons. To bask in her grateful gaze he would have found a loophole or exception, even bent the rules. Yet his hands were tied in the matter. All he could offer was solace.

" 'Tis not a reflection upon you, gentle lady. The entailment was drawn up a long time ago by the first viscount Shrewsbury. He came into the title through his aid to Charles the Second. Unfortunately, he was made to marry for it. The King's choice of his bride, a widow named Abbot saddled the first viscont with half a dozen young females from his wife's first marriage. I'm told such circumstance moved him to pen the codicil concerning dependents."

Japonica smiled into her lap. Though she could not approve of his recourse, had the codicil-maker acquired stepdaughters with Hyacinthe's coldness, Cynara's querulous temper, and Laurel's sly methods, she could find a bit of sympathy for the cause behind it.

"I can see we'll get no satisfaction here," Hyacinthe said frostily. "In any case, I have reached my majority and wish to collect my wedding portion."

To hide from her baleful gaze, Mr. Simmons looked down quickly at the document before him. " 'Fraid it's not that simple. According to the entailment you will come into a sum of money if and only if you wed." He ran his finger down a number of clauses before beginning to read. " 'Upon the occasion of a daughter's marriage, she shall receive twenty thousand pounds, to be paid to her husband in recompense for . . . .' " He paused as his cheeks pinkened. ". . . his unfortunate choice of bride.' "

"That's outrageous!" Japonica's forceful tone startled the solicitor as she came to her feet. "I am appalled you would read such tripe to young ladies!"

"We do not need you to vouch for us," Hyacinthe snapped. " 'Tis clear where your interests lie. May whatever Judas gold you receive bring you only ill fortune. We are going home. If you have any finer feelings you will be good enough to stay away." Her sisters followed behind her like so many goslings in the wake of a goose.

When they had departed, Japonica turned back to the solicitor. "You made a right hash of that!"

Relieved to be out of sight of Hyacinthe, he allowed himself the luxury of a shrug. "My dear lady . . ."

"Lady Shrewsbury," Japonica said with a lift of one eyebrow.

"Quite! Lady Shrewsbury," he amended as he came hastily to his feet, "I—I beg your pardon . . .

your ladyship," he added, noticing that her dark eyes were quite brilliant when moved by emotion.

"So then, what is to be done?"

"Why, very little, Lady Shrewsbury. The documents that accompanied your original correspondence uphold your claim that you are, indeed, the wife of the late Lord Alfred Abbott. That much his children will find indisputable."

"I very much doubt that." Japonica resumed her seat with hands folded. "If my stepchildren are an example of London nobility, I believe I shall be at the point of challenge again and again while I remain in this wretched country."

Mr. Simmons smiled. "You have a singular way of expressing yourself, viscountess."

"You mean plainly?" It occurred to her that Mr. Simmons had made the mistake that many people made upon first making her acquaintance. They took her silence to mean she had nothing to say, rather than as a nascent shyness. "Yes, I see that very little in London is said straightforwardly." Japonica took a deep breath and resumed her chair. "I do not intend to be taken by surprise by circumstance again. Explain in detail, please, exactly my situation."

Mr. Simmons lifted his arms in an expansive gesture. "No need to bother your head about such matters, my lady. That is my role. I shall be happy to serve your interests as I have served those of the Shrewsbury estate the last numbers of years."

Japonica eyed him impassively. Something in the solicitor's manner rankled. Perhaps it was his assumption that she wanted each and every matter cared for by him. Or that he did not believe her fully capable of understanding finance. He did not know that as a merchant's daughter, she had learned to keep records and balance books before her first menses and that she meant to keep a very strict account of the dispersal of her dowager's portion.

"Do sit down, Mr. Simmons." Her pleasant smile did not reach her eyes. "As you will be some little time explaining to me the full terms of the entailment, I wish you to be comfortable."

Mouth slightly agape, he did just that.

"Aristocrats!" Mr. Simmons muttered when, one hour later, he was finally alone with his cherished decanter of whiskey.

Imagine! A female who knew as much about debits and credits as he! There would be no paring of her cheese. Moreover, he suspected she meant for him to know it! Underestimated her, at every point. He only wished he could be present when Lady Abbott served Miss Hyacinthe her just deserts! No doubt of it, she would. And he had thought her plain. She was, when angered, quite striking. The red hair, it runs true every time, he thought belatedly. The little minx! She had set herself up quite nicely by marrying a doddering old fool. No doubt he had gone to his grave thinking butter would not melt on her tongue. Of course there was a puzzle in that thinking.

He poured himself the usual amount and then added a second measure to his glass. Between the visits of Lord Sinclair and the Abbott ladies he had earned the accommodation of his thirst. He hoped his wife had made roast beef and pudding. He had more than enough with which to entertain her through a substantial meal.

"First *he* don't want the title! Now *she* don't want the title!"

He would not have believed there breathed a soul on earth who would be willing to give up aristocratic status. Today he had met two.

"Flee the country, that's what they both want!" He

lifted his glass in salute to whatever deity had put the period on this day. "Aristocrats! High-fidgets and Bedlamites, the lot of them!"

Japonica sat in Mr. Simmons's private carriage, the offer having been extended to her when she realized that the girls had made off with the Shrewsbury chaise. But that was of little moment to her, not while Mr. Simmons's last and shocking revelation still rang in her ears.

"If one sister marries, she can then assume responsibility for the others. It is the only provision in the codicil that frees you from your obligation to them, my lady. Though I don't suppose . . ."

"Neither do I," Japonica murmured. Hyacinthe, a bride? She shook her head. Laurel? Perhaps, if she could be . . . . No, it would not serve. "There is no other loophole by which I may divest myself of this responsibility?"

The solicitor shook his head. "In short, the matter is closed, unless you should choose to leave England. In that case, you would forfeit all rights to the dowager's portion."

Until that summation, Mr. Simmons's measured explanations had cheered her considerably, for as a wedding gift her late husband had, as promised, ceded back to her the Fortnum fortune. So then, she was free to do as she wished. She did not need the dowager's portion or the title of viscountess. There was only one small blot on her freedom. If she left England as she planned, the Shrewsbury Posy would be left homeless and destitute.

"No more than they deserve!"

That ungenerous thought did not last beyond its formation. The sisters' plight was a great deal more serious than she supposed. The dowager's portion was in effect only as long as she remained in England. If she abandoned them, they would lose everything. As for marriage . . . Alyssum held the most promise. Yet such things took months to arrange, if they could be arranged at all.

She could not remain separated from Jamie for that long. The thought of her son squeezed hard on her heart. No, she would not stay long in England. The question is, what in good conscience should her next action be?

She turned her attention to the city moving slowly past her window. The din of the crowd, mixed with the sound of wheels and hooves traveling over cobblestones, was quite overwhelming. As for the air, it reminded her of nothing so much as a great room into which sooty smoke had backed up owing to a faulty chimney. Even at midday the sun was not visible, leaving the maze of busy dirty streets in a permanent state of gloom. So this was London.

She sighed and looked away. She must leave. She was within her rights to leave. Generations of Shrewsburys had dealt with the eccentricity of the codicil and somehow managed to survive. Who was she to try to subvert it? Jamie and Aggie waited for her in Lisbon. Oh, how she missed her son. No inducement in the world beyond her own sense of honor could have pried her away from him. How long would it be before Aggie's replies came to her letters? She did not know how he was faring, if he was eating, was growing, had sprouted a tooth. Lord Wellington had promised . . . !

"Oh!" She leaned forward suddenly and opened the window. There was one action she *could* take while she contemplated others. She had promised to send provisions to war-torn Lisbon. In her pocket were a dozen requests from Wellington's officers asking for everything from candles and soap to butter and cheese.

She rapped on the carriage roof and called out to the driver, "Fortnum and Mason in Piccadilly!"

Chapter Eight

"So kind of you to see me to my carriage, Mr. Fortnum."

"No bother, not for me 'Indian' cousin come all this way to see us." Richard Fortnum, great grandson of William Fortnum, the original partner in Fortnum and Mason, gave her a jolly smile. "Wish you'd reconsider me invitation to stop with the family while you're in town."

"You are too kind. Perhaps another time." Japonica turned and stepped quickly inside her borrowed carriage, welcoming its shelter from the snow that had settled over the city during the past hour.

"You will come again while in town, cousin?"

"I hope to. I will certainly inform you of my plans."

While the footman folded the step, Japonica sat back with a sigh, not knowing whether she had made a useful association or nearly given too much of herself away.

Before he shut the door the footman asked,
"Where to, my lady?"

"Indeed," Japonica murmured. She could not very
well take Mr. Simmons's carriage all the way to Croesus Hall . . .

"The Shrewsbury residence in Mayfair," she said
on inspiration.

"Very good, my lady."

As the carriage pulled away, Japonica leaned forward to smile and wave at her newly met relation.
"Good day to you, cousin!"

She had made no fuss upon entering the establishment but had gone directly to the office, where a
senior assistant took her order of enough supplies to
fortify an army—a comparison that was apt considering the amount she was asking to be put on various
British officers' accounts. She might have expected
so large a requisition would attraction attention. Or
perhaps it was that she signed it with her maiden
name. Sure enough, the senior assistant excused himself and within a few moments Richard Fortnum presented himself to her.

Proud to pronounce himself the new majority
shareholder in the grocery, he was all charm and ease
to learn that she was a distant relation. He showed her
to a private room where wine and cakes were served.
Cordially he plied her for news from abroad, expressing the desire, but for the press of business, to see
for himself the exotic sights of the Near East.

With as much reserve as was possible without being
rude, she had spoken generalities in answering his
questions about her reasons for being in London. Not
having mentioned at first that she was Viscountess
Shrewsbury, she could not see a reason to do so
afterwards. As she was leaving he asked for her London address that he might send an invitation to dine
with him and his family. Flattered, she had let slip

that she had no accommodations for a stay in London. Ever the gallant, he quickly suggested that she come and be a guest in his home.

It took her only a twinkling to realize that would not serve. But it left her with a new dilemma. Thank goodness, she remembered the Mayfair house.

Mr. Simmons had described the Mayfair house to her as one of the residences open to her as dowager. Closed these last two years during Lord Abbott's absence, he assured her it was still in good order, for he paid the wages of the caretaker couple who lived in the attic.

She sat back with a smile and opened the handsome tin of Portugal plums Mr. Fortnum insisted she take as a sample of their newest enterprise, Fortnum and Mason Preserved Fruits. For the short remainder of her time in England, she would have a house to herself. Away from the constant fracas of the Shrewsbury sisters! Irresistible!

"Bersham?" Japonica could not contain her surprise when her butler opened the door of the Shrewsbury townhouse.

"How good of you to anticipate us," she continued, as she pulled loose the strings of her damp bonnet. "However, your good intentions are for naught. The Abbott ladies have returned to Croesus Hall where I'm certain they will have more need of you than I."

"Thank you, my lady." The sad-faced man gave her a polite bow. "But I am not in London owing to anticipation. I was sent for."

"Sent for? By whom?"

"Viscount Shrewsbury, my lady. The summons arrived a quarter hour after your departure for town."

"The viscount is in residence? Best of luck! He is the very person I wish to speak to." She handed him her damp outer garments. "Please inform his lordship that I wait upon his convenience in a matter most urgent."

"He will not see you, my lady. I have orders that he is home to no one."

"I am not a guest. I am a relation," Japonica declared with more certainty than she felt.

The sound of raised feminine voices made her glance toward the closed doors of the first salon. "Is he entertaining guests already?" The idea pleased her, for it would seem to make him a gregarious and accommodating gentleman. Then too, the sooner they met, the more quickly the matter might be settled.

She patted her damp curls into place saying, "Don't bother to announce me."

"But—but, my lady," Bersham sputtered to no avail. She sailed past him and parted the doors.

"Do forgive my intru . . . ." The smile on Japonica's face froze. There sat the five Shrewsbury daughters squabbling over tea. The viscount was nowhere to be seen.

The sisters' heads turned the moment she opened the door, their expressions matching hers in reflecting unpleasant surprise.

"It's her!" Laurel turned to Hyacinthe. "I told you she could not be trusted."

Japonica closed the doors quickly behind her. "I thought you were returning to Croesus Hall."

"We thought *you* agreed to leave us in peace." Hyacinthe's cup made a distinct *click* as she placed it in its saucer. "Why ever are you here?"

Japonica swallowed her disappointment that the viscount was not present. "I have come to see the viscount."

"I knew it!" Laurel rose from the settee, scattering

crumbs from her lap onto the floor. "You have come to scheme behind our backs."

"He will not see you," Hyacinthe said with a finality that spoke of certain knowledge.

"And why is that?" Japonica moved into the room. "What have you said to him about me?"

Malice laced Laurel's smile. "Whatever makes you think we would speak to him of someone quite beneath our regard?"

Japonica tucked her thumbs into the crooks of her elbows, mimicking Aggie's stance when in high dudgeon. "So then you haven't spoken with him?"

"He w-w-wouldn't . . ."

"Peony!" her four sisters cried in chorus.

"He would not see you?" She gave Peony a warm look, for she had gained at least one ally. "But he will see me. I am the dowager viscountess. Unless he is married, I have the distinction of rank."

Laurel's gaze narrowed with the mention of the viscount's marital status. With her cheeks reddened by the wind and her hair loosened from her usually dowdy caps and bonnets, her step-mama looked, well, almost fetching!

"He's a doddering old fool. A confirmed bachelor." Laurel looked back over her shoulder for assistance from her sisters. "Besides, he is ill. Most likely it is the plague," she elaborated. "It's the pustules, you see."

"You have seen his pustules but not the man? However did you manage that?" Japonica inquired politely.

"Bersham told us that he is ill," Hyacinthe answered, giving her sister a withering look.

"He is ill," Alyssum said apologetically. "Bersham will confirm it."

Japonica gave the remaining girls a glance and realized that there was dissention in the ranks. Alyssum looked as if she had been weeping while Cynara possessed an expression that would spoil beets. Only Peony offered her anything like a smile, slight and guilt-ridden though it was. Yet she did not want to single the girl out, knowing that her eldest sisters would be certain to torment her for her broken allegiance.

"Cynara? Is my luggage still in the Shrewsbury chaise?"

Cynara hung her head. "Yes, miss."

"Good." Japonica's gaze next picked out Laurel. "I had a notion it might have been thrown into the Thames." Laurel reddened then glanced away.

Finally she turned to Bersham, who had followed her into the salon. "Have my things brought in."

"Yes, my lady."

"You cannot mean to stay here?" Laurel exclaimed in annoyance. "What about the fever beneath the roof?"

"Would you prefer that I accompany you back to Croesus Hall?"

Realizing she was outmaneuvered, Laurel plopped back down on the settee, her disappointment turned into a pout.

"As I thought. Until I have spoken with Lord . . . ." Japonica paused with a frown. "What is his name?"

"S-S-Sinclair," Peony supplied.

"Lord Sinclair. Until I have spoken with Lord Sinclair, you have my permission to remain beneath this roof."

"Permission?"

"How dare . . .' "

"Could she really put us out?"

Japonica turned and walked quickly away as the girls erupted in a cacophony of accusation, recrimination, and ill humor.

* * *

"So the widow arrives, as well. Confound it! The house becomes infested with Shrewsburys!"

Devlyn Sinclair sent his glass of claret hurtling across the room to smash into exquisite shards of crystal against the far wall.

"Those were Lord Abbott's favorite glasses," Bersham said quietly.

Devlyn swung around on the heel of one boot. "They now belong to me. I may break every damn one of them if it pleases me to do so!"

The old man lowered his gaze. "Quite right, my lord."

Devlyn swung his right arm across the tabletop where the remains of his dinner had been congealing, scattering china and silver serving dishes. Gravy and bones and bits of roasted potato flew in all directions before it all landed on the floor with a resounding crash. Only one of the three bottles of claret escaped his swipe, the one that still contained wine. Grabbing it up, he moved rather unsteadily toward the fireplace then sat a little heavily in a well-preserved Queen Anne chair.

Bersham winced as the antique chair's narrow legs creaked under the unaccustomed bulk. "You may wish to have a care, my lord." He moved closer as if he were readying to lift his master off the piece of furniture. "That chair's old and unreliable. Shall I have the footman fetch a more commodious one?"

Lord Sinclair did not answer. He sank lower in its depths and thrust his booted legs out toward the hearth from whence came the darkened bedroom's only light.

Hissing and leaping, the flames seemed to gather in the man's strangely golden eyes. But far more disturbing was the way the firelight played along the curve of the wicked hook thrust out past his right cuff. The effect quite unnerved Bersham but he dared not show it. No telling what the new viscount might do next in his inebriated state.

Drink was all Lord Sinclair had done since he turned up unexpectedly at the house in the wee hours. So said the pair of servants who lived in the attic rooms. Not knowing what else to do, they had sent for Bersham. All the Shrewsbury servants looked to the family retainer to guide them but, for the moment, Bersham was as wary as they. The last time he had set eyes on Devlyn Sinclair, a full ten years earlier, he was in full military uniform and as brash and arrogant as a young nobleman of spirit was wont to be. This harried and haunted-looking man with the scarred countenance and missing hand was a dangerous stranger to be watched and guarded against.

"What the devil do an elderly hen and her brood want with me?" Sinclair said suddenly.

"I could not say, my lord." Bersham wondered if he should disabuse his lordship's view of the dowager as ancient but suspected he would not be thanked for it. If present circumstance were any indication, he would soon dislike the new viscount as much as any man he had ever met, equal or superior. "Would you like me to inquire?"

"Good God, no! They are nothing to me! Nothing!"

"As you wish." Bersham moved to ring for a servant to pick up the dishes, barely able to contain a *tut tut* as he noticed the dent in the lid of one particularly fine piece of Charles the Second silver. He would have to set it aside for the tinker's next visit.

Pointedly ignoring the servant who came to right the mess, Devlyn rubbed the scar slanted across his brow behind which his head throbbed like a drum.

The more he tried to remember things the more it ached. He was the new viscount Shrewsbury. The thought would not stick. He could not remember the late viscount or this house, or even how he came to be here.

The solicitor attempted to explain it, something about his being seventh or eighth in a line of males that had dwindled rapidly over the years. "The last of the line of Shrewsbury," Mr. Simmons had proclaimed in officious tones.

"Better have said the last of a line of flaming madmen," he muttered to no one. There was little money in the inheritance and a great deal of debt and responsibility. The very house he sat in, built a hundred years earlier, was dilapidated, while its gardens sprawled out behind with a glory to rival the King's own. Lord Abbott's contribution to the science of botany, Bersham had proudly exclaimed. He had walked there awhile, hoping the fresh air would cool the pain. But London had little of that.

Devlyn lifted his right hand and stared at the despised hook. He did not like the way people stared at him when they noticed it, as if they feared he might turn and snare them on the end of it at any given moment. Mr. Simmons could scarcely look away from it. The one time he gestured with it to make a point, the solicitor all but swallowed his tongue. After he left the law offices he noticed that London's streets were full of the lame and blind, war-ravaged soldiers who had fared no better and sometimes worse than he. Yet his greatest loss was not a true war wound.

Swearing hard against a lack of memory, he turned the bottle up to his lips and pulled at its contents, drinking a good portion. Even so, he knew it would do no good. There were not enough spirits in all of Christendom to stave off the pain and rage gathering behind his eyes.

Inexplicable anger slithered and writhed through him until he gripped the bottle so tightly he felt he could crush it in his bare hand. Now he was to be plagued by relatives who would no doubt expect him to remember them.

"You say the dowager viscountess has come here to see me?"

Bersham swung around from his observation of the footman's task, more startled than he liked to be. The viscount had already asked him twice about Lady Abbott. It was the wine, of course. Wine's in, wits out!

He moved closer to the chair where his lordship still sat like a stone. "Not precisely, my lord. The viscountess did not know you were in residence. She came to town on business."

"Damn the dowager's privilege! I want no guests while I reside here. Order up their carriage and send them all packing!"

Bersham searched his mind for a prudent answer. "Lady Abbott did say she expects her daughters to return to Croesus Hall presently." Silence met his effort. "The journey is some three hours in good weather. A heavy mist such as has come on this evening could add half again the time. Now a good early start in morning . . ."

Lord Sinclair did not answer or move or even indicate that he had heard the old retainer. There was only unnerving silence underscored by the soft hiss of flame.

Bersham gave the signal for the footman to abandon what was left of his task. "If there be nothing else, my lord, we will withdraw."

Bersham retained all the faculties of his youth but had an old man's bones to deal with. He had only time to cringe in alarm when the bottle Lord Sinclair loosed flew past his shoulder and struck the door behind him, shattering and spraying the old retainer with it's contents.

"Out! Get out!"

Bersham just managed to pull the door shut behind himself before a second claret bottle shattered against the hundred-year-old carved oak door.

"Mad! That's what he be!" the footman cried like a scalded maid.

"Drunk!" Bersham pronounced with the wisdom of all his years of experience. "Madness is for commoners." The nobility could afford to label their excesses eccentricity.

Japonica was discovering that there were a great many ways to be uncomfortable in an English household. Croesus Hall, smelling of dust and cinders and dampness, had beds that seemed to be made of clumped sand. The Shrewsbury townhouse, the latest installment in her understanding of *Farangi* living, boasted a draftiness that had no equal in her experience. The wind whistled in at the edges of the windows, billowing out the heavy drapes spread across them in defense. Once the fire burned down, the downdraft in her small fireplace rattled like a loose wheel cover. The cold supper Bersham provided had soured her stomach, helped along by the news that the viscount would not under any circumstances see her or any of the Shrewsburys. She was still tossing when somewhere deep in the house a clock struck the hour of two.

The first cry sat her straight up in bed. Straining against darkness more like a blanket than a void, she listened for some sign of life within the house. Had she been dreaming?

The second cry, a man's roar of pain, cut off as it reached its keening peak and set her teeth on edge.

"Dear Lord!" she cried as she fumbled for the flint. Someone was being murdered under this very roof.

Her hands trembled so badly that she had to strike the flint half a dozen times before striking a spark that caught the tinder. As it did, a series of long moans began. She moved the tiny flame toward the candle by the bedside, and whispered a prayer for salvation against the horror unfolding beyond her door.

She was not a coward, but as she reached for her bed shawl and stuck her feet in her slippers she wondered if opening her door would be a wise thing to do. What could she do for the poor soul suffering at the hands of an assailant? She had not even a stout stick with which to arm herself. Grabbing up the slender candlestick, she looked about for something that might serve as a better weapon.

The sound of running footsteps sounded in the attic above and she realized in relief that the servants had been roused. From her baggage she plucked a small dagger Aggie had packed for her, "To keep away them thievin' English," took a deep breath of courage, and headed for the door.

No sooner did she lift the latch than five young women in nightcaps forced the door open.

Peony and Alyssum flung themselves on her, almost over-setting her. "Help us! Please!"

"Yes, save us!" Laurel shrieked. "We're about to be murdered in our beds!"

Hyacinthe, driven for once beyond her faint contempt, arrived with nightcap askew and eyes wide with fear. The candelabra she held swayed dangerously. "You must do something!"

Cynara, the last to squeeze through, closed the door again and quickly bolted it. "It's the devil come for us!"

"Hush, hush," Japonica commanded, though she felt as shaken as the young women looking to her for protection. She ushered them away from the door. "What did you see and hear?"

The cries started up again before any of the girls could speak. Peony wailed and tucked her face into Alyssum's shoulder.

"Someone's being done to death!" Laurel whispered as if afraid her voice might bring a similar doom upon her.

"Oh, miss, don't go out!" Alyssum cried when Japonica turned back to the door.

But the desperate cries were too much for Japonica to resist. Someone was in trouble. Someone must help. That someone seemed to be her. "Wait here," she said firmly. "Bolt the door behind me. I will return when I can."

None of the girls protested, but Peony blurted, "Oh, miss, do be careful."

Chapter Nine

Once the door closed behind her, her candle cast its feeble light a few paltry feet in front of her. Beyond that was blackness. Fear enveloped her for an instant, chilling her to the bone. Then a faint halo appeared at the far end of the hallway. In its glow she recognized the haggard face of the Shrewsbury butler. As she hurried toward him she saw a woman join him.

"What is going on?" she demanded of the stocking-capped Bersham.

"I cannot say, my lady." He indicated the double doors at the end of the hall. "That's his lordship's room."

"Have you been in?" she asked as moaning continued behind those closed doors.

" 'Tis locked, my lady, by his lordship's own hand," said the woman Japonica supposed to be the caretaker's wife. "My Jem's gone round to try the other door."

"Is there not another key?"

Bersham produced it. "But we've no right to open it against the master's wishes."

"No right . . . ?" A new cry cut through her question. She snatched up the key. "I have the right."

She saw frightened glances pass between the butler and woman. But the plight of the man beyond the door was more compelling than their apprehension.

"He must be ill or injured. Nothing to fear in that," she said to fortify herself, for illness was something with which she had experience. Still, her hand shook as she set the key in the lock and turned it.

The room was as dark and cold as a crypt. The fetid odor of illness reached her quickly, a sickly reek of retching and chamber pot. The unpleasant smells came almost as a relief. The occupant was ill, just as she supposed.

"Wait here." She squared her shoulders and lifted her candle to spread its light as she moved purposefully into the room. "Lord Sinclair?"

Her gaze quickly swept the space, seeking a figure in the gloomy corners. The doors of an old-fashioned cabinet bed hung open on their hinges. In the dimness beyond she spied the indistinct figure of a man who suddenly pitched forward, arms flailing. "Allah the Merciful, stop the pain!"

Japonica started. It was not just his actions but the fact that he had spoken in Persian that astonished her. She moved closer as he continued mumbling in a hodge-podge of Persian, Hindi, and obscure Arabic dialects she did not know.

"Lord Sinclair? Are you ill, my lord?" She pitched her voice at an unaccustomed octave and volume.

As if her words had shoved him, he tipped suddenly backwards onto the mattress, arched his back and dug his heels into the bedding. His face contorted

in the throes of a new agony as a harrowing bellow
rose up from him.

That unholy sound propelled her back a step. Perhaps she was mistaken. Perhaps he was not ill but
mad, suffering a fit!

She had never dealt with a lunatic but she had
heard that the mad were oftentimes dangerous and
unpredictable.

A hiss of pain issued from his lips as he began to
twitch. Every muscle in his body went rigid, and the
tendons in his arms and neck stood out in vivid relief.
Even as she reached for the dagger in her pocket he
cried out, "Allah be merciful! Take my life!"

The anguish of his despair touched her more
deeply than her own fear of who and what lay before
her. She replaced the knife and once again cautiously
approached the bed.

As the ring of her candlelight fell directly across
the bed he fell silent. Though he had sounded fully
alert, his eyes were shut. Was he asleep? Could any
nightmare seem so real to its victim?

"Lord Sinclair?" Her voice was softer now, for she
had always heard it said that startling awake a sleep-
walker might kill him.

He turned his face toward her but his eyes did not
open. With his black hair disordered by his thrashing
and his shirtsleeves dangling, he looked more like a
scarecrow than master of the manor. In the shadows
his face was strangely dark and deeply furrowed,
whether by age or torment she could not guess. He
did not look at all like an Englishman. Was this, truly,
the new viscount Shrewsbury?

All at once his chest began to move up and down
again in great heaves as if his lungs were about to
burst.

She quickly set down her candle and reached out
to shake him by the shoulder. The risk of death could

not be worse than the torment of his present state. "Wake up, sir. You are dreaming." When he did not answer, she repeated the words in Persian. "Wake up, *burra sahib*. You are dreaming."

His rigid stance collapsed and his body sank back against the bedding. After a long moment during which she held her breath, he opened his eyes. Dark with pain and unfocussed, they roamed aimlessly in their sockets until she spoke again.

"You must rest easy. You are ill."

He turned his head sharply toward her. When his gaze found hers it was she who whispered a frightened, *"Bismallah!"*

Golden eyes stared up at her, eyes she could never forget, eyes that had blazed through her every waking thought for months and still invaded her dreams when she was too tired to resist. The eyes of the *Hind Div*.

For the space of three heartbeats she felt herself swept back by a gale of emotion to another bed in another darkened room in a land far away. Those eyes had taunted and teased and beguiled and challenged and seduced her into the first act of recklessness in her once ordinary life.

The cold dank world receded until the fragrance of incense and exotic perfume seemed to fill the room. A warm breeze carried the faint pluck of a harp and shiver of a tambourine . . .

"No!" In panic she brought her hands up to her eyes. This must not be!

"What's wrong, my lady?"

The flat common speech in prosaic English spun her about.

In the doorway stood Bersham and the caretaker's wife. The world suddenly righted itself. Her mind was playing tricks on her. This could not be the *Hind Div*. This was Lord Sinclair, the new viscount.

"Nothing, nothing's wrong," she said.

Nothing's wrong. The words reverberated through her mind. But her pulse and her courage did not believe her head. Both galloped away, spurred by the shock, while her legs trembled with the urge to flee. Why had he spoken to her in Persian?

A moan from the bed sent her spinning in place. "Not possible," she said under her breath, and forced herself to take a step toward the bed. Yet, if she wanted to know the truth she had to look upon him a second time. She picked up her candle and approached again.

She paused just beyond his grasp and stared, her gaze as shy and alert as an antelope at the edge of a clearing. The longer she stared the less certain she became of her own instincts.

She had not really seen the *Hind Div's* face. Almost any kind of countenance might have been hidden by his cheetah markings. Yet there were differences. The *Hind Div's* skin was bronzed by the desert sun. Now that she held the candle closer, dissolving the shadows, she realized she had been mistaken about this man's coloring. He was as pallid as the sheet on which his head rested. Distorted by pain, the shape of his mouth was nothing like the one that had offered her such stunning kisses she could feel them in the pit of her stomach. She remembered the raven's wing blackness of flowing tresses. A strip of silver as thick as her thumb plowed through Lord Sinclair's short dark hair.

The need to deny fed her first judgments ever more excuse and contrast. Many Englishmen, military officers mostly, passed through Persia every year. The cleverer often learned the language of their regional posting. Unremarkable that he should know a few phrases. The man lying there so weak and pitiful was nothing like the all-powerful and dazzling being she remembered. The color of his eyes was coincidence. In every other way he was nothing like the man in whose bed she had lain captive to the rapture of his passion.

She was nearly convinced when he opened his eyes again and met her gaze. The jolt of his golden regard threw her into a panic as strong as ever. Could anyone who had witnessed it confuse that gilded stare? Who was this man!

To her amazement, he was first to look away. "Ah, *peri,* you come to torment me."

Was he still dreaming? She could not be certain.

"I am no fairy, *burra sahib.*" She reached out slowly and lightly skimmed her fingers across his sweaty brow. "Feel my touch. We are both real." And in being real, he could not be the *Hind Div,* she added in her thoughts.

"I am in such torment . . . ." He broke off to swallow. This time when he looked at her his red-rimmed eyes seemed to see past her into a realm she could not imagine. "No one can help me."

"As Allah wills it I will try." She did not know why they continued to speak in Persian but the language seemed to comfort him.

He tried to rise up on one elbow, the slow awkward movements of a man in pain. "I must escape!" He said the words so softly she was not certain she heard him correctly.

"Escape?" The influence of the dream must still hold his mind prisoner. "But this is your home."

"Lies!" Sweaty and shaking, he collapsed upon the bed.

The instinct to comfort drove her to rest a hand on his shoulder. She felt under her fingertips the hard muscle and bone beneath skin baked by fever. "I do not lie. You are ill, that is what causes your confusion."

For a moment the light in his eyes wavered like a gutted candle, his life force no more substantial than a flicker of flame in the wind. "If you would truly help me, *peri*, then stop the pain. Even if you must take my life, I beg you, end my misery!"

The hopelessness of his plea shocked her.

"My lady?"

Frowning, she turned her head toward the door where Bersham and the housekeeper still lurked. "Lord Sinclair is ill, Bersham. Fever has made him delirious," she said loudly. She directed her next words to the woman. "I need a basin of very warm water and soap. And you may tell the young ladies in my room to return to bed. It is only illness that awakened us all. Come in, Bersham, I will need your assistance."

"Very good, my lady."

"*Arrack!*" the viscount whispered hoarsely.

Bersham frowned as he neared the restless man on the bed. "What is he saying, my lady?"

"He is asking for strong spirits," Japonica answered with a bit of asperity in her tone. Now that she thought of it, the smell of wine was strong in the room. "Does he often drink himself into a stupor?"

Bersham answered with the tact of one who knew that the viscount was now his employer. "His lordship did enjoy the benefits of the cellar today."

"Perhaps too much so," Japonica answered as she noticed the claret bottles on the floor. This man might well be suffering the well-known terrors of a dissipated roué. Yet that would not explain the fever. Something else, surely, is wrong. "He has sweated through his shirt. We must change it before he catches a chill."

"Very good, ma'am."

But as the butler reached to unbutton his shirt,

Lord Sinclair suddenly lashed out at him. "Keep away!"

Bersham gazed uncertainly at Japonica. "If you hold his shoulders I will do it."

Before she could slip the first button free, the viscount rose up with a roar of rage. He knocked Bersham to his knees with a blow from his right forearm and grabbed Japonica's wrist in his left hand and pulled her down so close that she could feel his hot breath upon her face. "So, you have come back, *Bahia,* to kill me!"

That voice! For the space of five heartbeats—in which she heard Bersham's cry of, "Oh, my lady!"—Japonica wondered if he would try to kill them both. She did not doubt he was capable. Though he was feverish and trembling, the strength of his grip had not lost its power. Such outrage and pain in his expression! She could not say why she reached out to lay her hand against his cheek, whether she hoped to smooth away or blot out that terrible expression.

He flinched at her touch but did not move away. "Nay. I would never seek to kill you," she whispered. Her fingers slipped up over the contours of the deep scar at his brow. "No mortal can murder the *Hind Div.*"

He jerked at her words. "You know!" It was at once a question and an acknowledgment.

When he released her she did not move, could not look away from those black-fringed golden eyes. The *Hind Div* lived!

Shivering, she closed her eyes and slid to the floor.

Bersham was at her side at once, helping her rise to her feet. "Are you well, my lady?"

"Yes, fine," she murmured, but her gaze went back to the man on the bed. He had moved away, half turned his back and lifted his right arm to shield his face. That is when she noticed that no hand protruded from the right sleeve. Instead his arm ended in a stump covered by bloody bandages.

"Dear Lord!" she gasped.

"His lordship lost his hand in the war," Bersham said matter-of-factly.

Lord Sinclair shivered and then swung back toward the speaker, his arm just missing striking Japonica in the face. "Liar! You damned son of Satan." He thrust his maimed arm toward Bersham, his eyes blazing with rage. He spoke in Persian. "You took it, scourge of hell! The price of my resistance! You cut it off!"

Bersham skittered away from the venom in Lord Sinclair's voice and expression. "What's he saying, my lady?"

Japonica shook her head. "He believes—nothing." She could not say the words, that he thought they were his torturers.

Perhaps his enemies had captured him, as the Resident of the East India Company told her. Yet he had escaped. And here he was, in London, before her. A true conjurer's trick.

When she did speak she was amazed by how calm she sounded. She held out her dagger to him, hilt first. "You are safe. You have escaped. I seek only to ease your suffering. But you must trust me, *burra sahib*. Take this weapon if it will make you feel safe."

A spasm of emotion crossed his face, bringing into relief the long jagged scar etched like lightning across his brow. Then he very slowly reached out and touched her sleeve. "I do not think I have the strength left to deny you." He turned his face away. "Do as you will."

She looked down to where the broken nails of his left hand had left thin trails of blood on her night rail. A thousand questions sprang to mind. What had happened to him after they parted that night more than a year ago? How had he come to be in England? Was he really the new viscount?

Just as quickly, she realized what his reappearance might mean in her life. No, she could not think about that now. He had begun breathing heavily again, as if trying to prepare himself for more suffering. He was a man with a very thin grip on sanity.

"What do we do, my lady?"

She looked up, having forgotten that Bersham still hovered nearby. "We will continue."

Lord Sinclair did not stir this time as Bersham undressed him. She worked beside the butler without thinking about what would happen when her patient realized who she was. That would have to wait until he had recovered, if he recovered, his senses.

This is the *Hind Div!* Her mind could not stop teasing that thought but she refused to indulge it.

Moving quickly and efficiently, she slit the worn and frayed bandage that covered his wounded arm. Even steeled to the sight, she could not keep from gasping, "Dear Lord!" when she saw what lay beneath.

From elbow to stump his arm was swollen with bruises old and new. The mostly healed scar at the end of the stump oozed fresh blood. It looked as if he had been pounding it against the wall or some other hard surface. He had asked her to stop the pain. Perhaps he had been trying to do the same. It was the kind of thing an animal might do, an instinctive senseless attempt to try to numb the torment. But he had only made it worse. No wonder he was in agony. She would need to ease the swelling.

She glanced toward the draped windows. "Is it still snowing?"

"Most likely, my lady," Bersham answered.

"Then send someone into the street to fill a deep

bowl. And I need linen for bandages, and fresh bedding. Hurry!''

The familiar smell of incense awakened him. In the light of a single candle he saw her and smiled. She sat in a straight-backed chair, her head nodding forward as she slept. He could not see her face but the veil of tumbled pale red hair shielding her features was familiar.

He had dreamed her, willed her here. Not often, but when the torment of his affliction became too much, she sometimes came to him.

He did not try to reach out to her. She would never come near enough to touch. But he gazed at her, small and self-contained in the darkness, and was content with the knowledge that he did not deserve even this much.

If only he could remember who she was!

He did remember some things. They made him shudder. Horrifying remnants of the ephemera of his dreams.

She stirred at his moan. He bit his lip, ashamed to have disturbed her. She would disappear now. Regret dragged at him, so many regrets.

She stood up. Unlike the other times, she wore the black of mourning. His heart heaved in his chest. Had she come to tell him his life was ending?

He watched in silence as she moved toward him, afraid another sound would burst this precious madness.

Then she was leaning low over him, the cascade of her hair brushing his face. It was too much. A muscle spasmed in his cheek. The appalled push of tears brimmed in his eyes. He shut them briefly, hoping a blink would not cost him her vision. But she was still there, closer than ever before.

"Are you in pain?"

Pain? When she was here with him? There was nothing in him but this great swelling of gratitude.

He felt in astonishment the touch of her hand, more real than his own breath in his lungs. His teeth began to chatter.

"The fever's broken. That is why you are cold." She moved away, disappeared.

He closed his eyes, disappointment so bitter he could taste it.

"The fire is out," he heard her say from a long distance.

He could not believe it! She was climbing onto the bed beside him. He felt the warmth of her body as she pressed against his back and put an arm about his waist. "Is that better?"

Better than any feeling ever before in his life. But he could not say a word. The darkness was stealing over him. If this were death, he was content.

He reached out and touched the hand she had placed on his heart, murmuring, *"Alhamdolillah valmenah."*

Chapter Ten

Alyssum turned this way and that before the mirror, the better to see her face framed in a green silk bonnet with a large black velvet bow perched on the brim. "Is it not exquisite?"

"Fetching. A pity it does not flatter you," Laurel replied.

Alyssum's smile drooped. "What do you mean?"

"Very well, if you must have honesty. It looks like an overturned bucket on your head. You've not the countenance for it. Your features are too delicate. Now *I* have the chin and cheeks to balance the brim."

"You have cheeks and chins enough to balance an overturned barouche." Cynara puffed out her cheeks for emphasis.

"Oh, do be quiet." Laurel turned to the modiste who was supervising the fit of her new military blue spencer. "I quite detest children who fidget and fuss.

As if they have any pretense to fashion! I cannot think why they were not left at home.''

Japonica ignored this snipe at her decision to bring all the Shrewsbury sisters shopping on Oxford Street. After three wretched days under the same roof with Lord Sinclair, she felt as if she would burst if she did not get away.

She tried to keep her mind occupied by overseeing the sorting out of the Shrewsbury townhouse, which appeared not to have been properly cleaned in several decades. The moldy pile was not suitable for human habitation, a fact that seemed to disturb no one but her. So then, she instructed the caretakers to hire a dozen servants to help in the cleaning. As with the beginning of all such projects, the clutter and grime increased with their efforts. Dust and soot and cobwebs now filled the air. To escape the clutter she had suggested this shopping trip. It was also a chance to escape the possibility that at any moment she might turn a corner and run into Lord Sinclair.

The *Hind Div* was not dead! He was in London, beneath the very roof she shared. A changed man, surely, but one who would sooner or later remember when and how and where they first met. As if their last meeting were not embarrassment enough!

Japonica shuddered a little every time she thought of it. Bersham had found her the next morning, asleep in his lordship's bed! She had not meant to nod off, only to warm the man until he stopped shivering. But the night was very cold and the room so very dark and it seemed so natural . . . .

Japonica turned quickly to look out of the shop window, hoping none of the others would notice her blush.

Jamie's father was alive! But he must never know it.

That thought kept her so tied in knots she could

barely keep her wits together these last days. The fact that Lord Sinclair had issued orders banning everyone but Bersham from the sickroom did not ease her dilemma. Sooner or later, he would remember her and then she would have to face him. Unless she left London at once!

She was not quite so craven. But she did not have the nerve to return to the sickroom.

The Shrewsbury sisters, too, seemed under Lord Sinclair's influence. His unseen but daunting presence fostered a marked decline in their quarreling. Unfortunately, freed from Lord Sinclair's proximity, today they had reverted to old habits.

"What do you think, M-m-miss?" Peony had settled upon calling her step-mama "Miss" while her sisters went out of their way to avoid addressing her in any form. The child pirouetted before her in a high-waisted dress of palest pink with a blue ribbon under the bosom.

"It becomes you," Japonica said. "But you must scrub your neck before you wear it."

"Yes, you've got turnips growing in your ears and lice swinging from your curls," Cynara taunted.

"Have not!" Peony's lower lip began to tremble. "At least I don't have p-p-pimples the size of b-b-boils all over my face!"

"Brat!"

"Currant f-f-face!"

"Girls!" Japonica said sharply. She put a hand to her brow, aware of a vague throbbing there. She had promised not to interpose herself in the sisters' lives, no matter what they did and said. But two hours of shopping with them made her wish she had stayed behind to beat rugs. "I think it is time we collect our purchases and go."

Madame Soti, whose shop it was, chose this moment to intervene in this unhappy picture of aris-

tocratic family life. *"Je suis pret!* I have saved the best
for the last." She clapped her hands and two assistants
appeared carrying a ball gown from behind the curtain that hid the workroom. *"Enfin!* My latest creation!"

It was a gown of India muslin, the weave so silky
fine it drifted and draped on the breeze as the assistants swung it around to show off its lines. Gold lace
edged the very low-cut bodice and short sleeves of
the high-waisted frock. The skirt, worked with gilt
spangles in the form of tiny sprigs, sported a gold
beaded border of classic design with bouquets tied
with ribbons. White ribbon and more spangles decorated the hem. A separate train of similar design fell
from the shoulders.

"Oh, that's exactly what I want!" Laurel exclaimed,
reaching for it.

"This is perhaps *un peu vieux* for the mademoiselle
Abbott," the modiste suggested with a slight smile.

"She means you're too fat for it," Cynara stuck in.

"Scarecrow!" Laurel taunted.

Hyacinthe gave an impatient sniff. "Madame Soti
says the gown is meant for someone more mature."

"It is for the married lady." The modiste aimed a
knowing smile at Japonica. *"Cela fait beaucoup, mais
non?"*

With great reluctance Laurel released her grasp
on the gown.

The modiste's dark eyes moved back to the new
dowager viscountess. She had heard rumors of the
great *mesalliance* between the foreign commoner and
the elderly viscount Shrewsbury but none of her *ton-
nish* clientele had so much as caught sight of the
bride before now. What luck! The viscountess chose
her shop in which to do business. Not only did she
stand to make a handsome sum from dressing six
ladies, but once word circulated that she had spoken

with the mysterious stranger, her business would pick up considerably as London's gossips came to glean what information she had firsthand. But first she must make the proper impression on her new patroness so that the association might continue.

Though the new viscountess was dressed unfashionably in brown serge and her hair was nothing short of a fright, there was the distinct air of the lady about her; a gentility to her movements. It only needed teasing out. She swung the dress around for Japonica's view. "Is it not beautiful? So elegant! Fit only for the most perfect of forms. Perhaps Lady Abbott would care to demonstrate?"

"I?" Japonica said in faint surprise. "Oh no, I have no use for such a fine gown."

The modiste lifted one brow. "No use? But soon begins the London Season. You will have every need for half a dozen such gowns within a fortnight."

"I shan't be . . . . I shan't be so promoted," Japonica finished with a blush. She had almost blundered by saying she would not long be in London. She did not want to risk her tenuous authority over the sisters by reminding them that it would be brief. "I am a stranger, after all."

"*Au contraire!* A new face in town? A young widow of means with the hair *rouquin*? Madame will be favorite, *mais oui!*"

"Oh, Miss, why don't you t-t-try it on?" Peony encouraged.

"Yes, dear step-mama, why don't you?" Laurel cooed. There was nothing she would like better than a chance to make fun of her unwanted step-parent. An ill-worn ball gown would quickly show her up for the interloper she was.

"Well, I don't . . ." Japonica looked to the modiste for encouragement. "Shall I?"

Madame Soti and her girls nodded and clapped their approval.

She needed no more urging. She could not remember the last time she had had a new gown. And a ball gown made by a London modiste? Never!

Once in a private fitting room, Madame Soti helped her strip to stockings and chemise.

Rubbing the fabric of her client's serviceable undergarment between her fingers, the modiste clucked her tongue and said, "Off with it! We must begin with the skin!"

Several embarrassing minutes passed during which Japonica stood naked until she was dressed in new silk stockings with a blush of color in them held up by beribboned garters with rosettes. A short silk chemise, so sheer she could see the shadow of her form through it, barely covered the essentials.

Madame Soti prowled around her as she stood on a raised platform, one hand cupping an elbow while the other cupped her chin. "We shall need only the lightest corset, and no padding for the breasts." As the helper went for the garment the modiste smiled and patted Japonica's stomach. "Madam is to be congratulated on so quickly regaining her form after *l'enfant.*"

Japonica turned scarlet. "I—I . . ."

Madame Soti put a hand on her shoulder. "Ah, I am so clumsy. It must be my imagination. But I am old and wise enough to admit my mistakes."

Japonica stared into the woman's face searching for signs of duplicity. She saw only sincerity. "It is a very delicate and complicated matter, Madame Soti."

"Everyone in London has life matters both complex and delicate. A ladies' modiste hears many things and keeps silent that she may be worthy of a loyal patronage."

Japonica bit her lip but said nothing else. She had

no choice but to accept the woman's word for her discretion.

As she was being laced up, Japonica cursed her own vanity. It had not occurred to her that her body would give away her secret. If she had not wanted to try on the gown, her secret would remain her own. Now it was given to one with no reason to respect her privacy. She thought of offering the modiste a bribe but dismissed it. She might feel insulted after she had given her word. If she were not a woman of her word a few pounds would not mend her character.

When the gown had been lifted over her head and fastened up, she no longer cared what she looked like. "It is very nice," she said dryly without even a glance at the cheval glass. "But not for me."

"But madam must show her stepdaughters, surely, the lesson."

"Of course." She had quite forgotten the reason she had been persuaded to try on the gown in the first place. She stepped off the platform.

"But wait!" the modiste commanded and had an assistant place a pair of gold leather slippers before her. She clapped her hands and two other assistants hurried in with hairpins and a hot comb. Before Japonica could protest her hair was unpinned, rearranged, and caught up in a paste diamond diadem at her crown. Still another assistant brought out a pair of gold elbow-length gloves and slipped them up her arms. She had never in her life touched a rouge pot but said nothing as the modiste rubbed the sheer gloss across her cheeks and lips. The modiste might be a servant to the English aristocracy but within her own shop she was the general, martinet, and queen of all she surveyed.

As she worked on her newest client, Madame Soti began to compose in her mind the judgment she would repeat for certain privileged customers who would come into her shop in the subsequent days. "The viscountess is a natural for the fashions I alone can create for her. Slight of stature, *oui*. But such lovely shoulders and a bosom to put every young girl to her knees in prayer each night. In my hands, she blossoms! Blossoms! And a widow, so young! One senses this must be but a temporary tragedy. For who can resist russet curls to put the fox to shame?"

Finally she stepped back with a smug expression. *"Voila!* Now, viscountess, you are ready."

As Japonica entered the main shop, all eyes turned her way.

"I say!" A gentleman who sat in a corner of the main shop jumped to his feet.

Ladies paused in their shopping to glance in her direction and their mouths fell open.

"But you are pretty!" Alyssum cried, as if she had never before set eyes upon Japonica.

"Perfection, madam," the modiste said behind her. Every expression seemed to resonate with the compliment.

Flushed with embarrassment, Japonica turned and caught a glimpse of herself in a mirror. She moved closer, staring at what surely must be an apparition, for she could not believe she viewed herself. Yet it was her face and hair, altered by the cunning of professional care. For the first time in her life she appeared as she had never thought possible. She looked beautiful!

Peony came up to her, eyes shining as though she were witness to a vision. "Oh, Miss, you are the most beautiful lady in all London!"

"I wouldn't go that far." Laurel had expected the exquisite gown to show up the pretender in their midst. Yet, by some inexplicable transfiguration, the gown made Japonica Abbott stunningly attractive.

Was it the color or the cunningly cut bodice that gave her bosom an unexpected generosity or the style of her hair, which suddenly seemed quite gloriously red? She could not decide and the lack of explanation made her very cross. "She looks well enough, for a commoner."

"She looks like a f-f-fairy princess!" Peony exclaimed.

Cynara and Alyssum nodded in agreement. Only Hyacinthe sniffed and looked away, clearly as annoyed as her second sister.

"I will wrap it up for the viscountess," the modiste said.

"Yes, I will take it," Japonica heard herself say, when a second before she meant to refuse the gown.

"You said you will have no opportunity to wear it," Laurel reminded her.

"Perhaps not, but I shall feel better knowing I own it," Japonica answered. "Now what choices have each of you made?"

"Do you mean there are a few pennies to be spent on us?" Hyacinthe's voice carried throughout the showroom. "I rather thought our allowance was to be worn upon your back."

The insult drew a slight gasp from the imperturbable Madame Soti.

"Shopkeeper's brat!" Laurel whispered as she bent in close to Japonica.

As she was turning away, Japonica caught Laurel's elbow. "You may think what you will of me. But if you ever again utter one word against my parentage I very much fear I shall slap you soundly!" The shrill note in her voice appalled her but she had had enough.

"Now then," she said, taking a menacing step toward the taller Hyacinthe. "You will apologize."

Hyacinthe swelled up, her nostrils quivering. "I will never apologize to you."

"Then you will go directly to your room when we return and stay there until you find the decency to be heartily ashamed of yourself."

Though Hyacinthe's face flamed with color, she held her tongue.

No one said another word, but Japonica was shaking with fury when she returned to the dressing room.

As the modiste slipped the dress from her shoulders she met Japonica's tight-lipped expression. "The viscountess has the look of the lamb but the heart of the lioness. Bravo, madam!"

A few minutes later the very subdued Shrewsbury Posy and their step-mama stepped into Bond Street and into the rain while packages for each of them were lashed to the top of the Shrewsbury chaise.

Japonica wore a new green sarcenet barouche coat at the insistence of Madam Soti, who decried that she should be seen leaving her shop in a plain tobacco-brown walking dress. The color, a daring shade for one with hair so vivid, Laurel cautioned her, made her feel quite happy despite the miserable weather.

As she stepped up into the coach she heard the distant cries of a crowd. Curious, she turned to the postillion. "What is going on?"

The young man seemed surprised that she had addressed him but quickly answered, "The Persian ambassador's in town, m'lady. It is expected that he will create a spectacle wherever he goes."

A great cheer went up at the back of his words, drawing all eyes toward the end of the street. Japonica had read in *The Times* of the Persian ambassador's arrival but it had not made an impression on her until now. Homesickness arrowed through her. Too bad she could not call on him.

"Looks to be the crowd's comin' this way, m'lady. We'd best clear the street afore them," the postillion advised.

"I want to see the P-P-Persian," Peony said. "Oh, please, may we not wait and see the p-p-parade?"

"Yes, please!" three of the others joined in. Only Hyacinthe remained silent, looking as cross as a wet cat.

"I suppose," Japonica said, though she was not particularly pleased by the thought of standing in the rain when she had just recovered from quinsy. "I will meet you in the carriage at the end of the street." She climbed up and directed the driver to move on.

As the chaise moved away from the curb she saw her charges hurrying in the direction of the cheering crowd.

The driver turned off Oxford Street onto a quiet lane called Mansfield Street in Marylebone where they waited for the parade to pass. Instead, to Japonica's surprise, the noise of the crowd drew closer until curiosity made her drop the carriage window and look out.

A traveling coach passed her at a spanking pace, its fancy undercarriage and wheel rims splashed by the accumulated mud of a long journey. Midway down the street she saw it pull up at a lovely house of the distinctive Adam design. Doubtless in expectation of this arrival, servants ran from its white-columned portico with umbrellas in hand to meet the arriving guests.

She saw a handsome youngish man stand down when the coach door was opened. Striking even for a Persian, he was tall, with black hair curling beneath the edge of his brocade turban. He sported a thick flowing beard and wore robes so colorfully embroidered as to shame a peacock. Even in her life in Bushire, she had never seen his equal. Women were not, after all, allowed in the Persian court. Her father's tales were all she had of the Shah's royal palaces. The Mirza fit the tales like one of the characters from the oft-mentioned Arabian Nights.

As if on cue a crowd appeared, running from the direction the traveling coach had come, cheering as if the ambassador were a war hero or a member of the royal family. Banners magically appeared as people tied kerchiefs and other bits of cloth to sticks and canes and waved them overhead.

Japonica studied the faces of the other men climbing down from the carriage, searching for any familiar face from Bushire, but she could not decide which of the officers might be someone she had met before. Two were very young. The others wore the uniforms of His Majesty's Life Guards. Those not in military dress were clearly strangers. All but the Mirza seemed pleased with their reception. He stood stiffly for several moments before allowing himself to be escorted indoors.

Finally, her gaze lit on a tall, rail-thin man with black hair and a hawk-like stare whose own gaze was scouring the on-lookers. At the last moment her nerve failed her and as his gaze swept in her direction she sat back out of his vision.

Lord Sinclair was up and about, and in the company of Abul Hassan Khan. She was not wrong. The *Hind Div* had come to London!

Even as she drew in a shuddering breath, it was quite clear to her that she must make the first move. This game of nerves, if that was what Lord Sinclair was playing, had cut up her peace and had her peeping and starting at shadows. Even she had her limit of fear. So be it, she would brave the lion in his den.

If she were to be chewed up and spit out it would be at her own choosing.

"But when?" she murmured.

The chaise door swung open and her five charges climbed in, all talking at once about the amazing sights they had seen.

At precisely a quarter past three on the following afternoon, Lord Sinclair sat entertaining four fellow officers in his home. Though he had not wanted company, Devlyn felt compelled to play host once they arrived. For a quarter hour they had drunk his wines and eaten his biscuits as if this were no more than an "at home" for friends. Yet he was not fooled. They had come to him for a reason and he was curious. What would compel this uncomfortable truce between men who had not forgotten their last encounter?

Thanks to a note of warning from Winslow, he had been able to meet the Mirza's convoy on the outskirts of the city the day before and ride in with them. Yet he had returned to his own home only after the Mirza retired for the night.

"You look recovered from your fever." Winslow slanted a brief glance at Sinclair's right arm. Minus the hook, his arm ended in a neatly pinned sleeve.

"I look like hell, even on my best day," Devlyn answered shortly. "But you have not come calling for a reading of my health."

"We've come to lay your duty back at your door," Howe said shortly.

"And that would be?" Devlyn inquired softly.

"Keeping the ambassador's feathers unruffled. I wish you well of it. The man's skin's as thin as a newborn babe's."

"You saw how he behaved yesterday." Frampton

helped himself to another serving of his host's port. "Ordering the carriage windows rolled up when the crowds were cheering him. Damned impudence!"

"Hate to admit it but Howe's right," Hemphill said. "The Mirza takes offense at the least slight."

"And he perceives a slight at every turn," Winslow concurred. "Said he might as well have been a bale of goods smuggled into town for all the honor he received from the King upon his arrival. Goes on and on about the lack of an official welcome."

Devlyn nodded. "An *Isteqbal.*"

"He bloody well expected the King himself to be on the carpet for him!" Frampton said in disgust.

"That would be within his expectation. His family lineage is quite a bit older than the present king's," Devlyn answered blandly. "Why was there no official welcome?"

"Who knows the methods of the crown?" Howe groused. "Still, it don't serve for a foreigner to think he can dictate the terms of our customs."

"This is London, can you think of nothing with which to distract him?" Devlyn's voice was edged with indifference. "There are plays and pleasure gardens and gaming halls and mistresses enough to occupy any man with the Mirza's tastes and vigor."

"That's just it," Hemphill answered. "The Mirza has sworn by an oath to his sovereign. He cannot stir out of doors until he has delivered his credentials to His Majesty at his Court."

"And well you know the temperament of these Asiatics." Howe rolled his eyes. " 'Tis a diabolical yet subtly constructed device. By imposing his own house arrest, he hopes to embarrass the Court into acting quickly."

"I take it the delay is dictated by the King's health?" Devlyn said.

"Don't know and don't care." Howe sat forward

in his chair and jabbed a finger in Devlyn's direction. " 'Tis your headache. Our part is done. The Life Guards have more important duties to perform than minding a puffed up Oriental peacock."

"Walking the royal bitch, perhaps?" Devlyn smiled for the first time. " 'Tis noted in the news that Princess Amelia's lapdog has a new litter. That should keep a man of your capacity fully occupied."

"Now then!" Winslow said quickly as Howe muttered under his breath. "Someone's got to bring the Mirza round. Distract him. And you're . . . you're . . . ." A huge sneeze caught Winslow by surprise.

"Bless you," Devlyn said with a slight smile.

When he recovered, Winslow looked about, noticing for the first time the lack of window drapes and carpets in the room as well as the distinct smell of camphor and wood polish in the air. "What the devil are you about, Sinclair? No one redecorates in December."

"Spring cleaning," Devlyn answered with a sigh. "The viscountess's idea."

Howe looked interested in the conversation for the first time. "Is she the reason you deserted us en route?"

"Can't say that she is, as I haven't yet laid eyes on her."

"What?" The four men chorused in surprise.

"Not even a howdy-do?" Winslow pressed.

"She keeps to herself. As do I." Devlyn wished he had not brought up the subject. "There are five daughters to command her attention."

"Five?" Howe harrumphed. "Gad! She must be either full-sprung or wrung to a prune. Neither is meat to tempt my taste."

"Still, there might be a spark left . . . ." Frampton mused.

"Or desperation," Hemphill suggested. "Widows are often good for high jinx."

"And the ill-favored spinster." Howe chuckled. "They are so grateful for a man's attention they'll do anything. And I do mean *anything!*"

As the other gentlemen laughed at the bawdy jibe, Devlyn turned his head, for he heard the salon door open. Into the room stepped a young woman in a simple sarcenet gown and mob cap. "The room is occupied. Leave us!"

To his consternation she held her ground. "Forgive me, Lord Sinclair, but as you were entertaining I thought it as good time as any for you to introduce me to your companions."

Confounded, Devlyn stood up. "Why the devil should I wish to do that?"

She closed the doors behind her. "Because, as I am new to London, it is your duty to make my way."

"Let her in, Sinclair!" Howe had come to his feet, a wide grin on his handsome face. "Your hospitality's dull stuff. I prefer a bit of female companionship."

Devlyn's gaze narrowed upon the young woman who dared challenge his authority. "I do not entertain governesses."

For an instant she stared at him in amazement, then her expression cleared. "But of course you would not know, as we have not been formally introduced ourselves." She came forward with a smile and held out her hand to Devlyn. "I am Japonica Abbott."

"The viscountess Abbott?" Devlyn could hardly get the words past his surprise. Moreover, he left her extended hand hanging in midair, for this "widow" with five daughters could not be a day more than twenty.

"The very same, Lord Sinclair." She smiled at the stunned expressions on his companion's faces. "May I join you?"

"Certainly!" Howe and Frampton both jumped to their feet to offer their seats to her.

Devlyn, too, moved quickly. He walked purposefully to the door through which she had just come and set his hand on the latch before turning back to the room. "Gentleman, as you were just leaving, I shall be brief. Lady Abbott, may I present Colonel Hemphill, Captains Winslow, Howe, and Frampton. Gentleman, the viscountess Shrewsbury."

She curtsied as the gentlemen bowed deeply. Devlyn was not certain who was more annoyed and chagrinned, the officers or her. All faces were flushed with strong emotion.

As if he had not noticed a thing, Devlyn opened the doors and said, "Good day to you, gentlemen. I will join you in Mayfield Street for dinner. Meanwhile, Bersham will see you out."

Given no choice, they each murmured regrets and turned toward the door, all, that is, but Howe.

He approached the viscountess and reached for her hand. "Now that we are acquainted, Lady Abbott, I look forward to our next meeting."

With the deliberateness even Devlyn recognized as swagger, Howe saluted her hand. To his satisfaction she blushed and hastily retrieved it from him. Then she was not altogether a goose! Howe was a rotter where women were concerned.

Devlyn took his time in closing the doors. So this was the person Bersham had told him of, the one who nursed him through his first night beneath this roof. But she was young, a girl really! Chagrin, annoyance, and consternation vied for command of his emotions, for he retained the oddest memories of that night. Of a young woman . . . of her crawling into his bed . . . ! Good Lord! It must have been the fever.

He could not guess what thoughts ran through her

mind. Yet he knew enough of the ways of women to suppose she had not randomly chosen this moment to interfere in his life, not when several days of opportunity lay between her arrival and now. She wanted something. What? Only one way to find out.

He turned to her a blasé expression. "Now, madam, what the devil do you mean by barging into my private affairs?"

Chapter Eleven

Japonica wondered if she had made a mistake. She had thought these last days that she was the one avoiding a meeting. Yet when Lord Sinclair did not return the night before until after she had fallen asleep, and was gone before she rose this morning, the implication suddenly seemed clear. He must be making an effort to avoid her as well.

That realization—along with a generous glass of sherry from the sideboard in the dining room—had given her the courage to barge in upon the gentlemen so that he might not escape again. Staring at him now, she could not think of a single good reason for having wanted to do so. He eyed her as if she had slithered out from beneath a stone.

"I ask again. What the devil do you mean by this intrusion?"

Out of habit, she curtsied. "I wished to make myself known to you, Lord Sinclair, for two reasons."

"No one I wish to meet would make herself known in a manner so ill-bred and outrageous." He sounded as chillingly remote and condescending as the ancestral portraits lining the walls of Croesus Hall.

Japonica looked quickly away, intimidation warring with her natural dislike of those who used their superior status to quell the feelings of others. Her appearance could be mistaken for that of a governess, but now that he was aware of her position she would not be spoken to as if she were a mere servant.

"You may not wish to acknowledge the relationship but I assure you, as the dowager viscountess, I am well within my rights to enter any room of my own home at my choosing." To quell the shot of nerves that speech gave her, she moved to deposit herself on the settee. "If we are to toss daggers at one another it were better done at a civil level. Unless you prefer to make our conversation the stuff of gossip among the servants."

Emotion glinted in the thicket of his black lashes, reminding her of a jungle cat that had marked its prey. Reaching behind himself, he turned the key in the lock. The distinct *click* of the latch resounded very loudly in her ears. The stalking had begun.

"And now, madam," he said with deceptive deference when he stood over her. "Who, exactly, are you?"

In silence Japonica allowed her gaze to rest brazenly on him for a moment. Why was he maintaining the pretense that they were unacquainted? She was prepared to meet his angry surprise with accusations of her own, but with the craftiness of a predator he had moved into the position of aggressor and put her on the defense. How like the *Hind Div*.

Her heart gave a nervous start as she looked away, but her resolve hardened. No doubt he had a purpose in delaying the confrontation. Two could play at that game.

"Before we turn to other matters may I first inquire about your health?"

He turned abruptly away toward the hearth. "That is no concern of yours."

Surprised by his retreat, she pursued the matter. "Perhaps not, though I feel as if I had some little part in your recovery. At least we can be grateful there has been no repeat of the ordeal."

He looked up sharply. "What the devil are you prattling about?"

A flush of annoyance stung her cheeks. "My small skill as a herbalist may be of little note to you, Lord Sinclair, yet it was responsible for making you comfortable the first time we met. But then, you are something of an alchemist yourself, are you not? Potions in wine are your specialty."

His frown deepened into a scowl. "I haven't the slightest idea what you are talking about."

She blinked. Was this some new game of wits to lure her into a trap? Or was it his design to shame her by making her speak first of her seduction at his hands? Oh, but that was wicked!

She laced her trembling fingers together, more determined than ever not to slip into the position of pawn in a game at which he was a master. "Very well, let's discuss more recent events. You do recall how I came to be in your room the other night? How your cries roused the entire house? Do you not remember how we spoke and that I . . . ?" The puzzlement in his gaze increased with her every word until she did wonder at its purpose. "You do remember?"

His gaze danced away from hers as he moved to a humidor on a nearby table and opened it. He took his time in choosing a cigar and then looked up, pinning her with his oddly bright stare. "Madam, unless I have lost what little wit yet resides inside this skull, I would swear that I never before this hour set eyes upon you."

Japonica searched his face for a hint of a smirk, the gleam in the eye of a liar, the smug stare of the consummate bluff. She saw none of it. "You would have me believe you remember nothing? Nothing at all?"

He looked away. "I suffer lapses. There are gaps in my memory. Caused by my wounds." He again met her gaze with a thrust of emotion. In that golden glance she read the truth. He did not remember.

She stared with mouth slightly ajar, confounded by the revelation. He had knocked the pins out from under her, if he could be believed. The *Hind Div* was a master of bewilderment and obfuscation. Yet, if it were true that he had lost all memory—all memory of her—then she had nothing to fear from him.

Or perhaps she was wrong. He was not the *Hind Div.*

She closed her eyes, trying to recompose his features. If his lean cheeks were striped and the hard jaw stenciled by a thin beard, would they be . . . ?

"Where did we first meet?"

"What?" She glanced up warily. He had moved closer to her. Those eyes—she would swear she recognized them.

"You say we are acquainted." The muscles in his jaw bundled, etched for moments under his taut skin, and then eased. "Where did we meet?"

Panic stole over Japonica. Her throat seemed to close. *Steady on, old girl.* She could almost hear her father's voice warning her, as he often did, to keep her wits when she was about to make a mistake. It was not too late to retreat. Every one of her secrets remained intact. His weakness had become her advantage.

She sat up a littler straighter. "Before I answer I should like to put a question to you." He merely stared at her. "How often are you plagued by . . . lapses?"

Devlyn physically recoiled from the question. No one dared question him so directly about his infirmities.

"I have insulted you." She said it in a calm and composed voice. "I beg your pardon. I had not thought you would be so sensitive."

"Sensitive?"

Devlyn stared at her. He wished now he had paid better attention to the solicitor's tedious tale of how she had come to be a dowager viscountess. But he had been in the throes of a struggle with nonexistent memories that had erupted into blinding pain once he reached Mayfair. So it was she who had been in his room that night. Had she also climbed into his bed? She did not seem a bold baggage. To the contrary, she would seem the sort to turn her face to the wall at the slightest embarrassment. There were things here he did not know, things he suddenly wanted to understand.

No longer eager to be rid of her, he subsided in the chair opposite her, an unlit cigar dangling from the fingers of his left hand. "How old are you?"

"I am one and twenty."

"One and twenty."

He perused her slowly. Her figure, from what little he could detect beneath the drab ill-fitting clothing, was youthfully neat. The unexceptional face staring up at him might be quite pleasant if it were not so agitated. How vulnerable she seemed, her lower lip caught like a bite of ripe strawberry in her pearly teeth. What had induced this little wren to wed a man twice and half again her age?

The answer came quickly to mind. Money. Of

course. Mr. Simmons did mention the circumstances of Lord Abbott's second marriage. She had married a dying man for his money. As a rule such women were adventuresses, beguiling wenches of who-knew-what scandalous reputation, who played upon the vanity of elderly roués. Yet this women gave lie to the rule. The sprinkle of golden freckles across her nose gave her a certain charm and the intelligence in her fine eyes were certainly attributes in her favor. But in toto she lacked the style or beauty to lure a man's baser appetites. What, then, was her allure?

Devlyn sank a little lower in his seat, eyes half-shaded by his lids. "Tell me more about the other evening."

Unaware of the nature of the suspicions he had fashioned about her, Japonica recited the events as they unfolded from her point of view. She omitted only the two salient facts that might rouse his curiosity, which were that she suspected that he was the *Hind Div* and that they had conversed solely in Persian.

"Is that . . . all?"

"What else could there be?"

He noted her blush. She would not, then, mention climbing into his bed. And he was just unsure enough of his recollection to doubt the wisdom of suggesting that possibility to her. So innocent looking, she might swoon at his feet. But her apparent wholesomeness made him distrustful.

After a lengthy silence during which resin hissed as it boiled from a fissure in a log upon the fire, he finally spoke. "I suffer from headaches. There are moments when I am not in complete . . . command of myself." He hesitated, as if the words were hard for him to utter.

"Memory lapses and the rages, is that the summation of your symptoms?"

He smiled to himself. How quickly she pounced on the information, nay, prompted him to reveal more. She, no doubt, hoped to make use of this information for her own purposes. He was right to be distrustful of her when it was his inclination to be otherwise. That must be the source of her deviousness, to appear helpful when in truth she possessed the conniving heart of Jezebel.

He stood and took three steps toward her and held up his right arm so his pinned sleeve nearly skimmed her nose. "You've noticed my—infirmity."

Japonica hesitated. He towered over her like some vengeful deity, his golden eyes the only animated thing in his ghostly pale face. "You, of course, know the answer. I dressed your wounds myself."

Her answer seemed to enrage him. He snatched at the pinning of his sleeve, tearing and pulling at the fabric of his cuff until his stump was revealed. This time he bent down to bring his gaze onto a level with hers as he held his bared arm before her face. "Does it frighten and disgust you? Or this?" He touched the scar bisecting his brow. "Don't lie. I will know if you do."

She looked first at his ruined arm and then met his gaze with sadness. "Whatever discomfort the sight might give me it cannot be anything compared to what it must be to you, who deal with it daily."

Meeting her candid expression forced upon Devlyn the discomforting feeling he had been gauche. Because he could not remember, he did not trust her. Yet the little brown wren seemed to have no feathers to ruffle.

Unaware of his thoughts, she reached out and touched his wrist where the once swollen scar had begun to heal again. "Are you in constant pain?"

He jerked away from her as though she had clawed him. "Don't patronize me!"

Was his reaction one of thin-skinned pride or the beginnings of a rage he would not be able to contain? With a profound hope for the former she said, "You invited me to speak plainly. If you did not want to discuss it, you might not have brought it up."

Devlyn turned away. As he rewrapped his arm with the torn ends of his shirtsleeve he pondered how he might turn this new knowledge of her to his advantage. By the time he resumed the chair opposite her he had an idea.

He reached up and touched the scar seaming his brow. "I'm told the blow that cracked my skull made a madman of me." He looked directly across into her face. "What do you say to that?"

"That you are very lucky to be alive and in your right senses."

"How would you know these are my right senses? I might have been any sort of man before."

"I stand corrected." She did know what kind of man he had once been but she would not help him to those memories. "I must confess the idea of madness does explain one thing. The lack of kindness and tact in your rude and offensive manner."

Devlyn grunted and eased back in his chair, his gaze now half-hidden by lowered lids. Even if she were the most false jade in England, it had been some time since a lady had traded barbs with him. Most avoided his eye when they noticed his infirmity. The rest were made uncomfortable to the point of agitation. Not so Lady Abbott. The novelty of her entertained him and he was not quite ready to dismiss her.

"If you will linger about, make yourself useful. Pour me a port."

Japonica rose without a word to do his bidding.

While she was plying decanter and glass, he watched her as an unexpected thought shot through his mind. *I want her.* For the first time in months—years?—raw desire sprung fully realized in him.

All at once she did not seem so plain. He let his gaze linger over her, noting her narrow waist, the full swell of bosom as she bent slightly forward, and the push of hips outlined by her old-fashioned gown. He had already noticed the deep plush of her lips, a fullness he would like to sink his teeth into.

They were known to one another, had met twice. She said as much at the outset of their conversation. Was she insulted because he did not remember her? Or was it because he had forgotten how well he once knew her? That idea stung him anew. There did seem familiarity in the striking red curls. Something in the defiant way she spoke to him.

Dim recall stirred in his morass of lost memory. It failed almost instantly, leaving in its wake the first dull throb of a headache.

When she turned to hand the glass to him, something new caught his attention. "What is that you are wearing?"

"The usual custom of gown," she answered with a doubtful glance at him.

"I mean your scent." He leaned forward to catch another whiff even as she tried to back away. "What is it?"

"Oh that." Embarrassed, she reached up to touch first her cheek and then the tiny gold loop with a pearl drop in her ear. "A fragrance of my own making. The essence is cyprinum."

"The henna flower?" Devlyn's eyes widened. "Since when do English ladies wear such . . . ." He took a slow in-drawn breath of her heady floral perfume. It prompted half a dozen images of seduction, each more arousing than the one preceding it. "Strong," he said finally, "such strong scent."

For a fleeting instance Japonica saw desire in his expression, the desire of the *Hind Div.*

"That fragrance reminds me of . . . ."

She held her breath as his expression contorted with the effort of his thoughts. Was he remembering? She had not worn her personal fragrance in months, for it bothered Jamie. Only today, to bolster her courage, she had rubbed a little of the scented pomade into her wrists and throat. If it should be the thing that gave her away . . . !

". . . I cannot place it," he said finally, but his expression revealed that the search of his memory continued.

"Perhaps you've remarked it in the hallway these last days just after I've passed," she suggested, hoping to steer him from deeper memory.

"No, 'tis more . . . ." He stared at her as if he could divine the answer in her expression, ". . . profound than that."

"That is not surprising," Japonica answered, rushing to provide other suggestions of the mundane. "Herbs and fragrant oils are useful for so many purposes. Did you know camphor protects your stored clothing from an infestation of insects? Oil of cloves can mask even the odor of the privy. I intend to burn frankincense in all the cleaned rooms to dispel the lingering odor of decay . . . ."

"That is not the association!"

The dark look he gave her quelled her intention to continue in that vein. She backed toward the settee and resumed her seat.

Devlyn sipped his port and brooded. Damn his addled head! He could not remember! But he knew one thing. Hers was not a perfume for the meek and cowed young woman she appeared to be. It was the siren scent of allurement. His baser instinct was never wrong. So then, this was a game of wits between them.

He did not care who won, as long as he received as quickly as possible the pleasure of her spread beneath him. "You said you had two reasons to make yourself known to me."

"Yes." Japonica smiled, feeling on firm ground at last. "I wish to speak to you on the matter of Lord Abbott's five . . . ."

"*Aaaaahh!* Put it out! Put it out!"

The cry of anguish accompanied the sound of footfalls pounding down the main staircase.

"*Bismallah!*" Japonica sprang from her seat and hurried to the exit.

She opened the salon doors just in time to see Laurel sprinting toward the front door with some sort of burning torch raised over her head.

A hapless Alyssum ran behind, her arms outstretched imploringly. "It's mine! You can't do that!"

A chuckle of malice escaped Laurel as she reached the front door and jerked it open. "We've no choice. It must go!" Slinging back the burning object in her hand, she flung it with amazing strength through the opening. Alyssum's screech of dismay accompanied the trajectory of the burning missile.

"What is going on?" Japonica demanded as she reached them.

"I've saved us all!" Laurel declared and pointed out the door.

Japonica stuck her head out and recognized the half-burned object lying in the snowy lane. "That's Alyssum's new bonnet," she said when she had pulled her head in.

"I had to get rid of it. It might have burnt the house down around our ears." Laurel aimed a triumphant glance at Lord Sinclair, who had come into the hall to see for himself what was going on. "I've saved everyone here."

"Why was it on fire?" Japonica demanded.

"Laurel knocked my bonnet into a candle," Alyssum cried, for once moved beyond intimidation by her loss. Stars shone in the tears suspended in her lovely eyes. "It was the prettiest thing I ever owned!"

"If you were more careful with where you place your things it would never have happened," Laurel answered, but her gaze never left the face of the gentleman in their midst. "Isn't that right, Lord Sinclair?"

"I was careful. You moved it!"

"I did not touch . . . ."

"You did! You did," joined in Peony, who had arrived on a noiseless tread. "Laurel t-t-tried it on when Alyssum's back was turned."

"She tried to put it back before Alyssum noticed and it tipped into the lit candle wick," Cynara offered from the stairs where she was descending with Hyacinthe.

"No. She did it on purpose!" Peony cried.

"You little fool!" Laurel lifted her hand and smacked Peony full across the face. The slap resounded throughout the entry like the crack of a rifle.

Japonica grabbed the offender's arm as Peony's wail keened through the space on an unnerving note. "Don't you ever dare touch her again! Or I shall slap you in return."

That was all the fuel the moment needed. They fell to arguing, the noise of their hectoring voices rising into a crescendo of high-pitched cries.

"Get out! At once! All of you!" The sound of Lord Sinclair's voice cut across the noise like a great clap of thunder. In its wake there was only trembling and silence.

"Well?" The single syllable sent the sisters scampering up the stairs like leaves driven by a stiff breeze.

When they were again upstairs, Devlyn turned on

Japonica a look of icy fury. "You, madam, will follow me." He turned and strode back into the room they had exited. She followed, feeling at once foolish and furious that he had been witness to the fray.

"I am so sorry that you met the girls under these unfortunate circumstances. Generally they are quite . . . ." The sardonic lift of his brows made her falter over what she intended to be a tactful, if howling, lie.

He bent a jaded gaze on her. "If their manners are an example of your influence, then you are no fit guardian to them."

Though she resented the implication she ignored it, for his remark put them on the path of the matter she wished to discuss. "It is my every intention to disentangle myself from that position."

"No doubt both sides will benefit."

"In all fairness to myself, I am no kin to them. Someone of their rank and breeding should have their care." She paused. "Someone like yourself."

He stared at her for one long second. "I should rather be dragged backwards by a camel through fifty miles of jungle."

She pinched off her smile. "They can be a handful."

"From what little I have observed of their caterwauling they should better have been drowned at birth!"

Japonica gasped. "That is harsh."

"But true." His laughter was derisive. "There isn't enough merit between them to make one passable female. Thank providence they are not my responsibility."

That was not what she wanted to hear. Another tactic was in order. "It was their father's wish that one of the elder sisters be wed as soon as possible. In that, surely, you can be of assistance. For instance, were there not bachelors among the officers who visited here today?''

Devlyn stared at her as if she had sprouted horns. He was quite certain that matchmaking for Abbott's daughters was a ruse. Clever women were notorious for beginning in one place only to drive their argument ultimately in an entirely different direction. "Allow me to be blunt. I will not lift a finger to foist that menagerie on the least masculine acquaintance of mine."

Pricked by his snobbery she answered, "I shall be equally blunt. 'Tis your inheritance that beggars them. One might see it as the honorable thing to marry one of the daughters yourself."

He gazed at the toes of his boots as he drawled, "Madam, I would sooner wed you."

"Marry me?"

He had to admire her astonished expression. How well she played the ingenue. Marry her, indeed! " 'Tis strictly a manner of speech," he said coolly. "I should think you too much put upon in this business of daughters to wish yourself burdened by a new suitor."

Japonica felt her skin tingle to the roots of her hair. "Indeed, if you are proposing to play suitor to my widow's weeds."

He hid a smile at her indignant tone. Here, at last, was the temper hinted at by her mostly hidden cloud of red hair. It stirred him and that made him want to stir her.

"You are a viscountess yet you dress as if you were a governess fallen on hard times. What is this ridiculous object?"

He reached out too quickly for her to stop him and whipped off her mob cap. The gesture pulled loose her bun and sent flaming curls tumbling about her shoulders. She saw his eyes widen and this time there was no mistaking the carnal hunger of his gaze.

Outraged, her voice shook a little as she said, "You are the rudest man I've ever dealt with."

He dropped her cap at her feet and crossed his arms. "Believe me. I am an altogether ordinary sort of man."

"Yet I suspect you hope I will contradict you in that," she answered with stinging contempt. What arrogance the man possessed!

To her further consternation, he smiled. "You have leave to depart my objectionable presence."

Japonica looked away, realizing he had just maneuvered her into a corner. The last time he had done so it was the beginning of a bargain between them. This time she could not think of a single method by which she might engage him in a deal.

She bent to reach for her cap but he moved more quickly, scooping it up from the floor and then offering it to her with a flourish. She reached for it with two fingers, to make a point of not wanting to make even accidental contact with him.

Aware of the reason behind her action, Devlyn snatched it back at the last moment. "Come now. Will you give up your game so easily?"

Japonica met his amused expression with gritted teeth. Was his talk of lost memory only lies to lead her into some indiscretion? Or was this simply the true essence of the man reasserting itself? *You have yet to astonish me,* the *Hind Div* once taunted. Be clever. Think quickly!

Japonica folded her arms across her chest and spoke with a voice in utter contradiction to her pounding heart. "If I could make the Shrewsbury Posy unobjectionable to you, in say a month's time, would you introduce the eldest girls to London society?"

He smiled but it was not at all pleasant. "Madam, if you could alter them in even the slightest degree

from their ill-favored present, I might reconsider."
He moved forward, coming so close to her that she
was forced to look up at him. "But hear me well.
I do not expect this miracle. Therefore, until it is
achieved, neither you nor your brood are welcome
in my presence again."

Japonica's chin lifted a notch higher, affront in the
very line of her posture. "Give me one month. Until
then I bid you fair weather speed to whatever perdi-
tion you are bound!"

Devlyn's smile faded a bit when she had stalked
out. It was not often a woman, even a saucy ill-bred
one, got the last word.

"She did not address me as her superior," he murmured in afterthought. Much as he did not like being
a lord he was still aware of the lack of respect in
her manner. Did she see herself as his equal? He
supposed she was, as the dowager, his superior. Perhaps that was why she had expected he would remember her.

He did not remember her.

Even after her explanation of the events a few
nights earlier, he did not have the slightest clue as
to what else he should remember about her. But its
importance was there in her pansy-brown gaze. She
knew something that he did not. Something she
feared he would use against her. She had trembled
whenever he neared her. He wondered if she realized
it, that slight tremor of her lower lip when their gazes
met. Something quite remarkable occurred for him,
too. He felt as randy as a boy of seventeen.

The thing he had feared dead had but to meet
Japonica Abbott's gaze.

He had been fascinated by the way she kept reaching up to touch her throat or the tiny gold loop with
a pearl drop in her ear. The self-conscious gestures,
at once girlish yet entirely womanly in their seductive

power, had left him with a very solid reminder that he was a man and a man too long without the comfort of a woman's touch.

He smiled. He could not say he liked Lady Abbott or was even genuinely attracted to her. Yet he could not say that he was indifferent. Not when his body bloomed with evidence to the contrary. So then, what to do?

"What, indeed?" he murmured as he moved to ring for the butler.

Seducing the widow beneath his roof may prove a more complicated matter than it might seem at first suggestion. What to do with her when the novelty wore off? No, better not to spoil one's nest. There were women aplenty in London, more beautiful, more willing, more seductive than the little wren. The whim would pass. It would. As soon as he thoroughly exercised his own needs.

"My lord?"

Devlyn glanced at the butler. "Have the carriage brought round. Ah, Bersham. What do you know about our new viscountess? Was she much on the London marriage market before she snagged Lord Abbott?"

"Her ladyship is a stranger to England, my lord. Lord Abbott met and wed her while on his last sojourn in Persia."

Devlyn started. "Did you say Persia?"

"Just so, my lord. Lady Abbott was reared in the East India colonies."

"How did you come into this information?"

"Her ladyship volunteered it." Bersham permitted himself a rare simple smile. "The household is quite in awe of her. The manner in which she aided your lordship the other evening was nothing short of remarkable. Then to hear her converse with you most capably in that foreign tongue . . ."

"What?" Devlyn could not keep surprise from his tone.

"Lady Abbott said that in your feverish state you spoke to her in Persian." A tremble of apprehension shook old bones as Bersham beheld the arrested expression on his master's face. "I presumed, my lord, that you remembered."

"No." Devlyn looked down at the mob cap he held, a remarkable new thought in his mind.

So, it was just as he supposed. They shared a history older than the past three days. A colonist's daughter! They must have met in Persia. If only he could remember!

Pain pushed into his temples as it always did when he tried to remember. Reflexively, he crushed the simple lace-edged linen cap in his good hand. The action released the scent of a perfume as alluring as the ancient lands from which it came. The riddle of Lady Abbot was tantalizingly close. It teased his memory with the subtlety of the exotic fragrance rising from her cap. Wrapped in the feathers of that little brown wren was the spirit of an *houri*.

Something new stirred him, a thing that had lain idle this last year. The thrill of the hunt! He might no longer be a soldier capable of bringing low his chosen enemy. He might have no taste for diplomacy or politics. But he was no longer indifferent to possibility. Just now it confronted him in the form of the secrets of one small young woman, in whose gaze lay the key to a memory that he wanted very much to recall.

He smiled fully for the first time.

Chapter Twelve

Mirza Abul Hassan Shirazi, Envoy of the Qajar Shah Fath Ali—Sultan of Iran, Oibleh of the Universe, His Majesty the Padeshah of Iran—was ill.

The general consensus of his English hosts was that it was a malaise brought on by homesickness and his body's attempts to adjust to the intemperate cold of his hosts' northern isle. No amount of cajoling and entertainment could long lift him from his bed where he languished with the complaints of a fever and tightness of the heart. This condition could not be allowed to continue without the risk of drawing the notice of his ruler. Such concern had brought Devlyn to the outskirts of London and into private conversation with Sir Gore Ouseley on this Saturday morning.

Seated before an elaborately carved ivory chess set presented to Ouseley by an Indian rajah, they had closeted themselves in the baronet's gilt and green velvet library on the pretext of playing a game.

"We cannot afford a diplomatic incident." Ouseley, on the orders of King George, was attached to the Mirza as his *mehmandar,* or official host. "As you know, the Mirza refuses all invitations that require him to leave his residence until he has been formally introduced to His Majesty. The long distance from the Royal residence to London has made it impossible as yet to arrange the timing of a public royal audience. This causes talk. A few of the more radical gazettes have already expressed the sentiment that delay is a ruse to keep the Mirza under house arrest. If that were not bad enough, illness has curtailed the Mirza's enthusiasm for entertaining. If gossip should label him hopelessly ill it could spell disaster for the Anglo-Persian treaty. Bonaparte would like nothing better."

Devlyn nodded absently as he reached for a chess piece. The French treaty of '07 with the Persian Shah had not lasted six months. The Shah's renewed interest in an alliance with the English had their greatest enemy gravely concerned.

"Rumor is that London is rife with French spies whose sole purpose is to create havoc among England's allies." Ouseley smiled. "One hopes this news appeases your sense of futility with your post."

"To the contrary." Devlyn's tone was curt. "I believe both England and I would be better served by my return to India."

Ouseley frowned as he watched the younger man set his piece down on the board. "You were once of invaluable aid to the Secret Committee. A pity such services cannot be publicly rewarded. But I believe you have done your share."

"I should be more flattered if I could recall the service to which you refer." Devlyn indicated that it was Ouseley's turn.

"Just so." Ouseley reached for his pawn. "Memory remains blank, does it?"

"Too much and not enough." Devlyn had discovered that when he did not drink heavily, the rage that often accompanied his headaches remained within his control. But that was not the sort of thing one man confided in another. "It gives me no joy to play a guard dog who is all bark and no bite. I would rather return to my old duties for the Secret Committee."

Ouseley frowned. "My dear man, you cannot recall those duties."

"Were they unusual even for a seasoned soldier?"

"One might say they were singular." Ouseley picked up a pawn and fingered it thoughtfully. "Your duties were of a nature both delicate and unique. Secrecy was paramount. Alas, your injuries have made you . . . memorable."

Devlyn frowned and absently rubbed the right sleeve of his coat just above the place where his hook protruded. "No one will discuss with me the nature of duties I was tortured for and nearly died to keep from divulging. Do you not find that unjust?"

Without comment Ouseley slid his piece into place on the marble board with a smile. He was a diplomat, after all, and knew how to sail past dangerous currents. "I have noted how often the Mirza turns to you for small conversation when the days are dull. You share his love of eastern music and poetry, as few of us do. Your Persian is so fluent that he has doubted you are English."

Devlyn shrugged. "That, too, is a mystery. But I find that the words come when needed and the understanding is complete."

Ouseley nodded, for Sinclair's command of Arab and Indo languages was better than his own. "The Mirza is fretting himself to pieces. He has been in daily touch by couriers with the *Motamad od-Doleh* and the *Amin od-Doleh* who direct him to hasten his return. He fears each day that he remains in England causes him to incur the wrath of Ali Shah.''

"Well he might," Devlyn responded and quickly made a move on the board. "The Mirza lost an uncle to a fit of royal temper. He was boiled in oil, I believe."

Ouseley's face puckered in distaste. "There are fully half a dozen envoys of various rank who've been waiting months upon the King's pleasure. Yet they are amenable to London's pleasures. Hassan needs distraction." He smiled and moved another piece, exchanging it for one of Devlyn's pawns. "Female company, I should imagine, would be preferable."

Devlyn glanced up in unpleasant surprise. "You do not expect me to play the role of procurer for him?"

"No," Ouseley tugged at his chin, a sour expression on his face. "The Mirza would seem to be a rash fellow when it comes to oaths. He's also sworn to chastity until he has completed the task set him by his sovereign. Damned inconvenient! A few evenings at the opera followed by late suppers with chorus girls would considerably improve his mood."

Devlyn smiled but did not lift his eyes from the board. "It is for that reason his shah demanded the oath. A man in his prime, foresworn against female comfort, will be strongly motivated to accomplish his task."

Ouseley chuckled. "Wouldn't work for the British Army. We pay whores to travel with the army in order to keep our men motivated. Still, it is a point well taken. And yet, though the Mirza may not take full advantage, it does not follow that he is indifferent to the pleasure of female company. On more than one occasion he has remarked on his fondness for English ladies. I gather the diaphanous gowns so popular among our womenfolk strike him as a novelty worth frequent viewing. One longs to discover a stylish English lady of quality who would not be averse to sharing the occasional evening with our illustrious guest. She must, of course, be married. Youthful enough to be pleasing to the eye, yet have enough wits about her to be entertaining in her conversation, without being put off by his foreign manner."

"Your list of requirements is extensive."

"Of necessity. I'm told one lady visiting the Pump Room in Bath fainted at the sight of the Mirza's beard. Can't have a roomful of ninnies in decline at every moment of the evening." Ouseley leaned forward to better judge his opponent's tactic, for he had just lost a pawn. "Gad, we could use a lady who speaks a little Persian. The Mirza's English improves but slowly. Female companionship might spur his interest in our language."

Devlyn was not at all certain he wanted to attempt the idea that had proposed itself in his mind. "I may know someone."

"Capital! Mr. Grant, Chairman of the East India Company, and his deputy Mr. Astell have been invited to dine with the Mirza next week. We shall be glad to include you and your lady in the evening."

"I did not . . . ."

Ouseley lifted a silencing hand. "It's not a request but an order, Colonel Sinclair."

Devlyn let his annoyance filter through as a sigh before he said, "Very good, sir. But it cannot be accomplished today. I will need to travel out of London. And I am not persuaded she will agree. She is a widow and there are children to be seen to."

"Delightful!" Ouseley sat back with a smile of satisfaction.

Two hours later, with the Shrewsbury carriage following at a sedate pace, Devlyn was smiling as he strode down Bond Street. Well not precisely smiling, but buoyed by a sense of purpose, something he had not had in many months. It mattered little that the purpose was frivolous. It gave him an excuse to pursue a matter he had not acknowledged even to himself, the desire to effect another encounter with Lady Abbott.

He had been outdone when he learned that she had decamped with her charges the very evening of their meeting. That was a week ago. He meant what he said about her stepdaughters, but he had not expected his eviction to send her bolting from London. He thought she would remain in town, if not under his roof.

"Bedeviling woman!"

She had returned to Croesus Hall. Had she remained in town he might have found a dozen reasons and places to encounter her again. How could he go to Surrey without seeming to be following her? He could not. Until now. Ouseley had given him a reason.

He looked up as he was passing a modiste shop. There in the window was an emerald gown of such sheer fabric that it seemed a mere veil in which only the most daring of ladies would drape themselves. The thought of Japonica Abbott dressed in such a gown made his jaw drop.

A lady of style, Ouseley had said. Lady Abbott had no style, unless she be labeled an Antidote. If she agreed to help him she would need to be outfitted from the top of her head to her toes. And grandly, to impress the Persian taste for ornate beauty. 'Twas equally obvious she would need help.

Uncaring of the spectacle he made as a gentleman alone entering a ladies' shop, he pushed open the door and pointed to the gown in the window as the owner hurried forth to greet him. "Wrap that up."

The woman, sensing a man on a mission, smiled

warmly. "La, the monsieur has exquisite taste. A little something for his *chère amie,* perhaps?"

Devlyn's mouth firmed in a slight smile. "Are there other things ... ?" He waved an impatient hand around the shop, "Accoutrements?"

"Mais oui. Allow me to show the monsieur ..."

"Sinclair," he said firmly, bending over a case of beaded reticules. "Lord Sinclair."

Though he seemed in a hurry, the shop owner noted with approval that he had definite tastes. He took great pains in choosing the accessories of slippers, shawl, even stockings and a hair brooch with a feather. When they were done, he had a pile of boxes to carry out.

"A Merry Christmas to you, Lord Sinclair," the shop owner called gaily as he departed, her fake French accent abandoned in her delight at his spending. For, miracle of miracles, a nobleman had written her a bank draft for the entire amount. Unheard of!

"Christmas gifts! Of course!" Devlyn was feeling rather proud of himself as he looked around for the Shrewsbury carriage. Now he had the very excuse he needed to seek out Lady Abbott. How she responded to his proposal would tell him a great deal about the kind of woman she truly was.

"I am glad to be home." Alyssum smiled shyly and continued to plait silk ribbons into a band for the new bonnet that Japonica had ordered for her from London. It was not as pretty as the first, but she had a talent for dressing bonnets and had a particular reason for wanting this one to be especially fetching. "I should have been loath to celebrate Christmas anywhere other than our own sweet little church."

"Since when have you cared to attend church?" Laurel asked.

"Since there's a new vicar." Cynara smirked. "Alyssum thinks him quite dashing."

"A cleric?" The puzzled expression on Laurel's face was genuine. "I cannot imagine any lady being truly interested in a man who has dedicated himself to the troubles and ills of others. Shepherding lost souls calls to my mind a man minus all of the attributes I most desire in a husband." She ticked them off on her fingers. "A dashing air, a handsome face, and of course, a vast quantity of disposable wealth."

"Whose wealth is disposable?" Japonica questioned as she entered the morning room.

Unlike the first days, the elder pair of sisters no longer showed her open hostility. Since their return to Croesus Hall they had resorted to treating her with the indifference one showed to servants. They did not speak unless and until she did.

This morning they shared the usual conspiratorial glances before deferring to Hyacinthe, who bore an expression of amusement on her long face. "Laurel was discussing the merits of a fortunate match."

Japonica nodded. "I should be interested to hear what you believe would be an advantageous match."

"Naturally you wouldn't know." Laurel's smile mocked her. "Aristocratic women marry our own kind, gentlemen whose incomes are sufficient to supplement our dowries, and whose breeding and bloodlines guarantee a family lineage unblemished by scandal or shame or *mésalliance.*"

Japonica ignored this reference to her own marriage. "And have you found such a person?"

"Alyssum has!" Peony pinkened with delight at her mischief. "She's enamored of the v-v-vicar!"

"Tale bearer!" Alyssum flushed a painful shade of red. "If you say a word to anyone, I'll . . . ."

"What? Weep all over us?" Laurel scoffed. "I dare say you'd weep regularly, wed to a pious soul who spends his time and income among the poor. Might as well wed a commoner."

Again Japonica ignored Laurel's rudeness, for she had come here with a purpose. "How do you propose to find a paragon worthy of you?"

Laurel brightened perceptibly at this phrasing. "I shall find him in London during the Season."

"The Season," Japonica repeated and took a seat. "What, exactly, is the Season?"

The sisters quickly filled in the details, their replies tripping over one another.

" 'Tis the time of year when all the great and noble families come to London to share society—"

"Depends upon the opening of Parliament—"

"Not until the frost is out of the ground and the foxes begin to breed.

"Which means some families remain in the country until March."

"Others come to town right after Christmas.

"So many functions. Balls and routs, the opera—"

"Dinner parties and soirees—"

"In the spring, exhibitions and concerts—"

"Balls and the theater—"

"Dances and sporting events—"

"And balls!" Laurel supplied for the third time.

Japonica sat amazed by the emotions the very mention of the Season inspired in them. "And this is important for marriage?"

"Why, Miss, 'tis the only way to meet elegible parties."

"In order to form alliances—"

"In order to marry."

"Of course, one must be 'out' first," Hyacinthe pointed out.

"And that means?"

"When young ladies have reached the age of seventeen, they are presented to the sovereign at St. James's. Until they have had that honor they do not go out in society or attend dinner parties or receptions."

"All young ladies must meet the King?" Japonica said in amazement.

"All who have aspirations of a good match," Hyacinthe answered shortly.

"Then you have done so?"

Hectic color mottled Hyacinthe's cheeks as her mouth thinned with annoyance. "No."

"We are none of us 'out,' " Laurel said frostily, "for there must be a sponsor. I expect that will change now that Lord Sinclair is in town."

"Don't depend upon it," Japonica murmured under her breath.

She could not get the image of Lord Sinclair's mocking face out of her mind. It had followed her on the journey back to Croesus Hall. He would not entertain the suggestion of introducing his friends to her charges. Less likely he would be to sponsor the Shrewsbury Posy at court.

He does not remember me! Each time she recalled that revelation, the shock of it quite took her breath away and hurt her more deeply than she should have imagined possible. Her son's father lived, yet it could not matter to her a jot!

All at once she felt the inexplicable push of tears at the back of her eyes and realized that she was about to burst into weeping.

She stood up quickly. "I—I have something in my eye." She turned toward the door adding, "Excuse me!" and fled the room.

Once in the hall she pushed a fist to her lips to keep back a great sob. Sending a desperate glance down the hall she spied an open door at the far end. It led into the music room. She had just enough time to enter and close the door before her restraint burst and she fell against it and slid to the floor, sobbing as though the world would end.

Chapter Thirteen

For more than a minute there was only the wrenching sound of Japonica's hard sobs and the tingling fear that she might be overheard.

She did not understand herself at all these days. Frequently, and for no reason at all, she would suddenly burst into great weeping.

It must be that she missed Jamie. Nearly a month had passed since she left him behind. Would she seem a stranger to him when they reunited? Would he refuse to come to her? She spilled a few tears each time she finished one of her daily letters to Aggie, begging for details of her son's life. So far she had had no replies. Of course, Aggie had a small babe to care for and her writing skills were never strong. Yet the lack of mail did not entirely explain Japonica's moods.

Oh, how unfair life was! She had accepted her fate to bear a child with no father. She was prepared for every eventuality—except the possibility that the *Hind Div* still lived.

He did not recognize her! No, of course not! The loss of his memory aside, she doubted a merchant's plain daughter would have made much of an impression on the *Hind Div.*

"Governess, indeed!" she complained between sobs. His tactless comment, the least of her worries, had insulted her to the soles of her feet.

Rousing herself from the floor, she pulled a handkerchief from her sleeve and vigorously blew her nose. Why should his assessment of her matter? No man's ever had before. Not since she was sixteen.

"Insufferable man!" But it was a weak attack against a humbling truth she must now admit to herself.

She was profoundly shocked to discover that she was suffering from all the feminine weaknesses she had thought quite beneath her: pride, vanity, and the wish to be adored. She had not sought to make a good impression upon Lord Sinclair, but now she could not deny she had made a very poor showing as a woman.

"It doesn't matter, none of it!" she whispered. He could not remember Baghdad, or being the *Hind Div,* or the little *houri* who dared bargain with him for her life and lost her innocence instead. What matter?

She began to pace, hoping the exertion would stem her tears.

Amazing that they should meet again, thousands of miles from Persia! Astonishing that he should be the new viscount! Inexplicable that she should have wed a relation of his! It was as if the cosmos had concocted a great joke with which to torment her.

She moved to the piano and sat on the bench to

collect her thoughts. Of more import was the impossible bargain she had made with the man.

The cruel caricature Lord Sinclair had drawn of the five young women in her charge rang true. Then he had had the temerity to ascribe their lack of breeding to her own example. That stung. In fact she resented his remarks all the more because—*Because they are true.*

She took a deep steadying breath. No one could turn those sows' ears into silk purses in one short month.

"What is the matter, Miss?" Peony had stuck her head in through the door that Japonica had not heard open.

Looking away, Japonica smoothed her hand across her face, but she knew she could not hide swollen eyes. "I am just a little unwell."

"Was that a sniff? What could she possibly have to cry about?" Hyacinthe's voice would never be mistaken for anyone else's.

Japonica turned her head to find that all five girls stood in the doorway. No doubt this was what they had hoped for, to find her weeping with defeat. They would think it was their doing.

A final tear dripped from her chin onto her hand and the sight of it made her blaze with anger. How dare they feel that they were entitled to her thoughts and feelings when they treated her as if she were incapable of one and without the other! "If you must come in, do leave the door open. I can scarcely bear to be closeted with the five of you."

"What do you mean?" Hyacinthe asked as she came forward. "I demand to know."

"You smell." She rose to her feet to speak her mind before their shocked faces, to reduce them to tears like those that had just fallen from her own eyes. How smug the elder girls looked. But they did

Take 4 FREE Books!

We created our convenient Home Subscription Service so you'll be sure to have the hottest new romances delivered each month right to your doorstep — usually before they are available in book stores. Just to show you how convenient Zebra Home Subscription Service is, we would like to send you 4 Kensington Choice Historical Romances as a FREE gift. You receive a gift worth up to $23.96 — absolutely FREE. There's no extra charge for shipping and handling. There's no obligation to buy anything - ever!

Save Up To 30% On Home Delivery!

Accept your FREE gift and each month we'll deliver 4 brand new titles as soon as they are published. They'll be yours to examine FREE for 10 days. Then if you decide to keep the books, you'll pay the preferred subscriber's price. That's all 4 books for a savings of up to 30% off the cover price! Just add the cost of shipping and handling. Remember, you are under no obligation to buy any of these books at any time! If you are not delighted with them, simply return them and owe nothing. But if you enjoy Kensington Choice Historical Romances as much as we think you will, pay the special preferred subscriber rate and save over $7.00 off the bookstore price!

We have 4 FREE BOOKS for you as your introduction to KENSINGTON CHOICE!

To get your FREE BOOKS,
worth up to $23.96, mail the card below
or call TOLL-FREE 1-800-770-1963
Visit our website at www.kensingtonbooks.com.

Take 4 Kensington Choice Historical Romances FREE!

YES! Please send me my 4 FREE KENSINGTON CHOICE HISTORICAL ROMANCES (without obligation to purchase other books). Unless you hear from me after I receive my 4 FREE BOOKS, you may send me 4 new novels – as soon as they are published – to preview each month FREE for 10 days. If I am not satisfied, I may return them and owe nothing. Otherwise, I will pay the money-saving preferred subscriber's price plus shipping and handling. That's a savings of over $7.00 each month. I may return any shipment within 10 days and owe nothing, and I may cancel any time I wish. In any case the 4 FREE books will be mine to keep.

Name _____

Address _____ Apt No _____

City _____ State _____ Zip _____

Telephone ( ) _____ Signature _____

(If under 18, parent or guardian must sign)

KN052A

PLACE
STAMP
HERE

ll..l..lll..ll.l.l.l.ll.l.l.l.ll.l.l.ll.l.l

KENSINGTON CHOICE
Zebra Home Subscription Service, Inc.
P.O. Box 5214
Clifton NJ 07015-5214

not realize what she knew. They were unwanted by this world and had not the wits between them to recognize it. Over-bred, over-privileged, lacking in character and decency! They did not realize that she could, by simply walking out, leave them to well-deserved disaster.

The words swelled in her mouth, the bitterness of them, bile on her tongue. But she could not speak them. Hyacinthe's and Laurel's faces, puffed up with ridiculous misplaced pride, stopped her.

Despite their ages, they were only silly, ignorant young women. Oh, they acted so sure of themselves. This was their country, their home, and they thought themselves wrapped securely in the mantle of their aristocratic heritage. Yet if she abandoned them, they would be lost.

They are my responsibility. Her conscience would never long allow her to forget it. A month might not be time enough in which to spin them into silk, but she might just be able to dip them in gilt! But first she must gain control.

"Your hygiene, ladies, is deplorable." She heard her own voice as a distant calm and measured voice of sanity. "Beginning today, you will bathe twice weekly."

"Twice a week?" Cynara yelped as though she had been asked to jump naked into the snow-covered fishpond.

Japonica continued her speech as she moved toward them. "You will also wash your face, neck, and hands each morning and change your linen every other day."

"That is preposterous. No one bathes so frequently."

She paused before Hyacinthe. "There you are wrong. In Persia women spend many hours making themselves beautiful and sweet-smelling. In the best

Persian society, no one wishes to entertain people who smell like a pigsty.''

"Pigsty?" Laurel swelled up with rage. "How dare you! How d—"

"Pigsty!" Japonica bore down on the younger woman with a determined expression. "You may change your gown six times a day and waste good perfume, 'twill do you no good. Unless you rid your-self of the sour odor of turnips and horseradish which envelops you at the moment I very much doubt you will find many English gentlemen willing to come close enough to admire the effect."

Laurel sputtered and fumed but for once it seemed she had been reduced to silence.

Then her younger sisters did the unforgivable. They giggled.

Japonica turned quickly upon them with a smile. Alyssum, Cynara, and Peony at least were allies. "So then, we are in agreement. Starting today you shall practice how to walk and speak as young ladies. There can be no more running in the halls or shouting of any sort, indoors or out. You shall learn proper deportment in all social situations."

"We are not ponies to be put through our paces by the likes of you," Hyacinthe declared.

"No, you aren't as well trained as ponies. You are rude and ill-bred, a disgrace to your station in life. That must change." Japonica smiled, ready to offer a carrot on the stick. "Surely at least one of you aspires to being presented at court?"

"Court?" Laurel lifted her head from her pose of utter defeat. "Did she say presented at court?"

"What must we do?" The younger three asked, pointedly ignoring their two elder sisters' frowns of disapproval.

"You shall have to earn the privilege. It will not be

easy." Japonica lifted the piano lid. "Which of you plays this instrument?"

"I do," Laurel answered readily.

"We all play," Cynara corrected. "Monsieur Mallett was our teacher. Miss Haversham, a former governess, engaged his services."

"Laurel took the most lessons," Alyssum allowed.

Japonica noted the sly giggly glances that passed between Cynara and Peony but said nothing. "Very well. Play for us, Laurel."

Laurel dimpled. "Certainly. I am well versed in Mozart. But I dabble in Beethoven and Haydn as well."

"Mozart will do." Japonica took a place beside the pianoforte.

Laurel played with a great deal of elan and expression, all of it on her face. Her fingers, alas, were a different matter. They were ill trained, tripping over keys and keeping an uncertain tempo. Parts of the melody were incorrectly reproduced while other measures were skipped altogether. Yet she turned when she was done with a triumphant smile.

"You may be well-versed in Mozart but you play him exceedingly poorly," Japonica pronounced. "You need practice, my girl, and plenty of it."

Laurel sniffed. "How would *you* know what Mozart should sound like?"

Japonica chased the younger woman from the piano stool with a flutter of her fingers and then sat and played the same piece at the right tempo and with only a single mistake.

When she was done she smiled in self-satisfaction. "We have music teachers in Persia, too. When each of you can play at least as well as I, you will receive a hundred pounds with which to purchase gowns at Madame Soti's."

"Ooooh," chorused three of the five.

Hyacinthe sniffed. "I do not require new gowns, though I shouldn't accept your generosity in any case. It is not for you to distribute the Shrewsbury wealth as your own."

Japonica eyed the taller woman with the exact degree of disdain to which she was often subjected. "Do you never tire of being tedious?"

Hyacinthe flushed, an unfortunate reaction, Japonica thought, for it made her appear as if she had contracted hives.

Satisfied at last to have both her true adversaries on the defensive, she continued, hoping for a full rout. "Laurel, will you, too, toss my generosity back in my face?"

Laurel, who could not imagine rejecting any offer of a new gown, looked away from her eldest sister's frown. "I don't see what difference it makes who pays, as the money should be rightfully ours from the beginning."

Yet when Japonica turned away, Laurel shot her a hostile glance. She had been humiliated! She would find a way to repay the little commoner in their midst even if she must seem to bow to her wishes at present.

"I will practice first," Peony said, but Cynara beat her to the piano stool.

Watching as the maneuvering threatened to erupt into a spat, Japonica sighed. Her need of a miracle could not be overstated. "I will draw up a practice schedule for each of you and post the hours in the morning." She glanced at Hyacinthe, who did not ask to be excluded.

"Ow! You're pulling my hair!"

"Keep scrubbing," Japonica directed the frightened young maid who had been shampooing Laurel's hair. She had stirred up a mixture of camphor and borax solution to help cut through the greasy pomade the girls applied daily to their hair instead of washing it.

A little farther away, Cynara and Peony sat mute but miserable because coal oil, which had been rubbed into their heads as a delousing agent, dripped on the sheets thrown around their shoulders.

Two under-maids promoted from the scullery were using combs to untangle the washed heads of Alyssum and Hyacinthe.

"Faugh! You will yank me bald!" Hyacinthe thrust an elbow in the ribs of the maid working on her. "Stupid cow!"

"That will cost you one pound," Japonica said in a neutral voice. "That is four pounds so far this morning. At this rate you shall not have left enough of your allowance with which to buy ribbons, never mind a gown. If you are dissatisfied, you may comb out your own hair."

Hyacinthe crossed her arms. "I merely meant for her to have a care. If she is to be my maid, she will needs learn better."

Japonica saw this as evidence that Hyacinthe was not in opposition to the idea of her own personal maid. Vanity did have its usefulness.

The matter of experienced ladies' maids was one she could not mend overnight. It seemed the Misses Abbott had survived since nursery days by calling on whoever they could find to help them dress, or did for each other. From what she had seen, the English were often kinder to their servants than Persian masters but she would not tolerate meanness of any kind. Hence the fine each time one of her charges mistreated one of the girls.

The next hour went tolerably well. Only Cynara had to be threatened with banishment to the nursery in the matter of the tub. Who would have thought that a young lady of fourteen would truly believe that she could drown in four inches of water?

Afterwards, while they were still wrapped in sheets from their baths, she sat them down before her and opened the portmanteau with the Shrewsbury crest and took out several bottles and vials. "This is paste that each of you must put on your faces every morning and evening until I see an improvement."

Alyssum uncapped and sniffed suspiciously. "What is it?"

"A paste of almonds, lemon juice, and rose water. The order arrived from Fortnum and Mason yesterday. If you are very conscientious in your use, you will notice a great improvement in your complexions within a fortnight."

She unscrewed a second bottle and began dabbing it on Cynara's face. "This is a poultice of egg whites beaten with lemon juice and honey. It will fade the blemishes you have while the other will prevent more."

"No more spots for Cynara!" Peony sang out, and received a box on the ear from her sister.

"One pound!" Japonica merely lifted a brow before continuing. "I have made rubbing lotions which you are to apply after your bath to limbs and feet. Each of you has your own unique fragrance. Hyacinthe, yours is thyme. Lavender for Laurel. Mint, I think, for Alyssum. Rosemary for Cynara. And lemon balm for Peony. Another day I shall show you how to make it yourselves so that you may always have a quantity for your use."

Laurel appraised her step-mama with a jaundiced eye. "Why are you doing this?"

"Being kind and courteous and helpful? Why, to set an example. Now then, when you are all dressed appropriately for dinner, we will use the meal as a lesson in dining etiquette."

* * *

Japonica felt a certain pride as she sat in the dining hall surrounded by five scrubbed faces with shining hair set in simple arrangements. The faint odor of borax and camphor was a necessary evil. To her mind they had made a good beginning. After the meal, though, she meant to retire to her room with a glass of sherry and a book. Eight hours in the company of her still-recalcitrant charges was seven and a half past the limit of her easy tolerance.

"We begin with soup." She nodded to the footman who came forth with a tureen and began serving them.

"What is this?" Hyacinthe glanced up from the thin soup in her bowl. " 'Tis mere broth."

Cynara looked as cross as a badger as she pushed her bowl away. "I never eat broth!"

Laurel glanced towards the sideboard where several small dishes sat under their silver lids. "I do not see the Yorkshire pudding and gravy I ordered."

Unperturbed, Japonica picked up her spoon. "I took the liberty yesterday of reviewing the week's menus, as is my prerogative as the mistress of the household. There were far too many heavy sauces and creamed dishes and quantities of meats on the menu. I ordered chestnut soup with which to begin, to be served with a portion of pigeon and a roll. Several slices of lean beef with beet root and asparagus will follow. For dessert there are fresh pears from the Shrewsbury orchard and slices of Stilton cheese."

"No pudding?" the younger two protested.

Resolved to keep her temper, Japonica continued with her explanation. "I am surprised, Hyacinthe, that you have allowed such a shocking waste in food-stuffs. Were we double in number we could not consume the foods ordered each week. I have pared down the quantities to be ordered in future and shall put the money saved to better use.''

"You would starve us while you live off the profits!" Laurel sang out.

"It will be easier to deny yourself a little if you remind yourself of the reward you shall gain in a slimmer figure and better skin."

"Why should we all be punished?" Cynara snapped. "We are not all fat like Laurel."

"I'm not fat!" Laurel shrieked. "You are jealous because I have a bosom while you are flat, flat, flat!"

"Who can be jealous of a cow!" Cynara flung back.

Japonica, who thought she had endured the worst the sisters could offer, watched dazedly as Laurel went over to the sideboard and lifted the lid from the soup tureen then picked the dish up. It was not until she turned from the sideboard that Japonica realized her intent. "No! You will not . . . !"

She leapt from her chair but it was too late. The contents of the tureen had already taken flight behind a hearty toss. Most of it crested like a wave upon the table but the force of the heave was enough to catch those at the table in its back splash.

Cries of outrage more than fear of a scalding burst from the occupants at the table while the rolls prepared to go with the soup were hurled in Laurel's direction.

So much for clean bodies and shiny hair. All but Laurel stood dripping in the creamy residue of mashed chestnuts.

At that precise moment Bersham who, to her knowledge, should still be in London, flung open the doors of the dining room.

Startled by his appearance, Japonica cried, "What are you doing here?"

In a sonorous voice at odds with the wild scene,

the butler announced, "Lord Sinclair has arrived, Lady Abbott."

A footman stepped into the room carrying a stack of boxes tied with bright ribbons. Behind him came Devlyn Sinclair, his cockaded hat sitting at a jaunty angle upon his head. "Merry Christmas to you—!"

"Gifts!" The girls, spying the boxes and having heard the cheery note with which Lord Sinclair had begun his entrance, rushed forward to pull the boxes out of the hapless footman's arms.

Japonica could not contain her shock. Her mouth fell open in undiluted horror and then in consternation that surpassed every effort of civility.

She picked up the heavy silver ladle that had landed near her and marched toward her charges shouting, *"Sobhanallah!* If you do not step back at once I shall smite you heartily! As Allah is my witness!"

Chapter Fourteen

Appalling! Inexcusable! Unthinkable!

"I meant to strike them." Japonica looked down at the makeshift weapon in her hand. Her voice was as dull as her expression. "I should have."

She could not imagine why the viscount had not knocked them all senseless himself. The Shrewsbury Posy had snatched the boxes from the startled footman's arms before she could stop them. Then like the naughty girls they were, they dropped into curtsies and murmured thanks before fleeing with their booty. Their awe of the viscount, it seemed, came second to the prospect of receiving a new bauble.

From the corner of her eye, she saw Lord Sinclair advancing upon her. How handsomely he was dressed, in civilian smallclothes of buff superfine and a claret swallowtail coat. Had he dressed with such care just for a visit to Croesus Hall?

A giddy, ridiculous feeling sped through her. It

died the moment she spied the telltale gleam of metal at the end of his right arm and her gaze jerked up to meet the furious scowl upon his face. A shiver passed through her but she told herself that whatever he might be about to do and say would be no more than she deserved.

"This is an example of your new authority?" he roared at her. "I should have better command of a pack of wild mongrels!"

She lowered her gaze. She could not bear to look into his expression of accusation and disdain. "You mustn't beat them. I won't allow it. Nor will you lock them away with only bread and water. It is not that they don't deserve it, and more, but they are such foolish creatures. They do not understand the harm they cause. Motherless. And a father who could not be bothered . . . ." She let her plea trail off into a sigh.

"So you would defend them against me? With your ladle, perhaps? Madam, you run a household of most unusual style." His voice sounded tight, as if he were making an effort to keep from choking on his venom.

"Unusual?" Because she had just threatened her stepdaughters with a soup ladle? Because her dinner table overflowed with chestnut soup? Because she could not imagine a more horrifying and ignoble tableau than the one he had stepped into? Nor one more likely to wreck her fledgling plan to see a Shrewsbury daughter launched up on the sacrosanct Season?

The disaster was complete, the humiliation of her situation so much more than she had ever thought possible. Knocked to nothing, all her effort almost before it could be begun. Agitation bubbled up from the depths of her despair and spilled from her lips. She looked straight into his face and laughed.

She saw surprise register in his face for only an

instant before he shuttered all emotion. "You, madam, are in need of a drink!"

He took her briskly by the arm and steered her into her former chair.

"Sit down!" He reached for her wineglass. When he saw that the contents were contaminated by chestnut soup he tossed it from him. "Wine, Bersham! The best claret in the cellar!"

As the butler scurried away to do his bidding, Devlyn took Japonica—who was still laughing in evershriller lilts that sounded very much like hysteria—by the arm and lifted her to her feet. "Come with me, madam. We are in need of privacy."

She drank a little more of the wine than she meant to. She had, in fact, planned to drink none of it. However, the specter of Devlyn Sinclair shading her every movement was a very daunting thing. When she had drunk the first glass per his order he refilled it twice without speaking a word. She noticed that he did not touch a drop of wine himself.

At least he cannot this time have drugged it, she thought as a giggle escaped. Nor would he mistake her for an *houri* so beautiful a mortal man might be tempted to steal from her a bit of Paradise. Not when the drying patches on her gown were the evening's first course. She put a hand to her mouth but another small giggle escaped.

Devlyn lifted a brow. "So then, you are feeling somewhat the better?"

"Yes." The wine had given her a better lens through which to view the situation. Though he scowled as deeply as ever, the man standing over her seemed more exasperated than incensed. She would almost swear that a smile lurked in his gaze. Almost.

"Do you always call upon Allah in moments of great distress?"

She gazed at him, conscience-stricken. She had hoped he had not heard her. For a man who had lost so much of his past he did not miss much of the present. "It was my father's expression."

He looked as though he wanted very badly to press her about the matter but he only said, "You must tell me about that gentleman at some other moment."

Not if she could help it! "I am dreadfully sorry about your gifts, Lord Sinclair. Your kindness cannot be amply rewarded with thanks."

How prudish she sounded, governess-like, when at the moment she felt anything but straitlaced. She had to keep her admiring gaze from straying to the man beside her. "Though Christmas is a sennight away, I'm sure the girls have already opened them and will presently seek you out with their own words of thanks. They are not, I assure you, always so thoughtless."

"Thoughtless?" He rolled the word over his tongue as though it were foreign and completely incomprehensible to him. "Is that what you call that band of rabid bi—er, vixens who set upon me?"

"Dreadful conduct." Japonica went to gesture with her hand and found it contained a half glass of wine. A little of it splashed over the side.

"You've had enough." He reached out to take it from her with his hook. The touch of steel against her skin surprised her and she jerked away. The reaction caused more wine to splash upon the carpet. She heard him swear under his breath as he maneuvered the glass onto a tabletop.

She found it impossible not to stare at his prosthesis. She wanted to ask why he had chosen such a vicious-looking appendage, but there was such a thoroughly disgusted look on his face that she dared not mention it directly.

"You need a patch," she said aloud and then covered her right eye with her right hand. "Yo ho ho, and a bottle of rum!" Amused by her own temerity, she chuckled.

He frowned. "Yes, you've had quite enough wine."

Yet Devlyn was not altogether displeased. Most acquaintances and certainly strangers went out of their way not to meet his eye or to look at his hook. She had the spirit to not only look but to make fun of his infirmity. It was the wine, of course. She had drunk quite a lot. She looked flushed and happy, one might almost say radiantly at ease. Not quite pretty, perhaps, but something more, something he found enchanting.

He sat down across from her, prepared to carry on with his purpose. "So then, I have done your little family a kindness, however unintended."

Japonica nodded slowly, for she was no longer quite certain where her head met her shoulders. Why had she thought him severe? He was quite handsome, though not in any fashionably romantic way. If he would only cease frowning he would appear as charming as the *Hind Div* himself, she decided. "Most men know nothing of the lift to the morale it is for a lady to receive a gentleman's attention."

Unless her vision played tricks on her, his expression had relaxed into something near a smile. Not quite friendly, perhaps, but compelling, certainly. "I suppose that means I have misjudged you," she murmured in non sequitur.

"Does a bit of ribbon and lace mean so much?"

"For a young girl there is no better gift than a silly extravagance that she may wear to show off to her friends."

"I see." He looked away for a moment and then back at her. "The gifts were all meant for you."

"For me?" She cocked her head to one side, certain that her hearing was now as defective as her reflexes. "You brought gifts for me?"

The look she gave him made Devlyn uncomfortable. She appeared quite struck, and grateful. It came to him that this was not the kind of advantage he wanted with her. Gratitude, genuine gratitude, implied affection as well as obligation. He did not want her finer feelings. Pure self-interest motivated his largesse. "There is a purpose to them."

"Purpose?" It disturbed him almost as much to see the light fade from her eyes; turquoise ringed her dark irises. "You mean Need comes riding on the Gift Horse's back?"

"Precisely." He did not care for her phrasing, but it was the truth stated baldly.

He moved to pick up the box he had lain aside upon entering the room, and he held it out to her. "At least I was able to spare the main gift for its rightful owner."

Japonica stared at the gift without reaching for it. It was a lovely round box stamped with violets. A lavender-striped bow held it closed. "No one has given me a gift since my father died." She did not mean to voice her thoughts aloud, but at the moment it was difficult to distinguish what could be thought and not said. Then she shook her head. "I cannot."

"Did you not just tell me there lives no lady who can resist a box tied in a ribbon?" he said mockingly.

When she looked into his golden eyes she did not see the cold sarcasm of their last encounter, but a genuine desire that she accept. And something more, something she could not afford to examine. She took the box, set it on her lap, and folded her hands together. "So then."

He continued to stand over her, staring down. She really wished he would take two steps away. He must not guess what his nearness did to her.

"Will you not open it?"

"But if 'tis for Chri—"

" 'Tis for when I say! Open it at once!"

Even filled with wine she did not like to be ordered about. The fact that he was intimidating her, and in fact depended upon it to get his way, brought forth the rebel in her. "But I have no gift with which to return the spirit of the season."

Devlyn glowered at her, feeling none of the spirit of the season whatsoever. "You are being missish and ridiculous. Open the damned box!"

"One should not be sworn at over a Christmas package," she answered as she reached out to untie the bow. "It quite spoils the gallantry."

When she had pushed away the tissue paper she lifted out the gown by the shoulders, spilling the sheer emerald silk skirts onto the carpet. "Oh my! 'Tis quite—!" Struck dumb, she turned to look at him with an expression of wonder.

"So then, you like it?" He did not mean to sound harsh, but he wanted more than her awed silence as assurance. After all, he had made a right fool of himself by deciding that he should outfit her. The least she could do was let him know if his idiocy in choice far exceeded his audacity in daring to choose for her at all.

"What sort of need could such a gift assuage?" The moment the words were out, her mind supplied a suspicion. She glanced again at the diaphanous gown and then up at him, blushing deeply. "Oh!"

"Not the sort, by your expression, you are imagining." His own expression was severe. " 'Twas a spur of the moment purchase. Saw it in passing. Reminded

me of you. Your hair ... the color ...." The lift of
her brows embarrassed him into silence.

Japonica looked again at the gorgeous example of
feminine vanity and said in a dry voice, "This
reminded you of me." A smile tugged at her mouth.
"Perhaps you had been imbibing even more freely
than I have this night."

Devlyn could not prevent a guffaw of laughter. "I
had not touched a drop." Though at the moment
he was sorely pressed not to seek out a very deep
drink. He was heartily sorry he had begun this nonsense. The only thing worse would be to continue to
drag out the business. "The gown comes with an
invitation. To dine. Next week. In London. 'Tis is a
diplomatic affair, which you may find very dull." He
added each sentence as her face reflected a new question.

"I see." Heart pounding in slow but heavy strokes,
Japonica carefully folded the gown and laid it back
in the box. "I thank you very much, Lord Sinclair.
But I cannot accept such an expensive gift from a
gentleman."

"Don't be a fool!" he said roughly. "It is no lover's
token. We are now related." But he was not feeling
very familial toward her at the present. Seeing her
with the gown pressed however briefly to her bosom
had conjured in his mind visions of her in that dress
and very little else. Madame Soti had assured him
that stockings and a chemise were all that could be
worn under so sheer a gown. As he had bought stockings and a chemise, he knew how very little that was.
He wondered briefly what the Shrewsbury Posy would
make of the intimate apparel they had comman-
deered, then struck that disquieting thought from
his mind.

"I have a need for a companion for an evening.

Perhaps several evenings. A married lady of some good sense who will not embarrass me."

"After this evening's events I can only wonder at your certainty that I am that person."

He made a dismissive gesture. "Can't hold you responsible for the whole of their natures. They can not have been under your influence above a year."

"Less than a month," she replied. Not wishing to pursue the question that came into his expression, she hurried on as she retied the bow. "Still, there must be dozens of London ladies who . . . ."

"I don't know London's ladies. I have been soldiering abroad most of my adult life."

"The daughter of a friend . . . ?"

"Squire about a green girl who would most likely mistake the invitation as evidence of my pointed interest? Never!"

"A sister, cousin, a maiden aunt who . . . ?"

"I would sooner slit my throat."

Japonica smiled, hugely enjoying herself. "It would seem you've given the matter some thought."

"Extensive," he lied, for he had thought of her and only her from the moment Ouseley mentioned the plan. "Alas, madam, you are my last hope."

"How chivalrously put. I am charmed beyond imagining. Oh yes, quite put upon my head by your flattery."

"You may cut the caper, madam. It is clear you will have none of it." He reached out and snagged the box on his hook by the bow and lifted it off her lap.

Japonica met his angry stare and instantly regretted her hasty rejection of the gown. She could not very well admit that now. He might remember nothing of the past, but she did, and he had taken too much from her for her to accept anything from him. But his invitation had given her an idea.

"I have a suggestion which may supply the answer

to your need. I understand it is not the usual thing for ladies who have not yet been presented at court to socialize in public, but I suspect allowances are occasionally made. Why not allow Alyssum to accompany you? She is pretty and I find quite biddable when not surrounded by her elder siblings. Yes, Alyssum would do nicely. And if she should chance to catch the eye of an eligible bachelor . . ."

"Enough!" The look he flashed her was of such loathing that Japonica could not be certain if it was for her suggestion or her daring to presume she knew his needs. "I am not a marriage broker!"

"Then I don't know how it is to be done."

The treacherous tears that should have swamped her half an hour ago rose to the surface. She attempted to hold them at bay with fingers pressed to the corners of both eyes. "I would do it all myself but I have no entrée into London society. Without it, I fear I shall never accomplish Lord Abbott's dying wish. I have made such a mishmash of things. A ver-ver-veritable . . ."

"Are you crying?" Devlyn bent forward in suspicion. "You are not to cry, madam. I forbid it!"

"Bedeviling man!" She stood up, full of wine and indignation. "You are bad-mannered and ill-tempered, with no respect for the foibles of others. I do not doubt that you have few friends and no wife. What woman would care to deal with you?"

He tossed the dress box aside and took a step toward her, drawing her alarmed gaze unerringly to his gilded stare. "No doubt you think you could deal with me."

"Most probably. Though I dare swear it would not be worth the effort."

He smiled. "So then you have a little courage."

Japonica started. He had said those exact words to her the first night they met. And, as before, in this moment she wished she were a match for the lies in his eyes!

"You do not frighten me," she said because, as before, he did exactly that.

"Bismallah!" he murmured under his breath and took her in his arms. A strange look came into his eyes as he drew her toward him and spoke to her in Persian. "You disturb my peace of mind. I will know what secret lies behind your gaze."

The shock of his lips on hers lasted only a second, replaced by an overwhelming urge to discover if the reality of his kiss was as sweet a torment as her memory of the *Hind Div's.*

She was not disappointed. The enveloping heat of his arms, the tender warmth of his lips, the sinuous stroke of his tongue, she had imagined none of it. She was only amazed she ever doubted the experience. The wild impetuous being who once longed for adventure stirred inside her. But this time it was not with the curiosity of ignorance. This was longing wrapped in the power of recognition. Her woman's heart knew what he had yet to guess. This angry wounded stranger was her first and only lover. That connection was not broken. If only he could remember . . . if only she could tell him.

All too soon he lifted his head. Dizzy with amazement and warmth, Japonica gazed up at him. The passion kindling in his golden eyes was unforgettable. Once more she faced the *Hind Div,* sultan of the unexpected, ruler of mysteries locked away in her heart.

It did not last. As she watched, his expression changed by subtle degrees from desire and surprise to confusion then rejection.

"Sobhanallah! What madness is this?" He sounded angry, as if she had somehow tricked him into the moment.

A hot blush that had nothing to do with the wine suffused her skin. " 'Twas but a kiss, *memsahib!*"

Her reply startled him. "How is it you know Persian?"

Japonica searched his face. Had he remembered nothing? Oh, but she remembered everything, the feel of his skin against her own, the power of his body moving over . . . . For one anguished moment the truth lay on her tongue. No, she could not, must not help him to a memory that could destroy her. She looked away. "I might ask the same of you."

"I . . . ." The answer failed him.

She saw arrive in his expression sudden wariness and a trace of fear. The *Hind Div* had been many things: boastful, courageous, arrogant, derisive, mocking, and sensual, but never afraid or vulnerable. Then she remembered. This man was not like other men. He had no memory of his former self. She reached up and touched his cheek. "It doesn't matter."

Her gentle touch was too much. "Don't!" He pushed her away but his hook caught in the sleeve of her gown. As she stumbled back they both heard the sound of material tearing.

Japonica looked down and saw the left portion of her bodice was ripped, exposing the chemise and a good portion of her breast. Embarrassed, she quickly tried to press it back into place.

Realizing what he had done, Devlyn felt a shaming blush climb his cheeks and resented it almost as much as her power over him. Why could he not contain his emotions? Better never to have touched her. What little dignity he had managed to salvage from his wreck of a life was preciously won and very tenuous. Better she dislike him than pity him. "I will leave you now. And if you have any sense you will hurry to your room and lock the door."

She crossed her arms and lifted her chin. "Why is that?"

The intent to insult was bright in his gaze as he moved it slowly down her body, accompanied by the swipe of his tongue across his lips. "I am within an eyelash of tumbling you on the carpet. In your present state you would not seem to have the good sense to deny me!"

He saw his barb hit home, for the blush shrank from her cheeks. "Insufferable!"

"Remember that and keep away from me!" He turned his back, angry to be retreating but desperate to get away from the sight and taste and fragrance of her. God, how he wanted her! It coursed through his veins like liquid fire!

He paused at the door, hurling at her a challenge. "You will forget what just occurred."

"Certainly." Shocked by her own feelings, she knew she must get away, and stay away, from him. She bent and picked up the dress box he had cast aside. "You will be wanting this."

He made a slashing move with his good arm. "You will yet have a use for it when you accompany me to London tomorrow."

"I certainly will not."

"You will." He did not spare her another look and slammed the door behind him.

The sound of the slammed door reverberated in the stairwell where Laurel and Hyacinthe hid. They had braved the cold dark backstairs in order to spy through the servant's entrance to the library.

Hyacinthe nudged Laurel who was peeping through the keyhole as she longed to do. "What did you hear?"

Laurel straightened up from her crouched position and whispered, "He's taking her to London!"

"Are we to be left behind?" Hyacinthe questioned.

"So it seems." A violent jealousy convulsed Laurel's expression but it could not be seen in the blackness.

"Good riddance, I say." Hyacinthe sniffed. "My hair still smells of borax. Her potions make me itch. If she believes I will eat noxious greenery—! What?" she snapped, for Laurel had struck her on the arm to silence her.

"We have greater worries than a spoilt meal!"

"Why? What else did they say?"

"She will have his ear for the entire journey. Time enough to poison him against us. Is that not enough?" But Laurel had seen more than enough to scorch her to the soles of her feet. Lord Sinclair had kissed their step-mama! A thing so shocking to her sense of right that she could not bring herself to speak of it. Yet the image burned like carbolic acid in her mind. She had yet to set her cap for the viscount and the interloper in their midst had already outmaneuvered her.

"To think that plain, freckled-face slut—!" Laurel clamped her lips shut but her thoughts ran on.

She and her sisters had run upstairs to open their packages. Finding no cards, Peony opened the box that contained a silk chemise trimmed with bows and lace, Alyssum, pink silk stockings, Hyacinthe, garters with rosettes, Cynara, a hair clip with pink feathers and she, an India scarf. None but the scarf were suitable gifts for a gentleman to give anyone but his wife or mistress. Now she knew why. She had heard Lord Sinclair say they were meant for Japonica.

"Slut!" Laurel murmured. Gifts for Lord Sinclair's new whore.

How had that been accomplished? When had they had time? Laurel cudgeled her brain for the answer and could not come up with a single clue, unless it be that they knew one another before now.

"But of course! That foreign gibberish they had spoken to one another while entwined, it must be that they knew one another before this week."

"Entwined?" Hyacinthe whispered. "Whatever are you talking about?"

"Nothing." Laurel set her jaw. Ever since she was old enough to do so, she had craved worldly attention and harbored a vague sense of resentment that forces beyond her control had so far kept her from receiving her due. That resentment found resonance in the scene she had just witnessed. A corrosive anger against her step-mama churned in her young breast. "There must be a way to spike her wheel!"

A soft *shurring* sound like that of fur dragged along a wall caused Hyacinthe to grab her sister's arm. "What was that?"

Laurel shoved her away in annoyance. "Possibly a rat!"

"A rat!" Hyacinthe's voice climbed more than an octave in two syllables.

Laurel clapped a hand over her sister's mouth. "Come with me. We must send a letter to London. Several letters, in fact."

With little else to do in the country, letter writing had become Laurel's strong suit. She had a gift for barbed wickedness with which she entertained and appalled friends from her brief school days. In a quarter hour's time, she had penned the Shrewsbury solicitor, a distant relative in the House of Lords, and made inquiries at the Horse Guards about the new viscount. She did not know precisely what she hoped to learn by her inquiries. Yet she had worded them as a younger sister who harbored a vague unease about the two new people in her life. She wished to be assured that there was nothing, no matter how tiny, that should concern her. After all, there were still children in the household and the two adults sharing their roof were neither wed nor related by blood.

When the letters were done, she set the seal to them and turned to Hyacinthe. "Ring for a footman. The dinner hour is long past and we've not yet had a morsel. I need sustenance!"

Bersham came in answer to her summons.

"Ah, dear Bersham," Laurel said expansively, for intrigue had given her spirits a lift as well as increased her appetite. "My sister and I are in need of supper. Nothing heavy. Just a piece of capon, a serving of cold ham with egg sauce, and several slices of Shrewsbury cake."

"Her ladyship has set the supper menu," Bersham said, looking every bit as uncomfortable as he felt. "I will have a tray brought in."

"I do not care a fig what that woman has set. I will have what I asked for. Bring it!"

A pained expression came over the old butler's features. "I cannot go against the orders of the lady of the house."

Laurel exchanged glances with Hyacinthe, who rose to her feet and bore down on the old man like a full battalion. "Listen to me, you mewling old fool! She may be mistress now but she will not be mistress for long! When she is gone you will have to deal with me again. Do you . . . ?" Her gaze fell upon the salver he carried. "What have you there?"

"Letters for Lady Abbott," Bersham answered.

"Give them to me," Laurel cried, treading on her sister's toe in her haste to reach them. "Give them to me, I say!" When he did not immediately hold them out, Laurel snatched them from the tray.

"Lady Abbott's been waiting for an important post

for weeks," Bersham said in agitation. "I brought them with me from London for that very reason."

"We will see that she gets them," Hyacinthe said in a tone meant to squelch further argument. "Laurel will take them up."

Laurel studied the five missives in her grasp with a possessive intensity that neither sister nor butler could mistake for idle curiosity. She looked up suddenly, noting that they watched her. "Well? Be gone!"

"I will tell her ladyship to expect them directly," Bersham said pointedly as he reluctantly departed.

The moment he was gone Hyacinthe rushed up to her. "Who are they from?"

"I don't know." Laurel inspected each one again. "They were franked at a military posting in Lisbon."

"Lisbon? But she is from Persia."

"So she says. I have always thought her a liar and cheat. I think I should discover that truth upon opening them."

"You must not!" Hyacinthe looked horrified. "She will know."

"Do you think I care?" Laurel whirled on her older sister with a malicious smile. "I will do whatever I think fit to save the family from the clutches of an adventuress! And you will do nothing and say nothing to deter me. For if you do, I promise I will pay you back most unkindly!"

Stunned by her sister's unprovoked attack, Hyacinthe stared at her. "You would not!"

"I most certainly would!" Laurel squared her shoulders. At last, life had tossed into her lap a delicious morsel of intrigue. It almost quieted her appetite for other things. She tapped the letters against her lips murmuring, "I do hope Bersham will hurry with the supper tray. I am quite famished!"

Chapter Fifteen

Devlyn could scarcely believe he had allowed himself to be dragged to church. Not only was he not a particularly religious man—though there were few doubters on the battlefield—he did not like making an exhibition of himself. An exhibition was exactly what he had become. The number of worshipers had doubled between the singing of the opening hymn and the beginning of the sermon. No doubt reluctant parishioners sprang from their beds as word spread quickly to the village that the new viscount Shrewsbury was in attendance. A steady stream of latecomers now filled the pews to overflowing.

The Shrewsbury pew, with its ornate gate and velvet seat cushions, sat at right angles to the rest of the pews, giving the parishioners an unobstructed and continuous view of the aristocrats in their midst. It made him want to hold his hat up to protect his left profile, for the eyes glued to it were chaffing his temper. Though it could not be seen as it lay in his lap, he doubted anyone remained in ignorance of his missing right hand. It had already provoked one incident this morning.

Devlyn's lips thinned. Just as he was leaving the breakfast room the plump Shrewsbury sister, whom he thought of ungraciously as "The Goose," had approached him wearing the shawl he had bought for Japonica.

She had simpered and dimpled and made a general nuisance of herself in thanking him for the, "prodigiously delightful gift." All the while the minx kept drawing the shawl tight about her shoulders in a way that brought into prominence her ample bosom. It crossed his mind to wonder what delights of the feminine anatomy she might have displayed had she opened the boxes containing the chemise and stockings.

She had then looked at him in a knowing way and said, "I do wonder what you brought our *new* step-mama. She is such a wonder, our *new* step-mama. One would think she'd had a child of her own to practice upon. But, of course, that is impossible, isn't it? Such a good step-mama, to be so *new* at it."

He knew at once that her words were false. What he could not gather was why she had approached him. Then she let drop her handkerchief in the practiced method of flirtation and he understood. The minx thought to play at coquette.

Unable to ignore it, he bent to pick it up and handed it back to her. That was when she noticed his hook. The look of surprise on her face seemed genuine but then she began to screech like a scalded cat. Her swoon was a plop of ungraceful if deliberate design and he had been too annoyed by it to try to catch her. She did not, he noticed, bump her head when she fell.

Her eldest sister, the horse-faced dragon who now sat to his left in the pew, had entered in time to rescue her sister from the floor. No need to guess her feelings toward him. She sat so stiff and looked so severe that he wondered what would happen if he brushed her shoulder with his own. No doubt she would strike him with her reticule. As for the other three sisters, they had sat like toadstools in the coach, their gazes darting back and forth over his countenance like fireflies. The Mirza himself would not have been subjected to more ogling.

The only person who seemed less at ease in his company was the lady on his right. He had discovered in the last hour that Lady Abbott had a sweet husky voice, perhaps better suited to country tunes than hymns but he liked it. And she was nearly as fidgety as he. She kept folding and refolding her gloved hands and biting her lower lip. She was furious to be made a spectacle, of course. As was he.

He glanced over at her and not for the first time during the service, at the same moment she looked at him. He would swear she was seeking his assurance though her lips did not move. Courage, he offered her in a glance. It will be over soon. It had better be, he mused with a scowl.

It was her fault he was at the service. After the foolishness with Laurel in the breakfast room Lady Abbott had greeted him at the top of the stairs with the news that, contrary to his desire, she would not be returning with him to London. He did not recall exactly what he had replied but it set off a rather lengthy and loud debate which quite restored him from his black mood of the evening before.

A great deal of nonsense ensued as she railed at him and he roared back. When he sent Bersham to pack her bags she declared that Bersham might pack any number of bags but she refused to set a foot out of the door. He then informed her that if she did not get in the carriage when he ordered it, he would have her bodily carried to it by the footman.

Rallying with indignation she answered that she was a grown woman, married and widowed, and so free to do what she wanted and *not* do precisely the same thing. It was none of his business if she did not want to go to London. He retaliated with a great number of black looks and threats to shake her until she saw reason.

It was a wild scene, embarrassing and unnecessary, for in the end the younger three Shrewsburys had shown up and announced their intention of walking to church.

He had to admire Lady Abbott's quick wits. She had ushered the girls into the coach, drawn up in expectation of her accompanying him back to London, and ordered the driver to take them all to Ufton Nervet.

But now he had her!

A deep sound like a chuckle rumbled in Devlyn's chest. He noted her glance but this time he dared not catch her eye. Before he stepped up into the coach with a surprise of his own, that he would accompany them, he had set Bersham the task of packing her things and given the coachman instructions to pick them up at the house while they attended the service. Another carriage would see the sisters home. Lady Abbott would not be told this until she was once back inside the traveling coach, for he did not mean her to step down again until they were in Mayfair.

He smiled to himself. Rousing Lady Abbott's ire entertained him no end. When she forgot to be the dowdy dowager her face took on an animation that was quite fetching. That, and the kiss they had shared. She had kissed him warmly the night before. The more he thought about it, the more certain he became that they were not strangers. But why, if that were true, would she be reluctant to admit it?

He glanced down at his pinned sleeve. He did not intend to repeat the unfortunate mishap of last evening when he tore her gown. She did not seem overly concerned about it but even he understood that brandishing about that dangerous barb was not in the least romantic. Before them lay three hours alone in the coach bound for London. More than enough time for the beginning of a discreet dalliance. The mere thought of it was enough to stir his blood and tighten his groin.

Devlyn shifted uncomfortably in the pew, disconcerted that his present location had no dampening effect on his thoughts or his body's response.

The tedious sermon seemed longer than the average, followed by the inevitable passing of the collection plate. A last hymn and finally the service was at an end. He was delighted to discover that Japonica shared his disinterest in circulating among the congregation that waited as they passed out of the church. After a quick exchange with the vicar, she turned without pause and headed straight for the coach. He heard the whispers of the crowd and did as she did, nodded here and there, but gave no one leave to waylay them. He noted with an inward smile that two additional bags were lashed to the coach. The postillion held the door as she stepped up and then he entered behind her and pulled up the stairs.

Only then did she speak to him. "What are you doing? The girls are coming with us."

"Over my dead body," Devlyn declared. "London!" he called to the coachman and slammed the door.

Japonica gasped. "Open that door this instant. The girls are expecting to ride home with us."

"Bersham will see to them. In fact they are quite

preoccupied elsewhere," Devlyn answered and nodded in the direction of the church. There on the stairs Alyssum remained in conversation with the vicar while Peony and Cynara flanked her. Hyacinthe was speaking with a pair of elderly gentlewomen. Only Laurel seemed interested in the departure of the coach. She watched it roll away with a scowl of fury.

Realizing that her protest was for naught, Japonica sat back with a look of displeasure. "You are kidnapping me!"

He looked across at her and shrugged. "Call it what you will, you are coming to London."

"I have told you I have no wish to do so. If you do not stop this coach at once I shall launch myself through the open door with the coach at a full gallop."

He leaned toward her. "I am perfectly capable of sitting on you to prevent that eventuality."

Despite herself Japonica's lips twitched. "Wretched man!"

"Indubitably."

It surprised her to realize that she was enjoying their contest of wills. Still, it would do her no good to allow him the easy victory. "You cannot keep me locked up in London. I will leave at the first opportunity."

He reached for one of the coaching blankets of fur-lined velvet and unfolded it. "I have need of your company for one, possibly two evenings. Is your schedule so full or your disinclination toward me so strong that you cannot allow for one evening's duty in service of your sovereign?"

"Duty for the King? What possible duty could I perform for the King?"

He leaned forward and placed the blanket across her lap. "Ah, you are like all of your sex. Mention the monarchy and you are all ears."

"I suppose there is a condemnation in that but as I am too ignorant to appreciate it, you will need to explain yourself." She shifted in embarrassment as he began tucking the blanket in at her waist. "I can do that," she said suddenly, for he was tucking it around her hips with the seeming intent of moving ever lower.

Giving up, he leaned back and crossed an ankle over the opposite knee. "Women seem able to adjust every matter in their lives to accommodate an inconvenience that will raise them in society."

"And, of course, a man would never do anything rash in the name of his sire. He would never leave his home, seek out foreign lands, undergo shot and saber, risk his very life for that notoriously risky business called national pride."

Devlyn grunted and set his tricorn forward over his brow so that it blocked out the light, and the disturbing sight of Japonica Abbott.

Satisfied to have had the last word, Japonica settled back against the squabs of the coach. She was no fool. She had noticed her bags lashed to the coach and known what he was about. She had climbed in because she was more than a little curious to see London from a viscount's point of view. It had occurred to her that she might, despite his unwillingness to aid her, make useful social contacts if she accompanied him to London. Her sense of urgency in settling one Shrewsbury sister was compounded by news from Lisbon.

She'd had four letters from Aggie! The relief she felt reading them was so great she could not put them aside but slept with them under her pillow. Today they lay tucked against her heart.

Jamie was growing "fat and sleek as butter" Aggie had written, with a voice to match his appetite. The wet nurse claimed "the bairn suckles more than the twins at her last post."

Longing squeezed hard on her heart. She could not bear this! She was ready to abandon her promise and return to Lisbon . . . then what?

With each passing day her fear grew that word would sooner or later reach England that she had borne a son in Lisbon. She had kept first her pregnancy and then Jamie hidden from Wellington's officers but one never knew what might have been whispered about. Before speculation caught up with her she must leave England.

"You are deep in thought."

Lord Sinclair had set his hat aside and was staring at her with the bright concentrated gaze of the *Hind Div.* " 'Tis time we became better acquainted. For instance, I cannot even recall your Christian name."

She did not believe him, but why refuse something as simple as her name? "Japonica."

He smiled. "The bush with lovely red blossoms? A fitting if highly improper name for an English lady."

Japonica blushed. He had complimented her! But she must not take it to heart. Her mother had always clucked in fretful disappointment over the intemperate color of her hair. "I'm certain I've not heard your Christian name."

"Devlyn."

"Devlyn. That is a proper name for a gentleman to be sure." She cast a mirthful glance his way. "It means courageous, intrepid and chivalrous, which I suppose in your case is debatable."

His black brows lifted. "Debatable?"

"Inconclusive, open to interpretation, unresolved . . ."

He snorted with humor. "I did not ask you for an encyclopedia of interpretation. Do you doubt I am as fully courageous, intrepid, and chivalrous as any other man?"

Before she could stop herself, her glance took him in from head to toe. She looked away out the carriage window. "But my judgment would do you no credit."

Devlyn itched to grab her by the shoulders and demand that she explain that comment. But he dared not lay a hand on her, not when he trembled to do so much more. "What name would *you* give a male child?"

"What?" The question brought her startled gaze back to him.

"What would you name your son?"

"Why, I don't . . . ." How could he have hit upon the very last subject she wanted to discuss with him? Had he found her out? No, that could not be it. He would not be so cavalier about a discussion of a presumptive heir to his title. Yet the *Hind Div* might!

She glanced down then out the window, feeling the world drop away from her. "Why do you ask?"

The anxious note in her voice surprised Devlyn until he saw that her chin trembled. That tremble stirred not only his compassion but also less honorable emotions. How could one woman be so enigmatic yet so appealingly winsome?

"I but pass the time, lady," he said smoothly. "Idle conversation is difficult for one with no memory."

No memory! Japonica blinked. She was making a cake of herself for no reason. He could not guess her secrets, for there were no memories for him to attach to whatever he might have heard about her! She stifled her alarm and said in a measured tone, "James—Jamie, after my father."

"James. A good strong name. Two English kings shared it."

She shook her head. "I do not aspire to so lofty a

comparison. I am the daughter of James Fortnom, late of Bushire, Persia.''

"Persia." He repeated the word slowly, watching as her fingers curled into a stranglehold on her reticule. What made her so reluctant to talk about her family? The predator's instinct of sensing vulnerability in another set his interest in the topic. She was hiding something, something she did not want him to discover.

"So that is how you know the Persian language. Your father was, I suppose, an officer in the Indian Army."

"No, a merchant with the East India Company."

"Indeed? Are you perchance related to the English grocers Fortnum and Mason?" She nodded readily enough but there it was again, that cautious glance from beneath golden-red lashes. "Do you have many relations in England?"

"No close relations."

He was not so much listening to her answers as watching her. What a lovely mouth she had, full and ripe as a peach. "It must grieve you to be so far from your parents and your home."

"My parents are dead."

He saw misery in her expression and wanted to tell her that her secrets, whatever they might be, were safe with him. But that ludicrous notion vanished almost instantly. He did not believe he had ever been a man much concerned with the feelings of others. He wanted her, not her secrets. Desire pushed hard at him. "Were we acquainted in Persia?"

"I never met anyone named Devlyn Sinclair," she answered carefully.

That was not what he'd asked her. So then, they were known to one another in some fashion. But she was still too wary to confide in him. A wise man knew when to push and when to retreat, for the moment. "How did you meet Lord Abbott?"

Japonica resisted answering. Looking into his strong face with its proud expression she could feel again his kiss of the night before, almost believe that the intensity of that golden gaze was for her alone.

Foolish! Absurd! What would it gain her to encourage his interest? Only more grief and heartbreak. Even if marriage had lifted her to his class there were things about her he might never accept. There was Jamie. Without the buttress of his own memory, would he believe she bore him a son? Why should he? Even if he did, what would it gain her? He would be within society's bounds to think her little more than a whore and her son a bastard. No, better for them both if he thought of her as others did, an interloper, perhaps even an adventuress, who had duped a dying nobleman into marriage.

"I was asked by the East India Company to become Lord Abbott's nurse. I'm told it is not uncommon for an ailing elderly man to believe he is in love with the woman who cares for him. Some are foolish enough to offer marriage. Now if that is all, I am a little fatigued by the conversation." She looked out the window, hands clasped so tightly her knuckles ached.

Devlyn noticed her lips pinched white by nerves and regretted the direction the conversation had taken. He had not deliberately sought to push her away but he knew he had. No doubt she had suffered at the hands of gossips for her marriage. Bersham for all his tact had made plain the Shrewsbury daughters resented her with a rare hostility. Perhaps she expected that he harbored the same censure of her birth. How wrong she was! She was more than his equal in his eyes. She was a worthy companion.

Scowling, he joined her in a sightless gaze out of

the window where it had begun to rain harder than before. This pressing desire for her, this lust like a fever, had made him clumsy. Instinct told him he was not always so inept in courting the sentiments of the fairer sex. But at the moment her close proximity and her damned perfume were working to make a mockery of his self-possession.

"You are not to wear that scent in my presence again."

"What?" Japonica turned to look at him, for her thoughts had been as absent from the carriage as his were confined to it.

"You are never to wear that concoction of yours in my presence again. It disturbs me."

"Disturbs . . . ?"

"Irritates, annoys, irks. Are those sufficient words?"

"I see."

His gaze came around carefully to meet hers. "Do you? Do you really?"

He's flirting, she thought with surprised pleasure. No, she could not afford to respond. She jerked the edge of the carriage rug away from his legs, as if the merest contact with him was an insult. "If you find my presence so detestable why don't you take a horse and ride ahead?"

"The beasts do not care for my clumsy handling of the reins."

Before she could stop herself she glanced down at his right arm. "Could you not . . . ." The look of anger on his face made her swallow the thought. But another came quickly to fill its place, fired by consternation and fear. He had no right to speak to her as if they were intimates. "I shall keep my opinions of you to myself if you will so oblige me. I will wear my perfume when and where it suits me."

It was one provocation too many for Devlyn. "I

think you don't understand the nature of my torment. Let me demonstrate."

Grasping her by the arm, he dragged her until she was completely off her seat and halfway into his lap. "Now tell me you would not rather forego any bit of feminine vanity if you knew how much it rouses my interest?"

"I believe I should not be afraid to be myself, no matter the consequence," she answered over a heart beating so loudly she was certain he must hear it.

Devlyn could not hear her heart but he could see her pulse beat furiously in the indentation of her throat. The exotic perfume rising from her skin stirred him with the sweet aching that had become part of being in her company. Staring at her face only inches from his own, the absurdly red-gold filigree of the curls escaping her bonnet, it came to him that she had been in his arms long before last night, had kissed him with a passion that he sensed lived just beneath her modest surface. What difference if she would not tell him when or where or why? She was here, in his arms, and she was not protesting that fact. She had been a married woman, he reminded himself. There should be no false modesty or maidenly confusion once he made his declaration.

"I want you, Japonica. And I believe you want me. So then who will deny us?"

For a long moment Japonica held rigid in his embrace. Her hips were thrust against his thighs and every breath made muscles shift beneath her. He was real as he had never been before, a flesh and blood man, no phantom of her dream world or seductive conqueror seen through the haze of an opiate dream. She saw herself reflected in his gaze, saw all the longing in her expression she must never give voice to, and then his lips descended upon hers.

At that moment the coach lurched and swerved as

if making a sudden turn in the road. She heard the horses whinny in alarm and the coachman's hoarse cry and crack of his whip. The coach went over on two wheels, canting the interior so that she was thrown against the door and Devlyn rumbled after her. Then as if shoved by a strong hand, the coach righted itself, slamming back onto the paved road with a jolt that splintered the axle and wrung a cry from her. Even as Devlyn grabbed for her, she pitched forward and struck her head. Bright points of light sprang up in her vision surrounded by a field of black. She heard her name called repeatedly but it was a dim hollow sound like a voice calling down a well.

Cursing like the seasoned soldier he was, Devlyn pulled himself up from the floor of the coach and twisted around to gaze out the sprung coach door. On the road ahead in the slanting rain he saw the indistinct shape of two carriages. Closer by he could hear the Shrewsbury postillion and driver shouting and working to free the horses from their tangled harnesses.

"There's been an accident on the road ahead," he said. "Are you hurt?" When she did not answer, Devlyn swung round and looked down. Japonica lay at his feet. There was a bloody smudge on her brow and the thin trickle of blood at the corner of her mouth.

Quickly and with the precision of years of calculating the dead on the battlefield, his fingers slid round under the slender curve of her jaw to find the pulse. It beat quickly. Whispering a prayer of thanksgiving he squatted down beside her. As he did so, the coach moved to the accompanying creak of its suspension. To judge by the angle of the cant it had lost a wheel. He was not much concerned. What worried him was the stillness of the lady before him. Reaching out, he loosened the ribbons of her bonnet and removed it.

As carefully as he could he slid his right arm under her shoulders and lifted her up against his chest. "Are you badly hurt, my lady?" he asked softly.

Her eyes opened. He saw in them bewilderment and a touching pain. And then she said in Persian, "Is it you, *memsahib?*"

He frowned. "Who am I, *bahia?*"

A tremor of emotion passed through her, her lips quivered, and then she blinked. He knew the exact moment she recovered her senses, and with them the hesitation that seemed an innate part of her. "Why—Lord Sinclair."

He felt the anguish of the lost moment. That is not what she meant to say but he could not even guess how to discover what it was.

"We lost a wheel." He cradled her head against his chest with his left hand. Her satin-smooth skin felt as cool as ice. "Are you hurt?"

She shook her head a little. "Banged and bruised."

He did not believe her because she moaned as she tried to shift herself away from him. "Don't move." Carefully, he ran his hand down each of her arms and then strongly along either side of her body from underarm to waist.

"Does this hurt?" he questioned each time.

Each time she answered in a breathless, "No."

He pressed against her abdomen and then the small of her back. Finally he said, "Try to move your legs." He watched intently as she moved first the right and then the left. For the first time he smiled. "Perhaps you are right. You're not badly hurt."

But he did not like the way the bruise was blooming on her forehead nor the trickle of blood oozing from her lip. He touched her lip. "Have you loosened a tooth?"

Japonica felt around in her mouth with her tongue

then slowly moved her head in the negative. "Only bit my tongue."

The coachman stuck his head in the gap where the door had been. He looked stricken. "You okay gov'nor? Lady Abbott . . . ?"

"We're both well enough. A few bruises, that's all. What caused our accident?"

"Gor!" The coachman glanced back over his shoulder. " 'Twas a bad spill on the road, my lord. A phaeton clipped the mail coach. Tried to go round them. Swear I did! But we came upon 'em so sudden like. We lost a wheel, the road being slick and all."

"Go and see if you can be of help. I'll be right there." He looked down at Japonica. "Do you mind?"

"Not at all. I'll be fine, really." She sounded steadier and even smiled at him. "Little of consequence damaged other than my dignity."

He bent a hard stare on her, reluctant to release the woman in his arms.

Who will deny us? She had not answered his question but this did not seem the time or place to continue.

He shifted her onto the slanted seat and reached for the coach blanket with which to cover her. "Don't move. I'll be back in a moment."

He climbed out of the overturned coach into the misty day and headed toward the two vehicles on the road ahead. One was a massive coach, the other a slight large-wheeled racing equipage. It was a well-traveled road. Many who had been stopped by the accident were coming forth from their own vehicles to lend aid.

His own coachman met him halfway. " 'Tis a nasty business, gov'nor. The whip of the high flyer was badly injured when he was thrown."

"Then there's nothing to be done." Devlyn turned

back. "We've lost a wheel. I shall inquire as to whether another carriage can take Lady Abbott up."

"No need, m'lord. I've sent the postillion to ask. Only it may be some time before traffic is moving again, what with the weather and the wreckage to be cleared."

"Very well." Devlyn turned away and strode back to the coach. He did not think what the waiting would mean to his or Lady Abbott's comfort. It was cold. His clothes were slick with December rain. Sitting motionless would no doubt quickly become a great discomfort. He did not care. He climbed back in.

She sat on the slanted seat, her ankle propped on the opposite perch. "I did hurt my ankle. Nothing serious," she added with a quick smile that did not quite meet her eyes. He knew that she was thinking, as he was, of the seconds before their accident.

He moved carefully onto the seat beside her and rested his elbows on his knees as if he were weary. "We will be here some little while. We've broken a wheel."

"Then we are very lucky," she answered solemnly. "I heard the driver say someone was badly hurt."

"Fool in a high flyer trying to overtake the mail coach. Damn fool." He reached out and cupped her chin, turning it this way and that until he was satisfied that she had suffered no more than a single bruise on her forehead. Then he caught her by the waist and pulled her in against his chest. "We are lucky. Very lucky."

Japonica relaxed willingly against him. The tremble of feeling inside her was not all nerves. How solid he felt, warm where she was cold, strong where she felt weak, brave when she wanted to weep. And she could not tell him any of her feelings.

"You are cold?" He pulled the blanket up around her shoulders and tucked it close. "Is that better?"

She lifted her head from his shoulder. "No."

She saw the question in his eyes a scant second before he bent to her and his lips descended upon hers.

The heat of his breath came through parted lips, moist and hot against her mouth. The gentle flick of his tongue across her lips made her gasp and then his tongue boldly entered. The pleasure was too strong to resist. She reached up and encircled the strong column of his neck with her arms and gave into the desire to match his boldness, offering him stroke for stroke of her own tongue. His arms tightened about her, drawing her fully into his lap.

The spiraling dizziness of their kisses continued some minutes in silence, broken only by their sighs and gasps. His hand found her breast through her cloak and he stroked her softly as he pulled her against him. She turned into his embrace, wanting the feelings that she had never been fully certain of until this moment to go on and on. As his arms tightened about her she felt a hunger in him, tasted the delight of a forbidden night so long ago.

He lifted his head almost reluctantly, his hand coming up to frame her cheek. There it was in his passion-smoked gaze, the question she dared not answer and the one he very slowly put into words. "What . . . are . . . you . . . to . . . me?"

She turned her head away, anguish making her wince. "If you cannot remember, I cannot tell you."

"Cannot or will not?"

She shook her head, the bright red tangle of her curls tickling his face.

"Then I will have to discover the truth for myself."

He tucked her head beneath his chin and rested his cheek against her hair. She smelled of henna and tasted of Paradise. This time she had not pretended that they were strangers. He supposed it was a woman's prerogative to be mysterious where matters of the heart were concerned. And he was sure now that it was a matter of the heart. The rest could wait, even the raw ache consuming him. In this moment he was content for the first time in a long time.

Chapter Sixteen

"She don't look like a dowager." The tortoiseshell lorgnette rose up to cover a pair of eyes as pale a shade of gray as the day outside the Shrewsbury Mayfair residence.

Japonica could scarcely remain still as she was inspected from crown to toe and crown again by the tall elegant lady who had appeared in the entrance to the Shrewsbury dining room. The old-fashioned viewing device was an affectation, she decided, for the lady was in all other ways in the kick of fashion. She wore a long-sleeved walking dress of striped sarcenet and a scarlet velvet cap ornamented with rows of pearls and ostrich feathers that bobbed as she spoke.

When she was done with her inspection, the lady snapped her lorgnette closed by slapping it against her palm. "Devlyn, you may introduce me."

Devlyn, who had risen from his seat upon her appearance, looked as unruffled as was possible for a man whose supper had been interrupted by an uninvited guest. "You were told we were not at home, Aunt Lacey."

"Nonsense, Dev. I am family. I am famished, as well." The lady sailed up to Devlyn and turned her cheek, offering him its apple roundness that he dutifully pecked. Satisfied, she turned to the nearby chair at the table while a footman scurried to pull it back for her.

She favored Japonica with a sweet smile as she sat. "Don't look so worried, child. Devlyn is like a son to me and I've been these last twenty years a mother to him. But he's been very naughty. He claims he cannot remember me."

"It is not a claim, Aunt Lacey. It is a regrettable fact that I have lost years of memory."

"Fustian! You remember something. Did you not write me a fortnight ago to ask me to stay away from London? What is a mother to think but that you are in desperate need of her?"

"Mother or aunt?" Japonica whispered with a glance at Devlyn, for the lady seated with them did not appear to be a day older than he.

"It is a complex equation," Devlyn answered grimly.

Lady Simms shook her head, setting in motion not only pearls and feathers but also the ebony curls that framed her piquant face. "Do not mind his temper. Men are such difficult creatures. They bluster and blunder about then dare those who love them best to come to their aid." She looked back at Devlyn, her gaze as bright and direct as an owl's. "I have been in town two full days, yet they tell me each time I call that you are away."

"I have been," Devlyn answered shortly.

"I am mollified. You are here and I am here." She picked up the hastily laid napkin and shook it out.

"We shall sort the rest in a trice. Has the soup been laid?"

Devlyn turned to Japonica, his face a composite of consternation and fatigue, both of which she shared. "I had thought to spare you any further trying moments in this day but I fear it is not to be. Forgive the interruption of your meal and allow me to present to you my *aunt*, Lady Simms. Aunt, this is Japonica Abbott, dowager viscountess of Shrewsbury."

Japonica rose to her feet to offer the lady a curtsy. "It is a pleasure to meet at last another member of the Shrewsbury family, Lady Simms."

"We ain't kin." Lady Simms spoke in the abrupt manner of *beau monde*, all hauteur and censure, but Japonica found she did not resent the lady, for she was happily buttering a roll as she spoke. "I had heard the Indian Dowager was young, Devlyn, but this is ridiculous. How do you expect to explain a schoolroom miss to your acquaintances?"

"Do I need explanation?" Japonica inquired, though she knew she was not being addressed.

Lady Simms bent a significant glance on her nephew as she took a bite of her roll. "Not that I give a fig what you two have got up to. I can plainly understand why you shut yourself up with a ready-made mistress. Coming home to find yourself a viscount and nicely set up into the bargain with a widow under your roof? Too much temptation for a gentleman long absent from the niceties of civilized life. But to indulge your luck while all of London is agog with interest in her? It is just not done. Appearances, Devlyn! Appearances are everything."

"I don't understand," Japonica said, though she thought she did all too well. "I am thought to be Lord Sinclair's mistress?"

"Gossip," Lady Simms said shortly. "Devlyn's actions are those of a man in thrall to a woman. My dear, they say he is even dressing you." She frowned. "I do hope he did not choose that gown for you. It is much too matronly. But the green silk should be a dream. With your complexion and hair? *Faugh!* If I were you, I should drive about bareheaded in an open barouche every afternoon there was sun!"

"That is quite enough!" Devlyn had seen Japonica blanch and then color up as his aunt prattled on. "You entirely mistake the relationship between the viscountess and me."

"Do I?" Lady Simms's gaze ranged back and forth between the two. "Do I, indeed? Well, I beg pardon. Though it won't change gossip a jot. All of London suspects you share a torrid *tendre* given license by your proximity under the same roof. Then when you are seen buying her clothes? *Quel divertissement!* Of course, I must officially disapprove. Ah, turtle soup!" she cried in delight as the footman served her bowl. "My prayers are answered."

"What sort of mother are you?" Japonica questioned in distress at the many shocks she had endured. "That you would believe these aspersions against your son—or nephew . . ."

"We are actually cousins," Devlyn cut in, his expression an enigma.

Lady Simms's nod set pearls and feather and curls aswing. "Took Devlyn in when his parents died in the epidemic of '88. He was eight and I seventeen. I had just wed. My husband was kindness itself. We agreed to rear Dev as our own. He was a very clever if mysterious child, full of moods and prone to secretiveness. 'Twas a mother's part I've played, for I've never had children of my own. Both of us care deeply for Dev's future." She turned a warm glance on Japonica. "Do, we wonder, do you?"

"Of course," Japonica said slowly—the lady seemed as much an oddity as anyone she had ever met. "But let me assure you, Lady Simms, that we have not spent a single night unchaperoned beneath the same roof. My step-daughters have been with me the entire time."

"And quite a debauched picture that makes." She paused to swallow a spoonful of soup. "Of course, that sort of gossip will never reach my ear direct. But Leigh, my dear husband, is abuzz with *oui-dire* from his club. Some of it quite *outré*. Devlyn may have lived in the East these last ten years but it does not follow that he has developed the proclivities of a Caliph. Formed his own harem, indeed!"

"Enough, Aunt!" Devlyn had watched a sick look steal over Japonica's features and wished at the moment he could stuff his loquacious relative back into her barouche and drive it into the Thames. "You are distressing Lady Abbott."

"Am I?" Lady Simms looked utterly surprised. "But I have brought you the most delightful *on dits* upon which to dine. Are you not prodigiously diverted?"

Japonica could feel Devlyn's daunting gaze on her like the weight of judgment. She did not have the courage to look him in the face. Had he known what was being said? Did he care? She knew enough of the world to suspect that these rumors might improve his standing among the masculine set. But for her, and the Shrewsbury girls, it could spell utter social disaster. Seeking to learn the extent of the damage, Japonica asked, "As a member of the family, I am certain you were quick to defend Lord Abbott's daughters as well."

"Defend them? The Shrewsbury Posy?" Lady Simms shuddered. "It were a mercy they were not drowned at birth!"

Devlyn's snort of amusement reminded Japonica

that he had once made a similar observation. "Lady, surely that is hard."

Lady Simms squinted at the dish of lamb chops brought in to follow her soup. "Lord Abbott roamed the world while he was in it. Did it never occur to you to ask why? To get away from the coven of witches his blighted ballocks produced."

"Aunt, really!" Devlyn murmured.

She glanced over at Japonica, tongs poised to select a chop. "I have made you blush! Too few blush in the world today."

"You are wrong about Lord Abbott," Japonica said carefully. "He cared very deeply for his daughters. They were in his final words and thoughts."

"Well they might be, when he was about to answer for them to Saint Peter. 'Tis the curse of the Abbotts that they produced only harridans and stoop-shouldered men." She dropped two chops onto her plate. "Devlyn is what he is because he's so far removed from the direct line. 'Tis a mercy the main line ended with your husband."

The harsh words pricked the new protective sense Japonica felt for her new family. "Even if all you say is true, the girls are blameless in their heritage."

Lady Simms paused to look directly at Japonica for the first time. "That is a pretty speech. Had I not dealt with them my tender heart would be touched. I made an attempt to put a bit of town polish on the elder two last spring. Before the first day's shopping was done the younger became sick in the carriage, a bonnet was spoiled in a tussle at the haberdashery, and the eldest upended a teapot on a seamstress's head simply because of a pinprick! I could not bring myself to show my face in Madame Yvonne's for a full three months afterwards!"

Japonica noticed mirth in Devlyn's expression but he remained mercifully silent. "They have changed.

The girls have gained some maturity and government over their—ah, enthusiasm."

Lady Simms favored her with a fish-eyed glance. "I cannot imagine the stratagems that would be required to bring them up to the level of merest acceptability. I do not envy you, their new mama, one jot."

"Perhaps this lady is made of sterner stuff than their previous guardians," Devlyn suggested.

"She will needs be made of India rubber!" Lady Simms frowned as she stared at the dish of roasted potatoes. "No lady this side of the Channel would agree to the Devil's pact that marriage to Lord Abbott would have been." She looked across at Japonica as she spooned potatoes onto her plate. "By wedding you, a commoner, Lord Abbott provided his wretched brood a complaisant mama and a purse. The last act of a desperate man!"

Her selection made, she waved the footman away and looked again at Japonica, who was gasping in unspoken indignation. "Still, you've come up in the world, haven't you? Your dalliance with my nephew may not be entirely held against you. Given your lack of lineage it isn't as if you were destined to be accepted by the high sticklers. In certain circles of the *ton,* a notorious reputation isn't without merit. So then, where to begin with you?"

Japonica could barely speak past the insult choking her. "I suppose you mean well, Lady Simms, but I assure you your assistance is unnecessary."

Lady Simms glanced at Devlyn. "Is she always so stubborn?"

"Uncommonly," Devlyn answered.

One raven-black brow took flight as Lady Simms cocked her head birdlike in Japonica's direction. "I will say this on your behalf. You've drawn Devlyn out of his shell. Perhaps he tells his ladylove what he will not say to family.''

She turned her scorching glance on Devlyn. ''Amnesia and cracked brains. I don't believe in it. The truth is somewhere inside you. As for your infirmities.'' She picked up her gold-embossed fork and pointed first to his scarred brow. ''Of no consequence. In my father's day when dueling was every true gentleman's calling, a man without a scar was considered to be a coward or a clergyman. As for this!'' She jabbed the tines of her fork at his hook. ''Do you need advertise?''

Japonica was astonished that Devlyn allowed anyone to speak to him in so impertinent a fashion. Yet he sat in quiet repose, as if listening to a wiser voice, or even some sound altogether beyond them. She could find no equitable feeling in herself. She had just been called a whore and an interloper and now was being ignored. It was too much!

She stood up abruptly. ''I've had enough.'' The two turned sharp glances upon her. ''This is my home. Therefore I can speak my mind. Which is this. I am neither the wanton nor the waster you seem to believe, Lady Simms. Nor, I suppose, are you the inveterate gossip and spoiler you would appear.'' She saw Lady Simms's lips crimp at the corners. ''I am rather fatigued and would beg to leave you in the capable hands of your nephew.''

When she had gone, Lady Simms turned to Devlyn. ''I like her. She has spirit, wit, and courage. She will do very nicely for you.''

''She has already done very nicely,'' Devlyn returned coolly. ''She is a viscountess without my help.''

''She is a child, Dev! A lady so young and obviously untried is never long without a trail of randy suitors willing to make up for her lack.''

''Untried? Did you not just tell me half of London

supposes I have already ridden her to Londonderry and back?"

"Who listens to gossip?" Lady Simms set her fork aside with a sigh. "I never indulge in it."

"You show an unwelcome alacrity to poke your nose into what is my business."

"The presumption of age," she said carelessly. "After all, you asked my opinion."

"I did not."

"No? I must have read it in your face. Do give up that wretched scowl. You are a sour note in the sonata of life. Yes, you've been dealt with harshly by Fortune." She reached and covered his hook with her hand. "But answer me this, Devlyn. Was anything maimed, lopped off or otherwise put out of commission that would prevent you from making some undeserving lady's life a romp and a toss, with an endless nursery of swaddlings to show for it?"

Devlyn smiled. "Put that way, I should be congratulating myself."

She bent forward and laid her cheek upon his damaged arm. "Then my dear Dev, you have all that you need to be happy." She sat up and returned to her chop. "If it be true you've lost memory of years of your life it could prove a boon. Think of the ladies who will be willing, nay eager, to refresh your memory of them. 'Twill not be that prong," she pointed with her knife to his hook, "they will rush to hook themselves upon."

"You have grown into a bawd, Aunt."

Lady Simms laughed gaily. "It comes from being a politician's wife. Leigh despairs of me yet he will tell me the most wicked tales. Have you heard the story the Prince Regent tells about the prodigious size of his own brother's penis?"

"Aunt!"

"Very well." She reached for her wine. "Back to

Lady Abbott. She positively reeks of the middle class. If nothing else, that reflects poorly upon me. *Que faire?* I know! I will send my maid to her until I can secure a decent one for her." She frowned. *"Mauvais* relatives can be so vexing to one's social standing. I suppose it is too late to do away with the Shrewsbury Posy?"

Devlyn laughed for the first time. "Yes."

"A pity. But if we are to stem the talk against Lady Abbott she must be seen in town, instanter. Where will you take her first?"

"We are to dine with the Mirza tomorrow night."

Lady Simms's eyes lit up. "But that is wonderful! Few have seen him. London's hostesses despair of him. He declines every invitation. If Lady Abbott should be among the first to circulate with firsthand news of him . . ."

She broke off and reached out to pat Devlyn's chest just over his heart. "Oh, but that will keep. I am so very glad to see you, boy. I could not believe you were gone." She blinked back the tears that came into her eyes. "No longer a soldier but a viscount! How jolly! You are due a bit of happiness. Promise me you will seek it out. Or better yet, let Lady Abbott help you." She pulled away and returned to her dinner. "She is in love with you. Do you realize that?"

"I think you read too many novels," he answered neutrally. "Lady Abbot's feelings for me are decidedly other."

"For a man of experience and good sense, you are singularly lacking in discernment. Lady Japonica— gad, what a horror of a name!—wed an elderly man, a dying man. No doubt all her lofty dreams of romance remain intact. In fact, I should imagine if you have not done the deed that *she* is still intact."

The idea should not have shocked him. Devlyn knew every piece of the puzzle. Yet he had arranged them into a very different sort of picture. Wedded but not bedded. That would explain her wariness of him, despite their attraction. "Are you certain? I would swear . . ."

"Wishful thinking! Men make that mistake nearly every time. Assume the lady knows too little or too much, whatever best suits the gentleman's best opinion of himself." Her expression took on a rare thoughtful mode. "So then you have not bedded her. She did not strike me as a siren. Her looks are not those to attract the lusts of gentlemen seeking a meaningless liaison."

"You are right." Devlyn sighed. "She is more wren than raven."

"Did I say she's dull stuff? Nonsense! She's got pluck. Did you hear how she contradicted me when I attacked the Shrewsbury brood? There's passion in her, as well. I saw the way she looks at you, Devlyn. If you don't want her ruined, leave this house at once."

Lady Simms's personal maid assured Japonica that the hairdresser she had engaged was skilled in working with all types of hair. Yet she was in doubt about using his services. "Perhaps we should leave it as it is this time."

The maid's eyes grew wide. "Oh, my lady, do you think so?"

Japonica looked in the mirror. The Grecian knot she had attempted looked more like Vesuvius after an eruption. She turned to the hairdresser, a fellow in a wasp-waisted coat who wore his breeches too tight. "What do you think?"

He shook his head. "With your permission I will attempt something more complimentary yet demure. Lady Simms remarked that it won't serve upon your first public appearance to strive for the top kick of fashion.''

Japonica frowned. There seemed to be a formidable number of things that fit into the "Do" and "Don't" categories of being a London lady, many of which were beginning to pinch her like a pair of too-small shoes.

"Very well. You can do no worse than I have done and doubtless can do better.''

Japonica could not decide whether she liked or detested Lady Simms. Even if she had sent round her maid and hairdresser and two boxes of Belgian chocolates before nuncheon, the lady did not seem someone who could be trusted. Or maybe it was only that she resented the distorted public mirror Lady Simms had held up to the relationship between Lord Sinclair and herself.

Lord Sinclair's mistress! All of London speaks of it. A harem!

She could not long dismiss from her mind the strange and acutely embarrassing conversation of the evening before. It was shocking and mortifying, damning to others' reputations as well as hers.

Luckily Lord Sinclair had been absent from the house all day so that she had not been required to meet him in the hall or at any meals. She doubted she could have remained, otherwise. She had seen the annoyance in his expression the one time she dared glance at him during his aunt's recitation. But it gave her no real clue to his deeper feelings in the matter.

Her own feelings were appallingly obvious.

Before being accosted by Lady Simms at dinner she had thought the best and worst of yesterday had already been hers. Marooned for over an hour in their damaged coach, she had dozed in Devlyn's arms only to waken to the certain knowledge that her feelings for the man were exactly the reason she must never again allow him to touch her. Despite every caution and danger, she had become attached to a man she scarcely knew, and understood even less. Yet here she was, preparing to go out with him this evening as though yesterday and last night had never occurred.

"You are a fool, Japonica Fortnom Abbott!" she whispered under her breath.

Lord Sinclair had sent a note informing her to be ready to dine out this evening. A public outing, after what she knew was being whispered about them? How could he, how could she hold her head up?

"What of this, my lady?"

Japonica looked into the mirror and the reflection it offered made her smile. Her pile of irregular curls had been twisted into a curly topknot caught back in a silver net cap lined with purple silk and trimmed with a silver tassel that dangled by her left ear. "You are a wonder! Wherever did you find the cap?"

"Lady Simms had me bring it along." The hairdresser turned his head to one side and then the other. "You could crop the front a bit, my lady. But the color's good and the effect delightful."

"You have certainly helped me put my best foot forward," Japonica acknowledged. She hoped she could put on the proper face to go with it.

Minutes later she stood in her dressing room waiting to don her gown when lady Abbott's maid brought out the green silk.

"That is not the gown I laid out."

"No, my lady." The maid blushed and curtsied. "But Lady Simms was most particular that you wear this one. The other gown, while quite nice, isn't smart enough for dinner. Now this . . . ." She swung the gown out so the skirts danced across the floor.

Japonica bit her lip. According to Lady Simms,

everyone knew Lord Sinclair had bought that gown for her. If she wore it she would be stoking the fire of her supposed infamy. Yet the black frock she meant to wear was so dowdy. Some indignant and defiant spark took flame inside her. If she were to be thought a mistress, she might as well dress the part.

"Very well."

Devlyn appeared at the Shrewsbury residence a little before nine o'clock. He had moved out earlier in the day and dressed at his club. His aunt would be proud to know he had banished his hook to the bottom drawer of his highboy and ordered new shirts with the hem of the right sleeves sewn shut. He wished he could be equally proud of her, yet her behavior toward Japonica the night before had left him in doubt of her good sense. But perhaps he had been too long away from London and lost his taste for mocking wit and stinging humor. Certain that his aunt had inflated the public interest in the viscountess, he learned different before noon. Someone had set spark to wick over the matter of the viscountess and the smoke of that rumor was rapidly covering London.

While abroad during the day he learned he had the wagging tongues of Howe and Frampton to thank for it. They had told all over town how they had come to meet the dowager viscountess. His subsequent reluctance to partake of the public spectacle that was London society, coupled with the mysterious arrival of the "Indian Viscountess" as she was being called in some circles, had set other more malicious tongues wagging. As remedy, he could do no other than push them both into the spotlight and hope the truth would dampen speculation.

He poured himself a single small brandy as he

waited grimly for her to appear. He did not give a damn what people thought. But her? She had so many strikes against her, a widow, a colonialist, a common merchant's daughter wed to a dying nobleman twice and again her age; any of them was a daunting hurdle. Braced together they presented odds against public acceptance that an inveterate gambler might shy from accepting.

He finished his glass in a gulp and turned as someone entered the room.

The dress he had purchased off a modiste's mannequin now graced one of the best figures he had ever seen. Shaped to her bosom, it fell in sheer tiers that draped and clung to her hips and slender thighs as she approached. Her hair was caught back from her face in a net bonnet with short burnished curls framing her temples. The only discordant note in the whole picture of prettiness was her expression. Was it nerves or anger? He could not tell. But he knew he would have to do something about it.

She paused a few feet from him, her expression stiff. "You approve?"

"Turn around."

At once resentment brightened her dark eyes. "I am not a mare for sale on market day."

In answer he made a circle with his fingers. Though her expression retained its mutinous glare she turned slowly about.

As she moved, his gaze fixed for a moment on the thrust of her beautifully rounded bosom when she turned in profile and then on her superbly molded back and shoulders. How could he ever have thought her dowdy or plain? Dress the wren in peacock feathers and what a brilliant little bird she made! Was that part of the mystery he had always suspected? Or had he already known this about her?

He shied away from the temptation to cudgel his

brain for lost memory. Tonight he needed all his wits without the threat of headache and temper to distract him.

When she had come full circle Japonica held perfectly still under his golden regard. But her heart pounded with heavy strokes beneath her skimpy bodice. She felt naked and foolish. No matter what her mirror told her, she had yet to see a single glimmer of response to her display in his expression. Oh, but she had been wrong to wear it. She knew it!

"I will change."

"No." He reached out to stop her with the lightest of touches on her shoulder. And then he smiled full, the charm of it more potent for its rarity. "Forgive me. I am at a loss to convey my admiration, Lady Abbott."

She crossed her arms under her bosom. "You might have said so at once."

Devlyn gave a fleeting glance to the enticements she unconsciously drew to his attention and felt a quickening in his loins. If she realized how she affected him, he suspected she would refuse to go anywhere with him. Now, more than ever, he wanted to be seen in public at her side. "So then, you are ready?"

She nodded. "Will Lady Simms be joining us?"

"Decidedly not! She has been told to keep away from you."

"Why?"

Her beseeching gaze begged him to reassure her that his aunt's *on dits* were no more than wind whistling down a chimney. He could not. He would not know how much damage had been done to her reputation until she had spent an evening in society. How much crueler it would be to lead her out tonight without her guard up. Better she should go forth armed with righteous and wary indignation.

"I did it to protect my privacy." The anguish in her eyes increased and he wished instantly he had been more gallant.

Still she rallied almost instantly. "I suppose it does not matter to you how much Lady Simms blackens my character."

"Did I agree with a single thing she said?"

"You did not contradict her."

He felt a coward for not answering her genuine need to be assured but false hope was not his purpose. "Truth never spiked gossip's wheel."

The hope of rescue died in her dark eyes. "So then, you do not care that I am called your mistress and you are thought to be the debaucher of five young girls."

"Madame, if I thought that farce would be seriously accepted I should shoot myself. As I think it merely odious and tedious, I will continue to ignore it."

When she did not reply he turned and picked up a fur-lined wrap he had brought in with him. "You will need this. Snow is threatening again."

Japonica held still as he swung the cape about her shoulders. She wished she possessed his innate belief in himself. After all, what did it matter what London society thought of her? She had no real need of the trappings of an aristocratic title. Soon she would be away from here, and Lord Sinclair.

Devlyn watched outraged emotions play across her face, the struggle warming her cheeks with the color she had moments before lacked. His purpose was accomplished, if at the price of her liking. He should leave it at that. But he could not.

As she reached up to pull the cloak closed under her chin he covered her one hand with his and bent close to her. "You are beautiful. Has no one ever told you so?"

Japonica turned away. She did not want his com-

fort, did not want the warmth of his touch that made
her feel that her safety lay within his power. She could
not allow that. "Yours is too extravagant a compliment, Lord Sinclair, to be believed."

He caught her chin in his strong fingers and drew
her face up until she was looking into his eyes. "You
are beautiful. Believe it."

Quite before she was prepared for it, she was moving into his arms. There was plenty of time for her
to notice a dozen delightful disturbing things about
him, the crisp texture of his formal clothes, the whiff
of sandalwood rising from his warm skin, the powerful strength of his body held in check as he bent to
her. It was a light kiss, no more than the brush of
his lips across hers, but it nearly stopped her heart.

When he lifted his head, he was still smiling. He
took her hand and folded it in the crook of his arm.
"Come, Lady Abbott, we go to face London."

Chapter Seventeen

The façade of the house in Mansfield Street was ablaze with torches posted along the lane. Curiosity seekers, kept in check on the opposite side of the street by Bow Street Runners, gaped in awe of the crystal and gold and silver chandeliers on display through windows with drawn-back drapery. So many candles ablaze, more than two score East End households could afford to use in a year. Footmen flanked the entrance in new red scarlet coats. The livery had been delivered by the English government for the express use of those engaged in service to the Mirza. All onlookers remarked upon it at length, for red livery was reserved for the King and the Heir Apparent. The women gazed with great envy at the two rows of deep gold lace showing through their coats. Waistcoats of green and gold had the favor of the Dandies among them. All admired the tricorn hats cocked with gold lace. This mark of esteem and respect to a foreign ambassador was theretofore unheard of. Which, of course, increased the fervor to catch a glimpse of this mysterious being from Persia.

As the number of observers increased, so did the number of servants who hurried forth to welcome guests as they emerged from the carriages drawing up before the house.

"What place is this?" Japonica asked as she was handed down.

"Did I not say?" Devlyn replied in the most causal of voices. "We dine tonight as guests of his Excellency Abdul Hassan Khan."

"The Persian ambassador?"

He smiled at her incredulous expression. How could anyone so strong-willed and resourceful be at the same time so completely unguarded at a moment like this? He longed to touch her cheek with the back of a finger. Instead he merely said, "Courage, *bahia.*"

They were led into a room brilliant with candlelight reflected in the high-polished paneling and multitude of mirrors that doubled and redoubled the luminescence. With Devlyn at her side, Japonica was quickly introduced to a succession of gentlemen, many in full military regalia. Among them she recognized Lieutenants Hemphill and Winslow. They smiled but kept their distance, as did all the rest.

It dawned on her only as they approached the last group that she was the only lady in the room. Had gossip galloped so far that gentlemen would keep their wives at home lest they be insulted by her presence? Or was it simpler than that? She was a commoner and their wives refused to be introduced to her into circles where she did not belong.

"I am the sole lady present?" she asked quietly of the man at whose side she walked.

Devlyn looked down at her. "If so, the gentlemen

will be grateful. They need not divide their attention between you and their wives."

His reply did not answer her question but she noted he had gone out of his way to phrase his answer charmingly when most often he blasted her for a ninny. Was he trying to bolster her courage? Unless he, too, was dismayed by the results of the rumors his aunt had carried in and plopped at their dinner table like a proud cat displaying a dead mouse.

"I shall fetch you an orgeat," he said and left her side almost before she could refuse.

She watched him quickly leave the room, and looking around the assembly of gentlemen engrossed in conversation, wondered if she would be left to her own devices for the rest of the evening. She did not have long to wait for the answer. The doors to the main door opened and a footman made the announcement.

"His Excellency, the Persian Minister, Abul Hassan Khan."

Preceded by the heavy perfume of expensive incense, the man who strode into the assembly hall was as exotic as his name.

He was a head taller than those flanking him. His thick black beard, bristling, and glistening with scented oils, gave him a fierce appearance. Yet Japonica saw at once in his long-lidded dark eyes intelligence and humor to match his elegance and youth. A man in full vigor and much to be admired. The first man ever to compare to the *Hind Div*.

He wore a brilliantly embroidered gold brocade robe. Over his shoulders was a sable vest with skirts of emerald and red gold-embossed silk. About his waist was a thick scarlet band embroidered with gold thread. Tied over that a black belt bearing seals of state held suspended a gold and leather scabbard whose encased saber had a jewel-encrusted hilt.

Japonica felt an instant affinity with this noble stranger, a sense of familiarity that could not be real but which felt very much like a letter from home. When he spied her at the far end of the room and came toward her she sank to the floor as if greeting her own sovereign. She might be English by custom but she was Persian by place of birth.

"Who is this lady?" she heard him ask in Persian of one of his companions.

Keeping her head bowed in the manner of respect she nonetheless took the opportunity to answer for herself in Persian. "A handmaiden of Bushire, *burra sahib*. A thousand honors you do this humble soul by your notice."

She saw him take a startled step backwards. Because she was staring at his sapphire blue leather slippers with pointed toes she only heard disapproval in the murmur of male voices. She had overstepped the bounds of propriety by addressing him directly. Yet it seemed so natural to do so.

A hand appeared before her eyes. Large in size, it was smooth as a girl's and bore an ornate turquoise ring with a stone so large it covered the first knuckle of three fingers. "Rise, *memsahib*."

She took the hand he offered and rose to her feet but kept her eyes downcast. Nor did she speak again, for it seemed the entire room was watching them.

But the Mirza was not content with that. "You wear no veil, *memsahib*. Are you truly a countrywoman?"

"I am by birth and heart if not in nationality." Finally she dared meet his gaze. "One of the delights of foreign travel is the observation of customs different from one's own. Is not the English custom more delightful than one which keeps a lady hidden behind her veil?"

The indrawn breaths of those around her surprised her, for she had meant no insult in her challenge.

Men of the East admired women who were clever and flirtatious in their manner, as long as they did not incur a husband's wrath.

She saw a twinkle deep in the Mirza's eyes and knew she was right. "Indeed, the English custom is better. A veiled woman with downcast eyes is like a caged bird: when she is released she lacks even the strength to fly around the rose-garden." He leaned toward her, his beard coming within an inch of her face, and said in Persian, " 'Around the world my course I've set, Many great beauties have I met, Who stole my heart—never yet, Was any one like you.' "

"Ah, then it is true. 'A friend knows the voice of a friend.' " The familiar Persian saying brought an expression of delight to his handsome face.

"Alhamdolillah valmenah! I am presented with a lady who can converse with me as if I were at home." He threw back his head with laughter as big as the rest of him, a thing that enveloped the room in boisterous sound.

The men about him relaxed into smiles and chuckles. As long as the Mirza was pleased by the lady's unorthodox manner so were they.

"Who is she?" she heard the Mirza ask again, this time in heavily accented English.

"May I present Lady Abbott, your Excellency," Lord Sinclair supplied though Japonica had not seen him approach. "Widow of Lord Abbot, fifth viscount of Shrewsbury and former member of the East India Company's board."

"Ah, nobility," she heard the Mirza say with a smile. "Perfect."

She longed to glance at Devlyn and see if he approved of her actions but he was standing behind her and she did not want to offend the Mirza by turning away.

The Mirza slanted a glance down at her, his expression both imperial and lively. "In Persia a clever woman is sometimes rewarded her weight in gold, *memsahib.*"

"Then I shall eat well tonight, your Excellency, for I should wish to be worth a great deal."

"Delightful lady!" This time the Mirza clapped his hands to express his pleasure. Then he indicated that she walk beside him as they entered the dining room.

It was laid out in the Persian fashion. Persian rugs covered the floor upon which were placed deep red silk Ottoman cushions edged in three rows of gold lace. Low tables contained vessels of gold and silver and dishes of crystal and porcelain laden with delicacies, some of which she had never before seen. Inscribed on each plate and cup was the name of the Shah in gold lettering. Potted plants of fragrant cypress, juniper, citrus, and quince flanked the dining area while lanterns of pierced metal hung in the rafters, throwing designs of moons and stars among the shadows of the ceiling. At the far end English musicians played popular tunes.

The Mirza smiled, seemingly pleased with the preparations. "Tonight we dine in both the English and Persian fashion. My servants have prepared a Pillau. This perhaps you have enjoyed before, *memsahib?*"

"But a poor substitute," Japonica answered. "The honor of dining at the table of a host of exquisite taste and refinement will be a rare privilege."

"You will sit beside me for dinner."

"As you wish, *Burra sahib.*"

Lagging behind the Mirza and his newfound companion, Devlyn watched with an unexpected sensation brewing in his gut. He had hoped Japonica would be equal to the evening. He trusted her knowledge of Persian customs and language would ease the way. He expected her comeliness would be a respite for the Mirza's melancholy. He had not anticipated that she would be taken up so propitiously by the Persian nobleman. Nor that she would look upon her host with such undisguised admiration. How beautifully she smiled at the Mirza.

He knew her to be quick-witted. He, on the other hand, had seldom been the beneficiary of her charm and never her flattery. Yet in a few exchanges she so well stroked the Mirza's masculine pride that he was purring. She had never shown the flirtatious side of her nature to him, in fact had been at pains to eschew any art of feminine coquetry. He had not any inkling of its existence.

The discomforting feeling rising like bile in him was heretofore equally unknown but he recognized it nonetheless. He was jealous!

Sir Ouseley was beaming as he came up to Devlyn. "You have done well, my boy. Lady Abbot is the very answer to our prayers. My dear friend Hassan has not looked so contented in a fortnight. She is tonic for his Persian soul. Wherever did you discover her?"

"She discovered me," Devlyn answered dryly.

"Happy chance." Ouseley pulled him aside with a tug at his sleeve. "We, too, are in luck, at last. I am told, though not yet advised to announce it, that the King will see the Mirza next Wednesday. In the meanwhile we must thank our lucky stars we have Lady Abbott to distract him. Perhaps we may prevail upon her to visit him daily until then."

Devlyn was not at all certain that was a good idea. In fact, the longer the evening lasted the more certain he became that he had made a miscalculation. Seated to Japonica's left, he had a full viewing of the evening's events.

Watching them deeply engrossed in a private conversation that frequently brought laughter to the Mirza's lips and smiles to Japonica's, he wondered at their sudden and, apparent to all present, mutual regard. The fact that she barely reached the Mirza's shoulder even when seated meant that he was forced to bend close to exchange words with her. Certainly the Mirza was handsome and charming, rich and idle, and no doubt reminded her of her home. That did not explain her besotted expression. The whole exercise began to fret his temper.

Blissfully unaware of Lord Sinclair's dark thoughts, Japonica immensely enjoyed herself. No one had thought to engage her in true conversation in months. Never had she had the open admiration of a man of the Mirza's caliber. Even the *Hind Div* had thought her other than she was, disguised by stain and kohl and veil. For the first time in her life she was the center of a man's attention for no reason but her own self. A heady experience that made her reach often for her glass.

Devlyn told himself that it was concern for Japonica's new-budded reputation and not his own ire at being ignored that caused him to finally speak uninvited to the Mirza between the third and fourth course. She was monopolizing the man in a manner detractors might justly label impertinent. "We have not yet heard, your Excellency, what you think of English weather." Surely that was a safe topic.

"I am much disturbed by the English latitude," the Mirza began, lifting his voice to address the rest of his twenty-some guests. "The army of the day cannot long prevail against the hosts of the night. Their black-shouldered soldiers march steadily after the retreated sun even as it reaches its zenith."

"That is true, your Excellency," Ouseley answered. "But we have discussed this before. The days will dutifully lengthen."

"But how it this so?"

" 'Tis a seasonal battle, *burra sahib*, in which none may win the war," Japonica answered. "Though I have not seen it with my own eyes, I am told that in the summer the army of the day will overwhelm the hosts of the night with equal vigor. Late in the month of June it would seem the ebon soldiers remain in westward retreat for the whole of the day and night."

"Such is true?"

"But for a few hours in the deepest night," Devlyn concurred, "the summer sky is never quite dark"

"Amazing, this English island."

Amid chuckles and more general conversation, the evening progressed. There came only one brief moment's awkwardness, when the second main course was being served. The English course came first, a huge side of beef to be carved and served.

Japonica happened to look up at Devlyn's face as a slice was being carved for him that would require the use of a knife. She had seen him use a fork with his left but . . .

She put up her hand to deflect the carver who would have placed an inch-thick slab on Devlyn's plate. "Lord Sinclair will accept only the rarest cuts of beef. They must be tender, as well. As hostess in his home I have come to know his ways. He will not put a morsel of meat in his mouth that cannot be cut by the mere tines of a fork. His cook is quite distraught by the number of meals he sends back untouched." She knew she was chattering like a squirrel but something had to be done quickly. "Better yet I would suggest, Lord Sinclair, that you wait to partake of the Pillau." She glanced at Devlyn. "It is composed of rice and marinated fowls stewed together with spices. Its tenderness should more than meet with your approval."

Thus challenged, Devlyn bowed his head in acknowledgement of her suggestion. But a little later, when the Mirza's attention had been drawn momentarily away from her, he bent toward her and mut-

tered, "I do not thank you for that. I can manage
my own affairs."

"I am well aware of it," she said, smiling as though
they were exchanging pleasantries. "But I've heard
it said that the man of style in London is one who
gives grief to his tailor and his staff. As you manage
to give grief to everyone, I thought you should not
stint upon this occasion."

He gave her a glare that might have sent her scurry-
ing away had they been alone.

When the meal was done, the Mirza asked that
there be dancing. Though no one dissented, it was
obvious there could only be one couple at a time and
lady Abbott would always form one half of it.

"Can there not be some entertainment more general, your Excellency?" Japonica asked when she
caught sight of Devlyn's scowl. "I am but one lady.
How should I keep up with even one of these stalwart
soldiers, let alone your own august person? Rather,
burra sahib, if I might be allowed a small suggestion?"
When he nodded she continued. "A round of poetry.
A single dance goes as prize to the winner."

The Mirza gave her a sharp glance. "What a delight
you are!" Then to the general company he asked,
"Who will be the first to recite, that the lady may
choose her partner?"

Several gentlemen were game, reciting pieces from
their public school days of manly deeds or odes to
warfare and English pride of place, even a poem or
two of sacred prose. When the others were finished,
the Mirza clapped then turned to her with an intimate
smile. "Now it is my turn."

The Mirza recited a poem in Persian which most
of the party did not understand. Unfortunately, Devlyn was not one of them. She heard him mutter something too low to be understood and her discomfort
increased. The chosen poem was from *Ghazal*—a

romantic ode, the kind a suitor spoke to his ladylove. She was quite pink by the time the Mirza was done.

Pleased with himself, the Mirza rose from his cushions and helped her to her feet. "So then, *memsahib*, who gives the better recitation and is therefore worthy of your dance?"

Japonica recognized that there was only one answer to give and, in truth, the Mirza was the better orator. But to choose a piece from a romantic poet put her in an awkward position.

"Shall I not have a chance?" she asked. Seeing The Persian ambassador's brows rise in surprise she hurried on into a recitation of Hafez, the most famous of all Persian poets. " 'I remember the days when I lived at the end of your lane, Every time that I looked at your door my eyes shone once again, And I said to myself, 'Now I never will lack for a friend'—And we tried—how my heart and I tried!—But our efforts were in vain.' "

To her surprise the Mirza's eyes suddenly shone with tears. He bit his lip and then lifted a hand to his heart. *"Marhaba!* This lady is most attractive, eloquent and sweet spoken. I am deeply touched by the homesickness she feels in her exile. I will make the judgment that she is the winner and for her prize she shall be relieved of the burden of the dance."

Shortly thereafter, at precisely two of the clock, the evening was at an end.

To Japonica's surprise, the Mirza followed her to the door and saw to it that his personal servant placed her cape about her shoulders. "Did you enjoy yourself, Lady Abbott?" he inquired in English.

"Oh yes, your Excellency."

"Then you must come again to see me." He sighed. "I am most regretful that it cannot be that I may visit you for some little while. Until I have seen the English

King I have sworn not to set foot out of doors for any social purpose.''

"Then, if it please your Excellency, I should be glad to come and visit you again, though I doubt it shall long be that you remain housebound.''

He smiled at her. "When will you come to see me? Tomorrow afternoon? I often go riding for exercise in the park nearby. Lord Sinclair will bring you,'' the Mirza said in full confidence.

Japonica glanced at Devlyn for direction and though his expression was bland she knew he disapproved. She turned back to her host with a regretful expression. "Forgive me, your Excellency, but I have been hasty in over-presenting my freedom. I am spoken for tomorrow afternoon. I must beg your indulgence and cry off.''

A man not often denied his whims, the Mirza gave her a petulant look.

"Perhaps something can be arranged.'' Devlyn's voice was a dry as dust.

Japonica dared not look at him twice but her brain moved swiftly to back up his cue. "If it pleases your Excellency, I should be happy to join you for a ride the day after tomorrow. However, I must confess that I do not ride well. Perhaps Lord Sinclair would be good enough to play gallant and drive me about in his new curricle.''

"It is in the shop,'' he said shortly. "I may however offer a barouche.''

The Mirza smiled again. *"Marhaba,* Lady Abbott! Until then.''

They left quickly, Devlyn clasping her elbow in his hand as if she were a felon who might flee at the first opportunity.

He was angry, she realized. When was he not, she thought with a smile. So then, she did not care. Nothing would spoil her delight in the evening, not even the bitter man at her side.

The carriages were drawn up to the door in order to save them a drenching, for a chill rain had begun to fall. Devlyn helped her in with great care and ceremony. But once inside, he lost all civility. He flung himself onto the opposite seat and crossed his arms.

"Well, madam, I hope you are thoroughly pleased with yourself!"

Japonica noted the edge in his tone but decided not to indulge it. "Yes, it was a delightful evening. I can't think when I've had better."

"Yes, it was quite like watching a play." The scorn in his tone could have removed paint. "You have unsuspected talents. Who knew you could be Cleopatra to the Mirza's Caesar? We should have rolled you up in a carpet that you might have been unveiled at his feet."

Japonica glared him. His spiteful words were beginning to spoil her lovely mood. "You are dissatisfied with my efforts on your behalf?"

"My behalf? I asked nothing of you."

"Did you not bring me to the Mirza's home?" She leaned forward, her chin angled to provoke. "Was I not meant to entertain and make him smile and forget, for an evening, the dreary task that has brought him as far from his homeland as I am from mine?"

"I did not ask you to flirt with him until he is half in love with you."

"Oh, do you think so?" She leaned back against the carriage squabs. "How amazing that you should think it possible for any man to desire me. It was clear from our first meeting that you thought me a dowd unworthy of a glance."

"I never said . . . ." Devlyn stopped and swallowed

the lie. "Very well, but you must admit you were dressed like a governess, which was none of my doing. But tonight you dress like . . . ."

"A *houri?*" she suggested sweetly. "Which is your doing." She smoothed a wrinkle from her emerald silk skirts. "Was that not your plan, that the Mirza's gaze should not long leave me? Was I not but one of the many dishes set before him tonight to tempt his appetite away from the affairs of state?"

Devlyn simply stared at her, amazed that she had read so completely his duty when he had confided none of it to her. "You certainly took great delight in the task."

"Why shouldn't I? I have never been in a house so splendid, in company so splendid, with a man so splendid." She added the last as a challenge of her own, and greatly enjoyed doing it. For the first time she felt flush with victory and conquest, as a woman truly esteemed in a man's eyes.

"So then you are not averse to continuing in this 'duty' to entertain the Mirza?"

"Not at all," she answered, though she had no intentions of remaining in London to do so.

"You will not then be offended if the Mirza should seek from you more than smiles and poems? With royalty there is no such thing as an innocent flirtation. He is aware that you are a widow and therefore accustomed to a man's attentions."

"I am aware. He made his interest quite charmingly apparent." She pulled her fur-lined cape more closely about her shoulders while Devlyn stared at her as though he would like to box her ears. "Alas, he admits to a vow of chastity made to his sovereign that eclipses even his own inclination."

"He said that to you? *Bismallah!* And you said?"

Japonica hid her smile. "That I am just at the end of a year's mourning. While Persian women are chaste because they are forced to be, Englishwomen are chaste by choice. We are then free to go about in the world and treat all men as friends. The Mirza replied that he had never met an Englishwoman of such character and good humor. He would do nothing to set me to flight."

"You astonish me."

"That is because you expect so little," Japonica replied. "Were I a beauty that drew all men's eyes you would not be in the least amazed that I was clever and well-mannered. Or that other men thought me worthy of an evening's company."

"You think so little of me?"

"I think of you little, 'tis true," she replied, and then smiled for he looked so cross. "You do not see me as a woman unless ambushed by the realization, as when you saw me in this dress tonight. If a few yards of silk can so easily turn your head, then I am sure to lose you to the next shop of frocks."

Devlyn scowled. "This is a new aspect of your character. I am not certain I like it."

"Ah then, not to worry. You shan't long be forced to endure it."

"What does that mean?"

Japonica looked away from him. "Nothing, certainly. It must be the wine speaking. You must forgive me if I do not meet your every expectation, you have so many."

"You make me sound like a spoiled brat."

"And here I thought to make plain that you are a most difficult man to please."

This time he actually smiled. "Half the time I don't know whether to kiss or throttle you."

He said it lightly, so lightly than anyone who overheard it could not mistake it for anything but a tease. But Japonica found she could not smile back. The tease went too deeply into a matter she could not bare to contemplate.

Devlyn saw the cloud enter her eyes when he thought to make her smile and rail at him once more. What was this, the sudden pale look followed by a blush? Did she doubt he meant his words, or did she hope?

"I want to go riding tomorrow," she said suddenly. "Will you accompany me?"

"You know I don't ride."

She was silent a moment and then said, "Have you not noticed how the Persian Army's legions of archers hardly ever touch their reins? They ride full gallop into battle with both hands free that they might loose their arrows at the enemy. They control their steeds with their knees. A clever trick, would you not say?"

Devlyn did not answer. She was "managing" him again and that annoyed him. Yet, why had he not thought of that before? As a lad, he had often pretended to be a knight in armor with a shield in one hand and a lance in the other. A knight's horse had to feel his rider, and the rider urged his mount with his feet and knees. Yes, he could do that. But it did not please him to think she had thought first of what he had been too—well, too stubborn to consider.

Japonica watched him brood, wondering why she must always feel in the wrong with him. Walking about on cat's paws was not her metier. How like him to shout and then ignore her. But she did not want to be ignored just now, with wine and success humming in her veins. She wanted what she had had all evening, to be admired by a man, by this man who never seemed to look at her the same way twice.

She fluffed the curls at her brow with an impatient hand, using it as an excuse to glance at him. His expression in the shadows was not encouraging. She resisted the urge to kick him, but only just. "Will you sulk because you have succeeded? Or is it that I succeeded too well and you cannot admit that I am a thoroughly delightful and desirable woman?''

"Confound it!" He sprang forward, pinning her between the seat and his body by bracing himself with arms on either side of her head. "Will you prattle on in this manner until I am forced to walk home!"

Japonica shrank back against the squabs but the feelings awakening inside her were far from fear. "If you continue to assault me in this manner, I will gladly do the walking."

Her words seemed to surprise him. "I would never . . . ." Looking into her skeptical expression he thought better of finishing that sentence, and reared back and flung himself into the far corner of the opposite seat.

Heart jumping like an acrobat at practice, Japonica once more turned her face to the window, hoping the deep shadows protected her expression from his perusal.

"If you think—that by buying this gown—" She kept biting her lips, the words hard to speak. "—That you have bought me—my—you are very much mistaken!"

"I apologize. Deeply regret . . . ." He could not think of anything that would mollify the resentful accusation in her expression.

"You are no gentleman!" she said through stiff lips.

She was looking at him with all his imperfections. "No."

For the remainder of the ride Devlyn alternated between chastising himself for an idiot and her for a flirt. How could she ever look upon him as a man, one worthy of her regard, when she was perpetually at the ready to "improve" him like some schoolboy in need of polish? No, she would never regard him as he wanted to be thought of by her: as much the man as he had once been.

So far, he had avoided her pity. He did not believe she could hide that from him, not when her direct gaze offered up her every other thought. Only when they touched, even innocently, did the guard go up in her raisin-brown gaze. She did not want to be touched by him. Damnation! He could not blame her. He had never given her reason to believe that the feelings churning inside him at this very moment were real, and all for her.

"Fool, you!" he muttered.

When at last they came to her residence she barely touched the hand he offered to help her step down. "Good night, Lord Sinclair," she said in a rush of breath, and headed for the front door without bothering to look back.

She did not realize he was beside her until she reached the top step. One of the new footmen, on the lookout for his mistress, was there to open the door but Devlyn put out a hand to stop her from entering. "I should be grateful for a moment more of your time, Lady Abbott."

Japonica cocked her head toward him and saw that while anger still girded his expression there was a genuine request in his eyes. "Very well." She turned to the footman when she had entered the house. "Is the fire still burning in the library?"

"No, my lady, but it could be stirred up in a trice."

"Never mind. We shall contrive. Good night."

She waited until the footman left the hall and then turned to her unwelcome guest. "Yes? What do you wish to discuss?"

"Only this."

There was something like admiration in his expression as he reached out to curve his fingers under her chin. "I have misjudged you, once again."

His expression altered, became almost tender. "You possess a magnificence that you are most often at pains to disguise from me. You would have it that the world sees you as plain and uninteresting. It is you who are afraid to be what you know you are. That is what confounds and confuses and beguiles me." He smiled. "Why do you give more generously of yourself to strangers than you do to one who would be your friend?"

"You are impetuous to offer your friendship to me," Japonica said carefully, for his fingers were playing softly along the line of her jaw in such a manner that it made it difficult to think. "You may regret it."

He moved a little closer. "If I do, what matter except between the two of us?" His gaze fell from her eyes to her lips. "What if I were to kiss you now? What would you do?"

"Nothing, my lord, because you will not risk it. You need me to be companion to the Mirza. I doubt a momentary passion of the kind I'm told men are prone to will be allowed to get in the way of your good judgment."

"You almost persuade me that you are right. Almost."

She had not meant to issue a challenge but she saw at once that she had. He was already bending toward her. The only way to resist his kiss was to anticipate it.

She lifted a hand to touch his cheek a scarce moment before their mouths touched. This time there was no urgency or agitation in his actions, as if he was going against his own judgment in kissing her. She was conscious of him from head to toe, waited for him to draw her fiercely closer, to fit their bodies together as closely as their lips. But he did not. After several heartbeats he lifted his head. When he looked at her this time it was with wonder and a question.

She did not think about what she was doing, did not allow herself any thought, only feelings. It felt right. She turned slowly from him and began to mount the stairs. She did not look back, did not invite him by gesture or word, yet she sighed in thanksgiving when she heard his footsteps behind her. She moved quickly but quietly down the corridor to her room and then through her bedroom door. Finally, as she heard him close the door and set the latch, she dropped her cape on the floor and waited.

Chapter Eighteen

He moved in behind her slowly until the heat of his body reached out to her against the chill of the dark room. She did not speak. Could not think of a single thing she might say to him that would make sense of what they were doing. There were no excuses she could make to herself. Feelings guided her, a deep inarticulate need to alter the history between them. If she were being brave or utterly foolish, it did not matter. She would know in the next few breaths if something had changed between them, a balance had shifted, making possible a counterpoint to a night that he could not remember but one that she could not forget.

Aware of what she offered but doubtful of the reasons behind it, Devlyn hesitated to touch her. It made no sense after the evening in which she had been the center of attention of a dozen men more highly placed and better mannered, men far more charming than he. Whole men. And at this moment he hated them because of it.

She did not know that for the last few hours he had sat next her, mute as a eunuch in his admiration of her skill in entertaining a man of the Mirza's refinement. She could not guess that he had more than once briefly closed his eyes to better enjoy the fragrance of her perfume. It evoked in him a chimera of exotic places that remained shadowed, thrilling moments and desperate hours that had no real shape of memory but were all the more powerful for being insubstantial. He had allowed himself to think of all the things they might never be in reality. In his thoughts he had longed for this moment, and been just as certain that after this evening it would never be his.

Yet he could not turn away now from the woman whose presence tormented and teased and touched him in every hour since she had come into his life. So then, maybe she would stop him, stop them, from making a terrible mistake.

He reached out and slid his right arm around her waist, drawing her back against his chest. She trembled but did not resist. "Lady, I am all but mute before your courage. But, think what you do. It is not too late."

"I did not beg you follow," she said in a voice so soft a whisper would have seemed a shout.

"Did you not?" He smiled in the dark as he placed his hand on her shoulder and squeezed lightly. "Did you not without a glance dare me? Did you not without a gesture offer a way?"

She turned her head to press her cheek against the back of his hand. "Perhaps."

"Fearlessness is not the same as bravery. The brave soul knows the dangers and still feels compelled to act. Have you counted the danger?'' Why, he wondered, was he arguing against his own desire?

Japonica turned in his arms, glad for the darkness that did not allow her to be daunted by his gaze. "May a woman not be as brave as a man?''

"Lady!" That breathless sound spoken in his deepest voice took away from the word the distinction of class and left only the delight of a man who stands before the woman he desires. "I would help you be even braver, if you would allow it.''

A sweet sadness welled up in Japonica, the piquancy of his pledge bringing tears to her eyes. Because of him she had already done things that had forever changed her life. But he did not know that.

No! She brushed the thoughts from her mind with a slow shake of her head. Tonight, this night was for her alone. All she wanted was to be brave enough to be with him. "What would you have me do?''

Devlyn did not know her thoughts but he could guess the source of the struggle taking place within her. She was trembling now, little uncontrollable shivers beneath his touch. His aunt thought her untried. Her spirit in the face of that possibility drew from him a tenderness of which he had not known he was capable.

He pulled her closer until her cheek was against his chest and their bodies met from shoulder to hip. He reached up and slid off her net cap. He felt her hair fall free down her back. As her curls tumbled and bounced, they released the fragrance of a Persian garden.

He bent to her, bringing his lips to touch the shell of her ear as he whispered, "Do not be afraid, *bahia.* I will do nothing you deny me.''

He brushed his lips across her cheek until they briefly touched hers in the gentlest of kisses. The meeting of lips sent a shiver through her that was answered as a quiver in his lower belly. His mouth opened on hers and the urgency he sought to hold in check slipped a bit. Sweet! Her mouth was warm and tasted of the honeyed dates they had eaten for dessert. It was enough to tip his teetering emotions sharply toward passion.

Sensations of longing quaked along her nerve endings as his open mouth slanted over hers and then she felt him trace the contours of her lips with the tip of his tongue. Fear, anger, despair, and desire melded together under the heated persuasion of his kiss into a moment of longing so strong she did not want him to snatch that pleasure away.

She raised her arms, threading them between his to reach around and grip his back. His was strong and solid beneath the fingers she splayed across his shoulders, a secure place upon which to rest her troubled world.

She heard him expel a soft sound of satisfaction but it was quickly smothered as their mouths blended in kiss after long searing kiss.

Feelings rammed the barrier she had spent a year building against her own sense of self-mistrust and shame and betrayal. The *Hind Div* had come back to life, whether to save or damn her she did not know. And in this moment she did not care. She longed only to learn if the feeling, born of shame and on a night when she had no say in the matter, could be matched when it was her will and her desire and her need driving passion's onslaught.

Oh, but if she were wrong!

The door of conscience would not stay shut on her doubts. It flew open, forced by a gale of turmoil and second thoughts. What if in a few heartbeats he would have her skirts about her waist and she would discover that her passion too was a counterfeit? What if in an hour she knew she was, again, his fool?

With a cry very much like a wail, she tore her mouth from his and tried to break free. He let her go without a moment's hesitation.

She took several steps from him, breathing hard as though she had run a long way with the devil at her back. He said nothing for a moment and she was too daunted by her actions to think of anything.

"So then, you are afraid."

"Yes!" It was a quick desperate whisper.

"It is a lady's right to change her mind."

He sounded resigned, when she felt stretched across an abyss that would not allow her to move forward or back but might surely tear her apart if she did not choose. "Is it so easy for you?"

"Easy?" The word was spoken low but with such fervor that she did not doubt the sincerity of his passion. "Would you have it be easy?"

Japonica shook her head though she knew she must be nothing more than a dark silhouette in a room where the fire had died to embers. "I do not understand myself."

"Nor I." He sounded as bewildered as she did.

She knew she was not thinking clearly and that she needed to. But he had come up to her again, his arms slipping about her waist and that touch made her blurt out what she had not meant to say. "There was a man, someone once—before."

Devlyn's whole body came alert with her confession. "Yes?"

"He was quite dazzling." He heard in her voice the quiver of shame. "I should not have been alone with him. I should have been more wary . . ."

"He took advantage of you?"

"Oh yes." She sounded as if she was smiling but he knew that could not be. She angled a shoulder away from him and he released her regretfully but he could not hold her against her will. When she had moved a few chaste feet away she spoke again. "It was no brutal encounter but it was against my will. That will had been subdued by drugged wine."

The hair lifted on Devlyn's nape. Something familiar in this story. Something . . . if only . . . "You were drugged and raped."

He saw her silhouette start. "Rape is such a harsh word."

"Rape is a harsh deed," he answered.

She put a hand to her cheek. "I wish it were that simple. I wish I could know. I don't think I resisted him. I was curious, you see . . . curious." The word trailed out on a sigh of regret.

"But your will was tampered with." His said it flatly without the balm of pity.

"Yes." For the first time she looked back at him. "It was not my choice."

"A woman should always have a choice."

She stared at his silhouette, wondering if he meant what he voiced so readily. He had used the word woman, not lady. She had not been what society would call a lady until her marriage. Did he understand how much the distinction meant to her? Or was it only that he spoke without the knowledge of the blotted-out memory that would cast him as her defiler? "Why would a man treat a woman so?"

"Perhaps he feared her. Or sought to punish her. Or thought she was someone other than she was." He shrugged. "I do not defend him. I do not know him."

"Perhaps not," she said more slowly this time. But it was time for her to be certain.

She came toward him, her gaze searching the umbra for a glimpse of his expression. When she stood an arm's length away she could see his eyes shining like flames in his shadowed face. It was a moment of truth she thought she would have to wait until Judgement Day to confront. "He lived in Baghdad. His name was the *Hind Div.*"

"The name is known to me."

"Is it?" She felt as if lightning were about to strike her, so strongly did she tingle all over.

"The name comes to me sometimes in dreams." How distant he sounded when in fact he stood right in front of her. "A disembodied creature with the face of a cheetah. I thought it must be a nightmare of my battered mind's contriving." There was a bleak expression on his face, a deep sense of the doubt of his mind's workings. "I did not know there was such a man."

"Some would not credit him as wholly human," she answered. "They say he was a wizard. Some believed that he was a spirit, others the devil they called him."

"How did you come to know him?"

"I was sent to persuade him to help Lord Abbott escape from Baghdad after the French arrived. I offered him money. He required another sort of reward."

"Your virginity for your life."

Her virginity for three lives! She had not thought of it in quite that manner. "That was not the bargain we struck until . . . afterward."

Devlyn took a step toward her, half-closing the distance. "No wonder you trust no man. Little wonder you do not trust your own allure. It betrayed you once to great cost."

"My allure?" She had feared she might weep in front of him. Instead, laughter burst from her. "Do not toy with me. I am plain. Ordinary as crockery. I do not attract admiration. I do not . . ."

"Know your own value." He reached out and ran a finger down her cheek. "Light a candle, lady."

She did as he asked, putting to light the candlestick

that stood on the chimneypiece. The sudden brilliance made her blink but the room was large and the taper did not destroy the intimacy of shadowed corners.

Yet when she looked back, the man before her seemed changed utterly. Flickering flame exaggerated the contours of his face. Shadows etched deeper the twin smile lines that bracketed his mouth like the trace of a beard. They filled in the deep sockets of his eyes with smudges like kohl. For an instant she saw not Lord Sinclair but the fanciful façade of the *Hind Div* before her.

"Please," she whispered in choked anguish, and turned away.

"What is it?" she heard Lord Sinclair say, his deep voice echoing as a disembodied sound in the room.

Irrational tears pushed behind her eyes where moments before laughter had provoked her. Yet neither emotion seemed connected directly to her. They crowded in on her from another source. The warm firm pressure of his hand settling on her arm was the only real thing in the world she could believe in.

"Japonica?"

She looked up to reassure him that she was fine, but the words slipped right out of her mind as she met his gaze. The face of Lord Sinclair was again very real, with all its very human contours and shadings. Quite suddenly she was ashamed of herself, of what she had been thinking about, of what she had been willing to do with a man any sensible person would call her enemy.

Devlyn saw the beginnings of doubt gathering like sneak thieves in her gaze but he was not about to put off his original purpose. "Come, lady."

He took her hand and moved to stand before the pier glass in the corner, holding the candelabra so that its light fell on her face.

"Look there and tell me you see no charm of feature and deny the blush in your cheek, the brilliance of your eyes."

Japonica cast her gaze down. The power she had felt upon first viewing herself in full regalia had deserted her. Like the brilliance of her gown, dulled by the meager light, her confidence had deserted her. "I do not see it."

His hand came up and cupped her chin lightly. This time he addressed her in Persian. "The clever merchant displays his gaudiest wares to catch the crowd's taste for flash. The rare treasure, he keeps hidden from the eyes of careless passersby who would not value what they would buy. For the true connoisseur alone will he unwrap his rarest prize."

As he spoke he turned her face slowly back and forth, tilting it at different angles so that the light played along the curves of her cheeks, the glistening surface of her ripe mouth, and shone in her eyes.

"Look again, *bahia*, and see the truth. Only you have the power to bring forth the rarest treasure of yourself. I saw a glimpse of it tonight, as did every man present." His hand moved to her shoulder to turn her to face him. Distrust still shaded her expression but he saw something else, the beginning, perhaps, of hope. "Do you doubt what you saw in the eyes of the Mirza? Do you doubt what you see in my gaze?"

Yes!" she whispered raggedly because she feared to believe it.

But he only smiled at her and said, "Liar!"

Devlyn saw his reply made her blush. When she closed her eyes against his challenge, the curl of copper lashes against her soft cheeks distracted him. In the candle glow her hair had become flame, forming angel hair waves that billowed about her shoulders.

How could she think herself plain when she looked as she did at this moment?

He smiled, supposing he was as captivated as any man had ever been in the presence of a woman he desired. "You have always known the truth I speak and resented the noisy crowds who seek the easy prize and would not stop long enough to notice something more precious."

"Yes," she breathed. But she could not look at him.

He bent and kissed the edge of first one and the other set of her eyelashes. "I have stopped. I seek you out. I have come to learn the value that is you."

She opened her eyes and he saw in them a question. He did not know how to answer it, only pose another of his own. He touched a finger to her lower lip and rubbed gently there. "What is it you seek, *bahia?*"

Japonica saw desire in his face and no longer doubted its sincerity. But that did not allay her fears. He might so easily destroy her and all that she held dear, including this moment.

She looked away, wanting to escape the forbidden truth in his eyes. "This is foolish, my lord. We should not be here together like this."

"No. We should not." His finger left her lip and trailed over the smooth curve of her chin. It sailed light as a feather down the slim column of her throat and paused at the indentation at its base. "But we were not speaking of shoulds and propriety. There is only you and I. And no one to deny us."

"The world . . . ."

His finger rose to her lips to stop her speech. When she glanced up in affront, he smiled. "The world is not with us. There is only you." He lifted his finger from her mouth. "And I. For you I will be any and all you ask of me."

Japonica could not stop her smile. "I thought I

was the rare and precious prize and you the customer. Should I not seek to be all you seek?"

He smiled back, the mocking smile of the *Hind Div.* "You already are."

His hand settled lightly over the fullness above her low-cut bodice. "I would have *you.* What would you have?"

Japonica found she could not answer honestly. She pushed away his hand, the first act in turning away from him, but somehow she was turning to him instead, and he was reaching for her. She pressed her head to his chest and heard the pounding of his heart like surf on a stormy night. The brazen woman who had invited him to her room had vanished. If she let him see the feelings that hovered at the edge of every encounter with him, she would be lost. She could not want what her heart whispered above the beat of his. She wanted more than his body. She wanted his love. And that, of course, was absurd.

She should send him away, order him out of her room and her life. Instead, she held tighter to him and hoped he would not leave. Madness, surely. Somehow she must find a way to hold something of herself back or she would be lost.

Devlyn felt her clutching him, clinging like a child afraid of the dark. But he did not want her to yield to him out of fear or resignation. One man had taken from her what was her right to give. He must be certain that this time it was what she wanted and only what she wanted.

He pushed her gently away and she looked up questioningly at him. "I am a man missing his past, his hand, and his illusions about life. I can offer you only this night, in this place, as you would have it."

It took a great deal of courage to meet his gaze, and when she did, her voice quavered. "You ask what I want?" He nodded, no longer smiling. "Then it is simply this, my lord. I—I want to know what it is like to be with a man when it is by my choice."

The declaration set off fireworks in Devlyn's middle. "You wish me to make love to you?"

"Not love!" she said almost desperately. Why did he have to use that word? "I desire you." She tried to look past him, to remove if only a fraction of herself from the moment that had become too much. "All that you have said and done has led me to believe that you desire me."

Devlyn permitted himself a small smile. "Lady, you are too modest in your description. I very badly want to take you in my arms and kiss you until you can think of nothing and no one but me. And then I would help you to pleasure and help myself to you."

Japonica jerked in surprise that he spoke to her in Persian. It struck her that they had both been doing so for some time. So then it was like a dream, this moment, delivered in the poetic language as artificial as it was lovely.

She turned a little away from him. "You would pleasure me, *burra sahib?*"

"I would, *Uzza.* As if it would be my last deed on earth."

A renewed surge of daring curled through her. How easy to pretend that their actions could be as artificial and lovely as the language in which they couched their desire. In fantasy, any and everything was possible.

She looked back at him. "Where do we begin?"

It took Devlyn two heartbeats to recognize the subtle change. Not so much as a blink had altered her expression yet he felt it all the same. She had erected a shield. She might come to him but she would not yield all. He understood the source of her fear but knew, too, that it would be impossible for her to find complete pleasure if she held apart from him. If she would lie with him she must do so freely.

He put his arms around her, smoothing a hand down her back to bring her fully against him. "Do you hear my heart, *bahia*? It beats for you. You can alter its pattern by the slightest act. If you were to kiss me you would feel it quicken and know it responds at your request. Will you not try the simple exercise?"

"Very well." Japonica's gaze moved to his mouth. It was not so great a thing, she told herself. She had kissed him before. She lifted her head, closed her eyes, and found the shape of his mouth with hers.

He held still under the pressure of her lips, offering only dry warmth in return. After a few seconds she slipped away from his touch, a tiny frown of disappointment furrowing her brow. "If you are not satisfied, *bahia*, perhaps you should try another method."

Japonica considered his words. There was a better way but she did not know how to compel it from him. Always before, he had initiated the kisses that left her dizzy. Perhaps if she imitated his actions she might achieve his results.

She reached up and touched his face, fingers skimming along his lean cheek until they reached his lips. She paused, rubbing her forefinger against them until they parted and the heat of his breath caressed the tip. Leaning up on tiptoe, she quickly replaced her finger with her lips and covered his mouth with the open damp invitation of hers.

This time his arms tightened, drawing her hard against his body. Yes, that was what she sought. How warm and real he felt, his kiss so perfectly right. Her hands moved, fingers reaching up to plow into the thick hair at his temples, fingers tightening in his hair, as she held his mouth to hers.

She heard him groan in pleasure and felt a tiny sense of triumph in that response. Reluctantly she turned her mouth from his but she could not catch her breath.

Devlyn chuckled as she did so, as surprised by her passion as she. "More precious than rubies, a kiss from the right woman," he said against her hair. "Now let me show you that I may do the same for you."

His hand moved to her hair to angle her head slightly to better receive his kiss. His tongue found the edge of her upper lip and licked it carefully, once, twice, three times. He treated her lower lip to the same exotic stroking. Finally he took the fullest part of her lips between his teeth and sucked at them as if to draw juice from a ripe peach.

The effect of his kisses was dizzyingly swift. Several important admissions forced themselves to the fore of Japonica's consciousness. She did most decidedly want him to make love to her. She knew nearly nothing about how to encourage and return his caresses. And third, she wanted very much to learn.

He was smiling when he lifted his head. "Do you understand now? Pleasure may be given and taken on both sides."

She smiled back, but it was less brave than his. "I begin to understand. But there is more, surely."

"The lady grows greedy." He cradled her head in his hand and dragged his lips back and forth across hers, then again licked at them slowly and deliberately until she was so weak with desire she had to lean against him.

She did not resist when he unhooked her gown then pulled it away from her shoulders, freeing her breasts. He cupped one in his hand, grazing his thumb over her nipple and rolling it gently back and forth. When he bent his head to taste her, she arched under his mouth and whispered, "Oh!"

"You like it, my lady?" he murmured, his hand

finding and cupping the breast his mouth did not tease.

"I—yes!" It felt as if her body had caught fire. She could not keep still. She twisted and arched under his mouth and hand, trying to press closer to the source of the pleasure streaking through her. At the same time a blush flamed on her skin. Despite the pleasure, she felt silly and awkward and wondered if he found her response amusing.

But he did not laugh at her. He lifted his head and kissed her briefly. "There is so much more. May I show you?"

She opened passion-drugged eyes and said, "Yes."

His arms went about her, lifting her off the floor and up against his chest. The buttons of his coat pressed into her bare breasts, a sharp reminder of what they were doing, and then he was kissing her again, the sweetest, gentlest of kisses, as he carried her to the bed.

Devlyn laid her down gently upon the coverlet, following with his own body. He did not break the contact of their bodies but lay half over her, one hip and leg straddling hers. He saw that her eyes were wide open now. In their depths, behind the hesitation and confusion, lay the burning embers of a desire he longed to fully ignite. Still, he had not forgotten what she had said about her seducer and how he had robbed her of the right to consent. More than ever, he wanted her to feel secure in the possibilities of pleasure that awaited two willing partners.

He reached up and gently placed his hand over her eyes. "Don't be afraid, *bahia*. I promise you nothing will happen that you do not agree to." He added the touch of his mouth to first one corner and then the other of hers. "You are mistress of the moment. I follow your lead." He lifted his hand and very carefully stroked her cheek. "You are what I want. If you would have proof of my feelings, you need only look into my eyes."

Her gaze was as vulnerable as any he had ever seen. The look sent a quiver of desire through his belly that was one part longing and one part protective. "Truly?" she whispered.

Understanding that a demonstration of tenderness would be the best persuasion, he lifted his hand and held it a fraction of an inch above one bare breast. "May I touch you here?"

"Yes." She sounded afraid of the sound of her own voice.

"May I touch you like this?" His fingers began to work the peak with little tugs and gentle twists until it pouted proudly beneath them. His gaze never left her face, so he saw her mouth form an O of surprised pleasure. "You like it. You feel the pleasure I would give you."

This time she only sighed.

"There is more, Japonica, much more." Though he would have liked to set light to a dozen tapers that he might better avail himself of a long leisurely perusal of all that he wanted to touch and caress, he did not want to frighten her. There would be another time to undress her and let his gaze linger. Now he wanted only that she not be afraid of him.

"You are so sweet." He lowered his head and nuzzled the peak he had brought to standing, then slid it into his mouth.

Japonica turned into the embrace of his lips upon her breast, her thigh brushing the heavy corded muscles of his. The full swelling of feeling inside her made her want to wrap her arms about him and hold on forever. And so she did, clasping his shoulders so that her bare arms were filled with his warmth. What he was doing to her was so strange and so wonderful she did not ever want him to cease.

As he stretched out fully over her she welcomed everything about him, the scent of sandalwood rising from his skin, the slight abrasion of his beard upon her so sensitive breasts, the hard heavy weight of his longer, weightier body as he shifted his hips onto hers. With slow strokes he began driving his pelvis against her, pressing her farther into the mattress. As he did so a new hardness pushed against her lower belly. Curious, her hand slid down between them to touch it, only to draw away in disconcertment.

Devlyn lifted his head. "Would you know how a man is made?"

She had shut her eyes, and only shook her head.

"Are you certain?"

The regret in his voice made her look up into his face, at once familiar and strange. "I am afraid."

He smiled at her but there was a hint of mockery in it this time. "You frighten me, too. You are so lovely and taste so sweetly of passion that I dread to think I may not be able after all to best please you."

She frowned slightly. "Why so?"

His smile broadened. "A man who desires a lady is a prisoner to his passion for her. He cannot always control it. For instance, when you kiss me you make me hard with want of you. When you touch me—ah, then, lady, I am yours to command."

"Command?" A sly smile crept over her daunted expression.

"Would you have it so?" He took her hand in his. "You have only to touch me, stroke me, and know that it is true." He brought her hand back down to the placket of his breeches. "Unbutton and see for yourself what your kisses do to me."

For a moment her hand rested uncertainly on his rigid length and then she reached to undo first one button and then another. He raised up a bit to allow her hand to finish its work and then he felt himself spring free against her palm. She gasped but did not entirely draw away.

He kissed her again, a slow persuasive kiss of gentle supplication. "Do not be reluctant to touch me. I am only human," he said softly against her mouth.

Only human. Japonica wondered how she could ever have thought him otherwise when his human form was wondrous enough. She felt lightly along the length of his shaft and then closed her hand around the thickness of it. She felt his sharp intake of breath against her mouth. "Shall I stop?"

"Only if it pleases you," he murmured breathlessly. "But I beg you not. Know me and make me yours. I will deny you nothing."

As she caressed him shyly, he began again to touch and kiss her, her shoulders, her breasts, her belly. Everywhere he left the damp impression of his mouth, her skin seemed to burn. Those touches and kisses and licks and strokes quickly overwhelmed her and she abandoned her exploration of him to sink into sensation behind closed lids. Her senses filled with him, his taste, his scent, and his heat. It was as if he seeped into her pores and she would forever after carry a part of him with her. When he lifted her skirts, bunching them about her waist, and then cupped the bare skin of her buttocks in one hand, she thought she would swoon with the intimacy of the caress. But he was not done. He pushed a knee between hers and lifted her up so that she straddled his thigh.

"Don't fear me," he whispered against her ear. "You are meant to be touched here."

As he slipped his hand between her spread thighs and his fingers plied her most private place, Japonica gasped and moaned, feeling more wicked than she had thought possible. Her hips moved of their own volition to aid his stroking hand.

"Your body is ready for me, *bahia*. Are you?"

She looked up at him and whispered, "Yes."

"Open to me, sweet one, you are ready. I will not fail you . . . oh yes . . . that's it . . . so good. So warm . . . so wet and ready for . . ."

Past modesty or shame or fear, past all feeling except those that he provided with his hand and mouth, his body and words, Japonica abandoned herself to the moment. He was murmuring words to her in Persian, sweet husky pleadings, words of thanksgiving and encouragement. They were chest to chest and belly to belly. He lifted her hips once more and pressed between her thighs until he found the place he wanted.

She sobbed softly, her back arching in surprise as he slid into her. Her hands went automatically to his hips to hold him there deep within her. But he did not lie still. He surged deep within and then withdrew slowly, deliberately allowing her to feel every shift of muscle and tissue, and then he plunged again, slowly at first, watching her face and smiling at her inarticulate sounds of pleasure. Everywhere he touched her a new sensation registered. She heard his harsh breath in her ear, felt the bunch and stretch of the taut muscles of his back beneath her embrace, and marveled at the strength and gentleness of his motion. Finally the push-pull rhythm as old as life and as unique as the lovers who shared it caught them in its dance.

And then even that bit of separateness was gone. She was no longer feeling, but part of the feeling, part of him.

The perfect union became too much. Joyous and urgent need demanded release. When it came, the inexplicable spiraling release of ecstasy, she keened out her surprise and was echoed in his answering cry of gratitude.

Japonica was unaware of how much time passed before she felt herself again anchored to the earth. The candle had guttered out, the silence of the night broken only by the soft slow breaths of the man in whose embrace she lay gloriously and unashamedly naked.

"So this is how it is done? How everyone feels?"

Devlyn turned his head to look at her in grateful amusement. Never in all his life had he felt as he did in this moment with her, and he doubted, for all their boasting, that those most practiced in the exercise ever felt what they had just shared. If she had just discovered her capacity for passion, he had discovered in himself an emotion far deeper and more hazardous for the heart. Yet he hesitated to speak that truth for reasons he did not probe.

"It is often pleasant enough," he said carefully. "Easier for a man than a woman, I am told."

"Oh." So small a word captured exactly her expression, which was so eager and yet so shy.

He relented a little and took her chin in his hand. "As you now know, *bahia*, the lessons are simply mastered and the skill that comes with practice may provide its own enjoyment. But it is rare that feeling . . . ." He watched her gaze and so knew the exact moment when she began to understand him. "That feeling enters into the equation with such results."

"The key then is one's feelings?"

He nodded, wanting to tell her things he doubted she wanted to hear from him. "Did you think it only a man's pleasure?"

"I did not know." She rose up so that she could better observe his expression. "Are these feelings new to you?"

"These feelings . . ." Again reluctance held him back, the temptation to be less than honest when he had promised to be at her full command. So then the price of being with her was truth. "I would swear they are singular in my experience."

She folded her arms across his chest and placed her chin on them so that her face was only inches from his. "But you are a man of the world. How can that be?"

"Are you certain you want the answer, lady?"

Before she lost her nerve she whispered, "Yes."

He touched a hand to her cheek. "Memory is a tricky business and I have not even the usual recourse to it. Yet I believe the emotions I feel now I have felt before, but only with you."

Her pupils expanded, engulfing the plummy depths of her irises. He had shocked her and himself and he was only glad for it. "Will you not tell me if that is true?"

Japonica did not know how to answer, or even if she should. She looked away, staring off into the darkness that could not completely hide her thoughts. To tell him the truth would only give birth to more questions that she would not answer. "You sound regretful for your loss of memory, my lord."

He shook his head. "My only regret, lady, is that with both hands I might have loved you better."

She blushed so deep a shade she would have put holly berries to shame. "I do not think that I could bear to be loved better than I have been tonight."

He raised his eyes to the ceiling and exhaled a breath. So she would not yet tell him about their shared past. He was not a patient man but he could wait a little longer.

He rolled over and caught her to him. "It will be my greatest pleasure to love you as well and as long as you will have me."

As long as she would have him! Did he know what he offered? Did he even begin to suspect what her answer would be? *Love me forever.*

The words trembled on her lips. They deserved to be said, for they matched exactly the feeling welling up inside her. She had only to look into his eyes to know that what she wanted was reflected there with such passion as he had. But he had not spoken of love, only loving. And she was a woman, after all, and courage could take even a brave woman in love only so far.

She turned her head away, dusting his nose with her curls. "This is your proposition, that I will be your mistress for as long as it pleases us both?"

He did not answer at once. "If that is what pleases you."

"No." She rocked her head in the negative on his chest and answered with the truth. "No, if I were to be often with you like this, it would spoil me forever for any other man."

This time he took several shallow breaths. "Who is this other man?"

"There is none. Nor, until tonight, did I ever believe that there would be. But you have shown me something of myself and I shall be forever grateful to you for it."

"But if . . . am I not enough?"

She lifted her head, surprised by the strangled sound of his deep voice. "You are—everything. And that is why I must not become so attached to you. I would soon think myself in love and—well, then." She chuckled, though her words carried no amusement.

He tilted his chin forward to meet her gaze squarely. "Would that be so terrible a fate?"

Caught! She was caught in a trap of her devising. "No. It would not. But I must not love you."

"Must not love me?" His said the words reflectively. He lifted his maimed arm. "It is because of this?"

"Oh no." She reached for his arm and brought it

to her lips for a kiss. "It is what you are and in that calculation it makes no difference."

"So then, why?"

"I will not be your mistress." She looked away. "I wish you would not ask me again." She scooted back closer to him. "We have tonight. Kiss me and show me again how to make you happy."

She expected that he would kiss her and forget. But he looked suddenly more serious than he had been all evening. He touched her cheek, stroking back a handful of curls that had swung forward into her face.

"You have the power to lift my heart right out of my chest and take it with you. I bid you be kind, *bahia.*"

PART THREE

. . . what a mischievous devil Love is.
—Samuel Butler

Chapter Nineteen

Fortnum and Mason brimmed with activity the week before Christmas. Servants in livery, cooks with their kitchen maids, even gentry with baskets over their arms and maids at their sides jostled one another in order to have their turn at choosing among the various sundries and potables of the well-known establishment in Piccadilly.

Richard Fortnum made certain that his "cousin" did not, for lack of time or space or by oversight, miss any feature of his establishment. An initial awkwardness ensued when Fortnum overheard her being addressed by her maid as "my lady." Once Japonica confessed to her title of viscountess he made a quick adjustment and awarded her his instant deference. It was a singular privilege that nobility would deign to cross his humble doorstep. Add to it the cachet of being a relation? Now that was patronage. He took

it upon himself to give her a personally guided tour
with two senior assistants in tow.

Under escort, Japonica made her way through the
crush of shoppers and vendors, choosing decorated
tins of gingerbread biscuits and handmade Scottish
shortbread for the Shrewsbury Christmas. As she
walked among the busy counters absorbing the sights
and smells, homesickness struck her with unexpected
intensity. Praising her cousin's splendid wares, she
proclaimed the large well-stocked shop to be the clos-
est thing in London to the open-air bazaars that she
loved to browse in at home. Despite the chill, the
pungent aroma of foodstuffs filled the space. Aromas
from bins of spices and bowls of savories filled her
nostrils, reminding her of Bushire's sunny days
beneath vaulted blue skies limned by a warm sea
harbor. Stopping here and there, she passed barrels
of pickles and olives from the Middle East. Other
barrels contained filberts, walnuts, hazelnuts, cashews,
and almonds, shelled and unshelled. Threading her
way past barrels of sugar and salt and peppercorns,
past aisles of dried fruits from sunnier climes, she
came to gunnysacks rolled open to reveal dozens of
varieties of dried beans and peas with colors from
pearl to gray to green to speckled to red and black.
Sacks of meal and barley sat side by side with unmilled
kernels of wheat and oats.

Her favorite spot was the emporium where hothouse pears, dark-skinned plums and tart red apples
lay in straw-lined baskets. Beside them dishes of red,
black, and golden currants lay like shiny beads from
broken necklaces. Crocks of honey from such places
as Cornwall, Dorset, Newmarket, and the Scottish
Highlands filled shelves, all with labels touting their
special taste owing to the flowers the bees preferred.
On other shelves sat rows of ginger and apricot pre-
serves, along with creamy sweet-tart lemon curd and

rose petal jelly. Rows of ruby marmalade made from robust and bitter Spanish blood oranges stood beside jars of pickled green walnuts, sweet and sour cucumber, and figs marinated in West Indies rum. In another aisle she found tins of mustard and chutney and horseradish.

In the Tea Emporium she chose tins of Oolong and Keemun. Again and again she was urged to sample a pungent English cheddar or the blue-veined Stilton in earthenware jars. There were many more cheeses she had never heard of before such as Blue Wensleydale, Gubbeen, and Red Cheshire.

At the butcher's, she ordered a dozen dry-cured York hams, and crocks of smoked guinea fowl. In the readymade section there was caviar and smoked Scottish salmon along with game pies, patés, and raised salmon scallop pies. Nearby, live turtles and fish swam in tanks while waiting to be bought and turned into some fortunate diner's dinner. She chose instead oysters and salmon, both fresh and smoked, to be delivered to Croesus Hall, along with three large Christmas puddings.

After purchasing a paper twist full of chestnuts roasted to perfection in open braziers, she excused herself to her busy host and took a seat to open and enjoy the chestnuts in peace.

Quite by accident she had discovered a few days earlier that without Lord Abbott to order things, there had been no preparations made for Christmas at Croesus Hall.

Peony had been to the kitchen to ask when the currant tarts would be baked for the holiday, and returned with a tearful face.

"There were no puddings baked in October, Miss, nor mincemeat set aside to cure in brandy. Cook says the hams that hang in the smokehouse were not specially cured for the season. How can there be

Christmas without pudding? Oh, Miss, what shall we do?''

Japonica discovered that aristocratic households were no different from other sorts. Without a mistress or master in charge, no servant took it upon him or herself to see to anything. The cook claimed that she, "Wasn't to take it upon meself to see to the orderin'," and that the Shrewsbury daughters would not hear of the extra expense now that the dowager was in residence.

But Japonica was not too happy to allow the holiday to go unmarked at Croesus Hall and now that she was in London she could choose the best Christmas delicacies the city had to offer. Though they did not yet know it, the Shrewsbury sisters had extra reasons to celebrate, as had she!

She had awakened this morning to the amazing news that several of the wives of the gentlemen she met the night before at the Mirza's residence had left morning cards for her. Sir Ouseley's wife had written "at home" days on the back of her card. At first she was hurt that none of the ladies had actually asked for her until Bersham, bless him, patiently explained the custom of London cards and calls. Visitors often first left only their cards, signaling an acknowledgment that the homeowner was in town. She was expected to return the calls in the next few days but not actually meet any of the ladies save Lady Ouseley, because she had made known her "at home" hours. If the ladies then decided to actually visit her, it would be the first step in being accepted into London society. Only the first step, but significant.

Though they were not "out," Bersham agreed that Hyacinthe and Laurel could certainly be present during Japonica's "at home" days and accompany her on visits where only ladies would be present.

Japonica smiled as she chewed a peeled chestnut. Perhaps by the New Year the girls would have suitable connections to insure them invitations to balls and routs once they made their bow at St. James. It had even occurred to her how she might be able to remain in London long enough to secure the presentation at court for them.

Satisfied that the girls were well provisioned, she checked her list. She had given the roundsmen orders for baskets of food and drink to be shipped to Surrey for the laborers and cottagers who would come by Croesus Hall for their annual gift from the manor. She had also ordered enough to feed the tenants and tradespeople Bersham told her to expect for dinner on Christmas evening, a tradition that was observed whenever viscount Shrewsbury was in residence.

The viscount! Would he be in residence at Croesus Hall for Christmas?

She dipped her chin in the high collar of her fur-lined cloak, hoping the footman and maid who accompanied her would not notice the change of her complexion as blood warmed her cheeks.

When Devlyn left her bed a little after four of the clock that morning, she had not been thinking of the Shrewsburys or Croesus Hall. They had whispered and giggled like children as she helped him find his things in the dark. And while he puckered up as she helped him button his shirt and waistcoat, he did not quibble about her aid in fastening his breeches. In fact, she had had to push him playfully away with the admonition there was such a thing as too much ecstasy. Though if they had not feared discovery, she doubted either of them would have been satisfied with the amount they had shared so far. He promised to come the next evening to take her to the opera, that London might have its first public glimpse of her.

She had fallen into an exhausted sleep and awakened to the rapturous realization that the future she had not dared hope for might yet be. She did not expect marriage, nor would she accept the position as mistress. She had heard, even in her part of the world, of widows who kept discreet company with a lover. Perhaps he would accept something less than wedded vows not bound by vulgar commerce. But first, she must tell him about Jamie.

Over her ablutions she thought about how she might broach the subject of a son, *his* son. She could not very well do that until she had revealed yet another truth. He now knew that there had been a man other than the viscount in her life, the *Hind Div*. Was it not a short leap from the *Hind Div*—to who the *Hind Div* was—to the revelation that it was himself? Perhaps he would remember it all on his own. Perhaps not.

By the time she had dressed and sat with her cup of chocolate, the simple construction of revelation began to seem inadequate. In order for him to believe that he was Jamie's father, he must accept that he was the *Hind Div*. If his memory did not supply it, where could she find corroboration with which to buttress her truth? How would he react to the news when up to now she had gone out of her way never to admit that they were not strangers? Would he now think she had made a dupe of him?

By the time her chocolate cup was empty, her doubts were full to brimming. Even if he believed her it might take time for him to accept it all. There was only her word, and Aggie's. If he did believe her, what then? He would want to see the child. Therefore she must bring Jamie and Aggie to London!

Why had she not thought of that before? She would put them up in a small residence in London under an assumed name, somewhere nearby where she could visit every day and the Shrewsburys need never know.

Before she could change her mind, she had penned the note to Aggie and included a bank draft that would pay for their passage.

If in the end Devlyn would not accept Jamie as his, at least she would have her son close again. And if he did, Devlyn could enjoy getting to know his son in privacy. It was no one's business what they did. Once the first of the Abbott sisters was launched, she would not care a fig what London society thought of her.

At the last minute she made a final purchase before leaving Fortnum and Mason, a sack of musk which she would leave with her card as a present for the Mirza. Persian etiquette required a thank-you for his excellent hospitality of the evening before, though she would have done so anyway out of gratitude. The evening in the Mirza's company had prompted Devlyn to reveal, for the first time, the man beneath the enigma. Jealousy was, she was discovering, a wonderful motivator.

Devlyn strode past the Horse Guards, located between Whitehall and the parade ground of St. James's Park. He had been told he would find his fellow lieutenants in temporary quarters nearby. He came upon the address just as the two officers exited the doorway of the boarding establishment and turned in the opposite direction.

"Winslow! Hemphill!"

The two men swung about.

"Sinclair! This is a surprise."

"Didn't expect to see you about so early, Col— Viscount." Hemphill grinned. "Requires a moment to remember your title."

"Just going round to London Tavern for bacon and oysters," Hemphill added. "Join us."

Devlyn shook his head. "I would speak with you on a private matter."

"Step back into the parlor," Winslow suggested. "I'm sure the proprietor can secure us three glasses of port to tide us over."

When the port had been poured, Winslow raised his glass. "Before we begin I'd like to make a toast to the Shrewsbury widow." He had swallowed the salute before he went on. "Admit it, didn't recognize her last evening. Rumor would have it you're behind the transformation, Sinclair."

"You do me too much credit," Devlyn answered coolly as he noted the salacious smiles blooming on the other men's faces. "If all beauty required was a fashionable gown there wouldn't be a spinster in all of London."

"Too true," they chorused.

Frowning, Devlyn fiddled with his untouched glass. "Is there much rumor of that sort?"

"Rumor? Paint it scandal," Hemphill avowed. "The way she and the Mirza got on . . . . Spouting love poems at each other? A bit of luck, what, her arriving in London at the same time as the ambassador? The morning's *on dit* is that Ouseley's chosen the widow to be his secret mistress."

"All this before breakfast," Devlyn remarked in a low voice.

"Don't traffic in rumor myself," Winslow asserted, for he accounted Sinclair a friend and Lady Abbott was his married-in kin. "Still, it does strike one as odd that the Mirza should give her the whole of his attention for the entire evening."

Devlyn reached for his wine but did not drink. He knew a great deal about Japonica's fascinations. In fact, had been able to think of little else since he had left her bed. But she was not a mistress to be boasted about. All the more reason to end nefarious speculation about her. He could not come out and defend her directly without giving rise to another kind of speculation. And, there was the Mirza's reputation as well to be considered.

"Strange, that rumors should make counterfeit our first impression of her as a most unremarkable sort. I, for one, mistook her for a governess."

"So did we all," Winslow answered. "I quite believed the first account of her that Lord Abbott married her simply to provide his children a mother."

Devlyn nodded. "An altogether prosaic transaction. She was his nurse in Persia. Her way with the ill and young would explain her governess quality. Her life as a colonial explains her easy manner. Amid the formality of London one might misconstrue it as familiar and forward."

Devlyn saw doubt and disillusionment pucker his companions' expressions. He had only to seal shut their doubts on her character. "I will admit to being taken aback to learn that she is a relation of the Fortnum grocers."

"Mercantile class, do you say? Not even gentry?" Winslow questioned with a scowl of disapproval.

"We all know how morality-ridden the middle classes can be," Devlyn introduced as if in afterthought.

"Positively infested with virtue," Hemphill said with a grimace of dislike.

"Innocence is charming," Winslow concurred. "But save me from the pious!"

"As for the breach in the Mirza's vows, you have no doubt seen the results of a man condemned to be boiled in oil?"

Hemphill blanched.

"So then this business of lovers must be distorted," Winslow murmured.

"I don't doubt," Devlyn answered.

"A fellow would never be so lucky to actually find such flesh and blood temptation within his grasp," Hemphill said with a sulk of disappointment. "More likely she is one of those tiresome widows looking to wed again."

"Gad! Save me from all talk of leg-shackling." Winslow grimaced. "Mama will speak of nothing else since my return. 'Tis enough to send any man off to war again."

"If we are done with rumor?" Devlyn said lightly. "Which of you retains native connections in the East Indies?"

"I do," Winslow answered. "Not so much as you once did, o' course. Why do you ask?"

"I would learn the whereabouts of a shadowy figure who goes by the name of the *Hind Div.*"

Both men's expressions arrested in surprise.

"You're bamming me!" Hemphill said.

"Why do you inquire?" Winslow asked with a concerned look.

Devlyn picked up his glass and drained it without thinking. He had not expected he would need to explain his motives to fellow officers. He did not look at them as he said, "I believe I once knew the fellow."

"Welladay! I don't wonder," declared Hemphill, with nervous laughter.

Winslow's sharp glance made Hemphill swallow his mirth. "You remember nothing of Persia?" he asked.

"I have dreams." Devlyn gazed into his empty glass. For the second time in as many minutes he felt the discomfort of making a confession.

"I see." Winslow dragged the words out as if his mind were busily working out some puzzle. "What do these dreams tell you, if I may ask, of the *Hind Div?*"

Devlyn reached for the decanter of port and poured a full glass. "That I must redress a wrong. It would be paid at sword's point were I not incapable."

"A duel? With the *Hind Div?*" With each question Hemphill's voice rose until he ended in a whistle of amazement.

Devlyn slanted him a dark look. "I am in need of a few facts. If neither of you can help me I will turn elsewhere."

Winslow's gaze remained glued to Devlyn's face. "He was one of ours. An agent, don't you know?"

"The *Hind Div* is English?"

"As much as I or—you," Hemphill volunteered, and then cleared his throat nervously. "The devil of it is, we were never allowed to know exactly who he was until after he was dead."

Devlyn forced himself to take a breath. "If you knew he's dead, why lead me this merry chase?"

"Hemphill should say *reported* dead." Winslow took a cheroot out of his pocket and began nibbling on the end. "Thing is, old friend, the report of his death was premature."

"Then he lives?"

"As you live and breathe," Hemphill answered, amusement making the edges of his lips turn up. "Dash it all, Sinclair. Did you have to lose your wits?"

"I apologize for the burden it places upon our acquaintance." Devlyn looked suddenly alert. "Or is it something more?" He turned swiftly on Winslow, his expression struck by surprise. "Is one of you the *Hind Div?*"

Winslow fell back in his chair before Devlyn's gaze. "Faith, no! Do I look the sort to mark his face like a jungle cat or go unnoticed among the Persians and Indians?"

Looking at Winslow's light eyes and freckled skin and then Hemphill's sandy hair and complexion that colored up with every emotion, Devlyn grasped his meaning. "But you knew—know him."

"We know him." Winslow hung his head.

Suspicion lifted the hairs on Devlyn's forearms though he could not guess the nature of the danger he felt himself to be in. "Tell me everything."

"Steady on, friend." Winslow gnawed his lip a moment. "The doctors said we were not to press you with memories of your past."

"My past. A past that includes the *Hind Div?*"

Both men looked away.

Bile churned in his gut, but Devlyn did not quite believe. If it were true, surely the truth would register in his mind, some shred of memory would escape from the morass of lost thought to confirm it.

"I need confirmation."

"I can see how you might," Winslow answered. "There is something that might supply you with answers. We were given custody of it on your behalf. It's a small chest sent to the Governor General of Calcutta after you went missing last year. Delivered by agents of Zaman Shah of Afghanistan. In it was proof that you had been killed, or so we thought at the time."

Devlyn's eyes narrowed slightly. "What sort of proof?"

"Your severed hand," Hemphill offered, then hastily looked away from Devlyn's harsh expression. "Grisly business. It was given a burial."

"The hand still bore a ring, a large turquoise." Winslow paused to clear his throat. "Gossip said it had been stolen from the Zaman Shah himself . . . by the *Hind Div.*"

"What else is in the chest?"

"We don't know," Hemphill declared, for Devlyn's

tone was that of a man with a short leash on his temper. " 'Pon oath!''

"It's been in our safekeeping until such time as you seemed to require it."

Something moved in Devlyn's face, an emotion so terrible his companions glanced at one another in genuine alarm. "I require it now."

"I'll fetch it." Winslow sprang to his feet.

"I'll help." Hemphill bounded to his feet with equal alacrity. "Who knows but it might trigger a memory or two."

Devlyn watched them go, fighting the urge to stride after them so that he might put his hands on the chest all the sooner. Something held him back, something greater than the simple fear of the future. He felt the dread of the past dragging at his newfound joy.

Devlyn sat with his feet stretched out before him, a half-empty whiskey bottle at his elbow. Beside him lay an ornate turquoise and silver ring, a book of Persian poetry by Mullah Jami, and an unfolded letter. In the distance Big Ben struck ten of the clock. It was the hour to dine, dance, and visit the opera or theater. But he would not be going out this night. A rare and dangerous rage had him in its powerful grip. Even he was afraid of what might happen should he step outside his door.

The *Hind Div* was he!

Memory did not bolster that conclusion. Nor did feeling. The acceptance was more innate. Like his lost memory, he simply *knew* it was so.

Devlyn squeezed his eyes shut, not wanting to be distracted by his own view of the bleak world that was his room. Instantly there appeared before his mind's eye a pair of dark eyes feathered by red-gold lashes so bright they seemed unreal. Serious eyes, honest eyes, eyes that had looked all the way into his soul and knew the truth that lay hidden from his own psyche. He had read the truth in Japonica Abbott's gaze the first time she laid eyes on him but he did not recognize it. Her fear of him now had cause.

He was the *Hind Div!*

He came to feel the full revulsion of that truth by accident. It lay at the bottom of the box Winslow had handed over to him. Tucked into the leather binding of *Joseph and Zuleika* lay a thin piece of parchment that made the story damagingly complete.

He reached for it again, could not long keep from reading. In the last hours he must have read it a dozen times. But the words would not stick. The exact phrasing eluded his whiskey-soaked wits when he was away from it for more than two minutes together.

And so he picked it up and read it once again.

Dear Boy,

I have found for you a bride! Wondrous creature! She is that rarest of women: resourceful, levelheaded, and with a true loving heart. I send her to you for your approval. And then I shall borrow her back for a time. No doubt you've made an impression upon her to last a lifetime.

Until you are ready, she will be in my care.

But don't make her wait too long, my proud young cock. I would not like to think of her shackled to a less-deserving man.

George Abbott

Below, scrawled in another hand was the name JAPONICA FORTNOM. Japonica Fortnom was meant to be his bride.

Even now with damning evidence before him he

could not recall a single moment of the encounter that she had described to him the night before. He thought he had seen in her face what the admission cost her. Now he understood how miserably he had underestimated her courage. How could she tell her story to the villain in it and then listen to the very same man promise to help her overcome the greatest shame of her life?

Drugged her! She accused the *Hind Div* of that. This mysterious being who dealt in treachery and intrigue and guile and sorcery, must have found potions that served his purposes well. Too well.

Japonica's wariness, her evasions, her resentments of him all made sense. In fact, every encounter they had shared made sense save one, the hours he had spent in her bed. That memory, not twenty-four hours old, seemed to hold out to him a promise of a future he had never imagined. Now he did not understand a single moment of it.

"Damnation!" He reached for the whiskey bottle and swallowed a good bit of its contents. The beating at his temples for once was welcome, for it served as a companion to his painful thoughts.

What sort of thinking allowed a woman to welcome her defiler to her bed? He could not doubt the anguish he saw in her eyes as she told him her story. No one could lie that well. But what contortions of mind had persuaded her to surrender—no, encourage him to lie with her?

He sat forward so fast his brain seemed to career into the front inside of his skull, the impact creating radiant pain that made him gasp and swear again. But the salient fact survived even the pain. Perhaps Japonica Abbott had dared to beard the lion in his den because the lion did not know his own power over her. Defanged and unmasked by his lost recollection, what a pitiable creature he must seem to her after the terrifying spectacle he had once presented.

He had heard the talk among the officers on the voyage back to England of a foreign spy of such stealth, cunning, and treachery that some did not believe him wholly human. They did not even suspect that he was the man once known as the *Hind Div.* Even Hemphill and Winslow said they knew nothing—until after he was thought dead, after he was maimed and made useless in his former profession of spy.

Devlyn made a sudden violent movement with his right arm, as if he could dash away the torment building inside him. Useless! And pitiable, that's what he was. So impotent that even a gently bred lady whom he had once dishonored felt so little awe that she could use his weakened state to extract an ingenious and most subtle form of revenge from him.

"Exorcising her demon!" The thought made him laugh, but it was hard, bitter laughter with regret and recrimination as its chaser.

A woman scorned. He had treated her badly even here in England, dismissing her first as a governess and then calling her to account for her poor showing as a woman. Could any demonstration of his blind arrogance be more damning than that? Only perhaps, that he could not even remember her. Yes, he could well believe her ripe for revenge. He wanted it, too. Against himself.

He was ready to call out her seducer! Her defiler! The *Hind Div!*

How cleverly she had arranged it all. How sweet her vengeance must taste. Best of all he could not even blame her for it. She was a worthy opponent of the man he had once been.

He drank deep, trying to drown the feelings that stirred even in the depths of his humiliation. Despite all that he knew. In the face of reason and very good argument to the contrary, her vengeance was more complete than she might ever guess. For, last night, she had won from him his heart.

"Shall I stir the fire up again, my lady?"

Japonica shook her head. "No, Bersham, and you may retire for the night. I will shortly."

The family retainer gave his mistress a small smile as the clock on the mantel struck the hour as one A.M. "An unavoidable detainment, no doubt."

"No doubt," she agreed dully. "Good night, Bersham."

"Good night, my lady."

Japonica stood up and walked purposefully across the room. She would find another reason to wear the gown she had bribed Madame Soti to sell her though it was pledged to another customer. There would be other nights for the opera. Other nights for a small quiet supper like the one that sat congealing amid the silver, crystal, china, and lace of the table she approached. London was full of the kind of sperm whale tapers that had burned so low they had begun to sputter as she reached out to snuff them with her fingers.

She stared at the wax that came away on her fingers. There would be a perfectly good explanation for Devlyn's absence without even a note of regret. Something amiss, surely, yet reasonably explained. It would not be that she had made a fool of herself the night before. And that he, realizing it in the full light of day, had not known how to send his regrets and so remained silent even to her utter humiliation.

Could it be that she had made a dreadful mistake in believing that they had leapt some impossible hurdle as they lay in each other's arms just before dawn?

Would Jamie arrive in London to find no welcome at all from his sire?

"He has remembered!" The words escaped Japonica on a breath of horror.

Chapter Twenty

"She wants us to come to London." Hyacinthe's face shone with a rare smile of satisfaction. "We are to accompany her to an 'at home' with Lady Ouseley and another with Lady Hepple."

She laid the letter aside, her expression forming thoughtful lines. "Father knew Lady Hepple. He spoke frequently of her botanical gardens. Her roses are judged to be among the finest examples in the world. If I am not mistaken, he brought her a new specimen from one of his voyages. To meet her would be splendid. To tour her gardens? Singular!"

"I refuse to go." Laurel crossed her arms and shot her sister a dark glance. "This is another of *her* ruses. Nearly a fortnight and not a word? Now she needs us? It is a trick to lull us into the belief that she means well by us. She will merely use our presence as evidence of our support to advance herself in the world."

Jerked from pleasant possibilities, Hyacinthe stared at her peevish sister. "I see no harm in being introduced to two of London's hostesses. As you are at constant pains to point out, we must be known to exist before we can be introduced into society. I believe I shall take Lady Hepple a cutting from Father's . . ."

"I cannot believe you are so easily taken in!" Laurel jumped to her feet and began pacing the morning room at Croesus Hall. "There is a trap in this for us. Or this is a bribe."

"Bribe? For what possible purpose? We have nothing to hold over her but our dislike."

"You would be astonished!" Laurel turned quickly from her sister as Hyacinthe's brows peaked in a question.

She had not shared with anyone what she had discovered upon reading the letter stolen from Japonica. Hyacinthe had been so up in the boughs about the sin of theft that she had allowed her sister to believe she had delivered all five missives untouched. The shocking revelation contained in that purloined letter was too enormous to simply share with a sister. She had hugged it to her bruised pride, satisfied that a better moment would arrive when she might use it to smite the interloper in their midst.

Infuriation kindled in Laurel's breast. She was losing her sisters as allies just when she needed them most. The ninnies had begun to speak of their stepmother in terms one could only label as endearing.

"Deserters!" she murmured. True, Cynara's spots had begun to clear and Peony was louse-free for the first time in years. As for the regimen of bathing, it clearly had advantages. Her own complexion was smoother and brighter. And yes, it was nice to have a maid to boss and make demands upon, even if the stupid girl had not been successful in sneaking extra portions of meals up to Laurel's room. But none of it was sufficient to quell the great rage she felt each time that Japonica's name was mentioned.

It was not fair that *she* was in London receiving invitations that should rightly have come directly to Hyacinthe and herself. Surely any condescension shown their step-mama derived from the Shrewsbury name.

"Look what we have discovered!" Cynara burst into the room, all heels and petticoats. In her wake came Peony and Alyssum, looking apple-cheeked with December cold from their outing.

"Where have you been?" Hyacinthe demanded, for she had not given them permission to leave the house.

"To town, to see the vicar," Peony supplied breathlessly.

"To bring clothes for the poor to be distributed at Christmas," Alyssum added with a blush that deepened her high color.

"Never mind all that," Cynara said impatiently. "We've the most delicious gossip to impart. The vicar himself was kind enough to point it out to us. You'll never guess. There's a drawing of the Mirza and our Miss in the pages of a London gazette!"

"She is not 'our' miss," Laurel corrected crossly. "And what do you mean *she* is in the paper?"

"Well, not Miss precisely, but her likeness." Cynara held out the *Morning Post*. "See what it says right there."

Laurel snatched the tabloid from her sister and began to read the headlines. "There's nothing here but columns about Parliament, the war, royal decree, stocks, agricultural reports, and shipping discharges. Nothing about *her.*"

"Look inside!" Peony danced on tiptoe. "Y-y-you will see."

Laurel jerked open the paper so quickly it tore

halfway down the middle. Something did catch her eye. There in the upper left-hand side was a drawing of a tall exotic-looking man in brocade robe and turban and bushy beard. Beside him was the merest sketch of a young lady whose features were so indistinct as to be unrecognizable. A quick scan of the rest of the pages yielded nothing else of interest.

"I see nothing here about *her!*" Laurel tossed the paper aside in disgust.

Cynara scooped up the paper. "Here it is, under the picture of the Persian ambassador. The column is about the Mirza being given a private audience by the King at St. James's yesterday." She cleared her throat as if about to deliver a formal oration. "It reads . . ."

His Excellency returned to his house, where the crowd was so extremely great that it was impossible for his Majesty's footmen to get from the carriage, to open the carriage door, and knock at the house door; and had it not been for the vigilance of the Bow Street patrol, it would have been impossible to clear the doorway. The populace gave his Excellency three cheers again, upon his leaving the carriage.

"So what!" Scorn delineated every line of Laurel's expression.

"There's more. 'On his Excellency's return to Mansfield Street, he invited Sir Gore Ouseley and Mr. Morier to partake of an entertainment, called in the Persian language a Pillau. . .'" Cynara skipped a few lines. "Here it is. It says that among the frequent illustrious callers at Mayfield Street is the dowager viscountess Shrewsbury, formerly of Bushire, Persia. There!"

"Let me see that!" Laurel again snatched the paper and bent a hard stare on the article.

Peony reached under Laurel's arm to point at the drawing. "That is Miss b-b-beside the Mirza. We recognized the b-b-barouche coat as the one Miss purchased at Madame S-S-Soti's."

"Let me see!" Hyacinthe poked her head forward over her sister's shoulder and read the entire column for herself, clucking her tongue from time to time as she read it. "In the company of a heathen, our name attached to this—this . . ."

"The *Post* calls him a Noble Personage," Cynara interjected. "Indeed, he is quite handsome."

"He is a savage," Laurel declared, though she had gazed at his likeness long enough to be certain he was quite a tall, well-built young man despite his odious beard. What a jolly good showing she would have made of it had she been there beside the ambassador instead of Step-mama.

Jealousy boiled in Laurel's breast. She had made up her mind never to forgive Japonica for embarrassing her in front of her sisters over her appetite and dilatory performances on the piano. Resentment built against her stepmother for having stolen Lord Sinclair's affections from under her nose. Now to think that *she* had won the interest of a second high-ranking gentleman—even if he was foreign!

That last thought was too much for her. All the resentments, humiliations, and impotent rage of the last weeks built into a crescendo of feeling as she cried out, "It will not serve! Papa's name dragged about in the gazettes by that adventuress! I will see her brought low! I've the means to do it. You will see."

"What do you mean?" Cynara asked.

"You wouldn't do anything t-t-to hurt Miss?" Peony questioned in alarm.

Realizing that she was giving quite too much of her private feelings away, Laurel drew herself up and squared her shoulders. "I do not confide in children. Hyacinthe? You are right. We must go to London. Today, in fact."

"And so it is with most of Almina's friends." Mrs. Hepple smiled indulgently at her youngest daughter. "Eugenia Fawnsworth is engaged to Lord Averley's eldest son and Jane Simpson is known to be attached to the Carradine heir. The rest of our girls must look to themselves."

"I thank you for your advice, Lady Hepple, as do my daughters," Japonica said with a glance at Laurel who sat beside her with a cup of tea in one hand and a square of cake in the other.

"Think nothing of it." Lady Hepple eyed the diminished tray and said a bit wearily, "Another cup of tea?"

The usual quarter-hour visit had been extended indefinitely, it seemed, by her son's unexpected offer to show Miss Hyacinthe their newest hothouse collection. Lady Hepple had found herself in need of refreshment and so had gone against custom to order tea and cakes for her guests. Alas, her stream of acceptable conversation with strangers was running regrettably thin.

"You were saying, Lady Abbott, that you are new to London ways. Allow me to assure you that you have only to ask for my advice on all such matters pertaining to the debut of young ladies in society. I have launched two daughters successfully betimes. Almina will be my crowning achievement." She smiled again at the pretty petite confection of a daughter who sat beside her with hands folded calmly in her lap.

"You are to be commended." Japonica nodded at the Hepple's youngest child. From the pale gold curls at her crown, past eyes so bright a blue they seemed painted, to the tips of her tiny feet, Almina Hepple embodied nearly every mother's wish for a daughter. The picture was spoiled only by the complacent smile on the young lady's lips that betrayed to the exact degree how well she understood and enjoyed her advantages.

"Two daughters married in as many years." Japonica turned back to the self-satisfied mother and wondered if she had found a friend or a competitor. "I dare not hope to achieve so quick a tally."

"Tosh! I'm certain when this dreadful war ends, there will be gentlemen enough to go round." Mrs. Hepple leaned slightly forward in a confidential manner. "Meanwhile, I feel it my duty to offer a smidgen of advice. Launch no more than one daughter per Season. To do else would make it appear that you are anxious. Given the year she is sure to find someone. The selection of a proper spouse cannot be over-emphasized."

"Dear Step-mama is quite beforehand in that matter of advantageous marriages," Laurel said between bites of the new piece of cake she had selected from the tray circulated by the Hepple footman, who was dressed in rose-colored livery. "One might say *she* excels in the field."

"I daresay we mothers must all excel, in our daughters' behalf." Lady Hepple smiled uncertainly, for Miss Laurel was to her mind quite too coming for a girl who had yet to make her bow. Her forwardness was superseded only by her fondness for cake. The girl had consumed three pieces!

" 'Tis Fernlow I despair of. The dear boy won't hear a word in the matter of his own nuptials. Claims he's wed to his studies, which I am in all sympathy with. No one understands the needs of my roses, as does Fernlow. Yet he should have a wife to see to his own comfort. He protests he has met no lady who understands his passion for nature. He would hold out for a companion who would roam the world with him like a beggar but I tell him no genuine lady would wish to . . . ." Lady Hepple flushed up, the color decidedly at odds with her bronze taffeta costume.

"I agree, Lady Hepple. No *lady* would prefer the wilds." Laurel's smile bore a spot of cream from the pastry she had just consumed. "But dear Step-mama is of heartier stock than we aristocrats, Lady Hepple. Her people positively thrive in native climes. I should not but wonder after another generation there'll be scarce difference made between the heathens and them."

"Well, r-r-really!" Lady Hepple stammered. "I had not meant to make such a point."

"Oh, but 'tis true. Have you not read in the gazettes? Dear Step-mama prefers to spend her evenings in the company of the Persian Ambassador to every *civilized* diversion London might offer her." Laurel's voice took on the sugary coating of the too-sweet confection she had been consuming. "I have heard he keeps a *harem* and that his servants carry scimitars night and day and threaten to *behead* any who they believe is not sufficiently deferential to their master. I suppose dear Step-mama's *embrace* of such barbaric practices must be due to her foreign upbringing." She turned a spiteful gaze on Japonica. "Do tell us, Step-mama? Is the Mirza as imposing a figure in *private* as he appears to the public eye?"

The poor lady who was their hostess made a sound rather like a strangled gasp and reached for her tea, spilling a good deal of it on herself as she hurried to lift the cup to her lips.

As Almina offered her napkin in an effort to help her mother mop up the spill, Laurel sent her step-mama a second triumphant glance.

Laurel's animosity might have a better target, thought Japonica, had she not already been too heart-sick to truly care that she was being expertly cut up before an audience neither of them could afford to offend. But her feelings were running high in other directions.

Two weeks! Not a word. No note, or card, or a single flower had arrived from Lord Sinclair since the evening he had not appeared for the opera. The conclusion was undeniable. He had deserted her.

No one she spoke to had seen or heard from him. There seemed only two possible explanations for his desertion. He had recovered his memory and with it a renewed contempt for her. Or their night together had assuaged his carnal appetite brought on by jeal-ousy of Mirza Hassan. That done, he wanted nothing more to do with her.

She could not decide which scenario was worse. Both made her want to stretch herself upon the car-pet and weep until she was ill.

"I do wonder where Fernlow could have got to," Almina remarked when her mother had recovered her poise. "I am never so bored as when my brother is taken by the notion to lecture me on some aspect of botany. Poor Hyacinthe will have expired of bore-dom if he has chosen her to be his pupil."

"Nothing could be further from the truth, Miss Almina." Hyacinthe had appeared in the doorway with the Honorable Fernlow Hepple at her side. "I have passed a most delightful half hour among your roses, Lady Hepple. Delightful!"

The warmth in Hyacinthe's tone brought Japoni-ca's indifferent gaze to attention upon the gentleman who accompanied her eldest stepdaughter. Of medium height but slight of frame, the Hepple scion dressed simply in black. A head of thinning locks that looked more like a halo framed the serious but pleasant face of a man dedicated to the soil rather than the ribbons. His air of piety lacked only holiness. For his Grail, as his mother had already remarked upon some three times, was the creation of the perfect pink rose.

Not waiting for her hostess to rise first, Japonica came to her feet. "We must be going, Lady Hepple. You are patience itself to have indulged our company so long."

"Nothing so strenuous was required I assure you, Lady Abbott." But Lady Hepple looked relieved to have her guests announce their intention of a rapid departure. "You must come again . . . sometime."

"Indeed." When Hades is paved with ice, Japonica suspected. As she moved toward the doorway with Laurel bringing up the rear, she overheard Fernlow's conversation with Hyacinthe.

". . . Most edifying afternoon, Miss Hyacinthe." It did not seem to bother him that he had to look up to speak to her. "I shall look forward to receiving your father's notes on the subject of Oriental blossoms."

"I can't think of anyone more deserving with whom Father would have wished to share them." Hyacinthe blushed like a schoolgirl. "There are, of course, scribblings in the margins which you may find difficult to decipher . . ."

"I hope I may look to you for assistance should it be needed."

"Most assuredly, sir."

It crossed Japonica's mind, in light of Lady Hepple's declaration about her son, that he seemed extraordinarily genuine in his address to Hyacinthe. Matches had arisen from less commonality than a love of botany.

Yet it struck her like the blast of the windblown snow that greeted her exit from the Hepple house in Berkeley Square that she knew nothing about love and proper alliances. Curiosity, as well as necessity, had driven her to be reckless in the lair of the *Hind Div.* Compassion had goaded her into marriage with a man she respected and liked, but would never have thought to wed in other circumstances. A misplaced sense of duty had made her desert her son in order to try to secure the future of five ungrateful girls who had yet to benefit from her interference. Now, she could think of no excuse short of madness that had driven her to seek the embrace of a man she should by all rights despise.

Oh, but it was unfair! She did not despise him. She felt—no, what she felt she must not give name to, lest it truly drive her into insanity.

She turned her head away as the postillion stepped up to open the carriage door for her. A tear had escaped and slipped silently down the curve of her cheek. "I prefer to walk awhile," she said to no one in particular and set off at a fast pace through the lightened gloom of the snowy afternoon.

"You silly, stupid girl!" Hyacinthe declared after Laurel's smug recitation of her behavior at Lady Hepple's.

"There's no reason to pucker up at me!" Laurel answered and adjusted herself on the carriage cushions. "I did it for us."

"For us? Don't you realize what you have done? By ripping up *her* reputation you threaten to pull down scandal upon our own heads. We may never again be invited anywhere."

"You make too much of it," Laurel replied. "Once *she* realizes that she is considered an anathema to society and withdraws from London, we shall quickly recover. After all, she is nothing to us.''

"You are very ignorant of the world," Hyacinthe said crossly. "Ignorant and arrogant! I always said your temper would get the better of your limited good sense. I see I am right. If your meddling costs me the association of Lady Hepple I shall never forgive you. Our step-mama may not be precisely the sort of person we may wish her to be but she has been nothing but generous and, in the main, helpful.'' She nodded in concurrence with the rightness of her thoughts. "Woe to those who bite the hand that feeds them.''

"Don't you dare preach at me! I'm not the one with secrets! I am not the one who seduced Lord Sinclair beneath our roof. Who pretends to be better than her superiors, yet is no more than a whore!''

"What are you talking about?''

"So, now I have your attention. I know things, things she is at great pains to keep from us.''

"I wonder how that knowledge was got. By listening at keyholes? By thievery, and lying and sneaking and spying? Oh, those are wonderful traits for a young lady of Quality.''

"Never mind my conduct. Do you want to know what I know? It is this. Dear step-mama has a bastard child!''

Hyacinthe's eyes opened so wide they would seem to fall out of their sockets. "Dear Lord! Say it cannot be.''

"A son," Laurel confirmed, "named Jamie. I read all about him in one of those letters she received. He is not nearly six months old and living in Portugal with a nanny. I kept the post.''

Hyacinthe shut her eyes and let her head fall back against the carriage wall. "This will mean the ruination of everything!''

"It will ruin *her*." A smug smile wreathed Laurel's face. "Think when it's published abroad. The dowager viscountess Shrewsbury has borne a bastard."

"But then ...." Hyacinthe could scarce draw breath. "We have a brother!"

"Rubbish. The child is the result of a squalid liaison. Most probably Persian into the bargain. I've written to Mr. Simmons to get us proof!"

Hyacinthe opened her eyes and stared at her sister. "You little fool! Do you not see? If she has borne a son—six months old did you say? That puts his birth precisely nine months after the marriage. He could conceivably lay claim as the Shrewsbury heir!"

Laurel's smile faded as the full significance of the statement sank in. "Surely not! If she were after the Shrewsbury title, she had only to march into London with the babe at her breast."

"She must have reasons for keeping silent," Hyacinthe murmured.

"My point precisely! He is a bastard. So then, if we expose her ..."

"Do shut up, Laurel. We must stop these inquiries before they run ahead beyond our reach. Who else have you told of this discovery?"

"No one." Laurel looked as abashed as one who has pulled a joke only to discover that it is upon herself. "Oh, I may have mentioned the subject in passing in a note to Lord Shrewsbury."

"What?" Hyacinthe squawked and half rose from her seat. "The very person who has the most to lose? And who may pursue the subject of a public denunciation of our step-mama as an adulteress with a bastard? Well done, sister! You may be the very hook upon which will hang our eventual ruination!"

Feeling as if hornets from a dozen different directions were stinging her, Laurel swelled up and met her sister's glare of outrage with equal enmity. "So this is how you repay my efforts! That is very fine, I must say. I had not thought my own sisters would turn against me. After all, I did this for us. If you had not been mewling over that Fernlow fellow, you might have been present to see how she curried favor at our expense. Yes, I see it clearly now! I alone care what happens to the family!''

The crack of Hyacinthe's palm across her sister's face caught the attention of the postillion and driver but both thought they must be in error of the direction of the sound. After all, they drove two ladies through the streets of Mayfair.

Japonica found herself grateful for the Persian custom of drinking coffee, which to her mind was more warming and stimulating than the customary English tea. Soaked through by thick flakes of snow and icy puddles that seeped through her leather shoes, she was near tears when a strange coach pulled up beside her on Pall Mall. Its occupants, the Mirza Hassan and Sir Ouseley, generously offered her a ride.

She could not remember exactly what excuse she offered them for being found on the street. Something about shopping and losing her way. Her rescuers had been so appalled by her frozen state that they had pooh-poohed her explanations and busied themselves with tucking her into Sir Ouseley's Carrick coat and the Mirza's sable lap rug.

They gallantly offered to detour out of their way to drive her to her house, then suggested that, because the Mirza's residence was nearer and she was in need of a thorough warming, that she stop first there. Gratefully she agreed. Nothing awaited her at the Shrewsbury townhouse but stepdaughters she had no desire to face at the moment. Once inside the

Mirza's home, her coat, bonnet, and shoes were taken away by servants to clean and dry them.

Now, ensconced in the Mirza's salon, sitting among the cushions that he preferred to chairs, she felt at ease for the first time in two weeks. Thankfully, nothing more than her presence seemed to be required. The Mirza was in a talkative mood, regaling all within hearing of his various outings since his debut at the Court of St. James had released him from his self-imposed house arrest.

"The houses of London, though splendid, all look alike," the Mirza exclaimed expansively. "Therefore it is clever of each owner to paint his name above the door. Four stories, each of them, so that servants may share the roof of their masters at all times. Something that is not common even in the Shah's own capital. I find it convenient that stables and carriage houses are located behind each residence. And, too, the large round glass lanterns that are suspended from iron hooks above each doorway dazzle the eye. I have written to his Majesty, the Shahanshah, to inform him how truly amazing it is that in London winter it is so dark that the sun is all but invisible so that the lamps must be lighted day and night."

All shared a chuckle at his continuing amazement at the English winter.

"Convenient, too, are the shops," the Mirza continued. "I am told how each is designed to the requirements of its trade with a sign outside. Yet I am saddened by the evidence in this great city of so many drunkards, madmen, and thieves."

"What makes you believe so, Excellency?" Sir Ouseley asked in evident surprise.

"Why, the fact that every shop door stays shut, opened only to customers by the shopkeeper himself. In our country, wares are left in the open to be looked at and handled by all who pass by."

"Surely there are thieves, even among the Persians," another guest suggested.

"Of course. But the one caught thieving loses the hand that plucked the goods. Thereby serving as a reminder to all of the wages of his sin."

The mention of a lost hand bought Japonica's thoughts unhappily back to the cause of her dejected state. "Surely not everyone who loses a hand is branded a thief. For instance, Lord Sinclair."

The Mirza's mild gaze came to bear on her with an unexpected intensity. When he spoke, it was in Persian. "Lord Sinclair is a great and excellent man. Every great man has a great many enemies. It is sometimes the unfortunate fate of the great to fall into the snare of the envious."

Japonica knew then that the Mirza was aware of exactly who Devlyn was, though she doubted he would ever be brought to mention it directly. "I do not see Lord Sinclair about in the city these days," she said, hoping her observation sounded light enough to pass as mere conversation among the company.

"He is no longer in the city, Lady Abbott." When Japonica turned toward Sir Ouseley, he added, "Lord Sinclair crossed the Channel for France some ten days ago. I thought you knew."

"No." Japonica looked away and briefly closed her eyes, feeling as if she had been stabbed. Devlyn, gone from London! Gone from England! Gone from her forever. Without a word! Something seemed to crack open inside her and spill out all her heat so that she felt a sudden chill.

"The *memsahib* suffers a chill," she heard someone say.

The Mirza clapped his hands and a servant sprang forth to offer her a second sable robe to add to the one already about her shoulders.

She took it not because she needed it but because

even in her shock she was aware that all eyes were upon her. They would correctly interpret her brooding as the reaction of a jilted lady if she did not quickly distract them.

She looked up with a smile. "How like Lord Sinclair to neglect to mention to his own family the fact of his departure. It is the manner of a seasoned soldier, I presume, to leave without notice when he is bound for enemy territory."

"I was under the impression that it was a personal matter, lady." When she looked at Sir Ouseley again, he smiled. "But have every confidence that he shall return unscathed. Our friend is a man of many resources. Intrepid, would you not agree, your Excellency."

"Alhamdolillah valmenah," the Mirza answered with heartfelt voice as he gazed speculatively at Japonica. "But come, we make the lady sad with all this talk of enemies and intrigue. It is the duty of every worthy gentleman to bring forth a smile from a lovely lady."

He turned to the gentleman on his right, an officer in the Light Bobs. "Tell me more of this thing called a pocket watch, Colonel. I see that every man in England, whether of high or low estate, carries one. I would obtain one that I may better appreciate the importance of the regulation of everything from eating and drinking to keeping appointments. This strict keeping of hours is not, I suspect, good for the constitution."

Japonica continued to listen respectfully and smile and even offer a word or two when it seemed required but all the while she felt as if the fire lit more than a year ago inside her had burned out. No amount of sable or scented heat from braziers or even the benevolent smile of a handsome Persian courtier would ever bring it back to life.

When at the end of an hour her dry and refreshed

things were brought to her, she was almost as grateful for the excuse to leave the Mirza's company as she had been to accept it. Without the visit she would not yet know what had become of Devlyn or know that her hopes and dreams were once and for all at an end. Whatever reason he had given for leaving the country, she knew the real one. There was nothing to do after all but carry on with her new plan. Once she held Jamie again, even the pain of Devlyn's loss would be bearable.

As she stepped up into the Mirza's carriage for the ride home, she found herself agreeing with the ambassador's assessment of England as a frigid and gloomy place in which she would never again be truly warm.

"They await your return in the front salon," Bersham said as Japonica entered the townhouse.

"I am too weary just now to deal with the Abbott sisters. Tell them I shall be present at dinner, where they may plague me to their hearts' content."

"They are not alone," Bersham suggested in a tone that caused Japonica to halt with her first foot on the main stairs. "Mr. Simmons is with them."

"The solicitor?"

"Yes, my lady."

"They've thought of some new stratagem with which to confound me," she murmured. "Very well."

She entered the salon without delay, deciding that it was better to march straight into the enemy ranks.

"Good evening, Hyacinthe. Laurel. Mr. Simmons," she greeted the three people who sat for that instant frozen like statues about the tea table. "If this is another attempt to rout me by ambush I fear you find me extremely out of temper. Come quickly to the point, if you must, before I show you all the door."

Hyacinthe shot to her feet and moved forward, a look of terrible anxiety on her long face. To Japonica's surprise, she was even wringing her hands. "I— we have something to tell you. Laurel has done something—horrid!"

It is an interesting thing, Japonica mused absently, to discover that distress in Hyacinthe's strong features was an almost unbearably pitiful sight.

"I did not know about it. I would have stopped Laurel. Despite our—my previous enmity, I beg you believe me, I would have stopped her."

"I doubt that," Japonica said with some asperity. "What am I accused of now? Frittering away the household budget on diamond tiaras?"

Hyacinthe glanced back over her shoulder before continuing. "We have reason to believe—that is, Laurel had reason to believe. That is, she stole one of your letters . . . ."

"*Bismallah!*" Japonica's sudden ejaculation of emotion backed Hyacinthe up two steps.

"Allow me." Mr. Simmons approached, blushing, whereas Hyacinthe seemed dipped in ashes. "If you would be kind enough to come and sit and hear me out, Lady Abbott."

"You shan't be here long enough for me to take my ease." Japonica's gaze moved past him to where Laurel sat like a plump Medusa, awaiting her to turn to stone. The girl had no idea that she had had enough shocks this day to inure her against any more spiteful manipulation.

"So then," Mr. Simmons began again, "If you will indulge me, my lady. Miss Laurel Abbott has bade me make certain inquires of a most delicate nature." He reddened to a degree that would seem to be painful. "If your ladyship would like to seat herself?

No? Then I will of necessity press on. The subject of which is a child—a son, if your ladyship will allow the distinction—who is purported to be living in Portugal . . ." His obsequious tone died before Japonica's withering stare.

"You made inquiries. I see." Japonica's gaze moved from the solicitor to Hyacinthe.

"Do you have a son?" Hyacinthe whispered.

"Yes." Japonica smiled, amazed by how easy it was to at last tell that truth.

"I knew it!" Laurel rushed up to stand before her, spite and vulgar delight swelling her almost pretty face to an ugly proportion. "You mean to disinherit us. That's your evil plan!"

"If that were so, I should have brought Jamie with me to London in the beginning. But I have no wish to disinherit anyone."

"I do not believe you! I do not!" Laurel was shouting now, spittle flying from her lips. "I knew from the beginning that you intended us harm. I knew it!"

She swung round on the two other people present. "Did I not tell both of you that she had come to steal Father's legacy from us? If her bastard is allowed to inherit, we will lose everything, even Croesus Hall!"

"You are hysterical!" Japonica said with dampening contempt, but Hyacinthe and Mr. Simmons were staring at her in such appalled affront that she knew she had lost every inch of dignified ground she had gained these last weeks.

"I won't allow it! I won't." Choking on her rage, Laurel sprang at Japonica, who swung quickly out of her path. A moment later, Laurel was past her and headed for the door.

"Where are you going?" Japonica called out, alarmed for the first time.

"None of your business. You can't stop me!" Laurel called defiantly.

For one desperate second Japonica thought about calling for footmen to overtake Laurel and lock her in her room. Before the thought was complete she knew it would be futile. In a few hours or days the events of the afternoon would be all over London.

"I will go and try to reason with her," Mr. Simmons said and, bowing quickly, rushed from the room.

"I hope he is successful," Hyacinthe said in a voice that seemed to be starched with anger.

"He will not be," Japonica answered.

Soon the gossip mills would pick up scraps of whispers and mix them with conjecture, speculation, and envious devising to grind out delicious, titillating scandal meat. Whether she liked it or not she was about to be the most notorious woman in London.

"What shall we do?' Hyacinthe questioned in a hushed tone that implied that for the first time in her life she was at a loss.

Japonica smiled slightly. "We shall do what a great portion of London is about to do. Go home for Christmas."

Chapter Twenty-One

Japonica sat on a stone bench from which she had swept a dusting of snow. It was so cold that the flakes did not dampen the stone. After a moment she rested her elbows on her knees and balanced her chin on her fists and stared out across the lawn of Croesus Hall.

She had never spent a quieter or sadder Christmas, not even in the first year after the death of her father. This, the third day of Christmas, had dawned with the promise of being much the same as the previous two.

It was not for lack of trying on her part. Guided by Bersham's advice she had seen to it that the mantels and urns and main stairway of Croesus Hall were adorned with the traditional English cuttings of wax-leaf holly with cheerful red berries, boughs of ivy, branches of bay, and cuttings of evergreens. Mistletoe decked doorways and swung in swags above the arches. Thick creamy tapers lit from a special candle brought home from church on Christmas Eve flickered in the breeze of the passageways against the ancient injunction that no fire be allowed to burn out between Christmas and the New Year lest ill-luck befall all those beneath the roof. The infusion of green fragrance turned the house from what once seemed a dusty dank pile of stones into a wondrous green oasis. Yet, on this morning, she preferred the brisk chill of the out-of-doors. She hoped the clear cold would whisk from her mind the dull thickness that matched her mood. Nothing else so far had worked.

Mummers had descended upon the Hall the night before, having heard that Croesus Hall was full to brimming with food and drink for the season. The unbidden guests danced and sang and performed a rude drama about a pair of waggish lovers caught in the machinations of Napoleon and Nelson and saved, preposterously, by St. George. That had made her laugh in spite of herself. Yet as the Wassail bowl was being ladled out afterwards she could not for an instant shake the foreboding that disaster lay as close as the ticking of the next minute on the clock.

Though no one directly mentioned it, all those who gathered beneath her roof each night were keenly aware of the conspicuous absence of Croesus Hall's rightful holder, Lord Devlyn Sinclair.

Japonica shuddered and closed her eyes as a sudden breeze disturbed the already fallen snow and swirled it up about her so that flakes flew and resettled in her hair and on her eyelashes. Devlyn was gone for good. In all the unhappiness and uncertainty that seemed to lie in the days ahead, she could be grateful for that one fact. She would be spared facing him when he learned, as he eventually would, of the son

she had sought to hide from him. By then she would
be far, far away.

A very subdued Laurel had appeared the evening
before Christmas Eve in the company of Mr. Simmons, who hied right back to London to be with his
lady wife for the holidays. Laurel had said not a word
about where she had been or with whom she had
spoken but had gone to her room and remained
there until Christmas morning. She had accompanied her sisters to breakfast and then sat wide-eyed
when her gift from Japonica was unwrapped to reveal
the floral bonnet she had once admired in Madame
Soti's window. Quite surprising everyone, she had
bolted from the room in tears.

After breakfast, six very solemn Abbott ladies
attended Christmas Day services. The pews had been
trimmed with sprigs of holly and yew tied with bright
red ribbons to turn the church into a miniature for-
est. The only flurry of excitement came when Alyssum
stood up in the Shrewsbury pew to lead the congregation in song. Her clear light soprano soared above
the congregation's chorus like a flute. The effect
she had upon the vicar was apparent to the entire
congregation. He had stared at her as though she
were the joy of Christmas morning incarnate.

At dinner that night, to which the vicar had been
invited, Japonica doubted he or Alyssum heard a single word other than the ones they spoke to one
another. There, perhaps, she realized with a dull kind
of satisfaction, was a match that would be accomplished without adhering to the codified behavior of
London's *haute ton*.

Japonica blinked away tears of melting snow. Once
she had foolishly wished for adventure. Certainly she
had had her fill this year. The happiness and grief,
sadness and joy were so bound up together that she

doubted she would ever be able to extract one from the other. Yet all that was behind her.

The heaviness in her heart today came in part from the fact she had heard nothing from Aggie since she sent the letter and bank draft ordering her to bring Jamie to London. Perhaps the winter weather had delayed Aggie's reply. Once the first of her nurse's letters caught up with her, they had come in the post almost daily. The last, those waiting for her at Croesus Hall upon her return, were dated before her own post should have arrived in Lisbon. If she received no reply by the New Year, she would simply sail for Lisbon on her own.

It occurred to her only the evening before that she was not entirely unhappy about her imminent ejection from London's polite society. Though she had not wanted to admit it, even to herself, her fear of society's rejection was based in pride and her own desire to be part of it. From the moment she tried on that gown in Madame Soti's she had begun to want for herself things that she had never before considered important. But the ways of society exacted a heavy toll. The pitfalls were many and sometimes arbitrary, and she was too independent to long keep from committing one faux pas or another.

So then, she did not need society's stamp to return to her home in Bushire and resume the life she had been living before her fateful visit to Baghdad. The truth about scandal was that it only held sway in the fear of exposure. Once uncovered by Laurel, even the news of Jamie's birth no longer daunted her. Her old neighbors would talk and wonder and conjecture about her return with a babe in her arms. But who among them would dare question her openly about Jamie's parentage? None! And in time, something or someone else's misfortune would become fresh gossip to titillate and entertain. She was a skilled herbalist whose knowledge could be put to use in trade. She was not afraid to roll up her sleeves and rejoin the mercantile marketplace that had once been her family's life.

And Jamie need not lack, as she had not, for being born a commoner. She need not squander the considerable funds her father had left her. By the time Jamie was grown, he would have a thriving business to inherit. It was not a coronet but she had never really wanted that for him. She would be enough family for him, she and Aggie. If only they would arrive in England!

She was aware of a traveling coach passing in the distance long before she realized that it was coming directly toward Croesus Hall. In fact, not until she heard the blast of the postillion's horn, used to alert a household to an arriving coach, did she fully understand that she was about to have visitors.

She bolted to her feet, hoping against reason that this was Aggie bringing Jamie to her. But she quickly saw that the conveyance was not a mail coach or even a regular highway coach. The bright colors of the coach's compartment and its contrasting undercarriage were plainly on view as the coach made the final turn onto the drive. This was a private coach bearing on its door panels the shield of nobility. Still she hurried across the lawn to meet it as it rocked to a stop before the main entrance.

She scarcely had time to catch her breath before the postillion opened the coach door. The lady who stepped down from the interior wore an emerald green gown overlaid with a long silk cloak of scarlet superfine lined with fur. Her traveling bonnet was made of green and scarlet velours and sported two enormous white egret feathers.

"Lady Simms," Japonica greeted with an expression that was not entirely delighted. "This is a surprise."

"No more for you than I." Lady Simms looked up at the façade of Croesus Hall. "Gad! This Gothic pile never changes. Each time I visit, I expect Cromwell and his troops to descend upon me from the entry to lop off my head. You will need to brighten it up, Lady Abbott. I know the very architect, a protegé of Adam. I don't imagine Devlyn sees himself living here year around but you will find the adjustments the fellow suggests ever so accommodating to female sensibilities."

Japonica let the lady's chatter roll over her head until her guest came to take a breath where she could insert, "I regret to inform you, Lady Simms, but Lord Sinclair is not in residence at present. He is away in France."

"In France? But that is preposterous. Did I not but yesterday evening receive a letter in his own hand asking me to come this very day to meet him at Croesus Hall? Indeed, I did. But you look pale, child. Whatever is wrong?"

"Nothing," Japonica said faintly. "It is only that I had not been informed to expected so illustrious a guest." Devlyn was back? And coming here? "Are you certain he is expected today?"

Lady Simms turned a supercilious gaze on her hostess. "I may sport feathers in my bonnet but that does not make me a goose!" Immediately she relented with a sweet smile. "I should be quite put out, too, were I in your place and had not been informed of the arrival of guests. But here I am and we will make the best of it. I should be quite vexed with Dev myself had his missive not given me excuse to take leave of my husband's relatives. They are Scots. They come in lots of a dozen, don't you know. And a madder band of drunken gambling revelers you never met.

Night and day, they make no end to it! Fatigue plagues me constantly."

"Allow me to extend to you the hospitality of Croesus Hall," Japonica said wearily for it seemed, in any case, Lady Simms had come to stay.

"Spiced wine would be nice," Lady Simms commented as she climbed the stairs and entered the house. "Or a nice glass of sherry with biscuits. Did I say the Scots drink nothing but that noxious brew they make themselves and call whiskey! One becomes quite foxed without a pleasurable sip to be had at any point of consumption. I don't know but that the abundance of the distilled brew doesn't account for their decided lack of humor. Ah, this is better." She breezed from the entry into the main salon where a fire blazed. At the far end, the Shrewsbury sisters sat playing a quiet game of cards. "Ah, the Shrewsbury Menagerie," she mouthed in distaste.

The girls rose at once, resting their cards on the tabletop.

"Lady Simms, what a pleasant surprise," Hyacinthe intoned in an exact reflection of Japonica's own greeting. "Permit me to reacquaint you with my sisters." As she called each of their names, the girls dipped a curtsey and smiled and murmured appropriate greetings in well-modulated tones.

When they were done, Lady Simms turned to Japonica with raised brows and an arrested expression. "I am astonished. There must beat the heart of a Tartar behind your sweet façade. I made a bet with Leigh that you would be under the hatches with these harridans long before now." She reached for her lorgnette, dangling by a ribbon from her gown, and flicked it up to inspect each of the girls separately. As she did so she mouthed softly, "Quite remarkable! Exceptional! Astonishing!" When she was done, she turned to Japonica. "To a one, they seem in every way presentable."

"Thank you, Lady Simms." A week ago those words of confirmation of her achievement would have made Japonica warm with pride. Now they only echoed with the hollowness of a victory that could never be enjoyed. Devlyn was coming to Croesus Hall!

"Did Lord Sinclair say when we should expect him?"

"I never attempt to know precisely when the dear boy will show up." Her gaze flicked over Japonica's dress. "You would do well to change into something more cheerful, I dare say. An English gentleman likes to believe his household waits upon nothing so much as the hour of his return."

"Then England must be filled with disappointed gentlemen," Japonica said with some asperity. She turned to her stepdaughters. "Hyacinthe, ring for sherry and biscuits. Alyssum, show Lady Simms to a comfortable chair. Peony, find her a lap robe to dispel the chill of her journey." She allowed her gaze to pass unchecked over Laurel, who hung back with eyes downcast. "Now if you will excuse me, I will change into something . . ." she glanced at Lady Simms's stylish gown, "more appropriate for entertaining our guest."

"Stubborn pride," she heard Lady Simms's voice say softly at her back.

"I will pack and leave at once," Japonica said to herself as she reentered the entry hall. There was nothing to prevent her from simply walking away from Croesus Hall and all it represented. She could lose herself in the metropolis that was London as easily as a mouse in a hayloft. She would not be missed. All involved would expel a breath of relief, including her.

Her footsteps slowed as she noticed the front door

was again thrown open and through it could be seen the shadow of a second coach on the drive. A moment later, a man emerged from the shadow and she came to a halt, transfixed by recognition.

Devlyn had come to Croesus Hall! God forgive her, she still could not look upon him without such emotion that she felt choked by it. Tears rose in her eyes. He looked better than she had ever seen him, whereas she had never felt more wretched. He wore traveling clothes of a heavy great coat and chamois breeches and riding boots. His hair, a little longer, lifted in the breeze. His color was high and the easy smile that rode his expression took away years of care and strain. How could he be so happy? Of course, he did not yet know that she stood inside the doorway. Perhaps he thought he had frightened her away. Perhaps he hoped she had thrown herself into the Thames and had done with her miserable life that counted for nothing with him.

She felt her world turn over on itself and the madness she had so often spoken of in passing had at last taken hold. For he had turned back to reach through the coach door and when he faced forward again, he had in his arms a squirming bundle.

"No!" she whispered. She put up a hand as though to blot out the image but she could not look away. Like the condemned figures in paintings of the Last Judgment, she was drawn by an inexplicable horror to look upon the confirmation of her own damnation. The wind caught the upper edge of the blanket and flung it back from the cherubic face of her son.

The last thing Devlyn expected upon entering his ancestral home was to find Japonica Abbott spread upon the entry carpet in a faint. But his surprise did not last beyond the realization. He could surmise what had occurred and why. Cursing himself for not better judging the moment, he thrust his son into Bersham's startled arms and knelt down on the rug beside her.

He had just lifted up her unresponsive body and propped her head against his chest when Jamie let loose a wail of fright.

"Bounce him on your shoulder, man!" Devlyn ordered without a backward glance.

He noticed a dozen inconsequential things about her as he gathered her up against his chest. The satin of her cheek was cool as ice. Yet how warm and soft her weight felt against him, so natural and good he cold not resist embracing her more strongly than was absolutely necessary to hold her upright. She still smelled of henna, her personal perfume that, despite their surroundings, possessed the potency to curl deep in his loins as desire. He would have liked nothing better than to scoop her up and carry her away to a place of privacy where he might kiss her awake and then go on kissing her until they had satisfied every question and healed every hurt between them with loving touches. But, of course, that could not be.

Even as he bent to her the babe's keening wail drew curious people from all directions; among them, his own aunt.

Lady Simms sailed into the entry with a glass of sherry in one hand and a biscuit in the other. When she spied the tableau of the butler with babe and Devlyn on his knees beside Japonica, she stopped short.

"Dev, dear boy. Whatever are you about? And who is that sniveling brat?"

Devlyn smiled up at her. "Lady Simms, allow me to introduce to you James Michael Abbott, my son."

"Your son?" Lady Simms's astonishment lit her

whole face. She glanced from the wailing child to the lady being revived at her feet and back at Devlyn. "You fool! You thorough-going rogue!"

She lifted her wineglass and threw the contents in Devlyn's face.

Some of the sherry splashed across Japonica's face, rousing her. She lay blinking for a few senseless moments, staring up into the shadowed face of the man she had hoped never to see again. And then she remembered why he was here. He had Jamie!

A surge of panic spurred by pure maternal instinct made her reach up and grip his lapel. "You can't have him! Jamie belongs to me!"

"Ye're holding him too tight," Aggie cautioned as Jamie fretted and wiggled in his mother's lap.

"I don't care," Japonica answered, but attempted to accommodate her son's bid for freedom. "I may never put him down again."

"*Och*, ye will." Aggie smiled as she laid out fresh clothing for the child. They had been given the small room next to the dowager's bedchamber, which was large enough for Aggie and the wet nurse. Jamie was sleeping in his mother's bed. In the two days since their arrival they had been closeted away as if the rest of the world did not exist, yet both women were very aware that it did. Lord Sinclair had come to the door three times each day only to be turned away. And each time they felt the mounting anger in his tone and knew it would soon boil over into action.

If Japonica would not see reason on her own, Aggie decided it was time she forced her grand brave girl to it.

She stepped over to smile at the mother and child. "He's been after wanting yer arms about him these last weeks. Neither nanny nor I could long do to please him. *Och*, child, ye're not to grieve every time I speak."

"I'm sorry." Japonica wiped away a tear with the back her of hand. "I just can't believe that you and Jamie are really here."

"Ye've Lord Sinclair to thank for that." Aggie saw her mistress stiffen at the mention of his name, but went right on. "Without his lordship's aid we'd be in Portugal still. Never saw a man who could barter better. Yer father, rest his soul, included. And what language doesn't he speak? Portuguese to the Lisbon authorities, Basque and French as we traveled. I don't wonder but he could charm his way out of Hell."

Ignoring this, Japonica picked Jamie up under his arms and held him up so that only his toes brushed her lap. He chirped in pleasure to be held upright and pedaled his feet in the air, his pink mouth agape in a happily crooked smile that melted her heart. He was heavier than she remembered, his arms and legs filled out with deep dimples in his knees and thighs and wrists and elbows. And his once nearly bald head was sprouting tufts of dark curly hair. "He's grown, so, Aggie. I'd not have recognized him had you not been with him."

"Nae, lass, ye'd always know yer son. As did his father. His lordship never asked. Just took one look at our Jamie and then picked him up and said, 'Hello, son,' just like that. Mild as ye might ever want. Jamie took right to him."

Japonica looked away from Aggie. "He's not Jamie's father."

From the moment she spied Jamie in Devlyn's arms, an unreasoned fear gripped her that she might somehow now lose him to his powerful aristocratic father. She read the gazettes. Men could accuse their wives of adultery and have them locked away in prison or the madhouse with none to gainsay them. How easy would it be for a lord to take a child away from a commoner who the world would see as his low-born mistress. She did not know if she really believed Devlyn capable of such perfidy, but she could not endure even the possibility.

Aggie continued folding the babe's linen. "I said his lordship didn't ask me any questions. But he had a whale of a tale to tell. All about his lost memory and how he was once known as the *Hind Div.*" She cast a sidelong glance at the younger woman. "But I suppose ye'd be knowin' all about it."

"Not all of it," Japonica answered shortly and set Jamie back onto her lap. "Jamie's wet."

Aggie tossed her a fresh linen square. "Ye should hear his lordship out, lass. He's most eager to talk with ye."

"You better than anyone, Aggie, should know why I cannot."

"He's the *Hind Div* and I ken what that means to ye. But there's been such doin's since ye came to London that changes things a bit. The *Hind Div's* become a good and proper aristocrat what can give ye a good life. I ken ye've a bairn that's pined away these last weeks for a mother he scarce can recognize despite his longing for her. I ken his mother's in love with the man who gave him life . . . ."

"I do not love him," Japonica cut in, but Aggie didn't even pause.

". . . And Jamie has a sire who, without knowing for certain the child was his, crossed two war-torn countries to seek him out. That's what I ken. Jamie needs a father and ye a husband."

"Not this man."

"*Och,* well, if ye're goin' to be particular. Is it the cut of his coat ye don't like? Or is it his empty cuff?"

"You know it is not that," Japonica answered indignantly.

"I will nae lie to ye to spare yer feelings. Ye've the good of others besides yerself to think of. Ye've the look of a lass in love and he's the look of a man with a short leash on his temper. Simplest done is pair ye off and let time work out the rest."

Japonica shook her head. "He—he doesn't love me. We were together in London, once. He deserted me before he found out about Jamie."

"*Och,* that were simply mended, if ye were of a mind to make it so. A man's not a great complex beast, lass. It's for women to worry and fuss and devise and consider. A man's little more than what is in his heart and between his legs. If ye engage the one the other will come along behind."

Japonica smiled in despite of her reluctance to continue the subject. "You make men sound like dumb animals."

"*Och!* Dumb they aren't. Blathering on and on, full of shouts and oaths and threats. But that's all racket and ruckus." Aggie put her hand on Japonica's shoulder. "He's a man that loves ye. I would nae steer ye toward him if I believed else. Ye've only to see him with Jamie. He's a natural father and will become better as the days go on. But ye must act soon, lass. Men, for all they will deny it, are but thin-skinned creatures. They'll run away if their pride is bruised too often with no salve of a woman's lovin' to comfort them. Give him what he wants and what ye need, and what Jamie deserves."

Japonica squared her shoulders, a bleak expression on her face. "I cannot. It will never work."

Aggie shook her head. She had known Japonica since she was a wee bairn. She could be as stubborn in her indecision as any man who held to his heartfelt conviction. "Ye will have to speak to him sometime. Today, tomorrow, or the one after."

Japonica said nothing for a moment. There were

so many things she did want to say to Devlyn but she feared her strength was not equal to the daunting task of facing him again. "How did he know, Aggie? About Jamie."

"Isn't that something ye should be asking him?" When she did not answer Aggie clucked her tongue. " 'Twas one of yer stepdaughters. She wrote him after stealing one o' me letters."

"Laurel." Japonica sighed in wonder. There seemed no end to the girl's treachery.

"Aye, that's the one his lordship calls The Great Goose."

"She is a only a silly spoiled girl."

"She is a coldhearted, vicious creature," Aggie pronounced without mercy. "If she cannae ken the error of her ways, she'll poison every bit of happiness to come her way the rest o' her days."

Much as she resisted the idea, Japonica suspected Aggie spoke no more than the truth. "More's the pity. For I now think her sisters will do quite well in their world."

"No little thanks to ye." Aggie smiled at her startled expression. "His lordship spent many an hour in the coach holding the babe. With little else to do, he talked a great deal about ye."

Japonica blushed and set her son back on her knee. "I do not care for Lord Sinclair's opinion of me."

"I don't doubt. So I will nae be offering it."

There was a sharp rap on the door, followed by the imperious voice of Lady Simms saying, "Open this door at once!"

Japonica rose and went to it, released the bolt, and opened it a fraction.

Lady Simms's eyes narrowed when she noted Japonica's caution. "I have come to make myself known to my grandson. I do not thank you for the title. I shall be very cross about it for some little while.

But I do not intend the babe to suffer for his mother's insensitivity in attaching the odious appellation of grandparent to me." She stuck the silver point of her walking stick into the breech of the door. "Stand aside, Japonica, or I will do you a mischief, yet!"

Japonica saw a shadow move along the hallway beyond Lady Simms and her congenial expression altered. "Madame, do I have your word that you will not by trickery allow Lord Sinclair entrance, should I invite you in?"

Lady Simms eyed her with faint distaste. "I try to like you, girl. But you make it demmed difficult in this moment. I will not give my word and you will not ask it of me. Dev is the gentlest soul in the world, yet you treat him as a roué and a scoundrel when he is willing to make an honest woman of you."

"I beg your pardon . . ."

"Enough!" Devlyn stepped up behind his aunt and thrust his hand into the opening before Japonica could slam it. He glowered at her through the narrow space, the one golden eye she could see, blazing. "Madame, my patience is at an end. I wish to speak with you, privately. If you will not have it so, then we shall shout at one another through this damn door, but you will hear me out. Now! Which shall it be?"

Caught by circumstance, Japonica released the door and backed away. But she did not try to hide her fury as first Lady Simms sailed past her in a confection of lavender and crème and then Lord Sinclair presented himself, wearing a new suit of black superfine and looking as daunting as thunder clouds from a tropical typhoon.

"You will need a coat, bonnet, and stout shoes," he said without preamble. "I will wait for you in the entry below. You have five minutes." He touched his watch fob for emphasis. "Five."

"What a fine fellow he has become," Lady Simms

remarked when Devlyn had strode out. "Never seen him give a fig for style before." She gave Japonica a sharp glance. "This is your doing. Do not make a hash of it, girl."

"Now then," she said with a smile as she turned to Aggie. "Let me hold this little monkey who regales the household with so many squawks and screeches and wails at all hours."

Precisely five minutes later, Japonica walked beside Lord Sinclair as he led her down a walkway swept clear of snow to a small gazebo at the back of the rear garden. She was surprised to discover that shutters enclosed it and that a small fire had been lit at its center.

Devlyn watched her closely as they walked along, though he made certain she never caught his eye. She seemed smaller than he remembered, more self-contained, beyond his reach. In a few short weeks she had gone from the self-effacing manner of a governess to the untouchable regal bearing of an aristocrat. While he found the first annoying, he detested the latter. Neither was she the woman he had first glimpsed in all her glory at the Mirza's dinner and then later that night held in his arms.

He wanted very badly to break down this aloof demeanor but he knew if he pushed her too quickly she would flee and he would lose her once and for all.

"Now then," he said when she had seated herself in one of the two chairs that had been placed near the flames. "I would know your plans."

"Plans?" His question was not one Japonica expected. "I'm leaving."

"I see." He stood a little ways away, as if he did

not wish to come too near. "And you will do this in a month, perhaps, or when the spring thaw sets in?"

"Tonight." The declaration surprised her almost as much as it did him.

His dark brows shot up his forehead. "You're in no fit state to leave tonight."

Japonica folded her mittened hands together in her lap. "I think I may decide what I can and cannot do."

He stared at her for a moment. "Where do you propose to go?" His voice was unemotional again but he had grown very still, his deeply hooded golden eyes the only thing alive in his face.

"This has nothing to do with you," she said crossly. "Despite appearances, and your unwelcome interference, it has only to do with my desire to be away to my new life."

"Then you can at least wait until morning."

"No!" Japonica stood up and turned away from him. "I cannot in good conscience spend another night beneath a roof you share."

Devlyn heard in that confession the first glimmer of hope. "Very well. I will take myself off."

"You certainly shall not!" She turned back to him, a furious expression on her face. "You are lord of the manor. I am the interloper. An untenable situation that will only be made more suspect by every hour we share a residence."

"Neither you nor I have ever given a good goddamn what others may think of us. That much admit."

"You need not swear at me," she began.

"I will shout the roof down with invective if you persist in missish behavior!" he roared back.

"You may do as you wish," she countered primly. "This is your home."

He took a step toward her. "There are times when

I think I should simply abduct you. Then in peace we can roar and shout at one another until we are ready to assuage this passion that passes so often as anger between us."

She rose hastily from her seat. "You dare say that to me? After you now know all that has occurred between us? Even in Baghdad?" she added as a whisper.

He ignored this. "You must at least hear me out. I can imagine what you have thought of me." Her arch expression made him recant. "Very well, perhaps not entirely. But I am not insensitive to the sorrows and humiliation life can heap upon the unprotected. I cannot think what Lord Abbott was about, to send you directly into my path."

Japonica started. "What do you mean, your path?"

"That is right. You never knew what was in the message you brought me." His jaw hardened. "I wish to God you had. It might have kept you from me."

She hunched a shoulder in protective instinct. "You speak in riddles."

"Then let the riddle be answered." He took from his pocket and unfolded a small piece of parchment and held it out.

She read it twice before looking up at him with absolute astonishment in every curve and angle of her face. "What does this mean?"

" 'Tis plainly written."

She gazed at the paper a third time before saying, "You expect me to believe that Lord Abbott sent me to seek the *Hind Div's* help as a ruse in order to dangle me before your eyes like a trinket in a market stall?"

He smiled at her phrasing. "Diabolical, wasn't it?"

"Convenient. Too convenient." She loosed the letter from nerveless fingers and let it flutter to the floor. "I will not believe Lord Abbot would be so callous as to invite you to sample the wares he set before you."

For the first time Devlyn looked away from her. "I cannot remember even now all that happened. Once I discovered the letter I was able to piece together fragments of memory with the tale you told me." He looked back at her, his expression for once absent of hauteur. "It is no excuse but I believe that I must have been intoxicated by wine or the pipe to act so against decency after reading this missive."

"You did not read it."

His head jerked back. "What?"

Japonica's lips thinned. "When I gave the note to you, you tossed it aside. I was not certain you ever read it. Then, later, it did not seem to matter."

"Bismallah!" Devlyn bit out another curse. "It shows little to my credit but I am relieved to know that I did not act—knowing."

He again looked away from her. "The *Hind Div* was a law unto himself. By design a diabolical being: ruthless, treacherous, and without mercy. No less a creation would his equally merciless enemies fear. But I swear that as much as any man may know himself I would not willingly have debauched a virgin."

"Of course."

Her dull tone brought him up short again. "You think I am dissembling, do you?"

"I neither know nor care." She put a hand to her forehead and rubbed. "I dare say you were drunk. You drugged us both. But you were ready to do it! Even if you believed me to be the assassin you accused me of being, you were prepared to do to some other female what you did to me."

Devlyn had no answer for that.

"I don't bear you any grudge," she said wearily, wondering why he did not just walk away and leave her with her desperate thoughts. "I think I am past hating people, for there are so many to despise. There is Laurel, stupid foolish girl. She did not really understand the consequences of her actions. And now there is Lord Abbott." Indignation flared in her dark eyes. "To dare presume that he could choose at will a husband for me and send me to him unannounced and unprepared! He must have married me out of pity once we heard you were dead."

"I don't think pity was the motive," Devlyn said softly. "No man who truly knew you would need an excuse to want you."

Japonica did not meet his eye behind that speech. She could feel her anger giving way when she most needed its steadying influence. She crossed her arms before her chest. "It doesn't matter now. Nothing matters but that I made a mistake and compounded it by every decision since. I mean to go away. Jamie deserves better than London society would serve him."

Devlyn felt utterly defeated by her argument. It was one he had yet to solve. "I will not try to stop you going. Just tell me where."

"No." Japonica began to sway and gripped the back of a chair to steady herself. The glare of enmity she shot him prevented Devlyn from offering his aid. "I see no reason to tell you. I do not imagine you will see me again. Jamie needs his mother. He has been too long without her while she has tried to right a world that seems determined to go to hell in its own time." She swayed again, this time her voice all but inaudible. "I am so tired. I can't tell you how tired I am."

This time Devlyn did act, moving quickly to take her by the arm and force her to sit again.

When he had, he knelt down before her and took her chin firmly in his good hand. "Quite the little martyr, aren't you?" he pronounced. " 'I am so tired.

I can't tell you how tired,' " he mimicked her die-away tone and was rewarded by the rise of hot color into her too-pale complexion. Anger was better than despair.

Japonica pushed his hand away from her face. "I don't ever want to see you again." She looked away from him, feeling as if she were letting go of her last chance at safety. "I don't want anything of yours. I will make my own way. I will leave in the morning with Jamie and Aggie. I ask only one favor of you."

She turned to look back to face the man so close to her she had only to reach out to touch his cheek. Gazing back at her in mild bemusement was the one man on earth she should despise and loathe, and the only man on earth she had ever loved. "You must make no attempt to find me. Ever."

Devlyn smiled into her desperate expression. She was not indifferent to him if she could look so bereft in making that request. "Take your son away if you must. But know he is mine, too. And that in time I will come to claim what is mine. *All* that is mine."

"I wish you would not," she said in a small voice, and closed her eyes.

"I know you do. But in a while we will both feel different." He touched her cheek briefly and though she flinched he held his palm to her cool cheek a moment longer. "I think you have never been properly courted and I think I should learn something of the art."

When she lifted her head, he smiled straight into her startled brown gaze. "Do you think I do not know how difficult all this has been? That it is too much even now?" He reached forward and kissed her so softly she felt as if her heart would fly right up out of her chest. "Until another time, *bahia.*"

Chapter Twenty Two

Surrey, April

The morning was mild but promised to grow ripe with the heat and humidity of a temperate spring. The countryside bloomed with color both native and cultivated, from the tufts of red campion to new-green fern fronds and hedgerows of pink rhododendron. Rows of yellow and white daffodils planted along the carriageway to the main house nodded in the passing breeze. In the nearby copse irises thrust up crisp stalks that ended in stately ornate blossoms of blue and purple and gold. Within the ellipse, intricately petaled camellias bloomed full as any rose garden. Forced orange and lemon trees arranged in pots flanked the steps to Croesus Hall, filling the April air with citrus perfumes.

All of this and many other plans had been undertaken to provide a picturesque setting for the wed-

ding that was about to take place. As unorthodox as
it was unexpected, the middle Shrewsbury daughter,
Miss Alyssum Abbott, was about to be joined in wedded bliss to Mister Charles Repington, youngest son
of a baronet and presently rector at Ufton Nervet.

The villagers all agreed it was Miss Alyssum's lovely
song followed by his stirring sermon on the Holy
Family on Christmas morning that had set in motion
the eventualities of this happy occasion. A few sticklers whispered that it wasn't quite proper that the
two elder sisters had not gone off first, though. The
rest were only too happy to share in the joy of the
rector and his lovely bride.

Then, too, it had gotten about that the Honorable
Fernlow Hepple had been quite helpful to Miss Hyacinthe Abbott in her hothouse preparations for the
wedding. He had been seen riding over to Croesus
Hall some half dozen times to offer advice. The village
gossips were abuzz with conjecture about when a second set of nuptial banns might by posted from the
Shrewsbury county seat.

The two avid horticulturists were, thankfully, blissfully unaware of the vulgar speculation. The likely
connection had not proceeded so far in either of
their reticent minds. And there was plenty else to
occupy anyone with a direct connection to Croesus
Hall on this day. Most particularly involved in the
preparations was the lady of the manor herself.

Japonica stood in the sheltering shade of an oak
watching the best horsemen among her male guests
play polo in the park behind Croesus Hall. It was a
raucous game with many shouts and cries from the
players, crashing of mallets, and whinnying of their
mounts. An equal number of huzzahs and squeals
arose from their appreciative audience. The game
was just one of the entertainments provided for the

weekend party of guests who had come up from London for the celebration.

The Illustrious Stranger, as *The Morning Post* often referred to Mirza Hassan, was easily distinguished among the players and not only because of his long curly beard. He wore a riding costume of a red fur-trimmed short jacket and a long shirt of green quilted silk, billowing trousers, and gaiters over his boots. A scarlet sash wrapped his waist and his conical peaked hat was emblazoned with the crescent moon. His brilliance stood out even among the sharp coats and expensive finery of the many English military officers who had taken the field.

"See! Oh there, Jamie! Do you see how the ball speeds along when it's struck?" Japonica asked the child within her arms.

But Jamie's attention was otherwise engaged. He had spotted Peony's new pet, a liver-and-white cocker spaniel puppy that scampered toward them across the lawn. Having learned to crawl with great proficiency, he was anxious to try out his skill against that of the puppy and so he struggled to be put down.

Aware of his desire, Japonica bent and placed him in the grass.

Spying a potential playmate of the right size, the puppy dashed over and licked Jamie full across his face. In turn Jamie reached out and caught a fistful of dangling puppy ear and tugged until the puppy yelped.

"Oh no. You must be gentle, sweeting," she admonished as she pried his chubby fingers from the velvet-soft ear.

With the sense that discretion might be the better part with this new friend, the puppy bounced in and out of Jamie's reach so that he was forced to try out his hand-and-knee locomotion.

As she watched her son crawl away on the soft bed

of thick grass, Japonica was glad that she had not left before she had seen England in flower.

She had Lady Simms to thank for that. The eminently capable lady had first pointed out the unnecessary hardship Jamie would endure if she were to insist upon another long journey in winter. Japonica had not the heart for it, but she did not see an alternative. That was when the lady's wit had shone brightest.

"Dev tells me you fear the revelation of your natural child to London society," the lady had said the day Japonica planned to leave Croesus Hall. "I do not see the necessity of it. Aside from his family, who is to question his birth? No one who does not know the complication of it, and none do but family. Laurel has admitted as much. Dem foolish child! I should like to shake her twice a day, just to remind her of the harm she nearly caused. Scandal is all very well for the Hanovers. They are, after all, of vulgar Teutonic bloodlines. But it shall never taint our family line while I draw breath!"

Japonica smiled at the memory of the owl-eyed stare Lady Simms submitted her to during that fateful interview. "You are forgiven your error in breeding this once. As it was Dev who you helped to indiscretion, I judge it could not be helped. For I vow, I adore the rascal! As I will come to love his progeny. When he is in breeches, Jamie shall come and live with me for a month every summer."

To her question of Jamie's supposed parentage and what it would mean to Lord Sinclair if it became public, Lady Simms had been equally blithe.

"Dev assures me he shall have the matter in hand in due course. Meantime, I must return to London before Leigh sends the Light Bobs for me. I shall put it about that as the viscountess Shrewsbury has been happily reunited with family so little time—the perfect Christmas gift I vow!—she must decline all invitations. Who should question your desire to rusticate? I will further distribute your cards about town with the appropriate PPC writ upon them. What? It is French shorthand for 'I am leaving.' So much more fashionable when it's continental, don't you know."

Japonica had her doubts, but who could voice any objection when that lady had the floor?

If there was a hair in the cream it was in consideration of where Japonica and Jamie would live. Adamant was the only word to express her insistence that she not share a roof with Lord Sinclair for even another four-and-twenty hours.

Lady Simms again intervened by devising a plan with the viscount whereby Japonica, her son and the Abbott girls would remain at Croesus Hall. "Quite sensible when one has a babe to care for," she had assured Japonica. "Dev will live in town. He's never been one to rusticate for long."

And so it was agreed.

And just to make certain that the Croesus residence would settle into amiable family life, Lady Simms sent back from London an invitation for Laurel to winter with her. Only too glad to be away from constant reminders of her duplicity and reckless acts, Laurel packed and left before New Year's Day.

In one of her more recent letters in the constant stream she had begun sending Japonica after Christmas, Lady Simms had written:

"I fancy I was meant to have a brood, had Providence provided. Thus denied my own, I must be about the business of picking up the leavings of others and setting them to rights. Contrary to my first opinion, Laurel has proved to be biddable enough. Once she understood that her rations would be cut when she defied me! The girl lost quite some two sizes as she Adjusted.

Amazing what the want of a meringue can accomplish for one's Attitude. Having only the Past Experience of rearing a boy I now fancy myself to have become a Prime Whip in the management of Young Ladies!''

All had been nicely settled, Japonica mused as she kept a vigilant eye on her son. So nicely, in fact, that but for the occasional hamper sent by Lord Sinclair from Fortnum and Mason, she might have forgotten his existence. If she had been so inclined.

Instead she could not keep from brooding occasionally over his last private words to her. He had said that she had never been properly courted and he knew nothing of the art. Nothing else. Not that he intended to remedy the oversight, mend his lack, or even that he still had feelings for her. He had kissed her. And then made some vague, and to her womanly heart, evasive mention of "another time."

"What other time?" Japonica murmured to herself. She had courted patience, telling herself that the fact of his kiss was enough to keep her courage up. But more than three months had passed with only the briefest of weekly notes from him, apprising her of Shrewsbury estate matters and making inquiries about his "son's" health. A kiss was not words and the warmth of it cooled with each passing day. If this long distant politeness was his idea of courtship, it did not serve to secure her feelings or her happiness. The fact that he was now in residence, along with the whole company of gentlemen who had accompanied him to the wedding, including the Mirza, only made her frantic with frustration. So far, they had exchanged not a single private word. One moment she was certain the next time she was near him she would corner him and demand an explanation of his intentions. The next, when he did appear in a room full of people she all but ran and hid.

"He seemed in no hurry to speak with me," she murmured to herself, indignation fueling her thoughts. She had been as brazen as she knew how the night she had invited him up to her room. Where that courage had come from she would never again know. But she was done with taking the lead in the matter. If this reserved manner was indicative of his new style, she did not like it one tiny bit!

In the matter of Jamie he was far from reticent. According to Aggie, he had made thrice daily visits to the nursery to hold and cuddle his son. With each passing hour her resentment of that fact grew. But what to do about it all?

"If he expects me to speak first he shall have a long gray beard to keep him company!"

Japonica allowed her thoughts to drift off as she ambled after her son who had decided to show an interest in the polo fields after all, and had headed off in that general direction at a rapid crawl.

When the polo match was ended, most of the company strolled off toward the luncheon spread beneath a striped canopy with libations and such sustenance as might suit the fancy of her guests. That was where Aggie waited to take Jamie to the wet nurse. When she had handed him over, Japonica turned abruptly away from the crowd of well wishers, hoping to elude Lord Sinclair.

But Devlyn had already spotted her from his superior height astride his mount. In fact, he had kept an eye on her all morning to such a degree that he had missed a strategic shot when for an instant her actions diverted his whole attention from the game. She had bent over to pick up Jamie, presenting him with a magnificent view of the full curves of her flared hips revealed by the tight pull of her slim skirt. The sight pulled him up short and the game swooped past him and moved on.

When she stood up with the child in her arms, the breeze molded her skirts to her slender form and tousled her bright hair that she wore on this occasion in fashionable ringlets. He could not hear what she said to her son—his son. But he saw the babe's mouth open in a whoop of joy and then watched as she nuzzled the babe under his chin with her nose. The portrait of mother and child stirred something within him deeper than lust. It stirred up the longing to be part of that tableau. No, to have the right to be part of it.

The sight remained with him through the rest of the game with the certainty that she was all he could ever want in a lady.

But what of her and the kind of man she deserved? He had left Croesus Hall the last day of December uncertain he would make her a fit spouse, never mind a proper father for their child.

He had not even begun to understand the sort of person she really was until Laurel's note supplied him with the key. Written in spite in the hopes of doing mischief, that letter had saved him from making a terrible error in judgment. Going to Portugal to fetch the boy to her seemed the only way to begin to make amends. Then he was going to tell her his feelings for her after he showed her the letter that he found, from Lord Abbott. But she would not listen to him then and he could not blame her. In his self-pity he had treated her shabbily, standing her up for the opera without even a word of regret. And so he had left Croesus Hall on New Year's Day, hoping against reason that she would by word or action ask to see him again. The months passed and she did not.

"Stubborn," he muttered under his breath. And

so he had come here this weekend to find out for himself if there was a future for them.

Perhaps he would never regain his memory but the loss no longer plagued him. He had no need to drive himself half-mad with pain from his frustrated efforts to remember. With that realization the headaches had subsided. The most important piece of his past was standing in the field a little distance away. He had only to claim it.

When he saw her making a hurried if dignified retreat across the yard he spurred his horse forward. "Lady Abbott!"

As the rider approached Japonica lifted a hand to shade her eyes from the glare. What she saw startled her. Muscular and deeply tanned, he looked much as he had the first time she saw him. Four months growth had lengthened his hair into soft locks that curled about his temples and over his ears. All that was missing from his countenance were the cheetah stripes of the *Hind Div.*

When he reined in beside her, she nodded slightly in greeting. "Lord Sinclair."

"Lady Abbott." He could have wished for more warmth in her tone. But that would come, he told himself. For the moment he was content to gaze down at her and enjoy the view. She wore a high-waisted gown in a becoming shade of spring green and her hair seemed to have caught fire from the sun.

Disconcerted by his gaze, she asked, "Did you enjoy the game?"

"Not as much as my view at present," he answered.

Japonica frowned. It wasn't like Devlyn to make casual flattery. "Don't let me keep you. There will be hot water and towels aplenty to refresh you at the house." But she saw she was not so easily to escape his company, for the Mirza came galloping up to

Devlyn's side with a broad grin nestled in his black beard.

"You are to be commended, Lord Sinclair, for your great proficiency on the field." The Mirza did not seem in the slightest winded by his efforts. "Many a player would not be able to keep his seat in the midst of so mighty a fray."

"I have inspiration to guide me," Devlyn said with a quick glance down at Japonica. "It was suggested to me that I learn to ride like the horsemen of the Steppes who guide their ponies with their legs and feet so that they might enjoy the full freedom of their limbs."

The Mirza smiled down at Japonica in understanding. " *'Around the world my course I've set, so many beauties have I met, Who stole my heart—but never yet, Was any one like you.'* "

Japonica smiled and curtsied. "Your Excellency is too kind."

"I wonder, lady, that all of England does not lay its riches at your feet." He glanced at Devlyn. "A man could do no better."

"I have thought the same," Devlyn said quietly.

"Ah, but thoughts are not actions and therefore are of as little consequence as the effort required to think them," Japonica said glibly.

The Mirza laughed heartily. "Yet in this meadow many lovely ladies are gathered. The curved daggers of their eyebrows could draw blood from the hearts of the bravest men! I am completely captivated watching them ride and gallop. So much so that I must struggle to suppress my desires." He smiled archly again at Japonica. "Do you ride, Lady Abbott?"

She was in no mood to accept this outrageous invitation to flirtation but Devlyn had been so cold that even the admiration of a man she did not desire warmed her pride. She smiled back at the ambassador and addressed him in Persian. "I believe, your Excellency, that you put that question to me once before."

"Indeed, as Allah is my witness. But then as now you do not offer the reply I would like above all to hear."

"I do ride, sometimes, Excellency," she answered with a lowering of her lashes. "When the circumstance and the mount are right."

Again the Mirza threw back his head in laughter. "I stand in respectful awe of your discretion. And so I must console myself farther afield with poorer company." He offered her a slight bow from his saddle before turning his mount and riding on.

When the Mirza was out of earshot she looked up to find Devlyn's lazy golden gaze upon her. But she was not fooled. He was annoyed by the Mirza's flirtation and it pleased her no end that he should be.

"Will you not join the Mirza in his hunt for better company?" she challenged.

"I think I have already found that which I seek." Then he dipped his head to her. "Excuse me, lady."

Watching him ride away, Japonica just scotched the impulse to hurl a stone at his head. How could he leave her with no more than a few polite if enigmatic words?

The following morning the wedding ceremony took place. The registry signed by the couple, the guests repaired to the great hall for a wedding breakfast of tongue and roasted squab, rashers of bacon and ham, several dishes of eggs, broiled kidneys and oysters, a variety of breads, rolls, buns, and wedding cake. Several kinds of wines and ales and chocolate, tea and coffee completed the plentiful fare, all supplied by Fortnum and Mason and accompanied by no less than Richard Fortnum himself, who had been invited to the celebration as Japonica's guest.

Once the guests were served, Japonica slipped away for respite. She wanted solitude for her misery. During the ceremony she could not keep her gaze from straying to Devlyn, who looked remarkably handsome in his morning coat. Not once had he returned the flattery by looking at her. Instead he seemed to be in a world of his own, smiling absently at some particularly poignant thought, she supposed. It was all very vexing.

It was a beautiful wedding. Grander than any she would have wanted for herself, but lovely. And that was the problem. She had been a bride and was a widow and still she had yet to be wooed.

Most of the wedding party would be leaving Croesus Hall after breakfast and she had every reason to believe Devlyn would be among them. So then, she would not stand on the drive waving a lace handkerchief gaily as he departed.

"Bismallah!"

Self-pity was new to her but it seemed the perfect day on which to indulge in it. She slipped into the music room and closed the door.

She had not meant to be found sniveling like a schoolgirl. However, Lady Simms had a deplorable habit of nosing out trouble and so found her sprawled upon the piano keys where she had subsided after an unsuccessful attempt to play away her bad temper.

"Whatever are you doing?" Lady Simms inquired when she discovered her hostess in tears. " 'Tis much too late for regrets. The bride's been feted and is about to be bedded. One supposes a rector is man enough to do the deed. I remember one curate in particular whose wife, the poor pious soul, gave birth to sixteen children. One for every year of marriage, so I'm told. There's reason enough to weep rivers."

She glared at Japonica, who was still sniffing. "Do pull yourself together, dear. Ruins the complexion." She glanced about the room. "I was just taking a tour of the house. Never seen this particular arrangement. Suppose one would call it a gallery cum music room. Which makes it neither. Are you still bawling? What has Devlyn done now?"

"Nothing," Japonica answered miserably. "Nothing at all."

"Oh dear. That doesn't sound like my Dev. Rather expected he'd been pulling you behind doors for a thorough kissing."

"A kiss! What is a kiss?" Japonica sniffed loudly in complaint. "A woman needs to hear the right words."

"Dev is no more useless than the best sort of man, I suppose." Lady Simms moved to study the row of porcelain vases on the shelves that lined one wall. "I've never quite understood what it is that frightens them so. The words are not difficult to pronounce, not likely to be mistaken for a vulgarity or insult. 'I—Love—You.' Any child of two can manage the phrase."

"He—he won't say them. They are not in him," Japonica said then gulped. "I wish I were dead!"

"A lamentably execrable but not uncommon complaint of those with broken hearts. I never subscribe to the ailment myself. I've found it much pleasanter to be loved than to love. It alleviates the possibility of the symptoms you suffer." She peered hard at one particular vase. "That is *not* a Ming Dynasty vessel but a cheap Dutch copy! I've no doubt a great deal of money was wasted in the acquisition. Inexcusable!"

Diverted from her thoughts, Japonica rose and approached her uninvited audience. "Do you mean you've never been in love?"

Lady Simms spun about. "I mean, dear child, that you should never listen to me when I am being flip-

pant. I love Leigh to distraction but it would do him
no good and me a great deal of harm were he to be
in possession of that fact."

"I doubt that is true or factual in the least."

The masculine rejoinder took them both by surprise.

"Dev!" Lady Simms cried in delight. "About time,
I must say. The young are ever at the effort to appear
fashionably late when it is precisely on the dot that
a lover is wanted."

"You will excuse us, Aunt?" Devlyn held open the
door.

Lady Simms promptly sat down on the nearest
chair. "Not for all the world."

Devlyn's gaze moved to Japonica, his expression
not very inviting. "Come and walk with me, Lady
Abbott."

It was not a lover-like request but she could not
refuse without seeming equally churlish. "Very well."

They spoke not a word until they were well beyond
the sight and sound of the house, in the curve of the
ha-ha. The interval gave her a chance to surrepti-
tiously dry her tears, which she planned to blame on
the emotion of the wedding should he be so ungallant
as to inquire.

Finally, she could not keep from speaking any
longer. "You have had the chance to survey the
grounds?"

"A cursory one when I rode out this morning."
His voice sounded distantly polite. "All appears in
order. I shall look into matters more thoroughly
tomorrow. The Shrewsbury land agent is coming to
see me on Monday."

Monday was three days away. So then he was not
leaving directly. "Are you pleased with our efforts at
the house?"

"Of course." This time there was a distinct humor

in his tone. "Since you are moved in, Croesus Hall has become a veritable provincial idyll. The place fairly reeks of domesticity. All that is wanting is a parcel of children scampering about."

Japonica ducked her head so that he could not look into her face. "Your lordship will be thinking of setting up his own nursery soon, I suppose?"

"Something very much the like." Devlyn slanted a glance at her profile. How serious she looked. And she had plainly been crying. "I will needs be married, first."

"I see." Oh, she did see! He had found someone. A London lady! But of course! How could she have been so foolish as to expect anything else? The polite but distant inquiries. The thoughtful but in no way personal gifts he had sent could be shared equally among the family. *A London lady.* A beauty, of course. Accomplished, stylish, untouched by scandal. A true aristocrat!

She swallowed hard. "I hope you have had fair sailing upon the London Season."

"Tolerably."

Was that amusement or derision in his tone? Oh, but his smugness was not to be tolerated! He had doubtless found happiness. But if he expected her to wish him well, he could whistle for it!

"You have seen that Jamie is well?"

"Indeed. He grows so quickly I am in awe. And it is on his account that I would speak with you."

Japonica paused and turned fully to him, her expression guarded. "What do you want?"

Devlyn reached into his coat pocket and withdrew a legal document. "I have brought you papers certifying James Michael Abbott as the rightful heir to the title of viscount of Shrewsbury. It requires only your signature before it can be presented to the House of Lords."

Surprise held her silent only a moment. Then she backed up a step and shook her head. "It will not serve. Jamie is not entitled to inherit."

"Is he not?" Devlyn said mildly. "You would accept me as the rightful heir?"

"I do."

"Then who is *my* rightful heir if not my own son?"

Japonica bit her lip before saying softly, "Jamie is your bastard child."

"Never." He stared hard at her. "You were wed nine months when he was born. He is as legitimate as any person the world round may confidently claim to be."

Japonica shook her head reluctantly. "You are twisting circumstance to your own ends."

"I but report the truth. By omitting the exact details of the lineage we do no harm and yet protect our son's good name."

"Yet it will persuade people to think of you as less than you are, the rightful viscount Shrewsbury."

He smiled. "Do I need the title to impress you?"

"You know you do not!"

"By abdicating I lose nothing important to me." His smile deepened. "If you wed again, you will not lose the distinction of dowager viscountess Shrewsbury."

Japonica looked away from him across the lush green parkland. "I shall remember that, should the occasion arise."

"I hope you will." He angled his body around to bring his face into her view. "You may have need of the reminder sooner than you think."

She searched his face for any hint of doubt. "You would do this for my son? Give away your title?"

"In a heartbeat." He gazed at her with a smile of such tenderness that she thought she would weep.

"He is my child, too. I will not have the world call him bastard."

Japonica blushed. "I see."

Do you? He wanted to ask, but thought he would wait a little longer for she had yet to genuinely smile at him. "There is another answer. I could adopt him. As my heir he would inherit after me."

An odd shaky feeling invaded Japonica, a feeling so much more than gratitude as to make her wonder what it would be like to freely love this man. She knew how he felt about Jamie, yet he had not said a word of his feelings for her. He had not proposed marriage, but suggested an alliance. At least she believed he had. It must not be pity that would bring them together, or convenience, even for the sake of the child they both adored. If it were not for love, a word they had never spoken directly to one another, she would turn away from him again, even though it broke her own heart to do so.

She turned and began walking. "I have wondered since you showed it to me, why Lord Abbott married me when, if his letter is to be believed, he meant me to be yours."

"I have thought on that, too. He cannot have known about the child."

"No. And I would not have married him had I known."

He slipped his hand under her elbow to steer her off the path toward a folly in the distance. "You are too honest for your own good, Japonica. I believe he would have offered, just the same."

"Why?" The touch of his fingers was a memory that had occupied too many of her dreaming hours, yet she did not want to draw away from it.

Devlyn shrugged. "I will never have those years of my memory back but there comes to me from time to time things that feel like memory for all that they have no experiences attached. I believe Lord Abbott knew that I had disgraced you. Perhaps I wrote him of the fact. It seems the sort of bravado of which the *Hind Div* was capable."

"You believe Lord Abbot married me to protect my reputation?"

She tried again to pause to look at him but he kept her moving with a firm hand. "I don't know or care. But answer me this. Why did *you* marry *him?*"

For the first time Japonica faced that question honestly and the answer was so simple she did not have to think about it. "Because the *Hind Div* was dead."

He started but kept their pace. "How did you come to hear that?"

"I was told by The Company Resident the day I received Lord Abbott's wedding proposal. At the time the two did not seem to be connected." She looked up at him. "Now I see I was mistaken."

Devlyn smiled. "Then we have our answer. Or as complete a one as we are ever to know." He squeezed her elbow as he helped her over the threshold of the stonework edifice and into its shadowed depths.

Japonica turned away from him. "I will not wed you."

"I have not asked you, have I?"

She glanced back at him but could not be sure why he smiled. "You will. You will think yourself to do the honorable thing. And so I must beg you not to do so."

"Very well." He smiled at the drooping curve of disappointment on her mouth. "I am nothing if not honorable, as you know."

Japonica suddenly smiled. "You are a thoroughgoing rogue! I believe those were Lady Simms exact words."

"She should know. So then, you cannot expect a

rogue to honor a lady's wishes." He took her hand in his. "Or would you prefer me on bent knee?"

She snatched her hand away. "Don't. Don't tease me. I cannot take the teasing. Not from you."

He ran his hand lightly over her hair, smiling absently as he inhaled the fragrance of her, something he had missed doing for months. "Then let us not banter. Let us be in deadly earnest."

He took her by the chin and turned her face up to meet his. "I love you."

Her breath caught in her throat. The words she had so longed to hear were now pronounced. She threw her arms about his neck. "Say it again!"

He grinned. "Will you have me wear the words out?"

"Bismallah! You promised to do a little courting and you've done none of it."

"Agreed. So then let us begin." He bent and laid his lips against hers and said very carefully, so that the full vibrations of every syllable were felt against hers, "I . . . love . . . you."

Japonica felt wicked and scandalized and very, *very* happy. Who knew that one could make love in the out-of-doors in the full light of day within shouting distance of a wedding party that, thankfully, would never think to look here for them.

Above their heads vines laced the vaulted canopy of the folly and kept all but a few filtered sunrays from entering the chamber. Devlyn had spread his jacket and her spencer upon the wooden floorboards to make a makeshift bed that seemed to her as pleasant as a down tick.

Lying by his side, her fingers interlaced with his, she reveled in the passion so quickly spent between them. Other less volatile feelings lingered between them. The intense feelings of tenderness and protectiveness and this overwhelming vulnerability to another were a part of love, and of loving this man. That realization no longer frightened her. All the words had been said and, in the end, it was loving and being loved that led up to this moment of contentment.

She did not protest when he lifted her skirts a second time. She simply closed her eyes and gave in to the feelings that had first beckoned her into his embrace. This time there was only trust and honesty and the understanding of a future to be shared.

Later, Devlyn ran a loving finger over the telltale marks of motherhood he had not been able to see in the dark the other time they made love. He bent and kissed the faint striations. When her hand came up to hold his head to her belly, he smiled. She had no false modesty to interfere with their happiness. They would be very happy together, that they would.

"Why did you stay away so long?"

His voice came to her softly through the green shadows. "To give you time to be certain."

"I am certain. I always was. I did not enjoy a single moment of your absence."

"Good." He lifted his head, his golden cat's eyes shining in the umbra. "Then you will not mind if we are not seen for some time beyond the grounds of this estate?" He bent to kiss her mouth softly. "It may be some weeks before I am willing even to leave your bed."

Japonica chuckled as his crisp hair tickled her belly. "Do you not fear you will grow very tired of the same fare, my lord?"

"I should first grow tired of my own breath and body. So *when* will you marry me?"

Japonica smiled. "I suppose it should be soon."

"Very! I will renounce my supposed useful existence and lie about with my lady wife until I grow fat and weak and thoroughly useless for any activity beyond pleasing you." He smiled against her mouth. "You will soon grow, too, I should wager. If Jamie is any indication, it will take very little effort on my part to start you breeding again."

"Oh, then I shall grow round and slow and become quite out of fashion."

"Never with me, my love. Never!"

GLOSSARY

Abeyya—Robe that completely covers a woman's body
Alhamdolillah valmenah—Thanks to God's Grace
Ayah—Lowly servant
Bahia—Beautiful one
Bismallah—In the name of God
Burra sahib—My lord/master
Farang/Farangi—Europeans/European
Hind Div—Indian Devil, demon
Houri—Beautiful girl
Huqqah—water pipe
Inshallah—God willing!
Isteqbal—An official welcome by high officials for a
            foreign dignitary
Marhaba—Well done!
Mashrabiyah—Wooden screen
Mehmander—Host, a nobleman of high rank named
            to be official host
Memsahib—Lady, my lady
Mirza Abul Hassan Shirazi—Persian Ambassador
Peri—Pixie, fairy
Sahib—Lord, my lord
Sobhanallah—Good God!
Suq—Old market
Takhi-I-ravan—Persian coach
Uzza—Beauty

DO YOU HAVE THE
HOHL COLLECTION?